What others are saying..

When I first read this manus... ... ... for a prestigious writers' conference, and I completely fell in love with the writing, the characters, and the story. I knew then that this story was a winner and needed to be published. That's why I'm so excited that Mary Beth's exceptional talent is finally being shared with the world. I know that readers everywhere are going to enjoy this story as much as I did.

— Michelle Medlock Adams, award winning journalist and best-selling author

* * * *

In Through the Balustrade, master storyteller Mary Beth Dahl skillfully weaves a YA tale of good and evil set in the land of the Oblate, where lives are programmed, compliance is required, and difference isn't tolerated.

An otherworldly adventure, written with the brush of an artist...a movie of words you won't want to end!

— Vonda Skelton, The Bitsy Burroughs Mysteries

* * * *

There is a moment when you realize the things you have been taught all your life must be challenged. And your fear isn't enough to keep the challenge from beginning with you. Follow this story of multifaceted characters in a world of intrigue and wonder as they learn to conquer their fears, challenge their teachings, and discover the truth.

— Debbie Christian, mother of teens

THROUGH THE BALUSTRADE

M.B. DAHL

May God bless your gifts for his glory. Blessings and Peace! Mary Beth Dahl

TABERAH PRESS
GALAX, VIRGINIA

Through the Balustrade

Published by Taberah Press
An Imprint of Sonfire Media, LLC

974 E Stuart Ave, Suite D, PMB 232
Galax, VA 24333 USA

Cover and interior book design by Larry W. Van Hoose
Map of Oblate by Liz Dahl

ISBN No. 978-0-9891064-0-5

For Cameron, Elizabeth, and Julia

Table of Contents

Map of the Oblate

With Villages, Provinces, and the Balustrade

Hyperion and the Guardians retreated to the Oblate when the outer lands succumbed to mass destruction. The Oblate is surrounded by a wall known as the Balustrade, which separates and protects the villages and provinces from the destroyed world beyond.

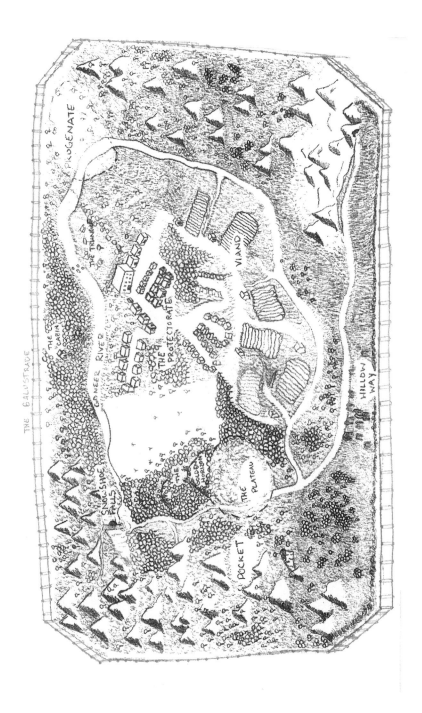

The Plebe's Common Guidebook to a Prosperous, Productive Life in the Oblate

Section I

Living above ground in the Oblate is an honor and a privilege. Do not take it lightly. Do not tread upon the trails and lanes of the Protectorate, Viand, and Plantanate Villages as if they were your reward for learning your skill and matriculating from your raising home.

If not for the care and divine protection offered to us by our master, Hyperion, we would all be lost to the world of desolation beyond the Balustrade. Follow his example of discernment and sacrifice, and commit these guidelines to your heart and mind.

It is not for you alone, that you live and breathe, but for all who occupy the Oblate. It is not for selfish gain that you work and toil, but for the betterment of a society. It is not for the accolades of an overseer or guide that you go beyond what is asked, but for Hyperion, the one who founded our world and leads us on to a better life, safe from the destruction in the outer lands and the lies that caused it.

For the good of all, we give ourselves.

CHAPTER 1

NOTHING SPECIAL

Seventeen turns of being groomed to a craft produced this graduation present—Roxan's own aboveground shanty. She blew a quiet kiss to her new home. It was perfect. The warm wooden walls, the dirt floor, the chair and table, the tall pantry case filled with food rations, all stood like guards silently upholding freedom. No one would burst through the door and yell about missed curfews or clothes on the floor. Things would be different here.

Roxan's cot creaked as she shifted to watch the soft hints of first light illuminate her tiny home. Despite being bolted to the wall beside the window, the cot wasn't as sturdy as the steel slab in her old room at the raising home. She didn't mind though. Creaks, dirt, all of it implied a new life, a free life.

Cool morning breezes blew papers from the shelf by the bed. Roxan drew the fresh air deep into her lungs. No more stale, oxygenated systems that depended on fans and siphoned hope from above. Open windows welcomed these busy molecules of freedom.

Roxan turned toward the breeze—and froze. A man draped in a black robe with a gold insignia glared at her through the open window.

Narrowing his gray eyes, he leaned toward her, as if he had every right to be lurking behind her cabin. A grin lifted his lips as the hazy implication of dawn swirled around him.

"You're nothing special," he muttered. She'd heard those words before, but not here. This place was supposed to be different. "Well?" He waited.

She didn't respond. This wasn't supposed to happen here. Plebes were free. No surprise inspections, no room intrusions. No one passing judgment. Plebes got their own shanties, their own little spaces where nosy rule enforcers weren't welcomed.

The man's robe rustled as he leaned in further, the scent of leather and mint clinging to him. "Nothing." His hot breath dampened Roxan's face as he drew the word out. Minty evil. "Roxan," he growled, "you're a waste of my time."

Even Nanny Skelt hadn't been so condemning. It wasn't what the stranger said, but the contempt etched in his clenched jaw and unblinking eyes.

Roxan tapped the headboard behind her until she landed on the switch to the solar rod. Not much zip was left, just enough to light half of the shanty and cast an eerie glow across the stranger's shaven face. The messy room drew his attention away. What was he trying to find anyway? Why was he here?

The questions wouldn't come out. Strangled by fear, Roxan concentrated on breathing. Cool fresh air filled her empty lungs. The oxygen helped to steady her, but it didn't slow her racing heart.

As she exhaled, a tingling rippled from the middle of her chest to the back of her head and to her eyes. She ran her fingers up the nape of her neck and into her thick hair, but that didn't ease the sensation rushing into her head.

The feeling intensified until a golden wave flooded the space around her, enveloping the stranger. It washed across him, outlining him with strands of gold. A series of scenes flashed inside the man's outline: a waterfall, a party, a crying woman, and finally a shadow of a creature—both man and scaled beast.

Shivering, Roxan covered her eyes with icy hands and willed the vision away. Not again, not here. She bit her lip and listened for a shift in the stranger's posture. Maybe he hadn't noticed. Sometimes people didn't see it. Sometimes it came and went before they ever detected the change.

As the prickly tingles faded away, she lowered her hands and met the intruder's gaze. If he had noticed the change in her eyes, he didn't show it.

A sharp knock sounded on the door at the other side of the room. The intruder's square jaw flexed as he glanced at the door. Whoever was knocking wasn't with him.

"Say nothing," he growled and held a glowing scinter toward her face. Purple, instead of the nanny guard's white, the implication from the light was the same. Every jab she'd gotten throbbed as he waved it in front of her. "Understand?" She nodded her compliance.

An artificial halo outlined the narrow door to the shanty, and in the solar rod's bluish light, her one-room shanty looked more like something from a bad dream than her new dream home. Sparkles of light, remnants from the tingling vision, twinkled like angry fireflies lost amid her clutter.

"Is anyone in there?" A man barked from the other side. He rattled the door handle and the light around the frame flickered.

Roxan sat mute, her back to the window. Any words withered in her mouth. Not that saying anything and defying the man with the scinter was an option. That kind of fight wasn't in her. She looked over her shoulder. The window intruder had gone.

Roxan leaned out the window. Only footprints in the wet grass remained. Maybe this was a normal custom in the Protectorate. Some cruel ritual to check out the new plebes. It didn't have to change anything. This could still be a fresh start. No one needed to know her secret. To them she could be nothing, as long as they left her alone.

CHAPTER 2

A COMPLETE IDIOT

The knocking on the worn door intensified. "423B7?"

Roxan reached for the L-shaped handle as her visitor plowed at her home with three more smacks. He grumbled, and this time she understood every derogatory word.

"Just a flash, please." Tears stood at the ready, but didn't venture out. Any more threats or weird eye issues, though, and the salty liquid would cloud her vision in a completely different way.

The intruder's words played again in her mind, "Say nothing."

Straightening, she tucked her hair behind her ears, rubbed her face with her hands, then turned the handle and pulled the door open. It squeaked and complained, which on a normal roll would have made her smile. The squeaks and kinks in things made life interesting. Today, though, she ignored the sound and faced the visitor.

"423B7?" The guy looked barely older than she.

She nodded her head to answer his question, at which he narrowed his eyes and glared. That look was familiar enough. It had crossed the face of every nanny she'd ever known. *Use your words, stupid girl.* For a split second, she considered slamming the door in his face. No more prisons, no more nannies, no more being told what to do all of the time. But she knew that wasn't true. Freedom still had its rules.

"Yes, sir." She spoke slowly and distinctly, meeting his chastising eyes. Tears still felt heavy in hers, but rebellion willed them back. This man would not make her cry. "That would be me, Roxan." She dropped the call number intentionally. "And you are?"

He took a deep breath and tilted his head to the side, lifting his chin a bit. "Your superior." Holding his glowing stave out, he illuminated his cover-up top and pants, revealing a patch with three golden lines and a star on his blue sleeve.

Glad she hadn't closed the door in his face, Roxan nearly danced with delight. "Blue? Our cover-ups are blue?" Seventeen turns in an orange cover-up made blue seem like finding out she'd be dressed in jewels on threads of gold. "It's like the beautiful sky." Looking out past him, she searched the foggy gray mist for the promise of a clear blue roll, which must have only annoyed him more. A storm cloud fell across his demeanor.

He jerked his light back to his face, then cleared his throat until she gave him her full attention again. "I'm Jonas, your guide."

"What's *your* call number?" The words popped out. The look on his face made her wish she'd thought about them.

"You won't need to know *my* call number." They both knew that might not be true. She would need it if she wanted to report him. She knew almost every nanny's call number in her zone at the raising home. Of course, after a while, they didn't take her complaints seriously. So, for now, she decided not to push it.

Jonas waved the light again. "You know you shouldn't make someone knock twice at your door. It's rude and inconsiderate. I didn't have to wait out here. I could have just come in." He paused.

Roxan ignored him. The evil intruder leaning through her window undermined any threat this man could have made, but she kept her mouth shut.

"You belong to us now," he provoked. "If you do your job well. . ." He glanced down at a file in his hand, obviously pausing for effect again.

He had a good-looking face, as faces go, framed by dark brown hair like hers, except his hair was short and stood up in the front. It looked like the reeds that lined the river, all stiff and standing bravely as the current rushed by. He was slightly taller than Roxan, thin, and smelled of detergent with a hint of vanilla.

"And it looks like you scored very highly. No reason why you can't do well. You shouldn't have anything to worry about." He found his place again.

"I'm sorry. Why exactly did you say you were here?"

His eyes flashed. "Since you didn't report last roll before sundown, I wasn't sure you had arrived. Here is your workstation and floor assignment."

He handed her a small sheet of paper with a list of rules on it and numbers at the top. "If you have any questions or problems, bring them to me. You should report to the Propagate work building as soon as you can. It's the tallest building in the village and the most prestigious." Roxan knew his type: arrogant, over achieving, and completely self-absorbed. He tilted his chin up, fitting her profile perfectly. "Any questions?"

"As soon as I can? I'm not late, am I? The directions the discharge nanny gave me said we had until the second horn. The first horn hasn't sounded yet, has it?" With her intruder this morning, maybe she hadn't heard it. Everything from when the first light woke her up to the scinter at her throat was a blur. It would've been easy to miss the drone of that horn.

"No, you are not late. But we do start working *before* the second horn." His serious eyes reminded her of a little one trying to convince a nanny he really needed another ration of chocolate. One eye twitched when he wanted to make a point, which seemed like every other word.

"We expect you to do your job and do it well. You aren't in your raising home. This is the real world, not that underground sanctuary you grew up in. If something breaks here," he pushed on her creaky door, "*you* have to see it gets fixed."

Roxan gaped at him. *Underground sanctuary? How could anyone ever think of the steel hallways, artificial lights, and stale air of the raising home as a sanctuary?* None of the words coming to her mind seemed to be appropriate to say to her boss, so she just shook her head. A curtain of long brown hair escaped from behind her ear, covering the right side of her face—she left it there, a screen for spying on this crazy person who thought a prison was some sort of paradise.

"You're going to have to deal with the elements also. Life outside your raising home is harsh. It's frigid in the cold season and insufferable in the hot one. You're lucky you arrived now. Enjoy it while you can. You should be getting new cover-ups soon." He twitched down at her toes. "And shoes."

What kind of point was he trying to make with that comment? He shut his file of papers and dropped his hand to his side like a sentry guard. "Okay, then, I'm done here."

While he had been talking, dawn had morphed into morning. He turned his stave off and snapped it to his belt. Still, he stood there looking at her.

Whatever he hoped to be hearing now escaped her, but she offered her best. "Okay then, thanks." Roxan reached for the door handle. It wouldn't seem inappropriate to close the door on him now. He did say he was done.

He fake-coughed. "Um. One more thing."

Roxan met his eyes full on. Her tears had long been chased off by annoyance.

He lowered his voice. "I noticed you're past seventeen full turns."

"That would be correct." She changed her focus to her dirty feet. He would have to bring that up, wouldn't he?

He continued to pry. "Why the delay in your promotion from the raising home? You had high marks on all your tests."

His detergent-vanilla odor stifled the fresh air. Roxan chewed on her bottom lip and balled her toes against the packed dirt floor. Seventeen wasn't that old. Besides, he had the file. He knew why it took so long, so she just stared back at him.

He twitched again. "Well? Why would someone as smart and gifted as you take nearly two turns longer than the normal plebe?"

"I, uh, had some problems."

"Problems?"

"A few."

"Well, I don't want any *problems*. Understand?" Jonas looked past her into the shanty.

Two stained, orange cover-ups, a half-eaten bowl of flakey stuff from the last roll of the sun, and all of the rocks, leaves, and interesting sticks she'd found on her exploring after she'd arrived were scattered around the tiny shanty. Her unopened handbook was wedged under the back leg to her wobbly table.

Jonas cleared his throat. "And you should make an effort to read your handbook. Not knowing a rule will *not* be an excuse for breaking one."

Roxan took a step back to block his view "Yes, sir." She filtered her comments. "I'll get right on that."

He pulled another handbook out of his satchel. "Here."

She took the book and thought she saw a glimmer of a smile cross his thin, solemn lips. Maybe there was more to him than arrogance and a mindless pursuit of success.

"Okay, plebe. For the good of all …" His brown eyes called her to attention.

"Oh, um … uh. I, no, we give ourselves." She sputtered the words out as if it were the first time she'd said them. "We give ourselves." She tried again.

"You'll have to do better than that, plebe." He grinned and twitched all at the same time. Roxan nodded her head and rolled her eyes. He didn't see her, though. He had already swiveled on his heel and was marching away.

She watched him disappear around the bushes toward the main corridor into town. Lifting her hands to her temples, she smashed the handbook into the side of her face and let out a yap. *How stupid! I didn't even get the mantra right. He must think I'm a complete idiot. There goes another first impression.*

A paper fluttered out of the handbook. Roxan snatched it up and shut the door. As the door creaked across the dirt floor, it made a fan imprint. She tiptoed around the design. It gave the dirt character and something to do in its stationary life.

Why'd he have to bring up my age? He couldn't be that much older. Hmm . . . maybe that was his point. Those stupid nannies. Not everyone fit into their mold. Do this. Do that. You're not tidy enough. Stop rolldreaming. If they'd paid half as much attention to the other students, they'd have noticed that people work at stuff differently. Disqualifying someone for having an unmade bed and papers on the floor seemed a bit neurotic.

She tossed everything onto the table, barely missing the crusty bowl, then plucked a Nutrivia bar off the shelf. A row of glass bottles lined the top pantry shelf. Not a lot of variety. Every bottle looked the same, clear liquid and a green label. At least in the raising home, there were three beverage choices, Vitawater, Calciwater, and Caftywater. Hopefully a few rolls of good work would earn enough merits to purchase fresh food. Making it on Vitawater alone seemed cruel.

She retrieved a bottle and returned to the table. Pushing the handbook aside, Roxan unfolded the thin sheet that had fallen out of it. A list of the provinces in the Oblate lined the top and then, in tiny print, a paragraph, in the form of a tree, took up the rest of the page. Intricate and artful, the word tree did not look like something Jonas would've bothered to do. But maybe there really was more to him than met the twitchy eye.

CHAPTER 3

THE UNGIFTED

Spray from the waterfall fell across Abiga's face. Her pallet lay ten meters from the downpour, but an occasional breeze blowing through carried a blanket of watery vapor with it. She didn't mind. It felt good. The others had gone farther back in the cave to inventory supplies. They didn't need her.

The freshly stuffed bedding hugged her. The smell of soft clover and milkweed enveloped her like the edges of the overstuffed material. It felt good to be cradled there, at least the pallet felt secure and light. Everything else felt heavy and suffocating, squeezing the oxygen and hope out of the air. She groaned as she exhaled.

Abiga watched as the flicker from the lumen danced across her skin. The scars on her arm glistened in the soft glow. Some of them almost looked like decoration, body art, but she remembered each terrible one. It had been a while since she'd gotten into a good scrape. She considered going out and looking for a fight. It wouldn't be hard to find one, but that would disappoint Altrist and the others.

She opened her hands and searched them for a sign. Her long fingers looked orangey-yellow from the swirling glow coming from the lumen. Calluses roughened the palms. Moving here had brought a lot more work, and this pack had definitely made use of her. They did more than that, though. They wanted her, loved her.

Abiga balled her hands into fists and tried to push away the dead feeling inside. *It's good to be here. These people seem different.* The light from the rear of the cave dimmed and brightened as her new pack walked back and forth, packing up the inventory of rations they would need for their trip. They accepted her and had no fear, even though they knew what she was capable of. It didn't make sense.

Quiet tears trickled away from her eyes and fell into her blonde curls. She wiped her wet nose on her sleeve and rested her head on her knees.

"Don't cry, Abiga." The soft voice broke her thoughts away, and Abiga turned her head, knowing she would see little Altrist. He touched her arm and said, "I think we should talk."

Most dark rolls he would come and sit next to her until she fell asleep. He didn't usually speak, though. Abiga brushed her tears away with the backs of her hands and scooted her pallet until she was sitting against the damp wall of the cave. Water from the wall soaked into her back, but she didn't care.

"What would you like to talk about Altrist?" She ignored the tears. Maybe he would too. "Is there more work to be done before we leave for Pocket?"

"I don't want to talk about that, sweet Abiga. I want to talk about you." Altrist came to Abiga's shoulder when she stood. His tog fell past his sandaled feet, and his blondish hair stuck out in prickles across his head. Although he looked like a boy, everyone knew he had seen more turns than anyone in the group. They treated him differently as if he were their leader. But he deferred that honor.

"Sweet Abiga, let's talk about you." Sincerity punctuated his words, like always, but she shook her head.

"Sweet?" The question came out sharper than she wanted it to, but what did it matter? "You know there's nothing *sweet* about me." She cut her eyes at him, but then looked back to the falling water. "What about *me* do you want to talk about?" He plopped down next to her, but didn't say anything. Abiga took a deep breath and pulled her darkest thoughts out. "Shall we talk about what jobs I'll be responsible for on our trip? Or were you thinking we'd discuss something from before?" She lingered on the word before. He hadn't brought that stuff up ever, but they all probably wondered about it.

"What's bothering you?" Altrist's bluish-grey eyes sparkled. "For too many rolls I've watched you fall asleep wet from your tears. What is it? Do you not like it here?" He looked so small sitting there, all huddled up next to her, his little legs crossed in front of him. The glow from farther back in the cave hung around his frame. Altrist always seemed to have a glow about him. Even if he were standing in pitch darkness, Abiga figured he would give off a light, somehow.

"I love it here." She spoke quietly, but she knew he could hear her. She cleared her throat and pushed the tears aside. "I'm fine. There's just a lot with us leaving. It's been hard getting ready. And I'm not crazy about going, anyway. Not that I'm not used to moving from place to place."

As she pulled away from the wet wall, the cold material clung to her back. "I liked settling down here with Thim and all of you. That's all." That should give him an answer he could fix and get him to leave her alone. Altrist cocked his head to the side and scrunched his face into a puzzled expression. Why wasn't he saying something? "Are you trying to read my mind, Altrist?" She searched his glistening eyes for some sign he could see into her head. He hadn't done that with anyone else that she'd noticed, but he had spoken his thoughts into her mind before. He did that instead of shouting. "Can you read minds too?"

"No." His berry pink lips mocked her. "No, I can't. Your mind is yours alone, but it wouldn't take a mind reader to know that you're hurting. What's really bothering you?"

He reached out his hand and rested it on her arm. Warmth surged through her chilled body, and it felt like the sun was sending its warm rays onto her wet back.

"Okay, that is one of my gifts," he giggled. "You can stay wet and cold, if you like." He lifted his hand away and the heat evaporated. She pressed his hand back down on her arm and smiled a thank you. "Okay, so what it is it? I can wait until the sun rolls back into the sky and even longer, if that's what it's going to take." He moved his hand up her arm and grew quiet. The sternness of his words didn't match the childish lilt in his voice, but Abiga knew he meant every word.

"It's hard, moving." It sounded even lamer when she said it aloud. "And, I don't get it. Where are we supposed to be going?" Trying to sound interested, Abiga shifted to face him. Altrist's hand dropped from her arm. Her rough cover-up felt warm and toasty now.

"Outside the Balustrade." He met her gaze, but she looked down and started picking pieces of straw off her lap. "Are you scared to go past the wall?"

Abiga scowled. "No. Why should I be scared? It's impossible to go through the Balustrade anyway." At least talking about the wall kept them away from what was bothering her. "Not unless that monster lets us get through it, and I don't think he's going to let *you* go anywhere without a fight."

"Is it the fight you're worried about?" He kept his eye on his target.

She shot right back, louder than she meant to be, "No."

Altrist nodded his head and rubbed his hand across his chin as if he were pondering some deep question. He narrowed his eyes, then launched another feeler. "I know you're good at fighting, but this won't be the same as going up against the Undesirables." Abiga shrugged. He plodded on, "The sentries are heavily armed, and Hyperion has his own set of *gifts*. It won't be easy, but we'll take care of you." He hit the mark, and she turned on him. The tears choked her throat, but she growled them away.

"I'm not scared. I've been in more scrapes than anyone here." She knew he understood her, but she kept on. "It doesn't bother me to kill a man if I need to. I'm not scared of the sentries, either. They depend on their scinters too much. Disarm them, and they go down quick enough." Her body trembled. "I don't need *you* to take care of me."

He held his arms up to surrender. "Fair enough. You're perfectly self-sufficient." Settling his hands in his lap, he probed on. "So what's the problem, then? You're a better fighter than any of us. You're used to moving around. That's nothing new. What is it?"

Abiga jerked her head away from his steely, blue stare. Her heart flitted in her chest. She put her hands on her hips, took several deep breaths, and focused on the falling water and not on the boy sticking her with questions.

His singsong voice invaded her thoughts again. "Okay, fine. Don't tell me. I get it. You're a wall. Fine, But at least talk with the Leader about what's bothering you. None of us should go it alone. It's too hard. Take it to Him."

It was as if Altrist had a map and followed all the right roads until he got to her heart. Abiga bowed her head. It took two flashes for the sob to build up inside her and burst out. She hunched over, covered her face with her hands, and gave in to it all. Altrist pulled her head to his chest and hugged her. His little arms had a firm hold. "It's okay, sweet Abiga."

She pushed away from him. Eventually, they would all need to know how she felt. But still, her mouth had a hard time forming the words. She scooted back and pulled her knees up to her chest.

"He doesn't want me." It came out in one breath, and it felt like the words swung around and smacked the air all out of her. Altrist remained quiet, concern in his eyes. "The Leader doesn't want me anymore. He did, early on. I met him, out there." She raised her hand and pointed to the waterfall. "But that seems like a long time ago." Altrist's silence confirmed her fears, emboldening her to go on. "You tell me to talk to him about what's bothering me, but what's bothering me is that I can't talk to him. He's not here. And he's given me nothing. Nothing."

Altrist reached over and brushed her curls away from her wet face. "I wish I could give you what you need to believe, but that falls only on you."

"Well, he could help that, but he doesn't. What's wrong with me? Why doesn't he want me?" Bile rose up within her, stopping her tears. Rejection tasted bitter. "No gift. He's given me no gift. After the waterfall, everyone said I would get a gift. They joked and even made bets about what it would be, and then they stopped because it's not going to happen. I don't get it. Everyone gets a gift."

Abiga lifted her hand and pointed toward the back of the cave where the others worked. "Liza heals and gets to evaporate into thin air and travel through space to who knows where, Anna fixes people, Grouper has the strength of ten men and the ability to sway a thousand, and you, look at you! I don't even know what all you can do. I just want something. Something to give me assurance that when I walked out under that waterfall it was real … that what I saw was real." She closed her eyes..

Nothing Altrist could say that would fix this. He couldn't offer her the proof she craved.

"What happened when you went through the waterfall?" His question caught her off-guard. Maybe he had doubts about her. Despair stepped over her frustration and took root in her heart. Meeting the Leader through the waterfall had felt real, but people tell themselves all kinds of lies. Maybe that's all that had happened. She had imagined it all. Altrist held up his hand and stopped her thoughts. "Try to remember. Sometimes it helps to go back to our roots." Abiga swallowed hard and closed her eyes.

Snapshots of her life popped into her mind: her mother, her first pack, playing in the woods, but then the scenes turned toward survival. She pushed away the worst image hovering in her memory. It tormented her, coming to her at random times. Pleading eyes and a gurgling scream. She forced it away and focused instead on the singular moment when her whole existence changed. The moment she decided she didn't want to go anywhere else.

"I stepped into the air." With her eyes still closed, she lifted her arms in front of her. She could see it clearly, as if she were standing there now. The spray of the waterfall warned her of the cave's edge. Grouper, Thim, Liza, Jahn, Anna, and Altrist stood somewhere behind her watching quietly. No one had ever loved her like they had, and they wanted her to join them. The Leader wanted her. They all seemed sure of that. Now, despair shadowed that joy she'd felt.

"I thought I was about to die, but if what you had told me hadn't been true, I would have wanted to die, anyway. So I went through the water, and I felt myself slip. As I reached out my hand, he took it from the other side. I can't remember his face, but he steadied me, walked me out from the water, and turned me around." Abiga lowered her arms and looked at Altrist. "At first all I could see was all of you standing, watching through the water. It didn't look like you could see me. You seemed to stare, not making eye contact, and then he waved his hand and the water turned into a fuzzy image, and I was standing there looking at myself, but it didn't look exactly like me. I was beautiful, dressed in white and yellow.

There were flowers, and I smiled. I've never been that happy. And then, he kissed me on the cheek and told me he loved me, and he would never let me go. It seemed so real. Look." Abiga held up the palm of her left hand. A faded circle with lines streaking out from it hid below the calloused palm.

"What's that?" Altrist took her hand and traced the circle with his finger. "Why haven't you shown us this before?"

"I don't know. He put it there. It's been there since that roll. It was much brighter, but now, it's faded." Abiga pulled her hand away from Altrist's warm touch. "I think it will be gone totally, soon." Altrist seemed to catch her thought, but didn't address it.

"I don't know why it's fading. But then there's a lot I don't know." He shrugged his shoulders. "That's part of this, not having all the answers, but believing, anyway."

"Yeah, that's easier said than done."

"Yep." His glow dimmed. "So what are you going to do?"

"I don't know. I won't stay where I'm not wanted." Abiga put on her strong tone, but her lower lip trembled. "I'll do what I can before I go."

Altrist scooted closer to her and propped his feet under him, meeting her eye to eye. "You're not the only one who hasn't gotten a gift, you know. Not everyone does. Several of the Outcasts at Pocket don't have gifts, and there are others, including Thim." Abiga had heard that before, but it didn't matter. She had to go with her own heart, and—for herself— she needed this. If the Leader couldn't see that, then he didn't love her as much as he said he did.

"I'm not asking for the world, Altrist." She ran her hand through her curls and leaned back. "It is what it is. I'll do what I can to help, but I'm not going through the wall unless the Leader proves it to me." Melancholy crossed his little face. She knew this would make Altrist sad, but he'd get over it. They all would, even Thim.

"Abiga," he whispered, but she heard him clearly. She shook her head and intended to tell him not to bother, she'd made up her mind, but he lifted his hands in the air and a glowing mist appeared between them, forming a sphere. "I'm not going to Pocket." A girl's face appeared in the glow, just a faint outline. "I've got to find this girl."

Abiga knew she wasn't an Outcast or an Undesirable. The girl sat by a willow tree, dressed in a blue cover-up, her straight, long chestnut hair blowing across her smiling face. She couldn't be more than seventeen or eighteen turns. A mindless member of that murdering world dressed up with cute little huts and following their precious Hyperion, the Leader's only adversary.

"What? You can't go after her. She's in a village. You can't go off, not now. Everyone needs you."

"Everyone needs her." Altrist threw his hands up, and the glowing orb with the girl inside dissolved as it rose into the air. "She has a gift. We'll need her help to get through the Balustrade."

She has a gift. Abiga mulled over his words. As their meaning sank in, her anger flew to the surface. "She's not even one of us!" A hush fell across the back of the cave and the mumbling from the others quieted.

Altrist lifted a finger to his lips shushing her. "Abiga, I haven't told the others yet. Please, let me tell them." His eyes and his tone flashed a warning to her. He rarely showed this side of himself, but she knew not to defy him. Laughter echoed from the back of the cave. They were oblivious. They had no idea what was about to happen.

"They need to know." Abiga jerked her head toward her friends.

"When are *you* going to tell them about your decision?"

"Don't turn this on me, Altrist. I would gladly stay." Tears threatened again. "But he's telling me he doesn't want me." She held up her palm. "I don't measure up."

"*You* don't have to." Altrist jumped to his feet. "They're going to need you, Abiga. None of them knows these woods like you do." She pulled a piece of straw out of the pallet. "It's your choice, sweet Abiga."

He walked to the opening under the spray of water and turned back to face her. She couldn't see his face in the shadows, and the roaring water drowned out his tiny voice, but then she heard him in her head. "We all love you, Abiga. It doesn't matter what you've done in the past or what will become of you on the next roll of the sun. In this very moment, you are loved. Walk away from that if you want, but know it's your choice." He disappeared into the darkness, but his words still hung in her mind.

They didn't make her feel better. Making a fist, she punched the rock wall of the cave. Pain shot up her wrist into her forearm, and she caught her breath, blowing out slowly. Cradling her hand up close to her chest, she nestled down into the pallet. She would help get the others to Pocket, but that would be it. After that, she would leave.

CHAPTER 4

SPUNKY

A shuffle outside the door followed by another hard thud almost caused Roxan to spit her Nutrivia bar across the table. She pushed the chair back and reached for the door handle. One thing about having such a small shanty, it didn't take long to get from the table to the door. Grabbing the handle, she whipped the creaky door open. No sense in making anyone knock twice. One lesson learned.

"Whoa! That was quick." A tall man, wearing a dark green cover-up, grinned as he spoke. "You must've seen me coming. Get up early to watch for the delivery man?"

"No, I … uh … well, my house seems to be very popular this morning." Tucking her chestnut hair behind her ears, she straightened her back and forced the partly chewed bits of bar down her throat. "And I didn't want you to have to knock twice."

"Oh, well, you're new here. Everyone always loves the new people. Give it some time, and no one will even notice you." He nodded toward the main road. People were starting to crowd it now. Blessed sunshine fell across his right side, making part of his face flush and the other side shadowed. His hazel eyes sparkled, and he jiggled the door, making it squeak louder. "I could fix that, ya know."

"Great," she knocked away his offer. No one appreciates the squeaky things. Leaning against the perfect door, she lost her balance and fell back through the doorway. "Um, and what do you want?" She tried to regain her composure by raising her voice. "You didn't come just to fix my door, did you?"

He gave her a "you-need-help" look, but didn't comment on her clumsiness. A handsome blanket of whiskers covered his solid face. "I've got your supplies, plus new cover-ups." He eyed her dingy orange cover-up. "I think these are a bright blue."

"Yyyes. Purple would've been better than this. But blue is perfect." She tugged at the crew neck of her bottom layer. Wrinkles from being slept in covered the top layer. The cover-ups never quite fit right on her tall thin frame. Maybe now they'd get her size right. And in blue. How wonderful. "Yours is green," she noted. "I've never seen a green one. Where are you from?"

He adjusted the box, pulled a paper off the top, and handed it to her. "Well, I travel all over." Something about him told her he didn't mind being asked questions. Maybe it was how his hazel eyes didn't look so vacant. "But I'm from the Viand Clan, for now."

She took a step to the table and signed the paper. "What do you mean *for now*?" The man cleared his throat and pointed to the line near the bottom, and Roxan marked through the first signature and signed it again. "I thought once you were assigned somewhere that it didn't change until you retired to the Plantanate." She handed the paper back.

He leaned on the door post. "That's usually the case, unless you've been misassigned." He didn't even flinch as he spoke. A nanny would have given him ten demerits for that comment, but out here in the free world, a person could say stuff like that and not get in trouble.

Roxan tossed her hair back over her shoulder. She'd go down that road too, talking about things formerly forbidden. "Misassigned? How can that happen? The Plateau wouldn't make that kind of mistake."

He chuckled, and then his shiny eyes grew serious and his voice softened to a whisper. "What do you know about the Plateau, girl? You've been tucked away underground for what fifteen or sixteen full turns? You do what they tell you and never question any of it. You don't know half of what the world is about." He didn't sound angry, more condescending. He set the box of her stuff in the doorway and walked down the short path to his cart, grabbing another box filled with blue cover-ups.

"It's seventeen, and this place seems perfect." Roxan raised her voice so he could hear her protest. "It's beautiful here—a wonderful change from that underground prison. This is nothing like the raising home. That place was repressive and inhibited everything about the human condition." Jonas's face flitted across her mind. *How could anyone think of the raising home as a sanctuary?* Even with having to work with dolts like that, this world offered more hope than the monotonous routine and sunless existence underground. Things would be different here. "The Protectorate is freedom." But a nagging recollection of the intruder clouded her tone.

The deliveryman's rugged face softened with a grin. "This place has its own walls. You'll soon find that out." He plopped the second box on top of the first. "It won't take long. And, I wouldn't be yelling that stuff out, if I were you. They don't take kindly to any negativity, and those raising homes in the Progenate are their pride and joy. The Protectorate, the Viand, the Plantanate—they're all glorified raising homes with one big shiny wall making the prison inescapable."

"What wall? The Balustrade? It's so far away. Does it even exist—a tall wall of mirrors? That's probably a story made up by the nannies." Roxan rolled onto her tippy-toes to meet her visitor's questioning eyes. "It doesn't matter, anyway. There are no walls in the Protectorate. Here I walk freely, and there's the sun." She smiled up at the morning sky as it cleared away the last bits of haze.

"You've got spunk, don't you?" The skin around his eyes crinkled when he smiled. He looked older than a plebe. He had to be close to the time of attainment. "But you'll see," he continued. "You don't need to go as far away as the Balustrade— and yes, it's real—to find that you're trapped here as well."

"Well, you must be close to being done here, anyway. I mean, what are you? Forty turns? You'll have attainment soon and be off to real freedom."

"Yeah, right. I'll have attainment soon. You can bet I've got my eye on that. But real freedom's going to take work. There's only one road to real freedom. And it's not for the faint of heart."

"Well, I'm done with being a prisoner to the demands of everyone else."

"Listen, Spunky, this place is twice as bad as what you had in that underground jail cell, and here the stakes are higher." He rubbed his hand across his stubbly head. "Here, you can fit into the mold and end up like everyone else or. . ." He paused, measuring her with his eyes. "Or you can make a bid for change. Stand out and get noticed."

"Get noticed? How?"

"I don't know," he baited her, and she waited. "Do something wild and crazy, but not too rebellious. Something that will get those wardens at the Plateau to notice you." He never took his eyes off her. "Like go out there." He nodded toward the wooded area behind Roxan's hut.

Roxan sighed at the bits he was feeding her. "What do you mean? Beyond the boundary line?" It's not allowed without a sentry escort. It's dangerous."

"It's not that dangerous," he smirked.

"How would you know?"

"Because I've been out there. Just into the woods. It's not that big a deal. Every sentry guard has to do it to graduate. So far all have returned." His smirk widened. "Except for one."

"What happened to him?" She held her breath.

"They think he got brainwashed by the wild people who live out there."

"You're making fun of me," she exhaled. "I believed you. You probably didn't even go out there, did you?" Straightening, she studied his face, but couldn't read him. "That's a crazy story. If you want to get noticed by the Guardians at the Plateau all you have to do is your job." She nodded toward his cart.

"Nope. You have it all wrong. Doing your job isn't good enough. You have to give them something they really want." His confidence annoyed her.

"It doesn't work that way, and you know it." Roxan tried to sound like she knew what she was talking about, but felt the prickles of uncertainty pulling at her mouth. "They do what's best for the good of all."

"Yes, sure they do, and we are all equal, aren't we?" Sarcasm again.

"You don't know anything about the Plateau. I bet you've never even been there." She lifted her head like Jonas had done. "Do you even read? Maybe instead of wandering around outside of boundary lines, you should read over the edicts from the Propagate. That's where I'll be working. Not everyone rises to the Plateau level. The Guardians choose the right people and leave the others right where they're supposed to be."

"You know all about it, don't you? Look at you. You're fresh out of the raising home. Shikes, you're still amazed you can see the sun for yourself and touch a tree." He waved a hand toward the woods. "When you get tired of thinking you know it all, I'll be around and I'll tell you what I do know. I'll even take you out there, show you around a bit." Pushing off from the door, he bowed slightly and rolled his hand forward as if he were presenting her with more than cynicism. "Now, now, Spunky, don't get mad. I'm the only one around here who's gonna tell you the truth and NOT tell you what to do."

The satisfied look of an argument won crossed his know-it-all face. Roxan ran her bare foot back through the dirt and tapped her toes on the ground. Between Jonas's arrogance, this guy's smug skepticism, and some stranger making threats, the roll wasn't going well. Keeping all of it in perspective quickly disappeared, and Roxan served up the only piece of ammunition she had.

"I've been to the Plateau," she blurted out with immediate regret.

The deliveryman took a step through the doorway, and leaned toward her. A hungry, serious look replaced his grin. "What do you mean you've been there?"

Roxan turned her head away. She felt his breath on her face, and for a split second the stranger from the window flashed across her mind. A thread of fear made its way up her spine and the back of her head began to tingle. *Not again.* Twice in the span of a slow flash would put her one freaky vision away from breaking her record. She pulled air deep into her lungs and forced the sensation away.

He straightened and stepped into the sunlight. If a person could give two totally different feelings without changing his expression, this guy mastered it. The hungry look still covered his tan face, but instead it was narrated by an apology. "I'm sorry. It's unusual for someone like you, fresh from a raising home, to have gone to the Plateau." He wanted more of her story, she could tell, but she didn't have much more to give.

"I was young, and I don't remember much," she censored herself. "They told me that I was there for the good of all." A tear annoyed her and rolled down her cheek. It flowed from somewhere deep inside. Somewhere she didn't want to go. "And now I'm here, and that's for the good of all too." She raised her head and met his cold-warm stare. "You would do better to live more for the good of everyone and not what you think will get you noticed." The tingling began again.

"Well, I was not expecting to meet someone who's been to the Plateau on my route this roll. How about that?" He looked her over again. "Can I ask you one more question?" He waited until Roxan nodded her head. "When you were there, at the Plateau, did the Guardians take you to Hyperion? Did you meet him?"

Roxan sighed. "I think I did. But I was little, and it all happened so fast. I'm not sure." She lifted a new cover-up out of one of the boxes he'd brought and hugged it. The material was surprisingly soft. The prickles weren't going to go away. Getting this guy to leave soon was becoming more urgent.

"Well, maybe you're just all kinds of special." He tapped his hand on the door, oblivious to the strands of golden light waving around him. "Listen, you should meet up with a few of us who are trying to make some changes around here." Roxan took a step back and nodded. Warmth spread across the back of her head.

He didn't seem to notice anything. "You might learn something, or maybe we'll learn something from you," he continued. "We meet at the end of the roll between twilight and the time that blasted horn drives us all back to our cells. Come to the amphitheater steps. And don't tell anyone. You're a fool if you think no one's watching. So keep it quiet." He winked and turned away, leaving Roxan standing in the doorway, a haze beginning to fall across all she could see.

CHAPTER 5

WHAT A WASTE

The feeling became stronger as she pushed the old door shut. Threading her hand through her thick hair and pressing her fingers to the back of her head didn't lessen the sensation. A warm cord of tingling wove its way through the synapses in her brain, converging on her eyes. It didn't hurt. But she shook her head to get it to stop.

As the line pushed its way to the front, heat spread through her eyes and the golden haze she'd seen earlier with the intruder fell across the interior of her shanty. She put her hand out into the vapor, but she felt nothing. This was different from the episodes she had when she was younger.

Strands of concentrated light weaved through the golden air like snakes making their way from the floor and into the walls. They branched out to four black boxes located in each of the corners of the room near the ceiling.

Roxan walked to the center of the shanty. The lines of light ran throughout the weathered walls, ending in a black cylinder directly above her head. Webs of light wound their way everywhere. One spot near the base of the left wall pulsated with a convergence of white light.

As all the cords of light united in one spot, the gleam pounded like a beating heart. Roxan stooped down. The walls of her shanty faded from view and she watched as the intertwined cords ran into the shanty on the other side of the grove of trees. When she stood up, she could see the lines running throughout the Protectorate—through buildings, under the river, and into the forest, where they disappeared into darkness.

The blackness twisted like a blanket in the wind, and as it moved, the lines flickered and spiraled upward. She followed them upward until they stopped, and a pair of deep, red eyes came out of the cover of darkness. Cat-like eyes with elongated irises and a black slit in the center. They looked at her, and she jumped back, hitting the wall. Everything snapped back to normal.

She slid down the wall and sat on the dirt floor, rubbing her face with her hands. "What is this? What's wrong with me?" Her questions hung in the air. She had no one to answer them. *Wait!* Pushing off from her spot against the wall, she grabbed her half-emptied bag of stuff and dug through her collection of broken pens, empty ink pots, and bottle caps. From the bottom of the bag, she pulled out a black book with a cord tied around it to keep papers from falling out. Folded long-ways, her release papers from the raising home stuck out the top of the book.

There scribbled at the bottom of the second sheet, Nanny Bala had written, *"Report all atypical occurrences to your guide or overseer."* No way. Taking something weird like this to Jonas definitely seemed like a bad idea.

She tossed the paper onto the table and tucked her black book between two boxes on her standing shelf. It blended right in. "Thanks a lot, Nanny Bala," she growled. That was no help. Telling someone she was seeing things definitely wasn't going to help get things off to a good start.

Pulling the box of cover-ups from the deliveryman over to her bed, she swerved making the pattern on the dirt floor a little more interesting. Her new blue cover-ups felt like butter—not the fake kind, but the real stuff. She brought the material to her face and inhaled its freshness. It smelled like the outside and didn't make that scratchy sound when she scrunched it.

She tossed her old orange cover-up onto the floor and slid the soft blue one over her head. It fit perfectly. The armholes weren't too tight, and it wasn't too short. She twirled three times and considered defying dress code regulations and going without the outer layer. Why cover such wonderfulness? No point in pushing things, though. At least, not yet.

Before she could adjust the top lighter blue layer, another thud sounded at the door. *Oh, what is this? You've got to be kidding me.* She fumbled with the ties as she hurried to the door. The side tie didn't wrap far enough around her waist. Evidently, village folks had fancier cover-ups that needed instructions.

Another soft tap sounded, but no one said anything. She gave the tie a yank, pulling it loose and losing her balance in the process. As she kicked her leg up, her foot slammed into a container on the pantry shelf, knocking the container from its perch, and spilling its contents across the floor. It clanged loudly as it landed on one of the six slate tiles lining the way to the bathroom, the only part of her home that had a floor. Of course, it wouldn't land on the quiet dirt. Roxan reeled back and fell into the table.

"Is everything okay in there?" A deep voice called from the other side of the door.

"Yeah." Roxan gulped and winced at the throbbing in her foot. "I'll be right there." She looked her toe over for blood, then hobbled to the door, and flung it open.

"What do you want?" She leaned against the worn wood and rested her injured foot on top of the good one.

The man in front of her wore a royal blue covering with a thick golden trim around the sleeves, neckline, and hem. Roxan met his serious eyes. This wasn't just anyone. This was a superior. A superior with a higher rank than Jonas.

She stood up straight and ignored the urge to apologize profusely. "Sir?"

"Good morning, Roxan. And welcome to the Protectorate." His warm tone filled the shanty. Roxan thought she felt the wood vibrating from his manly sound. "You are looking," he paused checking her out, "almost ready for your first roll of work." His countenance sent out an invitation for friendship.

"Thank you, sir," Roxan replied, trying to keep her eyes down. Strands of hair flew around her face. Her toe throbbed, but she ignored it, swallowed hard, and gave him her brightest expression.

He didn't look much older than she. He stood so tall his head almost touched the top of the doorframe. His thick hair framed his face. The sunlight played with the brown, bringing out golden strands flecked with red. The color almost matched his kind eyes. Brown with streaks of amber, green, and auburn.

"I'm Whitlock, your overseer. We missed you when you arrived. Could you not find the Propagate Buildings?"

Roxan resisted the urge to comment on the amazing stitchery on his cover-up top. The gold thread shined like real gold. "Uh, no sir, I saw the buildings. I just ... well, I'd never seen trees or the blue sky, and they said that we were to report to our shanties and get set up first." She felt her cheeks turning pink and wanted to put her cool hands on them but held on to the door handle, trying to keep herself steady and look more confident than she felt.

"Yes." He looked past her to the mess of food rations spread across her floor. "It can be hard getting your shanty set up for the first time."

"Yeah, I had a run in with the pantry shelf, but I think we're both going to get along fine." Roxan said, hoping Whitlock had a sense of humor. "Now that it knows who's boss."

"I think I can tell who won that battle. You are a force to be reckoned with." His straight white teeth lined up in his mouth. "My shanty is through there." Whitlock motioned to a small trail between the bushes at the dead end of her road. "And since you're on my way, I thought I'd stop off and show you to our building. Jonas is your guide, but he probably won't bother to start doing that job until you get into the office. He can be a bit ... well, let's just say he's very committed to the job."

Roxan's stomach twisted at the mention of Jonas's name. "Yes, he was here earlier."

"Oh, well. Don't let him get to you. His bark is worse than his bite. Besides, I'm the one you need to keep happy! And I don't bark or bite."

Whitlock was far too genuine to be an overseer. Power usually makes people selfish and little, not kind and big enough to see that other people have feelings. He could see. Roxan could tell. She also saw that his happy mood had some sort of shadow on it.

"Normally, I don't escort plebes into work, but I'm feeling especially charitable this roll," he declared. "I'll give you some time to put yourself together. Just step outside when you're ready. I'll be right here."

Roxan closed the door without a word. That seemed to go well. Whitlock noticed her potential already. And all with no eye weirdness or condescension. Things could only get better from here.

The reflection in her skinny mirror mocked her hopes. Her new blue cover-up was actually inside out. No wonder she couldn't find the tie for the top layer—the beautiful sky blue layer! Maybe Mr. Wonderful Boss hadn't noticed her inability to dress herself.

She flipped the top layer, grabbed a Nutrivia bar out of the pocket of her old clothes, and then chucked them to the corner. *So long, orange rags. Perhaps later you will get a proper good bye; something with fire might be nice.*

* * * * *

The wind blew against Roxan's face as she struggled to keep up with Whitlock. He had been talking nonstop since they left her shanty. At first she listened intently to his stories about past projects and deadlines, but the farther down the lane they went, the more she became distracted by the birds and flowers and even other people, so many people. Several men had the same tall-grass hairdo Jonas had sported. And most of the women had body art painted on their faces or arms.

Whitlock stood over six feet tall. Despite looking young, he carried himself with authority and confidence—something about his eyes and the angle of his chin. When the wind blew just right, she thought she smelled it, but it must have been the scent of the heavy, rich fabric of his fancy cover-up.

People along the way made a point either to say hello, or to cast a quick glance in Whitlock's direction—and then toward Roxan, with a look as if she were in trouble. She returned every look with a happy wave. Everything looked beautiful in the sunlight. People could contort their faces and toss up their breakfast, and it would still be picture perfect under a blue sky with trees swaying in the breeze.

"Good Morning, Whitlock." A familiar voice rumbled from a side street. Roxan turned from her thoughts to see the man in green pushing his cart alongside them.

"Hello, Mullin." Whitlock kept his head high, barely acknowledging Mullin's presence.

"What business do you have with Spunky, here?" Mullin didn't seem to be intimidated by Whitlock's position. He was oblivious to the people who had to go off the path to make their way around his cart too.

"This new plebe is going to be my lead recorder. Roxan, have you met Mullin?" Whitlock looked dismissively away from Mullin and faced Roxan.

"Uh, yes. He delivered my things." She blushed at the lead recorder comment and shifted her weight from one foot to the other, crossing her arms uncomfortably in front of her. There's never a good place for long arms.

Satisfied with her answer, Whitlock ended the conversation. "Well, good roll, Mullin."

"Well, all right then." Mullin made big eyes at Roxan like they shared some secret or something. Sarcasm dripped from every part of him.

"For the good of all …" Whitlock paused, waiting for Mullin's mandatory reply.

Mullin glared down at his cart. "We give ourselves. Good roll." He spoke the words dryly and darted his eyes to Roxan when Whitlock stepped away. She saw the faintest glimmer of a sneer cross his lips.

Turning his cart in the opposite direction, he wound his way around her. "What a waste!" He barely said the words aloud. But she knew he meant her, and she wanted to stay behind and ask him what that was supposed to mean, but Whitlock had already turned onto the side path.

"Do you know him very well?" Roxan called from behind as she caught back up to Whitlock's brisk pace.

"Who, Mullin? Everybody knows him. He's a supplier, so he gets around. I don't much care for him, though. I think he stirs up trouble," he declared.

"What do you mean?" Mullin seemed argumentative and arrogant, but not like trouble.

"Mmm. How do I put this? You know it's against the rules to talk about others." Roxan made a mental note to look over that rulebook. Whitlock paused in the pathway and skirted the rules. "But to speak in general terms, I would say that there are some people who simply refuse to be content. They find fault with everything and have an air of entitlement about them, as if we all owe them something. Perhaps he falls into that category. Eventually, those types end up spending time with the sentry guard getting an *adjustment*." As he finished speaking, he turned and took off again. Roxan mulled his words over before dashing after him.

"An adjustment? What's that?" Her voice sounded shakier than she felt, although a nagging feeling had crept into her stomach. *What else had she missed in that rulebook?*

"Don't worry Roxan." Whitlock slowed his pace. "The Plateau does what's best for us, and if that's helping certain people get to a place where they can see that, then it's only good. For our society to continue, we need the help of the Guardians at the Plateau ironing out the kinks and keeping people in line with our objectives. The rules are good, Roxan. They help give us meaning and move us forward. The sentries help 'adjust' that a little."

A blessed aroma came from the bakery behind Whitlock, but he didn't even seem to notice and kept talking. "In the raising home, kids went to solitary or lost privileges, but here the stakes are higher." Roxan bit her lower lip, and Whitlock stopped and rested his hands on her shoulders, compassion radiating from him. "Here, two steps outside the boundary could mean death and missteps *inside* the boundary bring a swift correction. It has to be for the good of all or it won't be tolerated. Anyone who thinks they know better gets an *adjustment*." He gave her a nod, as if to say, "You may not get it now, but you will." That didn't help the uneasy feeling go away, neither did the sweet scent of hot bread.

"Uh, sir. May I ask you one more question?" He took his hands off her shoulders and gave a glance toward the sky. She could tell he wanted to move on. "Please."

"Sure, Roxan."

"What is beyond the boundary line? Out in the woods? I've always heard it's dangerous and we shouldn't travel between villages without an escort. But why is that? What's out there?"

Whitlock stepped off the pathway to a bench nestled in between two trees. Motioning for her to take a seat, he waited for her and then filled up the other end of the bench. Even sitting, he looked tall. His hazel eyes flickered with that golden mixture of amber and brown.

"I don't know Roxan. I'm not sure what's out there. But I believe our leaders and trust them to know what's best for us. I don't know why they set some of the guidelines they do, but this is the world we live in. There are no other options." The warmth in his voice faded a bit, and he looked away toward the open field beyond the main pathway.

A bird flew onto the lowest branch of the tree near Whitlock and let out a chirp. "It's different being outside the raising home." He turned to face her again. "You need to read that rule book! Not knowing the rules will not be an excuse for you, and I know you've been a bit of a handful in the past. You will find things go much better if you simply do what you're told here and follow all the rules. Then there's plenty of sunshine to enjoy and no shiny walls to worry about." His eyes offered a testament to his kind heart. "Be careful, Roxan. Take a bit of friendly advice from me, and don't do anything to attract attention to yourself. They're going to be watching you. And, although there are some who aspire to be promoted to a position at the Plateau, you do not want to go there."

By the time he finished speaking, it felt like even the bird had leaned in to hear what secrets might be said. Roxan wondered if Whitlock somehow knew of Mullin's plans for being noticed, and then another question darted across her mind and jumped out of her mouth.

"Why would they be watching me?" A horn blasted across the village on her last word, scaring the little bird away. Roxan touched her hand to the back of her head where the tingly feeling had come from. Maybe they knew more than she thought they knew. Whitlock showed no interest in answering her. He stood, stretched his back, and stepped toward the path.

"C'mon, Roxan. We don't want to be late for your first roll." She followed him down the little pathway to steps leading to the Propagate Building. It reached up against the blue morning sky.

Whitlock waited for her, pushing the door completely open with his back and waving his arms in a rolling motion, beckoning her to enter. "Stop looking petrified. This is where you belong."

He led her toward the wide staircase in the center of the open foyer.

"Morning, Becka," he called to the receptionist.

The girl waved back and smiled, but cut her eyes at Roxan. She looked like she could be Jonas's sister. That would be weird. For that matter, the girl could be *her* sister. Roxan shook the thought from her mind. Whitlock wouldn't be answering any more questions this roll. And she'd drive herself crazy thinking about stuff like that. If she needed to know, someone would tell her.

The wooden stairwell led up to a balcony that surrounded the foyer. Doorways lined the balcony, and Whitlock headed toward the largest doorway, grabbed the golden handles, and announced, "You have arrived."

CHAPTER 6

DIFFERENT

Roxan stacked the last sheet of paper into her "finished" basket, then gathered her plebe handbook and the other paperwork she would need to read over in the dark side of the roll. She couldn't stop smiling. It felt great to be good at something. And being the best reworder on the floor meant she would be eating fresh fruit and baked bread before the end of the next roll.

The other plebes still sat hunched over their stacks of work. Roxan stood and leaned to look out the window. The rocks by the river called her name. Freedom meant when you finished your work, you were free to explore. And exploring meant wandering around without anyone watching.

"Where do you think you're going?" Jonas's nasally voice didn't fit the view from the window. "There is still work to be done."

Turning back to her desk, she grabbed and waved a stack of papers, crinkling the edges. "I've finished my work, sir."

"Well, there's always more to do. We're only done here when the sun sets." He tilted his head in his smug little way. Roxan held back the urge to argue with him. Instead, she took a deep breath and set the papers aside.

Jonas turned and waved his arm toward the other workers. "Here, why don't you help some of these other plebes finish their work and maybe we can all get out of here before the horn blows."

Roxan's heart sank. Everyone else had piles of papers left to copy, and not a single worker had even been able to understand the assignment without asking a dozen questions. Several shot her a look that told her to stay away, and the others either didn't look up or looked like they were on the verge of tears. *Ugh.* Three rolls of the sun and she didn't know even one of their names and wanted to keep it that way.

Whitlock had his back to the office. The window wall separating him from the work floor was always open. Roxan tossed Jonas a smug smile and twigged it toward Whitlock's doorway. Maybe he would see the value in rewarding hard work, instead of piling more on.

He didn't notice her as she stepped inside. "Excuse me, sir."

"Yes, Roxan. How are you?" The seriousness in his face disappeared when he saw her. "Has another roll of the sun found you rising above the chaff?"

"I don't know about that sir, but I have finished rewording the Plateau's guidelines concerning hairstyles and body art and finished the template for the printer before anyone else finished their assignment. I was wondering if I might do something to assist you." Out of the corner of her eye, she saw Jonas approaching the doorway. But Whitlock ignored the little pipsqueak.

"Impressive, Roxan. Very well done." Whitlock beamed as he placed the last stack of bound papers in a tan rectangular basket. "As a matter of fact, if you don't mind, you can take these flyers around to the shops in the village. Every shop needs to get one stack and a scroll. It's a lot of walking, but somehow I don't think you'll mind being outside."

His eyes floated to the glass window filled with blue sky and puffy white clouds and then came back to rest on Roxan. The spark she saw there turned her jubilation into triumph. Everyone's eyes were brown or hazel, but not everyone's were like Whitlock's. His eyes seemed to see some of the same amazement in the world around them as Roxan did; she liked him better and better.

She let out a wispy hum and reached for the basket. "I would definitely not mind delivering *your* flyers, sir."

Jonas slid past her, gently patted her arm with his hand, and gave her a reproachful look. "Sir, I had thought Roxan could help some of the other plebes with their work." He placed his hands on the edge of the basket and his eye twitched slightly. "I'll be happy to deliver these for you." He nodded his head to dismiss her back to the dreary workroom, but Roxan stayed put. A look of annoyance flickered in Whitlock's sweet eyes. She held her breath and waited.

"That won't be necessary, Jonas. Roxan's got this covered." Whitlock lifted the basket away from Jonas, deposited it in Roxan's open arms, and gave her a friendly wink. Without another word, she smiled and exited the office before Jonas could protest. The basket was heavier than she thought, but she waited until she had exited the workroom to adjust her grip. Small, stiff cards, the size of a hand, filled the basket. Each supplied the same message:

Plateau Guidelines

Shops should operate for the good of all.

No shop should provide any good or service to anyone who has not received the proper number of merits.

Each shop should close its doors at the warning horn.

No Exceptions

All bookkeeping records should be submitted at the end of each moon cycle. Failure to do so will result in the assignment of a sentry supervisor until privileges can be reinstated.

Beautifully scripted lettering displayed each message, and from the looks of it, the same person had written all of the cards. There couldn't be that many shops in the Protectorate. Roxan regretted not asking more questions about her assignment. She paused at the top of the stairwell and lifted the top layer of cards; underneath were scrolls that were rolled and tied together with leather. Each scroll had a shiny plate on it with the name of the shop engraved into it. *Ah, each shop gets a scroll and a card! I can do this.*

Roxan lifted the basket to her chest, descended the staircase, and headed for the large glass door and the great outdoors. A fresh breeze, filled with the hint of some yet-to-be-found-out flower greeted her as she stepped out into the sunshine. An orangey-brown butterfly shared her joy. Free at last.

The river flowed on the other side of the field. Roxan stepped from the path into the grassy bowl. The river had to be the boundary line for the village, but the map was probably in her handbook, which she'd left on her desk. The woods beyond the river looked untouched and mysterious.

A large boundary sign stood at attention in the center of the field. Even from a distance, she could tell the forest was off limits. A thick red line followed the field side of the river. The red lines aren't to be crossed. Oh well. It's hard to complain when a few rolls ago, the ceiling was steel, and the only light came from a thousand solar globes. Stupid raising home.

Puffy white clouds meandered through the blue sky. Roxan plopped down and sat the basket aside. "Clouds are incredible," she whispered to herself. Huge billowing white blobs. Pictures hadn't done any of this justice.

Roxan shook her finger at the sky. "Just don't stick around when the warning horn blows. Please, no clouds in the darkness." Clear skies would make for a much better viewing of the moon. It was supposed to be a full moon too.

"Whoa! Who are you talking to? You're looking serious." Mullin nudged the basket with his booted foot. "How's that lead recorder thing working out for ya?" A strong smell of jerky, mixed with cinnamon and sweat, accosted her.

"Uh, it's fine." Lifting the basket, she jumped to her feet and hurried back to the path. Mullin stayed in step with her, his worn wooden cart squeaking as he followed.

"Fine, huh? Whatcha doing? That old Whitlock got you doing his bidding?" He smirked and kept his sarcastic eyes on her. "Or are you contemplating sneaking off on a little woodsy excursion, Spunky?"

"I'm delivering these flyers to the shops in the village. Not that it's any of your business. Whitlock was doing me a favor." Roxan met his eyes. How could a person be warm and inviting and mysterious and questionable all at the same time?

Mullin pulled his cart around, blocking part of the path and annoying a line of shop girls with curlicues painted on their cheeks. "A favor? How's that?" he asked. He pulled a red apple from a sack in the cart and took a smug bite. "I've never heard of overseers doing favors for anyone but themselves." He chewed as he spoke.

Roxan eyed the apple. "He knows I like it out here, so he gave me a job to do outside. I don't think he's like other overseers."

Mullin sat down on the edge of his cart. He, evidently, had no need of an overseer to give him a break. His face looked brown from too much sun, and his closely set hazel eyes stayed fixed on her.

Roxan took in another bolt of the fresh air. "It's beautiful out here. *He* can see that."

"Yep." Mullin's dirty-blonde crew cut looked golden with the sunlight falling across him. "It's lovely." He took another chomp from the fruit, then coughed out an apple-filled laugh.

Roxan couldn't take it anymore. "Are you kidding me? What's your problem? You've got it made. You get to travel around, meet lots of people. You practically get to be your own boss." Mullin smiled at her and waved the apple back and forth. She bit her lip and sighed. "I don't know why I even bother talking to you."

"Whoa, calm down there," he backed down. "Didn't mean to get you all charged up." He must have noticed her eyes on the apple, because he held it out as an offering.

Thankful his tone had changed, she gingerly picked the scrumptious fruit from his hand and just looked at it. Red and juicy. Sweet and fresh.

"Never had one, eh?"

She nodded, keeping her eyes on the fruit.

"Yeah, those gummy fruit squares they give you at the raising home aren't even close to the real thing." His tone changed from sarcasm to something deeper, almost entreating her. "Roxan, there's so much you haven't seen yet."

She heard him, but this was her first taste of a real apple, a monumental moment. And, as she did with all monumental moments, she closed her eyes for a second, trying to stamp into her memory the exact place and situation of the event, so she'd have it in the scrapbook of her mind. Then she took the bite. Juice sprayed into her mouth, and she tried to contain her joy.

Mullin kept talking, stuck in his own world and, evidently, oblivious to the great thing taking place inside her mouth. She was halfway done when he coughed and got her attention back.

"You're right," he agreed. "It is beautiful here, and I do have a good job, but I'm not my own boss. I answer to a guide who answers to an overseer, and so on and so on. And none of us ever really gets to do what he wants." His hazel eyes lost their green and turned toward a grim brown.

Torn between the apple and his sad countenance, Roxan savored the bits in her mouth before holding the precious fruit up. Just another roll and she would have enough merits to get her own apple.

Mullin waved her off. "You can keep it."

Cradling the fruit in both hands, she took another bite.

"Roxan, you've gotten me to thinking."

"About what?" A piece of apple almost escaped out the corner of her mouth.

"Well, about how great it is here, except for a few things. But maybe we could get some of those things changed." He was serious. Who would have thought a delivery guy would get so philosophical about social issues. He stepped closer and whispered in her ear. "Maybe there's a way to show them that we're more than just a bunch of mindless machines, churning out work until we *graduate* to the Plantanate. Maybe we could at least change having to be in every roll when that horn blows or being stuck inside that confining boundary line."

She didn't wait to finish chewing. "Are you crazy?"

"I might be, if I were thinking about doing this on my own, but with you, there might be a chance. You've actually been to the Plateau."

"I was a child."

"Exactly, and Hyperion took a special interest in you."

Roxan froze. A bad feeling sat in her stomach. This wasn't the kind of stuff she wanted to talk about, but the stuff she wanted to ignore, to keep secret. Yet she was the one who'd blurted it all out. Why did she have to tell him she'd been to the Plateau?

"What?" He drew her back, "Why the frightened eyes?"

A shockwave went through her when he said eyes. It was time to take the conversational defensive. He'd already gotten more out of her than she'd wanted to say. Time for him to start answering some questions. Wiping her mouth with her sleeve, she stood on her tippy toes to look him in the eye. "What do you think you're doing?"

"Settle down, Spunky. I'm not going to make you do anything you don't want to. But you've got to know that going to the Plateau and meeting Hyperion means something." He kept prying at her secrets.

Roxan shuffled her new sandals across the well-worn path. Just walking away probably wasn't an option. And for the first time ever, she didn't know how to divert the conversation. A light tingling started in the back of her head again.

Mullin kept talking, oblivious. "I'm actually surprised you're not more interested in all of this. If it were me, I'd be asking some questions, talking to people. Have you?" He broke into her tingling head.

Roxan met his question blankly. She was busy trying to ward off another episode with her eyes. Twice he'd been around when she needed him not to be.

"Have you, Roxan? Have you spoken with anyone else about all of this? Maybe your overseer? Or someone else who might have known about it?"

She shook her head. The warmth receded, and as the prickles eased up, her mind jumped into gear. "Why all the questions? You know, we're not really friends, you and I. Don't go thinking I'm going to help you do anything subversive. I'm here to live, do my job well, and enjoy all of this."

A smile made its way to her face. "So why don't you do your job and let me get back to mine."

"I don't mean to press. I believe there's more to you than you think, though. You may not even know what it is yet. But I think there are some others who do." The muddy mix of color in his eyes moved out of the way for his large black pupils, and Roxan swallowed the last bits of apple that had pooled in the back of her mouth. It was hard to hold his gaze, but equally as hard to look away.

Consideration replaced the urgency in his voice. "I know you don't believe me. But there has to be some part of you that sees it, that knows. You're different." He paused. Other plebes walked around the cart, but Roxan only watched their feet go by, not their faces. "Listen, I could be totally wrong about all of this, but I don't think so. People don't just go to the Plateau. It's a big deal. But if you don't want to know about it that's fine. I only wanted to help. That's all."

"How? How can you help me?"

"I'm still working on that. I can't talk about it here." He took her by the arm and pulled her to the side wall of the Baker's Shoppe. The shaded stone cooled her hot back. An alley about a meter wide separated the bakery from the packaged food dealer. Mullin blocked the exit to the path. "Would you meet me somewhere? I need to do some research. If I find out anything, I'll send you a note, and then we can meet."

"Where?" Roxan dropped the sticky apple core and adjusted the basket of flyers. She'd almost forgotten about her job. "At one of those meetings you mentioned earlier?" Tiny barbs poked at her neck, and a warm sensation enveloped her ears and slid toward her eyes.

"No. I don't think that little band of free thinkers will appreciate you. I'll be in touch. I'll let you know where we can meet. Roxan, be careful who you trust. I'll find out what I can, and I'll help you. Until then?" He gripped her arm tightly, almost causing her to drop the basket.

"Until then," she whispered back, but he had already stepped into the stream of people on the path.

A golden ray of light pushed past her will and threaded out from her eyes toward him as he turned toward her work building. The strands silhouetted him, a blackened, faceless figure, wheeling a cart away.

CHAPTER 7

OPERATION DETHRONE-THE-OVERSEER

Sunlight faded from the empty workroom. Jonas tossed his scribbling into the refuse bin, and rested his hand on the shiny wooden desktop. He drummed his fingers as if they were marching in place, and used his other hand to prop up his head. This entire roll had *not* gone according to plan.

Stacks of completed assignments sat at the corners of each desk. That would normally give him a sense of pride, but not this roll. The sting of being ignored smarted. Roxan had been able to defy orders and get her own way. And Whitlock fell for it all. She had obviously made it onto his "best" list. That made her a rival, not an associate, no matter how talented she might be. Her little power play with the flyers needed a response, a counteroffensive.

Jonas stopped drumming and balled his hand into a fist. His back stiffened. Roxan didn't know who she was dealing with. Obviously, this sort of stuff had worked for her in the raising home. Nannies could be easily duped. But she underestimated him if she thought he would let something like that go. He could make her life miserable, and Whitlock would never even know.

The quickly fading plasma globe cast an orangey glow across the empty assignment board at the front of the room. Jonas scanned the workstations. Each one marked the work area of a half-witted, thickheaded, mediocre technician. And they all answered to him. They knew their place. Roxan would too, and once she got that figured out, she could go from opponent to ally. It would be good to have someone on the team who actually had talent.

What is he doing in there? Jonas cut his eyes toward the overseer's office. Whitlock had been hunched over his desk, ever since the last plebe had cleared out and headed for home. *Why hasn't he taken off like usual? The first warning horn's already blown.*

Twilight cast shadows across Whitlock's face. Framed by ribbons of pink and red in the fading sky, his silhouette looked majestic—the striking form of a mighty leader arched over his work. Jonas rolled his eyes. *That should be me in there.* It would be—one of these rolls. Whitlock didn't deserve the position. He had no ambition, no drive.

Jonas clenched his teeth and a spray of dissatisfaction filled his mouth. Whitlock owned the honor of being the youngest overseer to ever be appointed, but that would change. The Guardians would eventually notice whose name was on most of the projects, and who was making this floor into a powerful machine.

Jonas took out a red appointment card from his desk drawer. The first stage of his attack was scheduled to begin at the start of the new cycle. *Operation Dethrone-the-Overseer* had already begun. Whitlock's high intelligence may have put him leaps and bounds ahead of everyone in his office and probably in the Protectorate, but it wouldn't save him. Jonas closed his drawer, locked it, and tucked the card in his pocket.

"The work roll's over, Jonas," Whitlock grunted as he breezed toward the exit. And his lack of curiosity served Jonas well. The overseer left without looking back or offering another word. His genius was accompanied by a simplicity that kept him believing everyone was on the same side.

Jonas pushed himself away from the desk and rounded the corner into Whitlock's office. The brilliance of it shocked him. He could look into the office from his desk all roll long, but rounding that corner and walking in always filled him with awe.

The last visages of dusk illuminated the horizontal windows that were the better part of two walls in the room. Whitlock's entire office was one big window. No curtains, just lots of glass. The entire grassy bowl could be seen, even to the edge of the Triangle Park. Jonas grunted at the view and headed straight to the desk chair.

Smoky air seeped through the cracked window behind the desk and left a bad taste in Jonas's mouth. That mixed with the freshly cut honeysuckle on the desk made the room even more like someone's sitting room than an office. Offices should be filled with the scent of paper, ink, and sweat, not smoke and flowers.

The smell of leather, however, should be part of an overseer's sanctuary. Jonas drew in a deep breath and smiled. There it was. Whitlock's chair—thickly stuffed leather, dark brown and the perfect symbol of power. More than a seat, it served as the throne, and its owner ruled as the king in this little corner of the Protectorate.

Jonas glided to his favorite spot, then straightened his back as he settled into the chair. The workroom lay before him, and his reflection superimposed itself across the view. *Ah, this is where I belong.* Whitlock always kept the shutters to the window overlooking the main office open. He liked keeping an eye on all of his *dear* workers. That would change if Jonas were overseer. Keeping an eye on *his* employees would be more than staring through a window. There would be no doubt of that. There were other ways to find out what people were up to. He patted the card in his pocket.

Jonas pulled in another breath and exhaled the annoying scent of honeysuckle hovering in the air. This office would be his one roll. And maybe, if Roxan were worthy, she could be his second-in-command. But first, he needed something to subdue her childish rebellion.

Whitlock's desk creaked as Jonas pulled himself closer. The slick, black surface held only the vase with honeysuckle, a nameplate, and a stack of papers. He swiveled around in his sweet throne and pulled open a cabinet drawer in the credenza. It rolled out slowly, revealing numbered files, fifty-six, all neatly labeled with the names of each plebe ever assigned under Whitlock. *Okay, Roxan, now it's time to find out why it took you so long to graduate.* The plebe sheet hadn't given much information except for her age, number of infractions and a few other benign notes.

Jonas grunted at the empty space where Roxan's file should be. He slammed the drawer and spun the chair around. "Where is it?" His voice trailed off as he noticed a file under the papers on the desk. "Mmm ..." He moved the papers to the side and saw the label—"Roxan 423B7." A handwritten note was attached that read, "Plateau bonded/Eyes/???"

"So, the big guy's got questions about her too," Jonas whispered. If Whitlock doubted Roxan, it would be easier to displace her or even remove her to an entirely different unit if that proved to be the best option. He had seemed bothered by something when he was all hunched over his desk earlier. Maybe the situation would resolve itself without much interference.

Jonas flipped the file open and examined a small picture of Roxan as a child. A shiver ran down his spine. Something about her seemed off. The little girl looked defiant. Her chin pushed up and her eyes narrowed, looking straight at the camera—her long, brown hair a tangled mess. Someone had scribbled words, dates, and times below the picture, but Jonas didn't know their significance. One of the words, *Clingman*, rang a bell, but he couldn't pull up its meaning.

A long blast of the second All-In horn blew away the silence in the room. Jonas didn't flinch, though. All-In had proven to be his friend. While the others cowered in their shanties and huts, he found his way around the rules and used the dark roll to gather information. He knew a secret way back to his shanty, so the sentries wouldn't nab him for being out, and he also had a Roll-Expansion Card saved for special occasions.

"Something's up with you, Roxan," he deliberated with himself. This stuff smacked of secrecy. According to the dates in the file, three seasons were missing from Roxan's training, nearly an entire turn.

The last page was a large picture of Roxan's group. The symbol at the bottom of the picture indicated it had been taken right before her advancement. Tall and thin, she stood out among a sea of orange cover-ups. Older than her classmates, she also seemed to be set apart from them. They all stood facing the camera, smiling, with their hands clasped in front. But not Roxan. Her eyes looked away from the camera. She looked off as if she were staring at something on the shiny steel ceiling. And her hands were clasped under her chin.

Jonas propped his elbows on the desk and rubbed his temples with his fingers. A pinch pulled at his neck. His stomach acids gurgled and churned. They would be headed up his esophagus soon enough, burning their way to his throat. He pulled open the cooler and snatched a bottle of

Calciwater. Whitlock wouldn't miss it, and the milky liquid worked faster than the pills the clinician had given him.

He took two swigs, closed his eyes, and rested his head on the back of the chair. Eyes? Plateau bonded? This puzzle needed more pieces. But finding those pieces was a puzzle in itself. No one was going to be answering the questions he was having.

A chair scraped across the floor in the outer office. Jonas popped forward, bumping the Calciwater, but catching it before the whole thing spilled. Someone else was here. That could only mean two things. Sentries, or Whitlock had returned—neither was good.

Voices echoed off the black walls of the workroom, and the beam of a high-powered stave cast long shadows across the stations. Jonas ducked down beside the desk. The sudden movement, combined with his racing heart, almost brought the churning milky substance back up, but he cupped his hand over his mouth and took a few deep breaths. No one had seen him.

He pulled the Roll-Expansion Card out from under his cover-up top. Three of the six stick figures were marked through with an X. If he needed to, he could use it to excuse his missing curfew.

Two shadowed figures worked their way down each row of desks. The one leading, holding the light, wore the leather cover-up of a sentry. Jonas couldn't make out his face, so he crawled to the doorway, keeping his head close to the floor.

"This is it. Her desk's in the back corner. . .over there." The man behind the sentry spoke.

"Shhh. Keep it down," the sentry scolded.

"Why? Nobody's here. You worry too much."

"Listen, Mullin. If we are caught here, I'll have to write you up. There will be no explaining how I'm here with you." This was no plebe sentry. Anyone with as much gold trim as on his cover-up had to be on the job for at least five turns.

"Okay, fine. But don't doubt the expertise with which I can weave a story, especially around most of your dubious comrades." Mullin chuckled as he spoke. "Look! This is it." The two men stood next to Roxan's desk. Jonas couldn't see what they were doing without crawling closer.

"There's nothing here." The sentry sounded annoyed. "This is a waste of time. This girl isn't anything special. I told you I've already checked her out."

"Staring at her through a window isn't checking her out. It's stalking," Mullin said. "You can't tell much from only observing. You've got to actually talk to her." He rummaged through her desk drawers and papers. The sentry stood in the aisle between the workstations. Big and bulky, he didn't look like someone you'd want to talk back to, but Mullin pushed on, "What if she'd seen you?"

"She did." He cleared his throat with a laugh.

Mullin got still. "Are you crazy?"

"That was the quickest way to see if she had a gift, but nothing happened. She froze," he sneered. "I don't know why she's on the list, but with fifteen names to investigate, I'm not going to spend any more time on her." He pulled out a small scroll and unrolled it. "Looks like there's another one in this office I need to check out."

"Who?"

"Whitlock. He's the overseer." The guard turned toward the office. Mullin shoved a drawer shut and followed.

"An overseer? How could an overseer be on the list? Aren't those guys just like us?" Mullin bumped into one of the desks, knocking papers on the floor, but didn't bother to pick them up.

The sentry stopped. "Fix that," he grumbled, pointing to the papers. "No one's just like us, Mullin. Overseers are good rule followers, but they aren't insiders. I've known a few to stray off the path and start trouble." Mullin picked the papers up and tossed them onto a different desk.

"I've never heard of any."

The sentry grunted at him and headed for the office.

Jonas checked out his options. Other than under the desk, the only other place to hide was a tall cabinet situated between the two vertical windows on the short wall. Whitlock had made the decorative piece of furniture. The elaborately carved doors hid only empty space inside. He reached the cabinet as the sentry's light invaded the room. He slipped inside, but left the door cracked.

"Whoa. Now, this is an office." Mullin walked in as if he belonged there. "Who is this Whitlock guy, anyway?"

"He's not anyone. He's supposed to be good at what he does, a genius, but he's also by the book. It doesn't make sense for his name to be on a traitor list. He has no connection with anyone outside the boundary. I don't think he'll be very useful."

"I don't know why we don't go out there and hunt them down." Mullin pulled drawers open. "I mean we've got the fire power. Why not cut them all down?"

"It's not that easy." The sentry lifted the file from Whitlock's desk. "Well, it looks like Mr. Whitlock does know something. She's Plateau Bonded."

Mullin swung around from the back table. "What? Then why isn't she there?" The two men hunched over the file.

The sentry tapped the file and grumbled, "She's hardheaded. They turned her away for being unorganized and unfocused. They wanted her. They're waiting till her kinks get worked out."

"Look here." Mullin pulled the light closer to the file. "Clingman." His voice caught as he spoke. "That must be it."

"What?"

"She said she went to the Plateau when she was a little one. This must be why." Mullin spoke slowly, as if he were pondering something in his head.

"How do *you* know that?" The sentry put his hand on his scinter and growled, "I told you not to talk to any of these people."

"She's on my route." Mullin held his hands up. "All innocent. She doesn't know anything. Besides, I think she likes me." He turned back to the papers and flipped a page over. "What was it? Clingman. That's serious. She seems normal to me. What do you think they found?"

The sentry snapped the file closed and pointed to Whitlock's note attached to the front. "Her eyes. It was her eyes." The two quietly looked through the rest of the file without another word. They obviously understood something deeper in the words than Jonas had.

"Well I guess that's it, then." Mullin took a step and plopped down in Whitlock's leather chair. "I'll have to lure her out there."

"You stay away from her." The sentry spoke firmly. "I mean it. We'll take it from here. This is over your head." His condescension landed squarely on Mullin, propelling him from the chair.

"What? You can't keep me out of this." The chair slid back, hitting the credenza behind the desk. "What are you up to, Jasper?" Jonas held his breath at the mention of the sentry's name.

"Are you threatening me?" Jasper lit his scinter. "Are you questioning *my* motives? This is only about devotion, following orders and supplying the Guardians with information to make the best decisions—and give Hyperion the course he wants."

Mullin backed away and mumbled, "So it would seem."

Before the words were out of his mouth completely, Jasper had grabbed him and slammed him against the one patch of wall that wasn't made of glass. Mullin didn't resist, but kept his composure, despite the sentry's forearm pinning his neck to the wall.

"Stay away from the girl," Jasper warned. "You try to use this for your own advantage, and you'll go down."

"Okay." Mullin strained for air.

The sentry loosened his grip and stepped back. "Don't mess this up, Mullin. You may have gone out there a few times, but you have no idea what they're capable of or what they're planning." Mullin rubbed his neck and didn't say anything more. Jasper grabbed the light from the desk and headed out. "C'mon," he ordered.

Mullin growled softly to the empty room, then walked away.

Jonas crawled out of the cabinet and sat in the silence, replaying their conversation in his mind. None of it made much sense, though. Why would Roxan and Whitlock be suspected of being traitors?

Jonas lit his stave and checked the appointment card. He couldn't wait until the next cycle. He needed to make his arrangement with Wortman before the sentry could take Roxan.

CHAPTER 8

THE OTHER WORLD

"What are you up to?" Abiga could barely hear herself across the roar of the pouring waterfall. Altrist looked funny. He had a gray blanket draped over his shoulders and a red scarf wrapped around his neck.

"I'm going to the edge of the Protectorate and try to see her." He pulled on brown gloves with the fingers cut out. Jumping up from her pallet near the warm lumen, Abiga got right in his face.

"What? Altrist, you know how dangerous that is. If she's supposed to come here, won't she just come? Won't that happen without your help? There's no need for you to be careless." She turned back toward her little corner of the cave.

"I know. But I'm tired of waiting around. I know I'm supposed to bring her here, so I might as well get on with it." Altrist touched Abiga's shoulder and turned her around. Water glistened in his spiky blonde hair. His deep blue eyes filled with a watery sheen. Abiga had never seen him cry, except once when he laughed so hard at Thim and Grouper's horsing around. "Please, Abiga. You need to let go."

"Altrist, I don't know about this girl, but I do know that you put us all in danger when you go to the Protectorate." It was time to pull out her list of arguments. "That world isn't for us. I've seen it firsthand. There are sentries all over the place down there. Leave it alone. They've all made their choice. They don't want to know the truth."

She held up her arm and folded up her sleeve. The scars spoke for themselves. Sentries had no regard for what's right, only serving their master. They attacked Undesirables for sport, killing off the weaker ones. They carried out their evil orders with zeal. He had to know all of that. Maybe he needed reminding.

"It's not only the Undesirables they hate. They hunt us too," she continued. "They hunt for you." Had he forgotten that? There were only two beings like him in the entire Oblate. Maybe only one. The other, a girl, didn't have the same abilities. Without Altrist to help them understand the Leader's orders, they would be lost. "How can you do this to us? Will you waltz right up to their doorstep? Offer yourself up without a thought to what will happen to us without you?"

"I know all that Abiga. I'll be careful." Altrist lifted his gloved hands into the air. "I do have gifts that can help, you know." A light glowed from his hands and fell down across his body until he had completely vanished from view. His voice chimed up from behind her. "I think I can elude the sentries if I need to."

"You can't easily do that within their boundaries. Besides, that's not the point Altrist." Abiga turned and pulled the red scarf from his neck. "If you draw attention to yourself, then they're gonna come looking for you, and you may be able to get away, but it's gonna be hard to hide a group of fifty-some Outcasts making a run for the Balustrade. You put us all in danger." She poked his little chest with her finger and dropped the scarf at his feet.

"The Leader will see the Outcasts safely through. Honestly, Abiga, you have to stop depending on your take on things and start acting on what you believe." Altrist rarely scolded others, and the sting of his words hit their mark.

She pulled out more ammunition. "We can't help them. They don't want our help. This girl doesn't even want your help." Abiga's hot face didn't match her ice-cold hands.

"How do you determine who does and does not want our help?" Altrist took her hand as he spoke, but she pulled away from him. "How do you know who will hear the truth and embrace it and who will run or fight? We can't know, but that doesn't change what we do know. I know my path. Now, quit trying to stop me."

"What about my path?" She cried. Her curls bounced, punctuating each word. "Don't you even care about me?"

"I love you Abiga. You are like a sister to me, but I can't fix your problems, and my staying won't fix your problems. You have to figure this out for yourself." Altrist reached down and picked up the red scarf. "So you think this would be a bad idea?"

"Yeah." Abiga wiped her face with her sleeve. None of her arguments had worked. But she still had one more. "You have to tell them." She nodded in the direction of the others, who were eating breakfast in the back of the cave. "I won't keep this secret any longer. They all think you're coming with us. You tell them or I will."

She couldn't believe her voice sounded so steady, but the anger at his abandoning them had not subsided since he had told her three rolls of the sun ago. It had been simmering. "As a matter of fact, why don't you do it right now?" She grabbed his little hand and headed down the short tunnel to the smaller chamber where the others sat.

"Everyone. I think Altrist has an announcement he'd like to make." Abiga let go of his hand and took a step to the side. Altrist's white skin and blonde hair glowed in the dimly lit cavern. The others stopped their chatting and turned their eyes to him. He gave Abiga an angry sideways glance.

"Well, I hadn't planned it this way, but. . ." He took a step closer to the small group of Outcasts. "I guess now is as good a time as any."

Abiga looked around the table at the faces she'd grown to love. Grouper sat at the head of the table. He needed the extra space for his large arms. Having served as a sentry in the Protectorate, Grouper knew the dangers Altrist would find and bring on them all if he wasn't careful. He would be the best bet at convincing Altrist not to go. Liza sat next to Jahn, like always. On the other side of the table sat Anna, the oldest of the group— not including Altrist. No one knew how old he was, and he kept it that way.

Thim sat next to Anna. His eyes were fixed on Abiga, not Altrist, but she refused to look at him. He wouldn't approve of her forcing Altrist's confession like this, but she also knew he'd forgive her and make up before the roll ended.

"I'm leaving," Altrist, blurted out. Everyone froze, cups and forks paused on their courses. "I won't be going with you when you leave for Pocket. I've got something I must do here, and if it works out like I hope, I'll join you later, and I won't be alone." He winked and smiled. His words crossed the border of every mind in the cavern. Abiga watched them process the news.

Grouper spoke first. "Where are ya going?" The words bounced around the rock walls. Abiga looked back and forth from Grouper to Altrist. This would be it. Grouper would have something to say about Altrist traipsing off to the Protectorate.

"Well, I don't plan to leave our boundaries, but for now I'm going to the edge, near the line to the Protectorate." Altrist held up his hand holding his finger and his thumb close together. "Just this close, but not within their boundary." Abiga searched the faces of her friends, hoping to see her concern mirrored there.

"Be careful." Grouper returned to his bowl of oatmeal with berries. Abiga's heart sank. Maybe someone else would speak up.

"Yes, be careful!" Liza chimed, sounding more like a happy bird than a concerned friend. Abiga cut her eyes to the playful admonisher. Annoying.

"Who are you going to see?" Anna cleared several bowls from the table. She had grown old within the Protectorate and still had connections there. She had discovered their lies and escaped before they threw her out, like they did with everyone who ceased being productive. Outcasts had found her before the Undesirables did. And she had been a part of them ever since. She said that somehow she always knew there had to be more, that the Leader had created a space within her that drew her to the truth. Abiga thought the older woman was terribly lucky. She had received her gift immediately, even before she went through the water. Anna could heal a person of about anything with only her warm touch.

"A girl." Altrist pulled out a chair from the table and sat down. "I don't think you would know her, Anna. She's fresh from one of the raising homes." Liza handed Altrist the berries and some bread.

"Where will you meet us?" Jahn scooted the lump of butter toward the old boy.

"I don't know. If not at Pocket or Willow Way, then at the Balustrade." Altrist took a slice of bread and buttered it, laying a coating of berries to one side and then folding it over. "What is it, Anna?" He didn't look at her, but evidently he sensed something in her expression.

"Will anyone else from the Protectorate leave with us?" She smiled, but her eyes had a distant, sad look to them that betrayed her.

"I don't know. Everyone has his or her own path to follow. Mine only seems to be leading to this girl. We must all trust the Leader right now." He put his berry sandwich down and placed one hand on Thim's shoulder and the other on Jahn's. "There are a lot of unknowns in this, but he wouldn't ask us to do something and then desert us. You will need to watch out for one another, stay together, and keep an eye on Abiga. At least until she gets her gift."

Abiga's eyes flooded again. Her efforts to sabotage Altrist's trip had failed. Of course it didn't work. The other Outcasts didn't have as much to lose by Altrist's absence. They each had their own gift—their own way around the dangers in the world. And now he asked them to babysit *her*. He was deserting her and leaving her care to them.

"I can take care of myself." She spat the words out across the table. Thim started to say something, but she spun around and tore through the tunnel.

Light poured through the waterfall. Morning was well underway, and they would all be leaving soon. She crammed her few belongings into her drawstring bag made from an old cover-up. Nothing good ever lasts. Slipping through the break between falling water and rock, she decided to wait for the rest at the trailhead for Pocket.

Twig-covered and rocky, the path to the level ground above the waterfall would have been completely hidden to anyone else, but Abiga knew it well and took it twice as fast as normal, propelled by anger. A bitter taste filled her mouth, the flavor of disappointment mixed with rejection.

"It's not fair." The rush of water drowned her shouts of anger. "It's not fair."

"What's not fair?" Altrist's voice came from inside her head. He had followed her out.

"Please don't go." She turned to face him. In the bright sunlight, he looked pale and fragile.

"Abiga, why are you fighting me on this?"

She pressed her hands to her face and shook her head back and forth.

Altrist spoke into her thoughts again. "I love you. We all love you. You will not be alone." He pressed his little hand to her shoulder. She couldn't bring herself to look at him. It hurt too much. "Please, Sweet Abiga. Don't let this thing with the gift keep you from what you know is real. I'm not the answer. You already have all you need." He kissed her hand, and a warm breeze blew across her. He was gone. He didn't wait to hear anymore of her protests. He left her there.

The others called to her from the cave. Thim made it to her side first and gently draped his arm across her shoulder. Abiga leaned into him, trying to push the tears away. *Had they all followed her out of the cave?* She didn't look up, but kept her face buried in her hands.

"Abiga." Thim leaned close to her ear. "Are you okay?"

"I'll be fine." She wiped her eyes and looked up the pathway to the thicket of trees at the top. "I just didn't want him to go."

"Me neither." Liza chimed her agreement. "I hate making these kinds of trips without him."

"You've done it before?" Abiga turned. They had all followed her onto the narrow pathway. She squinted from the sunlight. Smiles and sympathy colored their sweet faces. They stood single file on the narrow trail, almost on top of one another trying to get to her.

"We made it six cycles ago." Liza punched Abiga in the arm and gave her a wink. "He had said then there was someone he needed to meet, and now we are all very glad he did." Abiga knew what she meant. Six cycles ago, Altrist had found her. They all pressed in closer, to squeeze her arm or pat her.

"You're going to be fine, kid." Grouper put his large arms around all of them. Abiga immediately felt a peace envelop her. He used his gift liberally. But it felt good to have the pain give way to a sense of comfort. Cocking her head to the side, she gave him a knowing smile. "Hey! I'm doing what I can for you," he said. "If you want, I can get you so happy, you'll want to skip all the way to Pocket."

"I don't think you're that good." Abiga shook her head and laughed.

Grouper released the Outcasts and patted Abiga on the head. "Probably not." She felt the wash of love flow over her and flashed her questioning eyes at Grouper. "Hey, I'm not making you feel anything that's not already here. I'm only turning the lights on for you."

"Thanks, you guys. I ... " She wanted to tell them she loved them, but the words wouldn't come out. Love had been a bad thing until she met them. They changed everything about the way she saw the world. "I ... you know."

"Yes, we know." Liza threw her arms around Abiga, making her take a step back. "We know." Despite her small size, Liza had a firm grip, and Abiga returned her hug.

The others chuckled. Complete opposites, she and Liza had to look funny hugging each other. Abiga stood a full head over Liza's little frame, and her blonde curls looked nothing like Liza's long, straight, black hair. Liza was beautiful too, big eyes, plump pink lips, and no scars. The two would never be mistaken as sisters.

Abiga took a step back, looked at her little adopted family, and the gloom returned. She couldn't look at them without seeing their gifts, and that made her sad. Grouper was strong and could make people feel comfort and hope. Jahn could sing and paint. And Liza, her gifts were the most enviable. She could heal people with her touch, like Anna, and she somehow got from one place to another in the blink of an eye.

No one else could do that except Altrist, and even he couldn't get as far as she could. The only bad thing about it seemed to be Liza's lack of control. She couldn't make herself zip away. It would just happen.

Thim was the only one of them that didn't have a gift. That stung Abiga, too, though. He didn't mind it. He said that not having a gift was a gift, but she couldn't see it that way. It left her empty and wanting and questioning whether or not she belonged.

She would help them get to Pocket and then leave. It wasn't their fault the Leader hadn't given her a gift. They were precious, and time with them had been the richest part of life.

Abiga held back her tears. "Thank you," she whispered. They smiled back, not seeing the depths behind her words.

"Well, you dears," Anna's sweet voice crackled as she shouted over the powerful water, "we'd better get a move on it, if we're going to make it to Pocket in plenty of time to help them with their supplies."

Everyone made their way back into the cave to clean up after breakfast and gather their things. Abiga followed. Another cave, more like an overhang cut back into a bluff, Pocket housed about twenty-five other Outcasts. And between the two base camps, Pocket and Snowshoe Falls, ten mini-camps were hidden. They would stop at each camp, gathering Outcasts along the way.

The hidden sites weren't easy to find. Abiga only knew where five of them were. Grouper knew most of them, but needed help from the Pocket Outcasts to find one or two. Altrist had been clear that all the Outcasts needed to know about the plan to leave. Whether they decided to go or not was up to them. But they needed to be told.

Abiga pulled out a map drawn on a piece of fabric. She knew the woods like the back of her hand, but she had never been as far out as the Balustrade. They had five rolls of the sun to gather all the Outcasts and get to the wall. Grouper could help them there. He's the only one who'd ever been to the wall anyway. After Pocket, she would leave.

"Whatcha doin'?" Thim popped over her shoulder.

"Oh, nothing. Just looking at this old map for the hundredth time." She folded the map and put it back in Grouper's pack. "You know this seems crazy, right?"

"Yeah, like most of the things we do." Thim fiddled with his backpack. His sandy brown hair was combed toward his tanned face. Pulling the tie loose from his gray tog, he draped a thin green blanket across one shoulder and then used the tie to fasten it onto his sturdy frame. "Are you ready for this?"

"What? For leaving everything for the great unknown? Sure. I'm raring to go." Abiga rummaged through a chest of unclaimed things. One smelly blanket, a few cups, and some other odds and ends had been left behind for good reason. She already had everything she wanted, but she needed something to make her look busy.

"Yeah, I know what you mean. But at least we're doing it together." Thim finished strapping on his travelling gear and grabbed something from his bag. He was clumsier than usual. Something was on his mind besides the trip. "Abiga," he whispered.

She stiffened and gripped the chest, not looking back. She hadn't told him her plans, because he would've argued, and she didn't need that. Still, a little bit of honesty would have spared him now.

He touched her arm and turned her toward him. "I have something to ask you." A little wooden box sat on his palm. Reaching down, Abiga snatched up her pack and stepped around him. Ignoring him wasn't going to work this time. But she needed space.

She waited for him to face her before she spoke. "Not yet, Thim." A spark of surprise flashed into his eyes.

"Why not? Now's as good a time as any." His voice cracked into a whisper. Grouper came out from the back of the cave and dropped a crate of food and cooking supplies. He would "feel" what was going on and give them plenty of space—just what she didn't need right now. He turned and left quietly.

She watched him disappear down the tunnel before she spoke. "I can't think about any of this right now. I've got some things that need to be resolved." Her eyes connected with his, and she hated the sad understanding she saw there. "But later, definitely." Maybe offering a little hope wasn't so bad.

Thim made a move to say something more, but she stepped back and yelled into the darkness toward the back of the cave. "What's taking you guys so long?"

Anna and Liza came out of the darkness. Grouper and Jahn followed behind. They all grinned, misfiring with their premature celebrating.

Abiga broke the grinfest. "Well, what? Let's get moving." Their smiles fell, and they made small talk as they gathered the last few things from the outer cave. Abiga headed for the open air. This time they could meet her at the trailhead. Brushing by Thim, she made it to the opening just as Liza called out and put her hands over her stomach.

"Oh no," Liza winced. A light began to glow from her hands. "I'm sorry you guys. I can't stop it." As the light expanded to cover her, she closed her eyes and fell back, but before she hit the ground, she had disappeared.

"Where are you going?" Jahn ran toward her, but his arms caught only empty glowing air. This hadn't been part of their plan.

Anna broke the shockwave connecting them to disbelief. "Well, I guess that staying together thing isn't going to work out so well. We'd better get going." She motioned toward the trail. "For all we know, Liza's already at Pocket waiting on us now. We'll have to thank the Leader and hit the trail."

They grabbed their gear and filed out of the cave in silence. Abiga hung back, staring at the spot where Liza had been. "Thank the Leader." How could they thank the Leader for making things harder? For the first time, she realized her dear friends would never understand her questions.

The things they couldn't explain were attributed to the Leader as either ways for him to teach or help them. Even the bad stuff came from him, not to hurt but in some crazy way to help. How does that make sense?

They would never understand the emptiness she felt from not getting a gift. To them it was simple. If he wanted her to have a gift, she would, and if she never got one, then it wasn't something he had planned for her. And that would be that. But that wouldn't be enough for her. And eventually, they would get tired of her questioning them. There would be an unspoken expectation of agreement or else she would have to leave.

A gift wasn't too much to ask for. Abiga checked the fading image on her palm. The Leader would do this, or she wouldn't follow him.

CHAPTER 9
BLINDED

Jonas's red face made missing the sunrise an even swap. The colors were similar. Roxan bit her lip to keep her glee in check. He almost didn't notice her when he burst through the heavy wooden door, whistling to himself. He didn't seem like the whistling type. Happy people whistle. Grumpy, uptight, know-it-alls scowl, complain and make "tsk, tsk, tsk" sounds.

His cute little tune turned to a grunt, though, as Roxan caught his eye. She popped up from her desk, called out a cheery greeting, smiled, and waved. "Good roll, Master Jonas. Isn't it great to be one of the first in to work?" He didn't answer her. He marched to his desk and slung his satchel down.

Roxan pushed the window next to her desk up. Fresh air and mission accomplished. After he'd gone out of his way to greet her at the door the past four rolls, it seemed only fair to greet him back. Of course, to make it even, she should've lectured him on punctuality, and on how "no time is too early when there's work to be done." But that might have made him explode. His pouty, angry, face hit the spot. And she settled down in her chair to watch the fun continue.

"Jonas." Whitlock's voice boomed across the work area. "Get in here."

Roxan nibbled on a honey wafer and moved into a better position to watch stage two of her make-Jonas-miserable plan.

As he glanced at her from his desk, she flashed her happiest grin. This had been much more fun than pulling a prank on a nanny. And it had all worked perfectly. She couldn't have orchestrated it any better.

The shutters to Whitlock's office were open, as usual. Her splendid overseer was right where she could see him. The sun hadn't made its way over the far hill yet, but when it did, it would spray its rays through those glorious windows and across Whitlock. When the light hit him, he looked more like perfection than simply a man.

"Roxan? What are you doing here?" Norwood, Jonas's second-in-command, hung her satchel on a peg in the front and marched back. Roxan braced herself. A copy of their guide, Norwood made it a priority to anticipate Jonas's every need, even picking up the slack harassing people when he wasn't around.

"I work here," Roxan responded, keeping an eye on Whitlock's office.

"Yes, I know that, but why are you here so early? We don't usually see you until right before the late horn blows."

Roxan wanted to put the stiff replica of meanness in her place, but she held her tongue. Norwood would have to wait. Jonas needed to hear the news first. "Is there a problem?" She redirected the questioning. Norwood had no chance in a conversational skirmish.

The hollowed underling knew it too, and backed off. "No, there's no problem. I'll get you your orders for the roll."

"No need for that Norwood. Master Whitlock has already given me my orders."

"Okay, then." She cast a glance toward the overseer's office, then went back to the front.

"Yeah, you go figure out what your orders are," Roxan whispered, and then watched as Jonas finished putting away his things. He always did whatever he could to make Whitlock wait. Of course, if anyone dared to not jump when he called, they would get a loud and condemning lecture on the proper use of their time. He must have sensed something though, because he only unpacked his satchel before going to their master.

Whitlock's expression moved from tired to serious, until he glanced out the window toward her. Meeting Roxan's eyes, he nodded, smiled, and motioned for her come to his office. This would be it. Jonas was about to hear the worst news he could possibly imagine.

Whitlock had probably already told him about the Plateau's special work order issued long after All-In. And, of course, at the mention of the Plateau, Jonas's attention would be completely captivated. His desire to be part of higher management glistened in his eyes like a little one's at the sight of the treat cart.

Roxan floated from her desk to the overseer's office door, her heart pounding in her chest. Although this all seemed like a great plan, she knew Jonas. If there would be a way to cover her blue sky, he would find it. And she wasn't so sure she had what it would take to keep him in his place. But that would be part of the game.

"So, Jonas, I've decided," Whitlock came around his desk to stand next to Roxan, "to make Roxan the lead on this project."

Jonas stiffened and pressed his thin lips tightly together.

Whitlock continued, "I'm putting *her* as lead on the Plateau's latest work order and you will serve as second." Who knew getting to work early would afford such privilege! Roxan tried to look directly at Jonas, but she couldn't without breaking into a goofy smile, and now was not the time to laugh in his face. She could do that later, in private.

"Yes, sir," Jonas replied.

His shaky voice surprised her. Catching his clear eyes, she saw something new in him: bewilderment, and something else. Yesterroll, she had caught him staring at her more than usual, but she couldn't match the look in his eyes now with anything she'd encountered before. Standing there, still wearing his jacket, he looked lost. His hair didn't stand up so much in the front, and his bushy eyebrows went up instead of down. She pushed away the urge to feel sorry for him.

"That sounds good." Jonas smiled and gave her a nod. "Now, if you'll excuse me, I'll go get ready." As he passed, the stringent smell of cleanliness with a hint of vanilla enveloped her.

Whitlock returned to his chair, sunk into it, and sighed. "Well, that went better than I thought it would." His long fingers threaded their way through his messy hair. "I was ready for an argument. Alright, then, I think I'll leave things in your capable hands and go back to my hut and get cleaned up." He reached for his satchel.

Roxan started to leave, but then turned back. "Sir?" Whitlock looked up. He looked like he could fall asleep right there. "Are you sure about this? He does have tons more experience."

"You're the one for this, Roxan. I'm sure." He jammed some papers into his satchel, and she could tell she wasn't going to get anything else out of him.

The outer office was empty as she tiptoed back to her desk, reality beginning to hit her. As fun as it would be to give Jonas orders, she didn't have the experience to handle a project of this magnitude. What was Whitlock thinking? Her stomach twisted into a knot. The new assignment lay on top of the mess on her desk. It was out of place. A fancy order, directly from the Plateau lying on a bunch of papers with water stains and crumbs on them.

"Census of all souls to be taken on the first roll of the new moon.

Everyone will be counted, described, and tested. No exceptions.

Testers and counters will be sent from the Plateau during the full moon and should be housed by village officials.

Sentries will aid in the census and be available to remove anyone who does not comply.

It gave her the creeps. They would be interrogating everyone in every village. It didn't make sense, but it would be her job to make people feel good about it, to not argue with the intrusion.

Is that what she had to look forward to until she reached attainment? Lying to people, bending the truth to make it go down smoother? How crazy! She would never be allowed to voice her own opinion, because doing that would land her in a cell getting an adjustment, whatever that was.

She read it again. Nothing could be done about it. People should get mad about this intrusion, but she knew they wouldn't. People did what they were told and trusted the Guardians and replicators like her. They trusted her to tell the truth and stupidly believed she would present the facts in an unbiased light.

She lifted a stack of papers scattered on her desk and pulled out a note she'd found under her lunch sack last roll. Mullin had crossed her path every roll of the sun since her arrival, but this was the first note he'd left for her.

After their third meeting, she began to trust him. He was different, unpredictable, and enthusiastic. And he always had something nice to say about her. How smart she was, or how pretty she looked. He thought she was special.

If he'd given her a chance the last time she saw him, she would've told him about the visions. But their walk had been interrupted when two sentries came onto the trail. He hurried off, said the sentries had it out for him. That was the last she'd seen him.

A picture code decorated the front of the little piece of paper. Mullin had drawn it in red, almost like the order from the Plateau, except it didn't glisten when the light hit it. His paper was heavy too. The picture code was easy to figure out. He wanted to meet her by the river, at twilight this roll of this sun.

Roxan held the note next to the order sheet from the Plateau. Maybe Mullin would have some advice about all of this lying. At least she could talk with him about it. Whitlock evaded her questions. He answered her with long-winded stories and anecdotes.

Life out here was a bit more complicated than she'd anticipated. Maybe the plan to put Jonas in his place wasn't so brilliant after all. Between him picking on her and Mullin trying to convince her that being taken to the Plateau was significant beyond measure, the sky wasn't quite as blue, and the birds didn't sound so happy.

"Well, it looks like we'll be working together."

Roxan jumped as Jonas stepped beside her. He seemed to move about like a one of those little black bugs in her shanty, here one flash and gone the next. "Uh, yes, it does." She returned Mullin's note to its hiding place.

Jonas wouldn't notice it, anyway. If it didn't have a mirror or the seal of the Plateau across the top, he didn't pay it much attention.

"May I see the orders?" He reached past her and took the paper from her desk, giving a nudge to the stack that remained. "Good grief, Roxan. Your desk looks like a storm blew through. I'm going to have to write you up for this mess."

She turned her head away and rolled her eyes. So the game is on, eh. He must be over the initial shock of Whitlock's news and ready for a fight. He looked polished again, his grassy hair standing straight and his perfect jaw set.

"Well, it looks like we have our work cut out for us," he stated, placing the orders back on her desk.

Roxan checked his face for the same annoyance she'd had over the orders. Maybe he wouldn't like lying to people either. "What do you mean?" She reached around, grabbed her braid, and smacked her palm with it. Best to lead with a question and not give away her thoughts.

His eye twitched. "Most people won't like to go through mandatory testing. We'll need to make it sound appealing, as if it's to their benefit." Nope, he was going in a different direction.

"I thought we would write the order the way they have it, just simpler." She tossed her braid around to her back and straightened one of the piles on her desk. "You know, if people don't like it, then that's the Plateau's problem."

Jonas took a deep breath and slowly blew it out. The sweet smell of orange hovered between them. Then he gave her his classic "you're stupid" smile and jumped into his twitchy, lecture format.

"Noooo, Roxan. The Plateau requires that we bridge the gap with the people. They tell us what they need from the people, and we produce materials that create the illusion for the common man that this was his idea. It's fairly simple. Think of it as advertising." Quite proud of himself, he puffed his chest out and raised his chin.

It made her sick, though. "Or slanted reporting," she mumbled. He heard her, but ignored it. Norwood, his second-in-command, had entered the workroom and stood by, waiting. Her short blonde hair was as close to a crew cut as it could get, and the extensive body art on her neck and arms almost looked like it moved as she gritted her teeth impatiently.

"Meet me in the conference room to work out the kinks," he ordered as he met Norwood halfway up the aisle. He only liked that glorified plebe because she did everything he said without questioning any of it. It was almost creepy.

Roxan lifted the Plateau order from her desk; it felt heavy. The joy of putting Jonas in his place was quickly waning. This would be a long roll of the sun.

* * * * * *

Cold air blew through a vent behind Roxan's chair. Jonas twisted knobs by the door to get the artificial lighting to glow brighter. No sunlight. The door didn't even have a window. A black topped table took up most of the room, leaving only enough space for chairs, a cooler, and one wooden case housing a shelf of scrolls and a basket of snacks.

Between the humming of the cooler and the buzz of the fancy plasma globes, a headache was inevitable. Being sealed in this plasma-lit tomb with a power-hungry moron until this idiotic job was done might be the worst thing to happen since Nanny Skelt ripped up all of Roxan's pictures from the villages.

Jonas took the seat at the head of the table. *Of course.* Roxan wanted to bang her head on the cold, black surface. *What was I thinking? Making Jonas miserable only diminished the quality of my life. I should have seen this coming and stuck to keeping a low profile.*

"Okay," Jonas spread papers across the table. "We'll need to choose a texture of paper and even a color that will convey comfort and authority."

"What?" Roxan knew she was giving him her "you're crazy" face, but he needed it. He seemed perfectly serious. She lifted a sheet of slick paper and dangled it between two fingers. "Just pick one, who cares?"

Jonas heaved another orangey sigh and twitched his eye. The eye-twitch had actually grown on her. It served as a warning that another condescending lecture was on the way.

He snatched the paper from her hand. "Roxan, do you have to be so difficult with everything?" Although his eye still twitched, his tone had changed. No condescension. Something was different, almost friendly, like there was a laugh in there somewhere. "We have three rolls of the sun to prepare this for distribution. I can't spend a lot of time arguing with you or teaching you how to do this." His chiseled features softened up a bit.

Roxan settled back in her chair. Something wasn't right, but she couldn't place her finger on it. *He's being way too nice.* It put her on edge.

"Wait a flash. I thought I was lead on this project," she blurted out. "Aren't you supposed to be following me?" Sitting up in the cushioned chair, she avoided eye contact and moved several sheets of paper around in front of her.

Jonas reached across the table and touched her arm. Roxan stayed the urge to pull out from under his touch. This was all too weird, a clear invasion of personal space.

"Well, that's what Whitlock said, but let's face it. He's not thinking straight in regard to you." His friendly voice had a deeper, richer tone—so much nicer than his usual higher, whinier nag. "Roxan, you're not ready for this project and we both know it. If you want to do what's best, you'll do what I say. And, maybe, we can both come out ahead on this." He ended his response with almost a smile and a squeeze to her forearm.

Baffling. Settling back into the chair, she kept her mouth shut and lifted up a creamy, linen-textured paper. "Here."

Jonas lit up. "Ah, I thought that was a good choice myself." He flashed a not-before-seen toothy smile, and then set off lecturing about how the success of many orders hinged on picking the correct paper.

She halfway listened as she drifted back over their conversation, dissecting his comments. Something still wasn't right. Her mind worked backward from his last request to her questioning him. *Ah, that was it!*

Jonas stopped his lecture and began scribbling furiously on a long sheet of white paper. For the first time since she'd met him, she contemplated a truce. He worked hard and never asked others to do things he wouldn't do himself. Handsome, confident, and strong, he wasn't half-bad. He must have felt her eyes on him, because he caught her gaze and met it warmly. Still, forgiveness wasn't her strong suit, so she waved off the truce idea.

"What did you mean about Whitlock?" The words came out harsher than she meant them. Jonas's brown eyes searched her face, and he shrugged off her question, but she wasn't going to let it drop. "No, what did you mean when you said Whitlock's not thinking straight?"

His expression shifted. A cloud crossed his countenance, and an angry twitch took over his left eye. He had to be spinning another take on what he'd slipped in saying. The Plateau had forbidden workers to speak poorly of those over them—it was too divisive and slowed productivity. *Formal complaints can be filed with the appropriate people, but nothing derisive can be said under any circumstance.* She'd been studying the handbook.

"You know what I meant, Roxan." His jaw flexed.

"No, I don't, Jonas. I don't know what you meant at all," she returned. A few rolls under his tutelage and she'd been able to find her ability to meet him on level ground. Jonas leaned toward her. The cloud on his face took an evil glint, and he shook his head slowly. If he were a wild animal, this would be how he'd look right before he pounced for the kill.

"It's obvious. Whitlock finds you interesting, intriguing, and even vaguely attractive, and he's going out of his way, to the detriment of this office, to keep you happy."

He didn't touch her, but Roxan felt like all the air had been knocked out of her. "Don't look so surprised, Roxan. You had to know. How could you not know, the way he watches out for you. What is it about you that makes everyone else want to take care of you?" He stopped. "What?"

"Vaguely attractive?" Roxan looked up at the singing lights. The words stuck in her head.

"Ugh. Forget it." He picked up his pencil and focused on the paper.

Roxan inhaled deeply and exhaled with a smile. *What a sweet development!* It hadn't occurred to her before. Sure, Whitlock watched out for her and always appeared happy to see her, but attracted to her? Jonas shifted in his seat and grumbled. But Roxan ignored him. Could a matchment with Whitlock be possible? He could request it. He could petition for her. Maybe they could be paired together for a short while.

Jonas smacked his hand on the table. "There's no way the Plateau will match you two." His chocolate eyes narrowed, nothing twitched. Anger radiated from him.

Roxan put her hands up to her hot cheeks and searched for a response to his anger. Did he hate her so much that he couldn't imagine anyone ever wanting a matchment with her? It was one thing to pass judgment on someone's work, but quite another to not find any value in the person. She hadn't even hoped for a matching, ever. But someone could make a request. It wasn't impossible.

He must have seen she was weighing the possibility of it. "It won't happen. Leave it alone."

"It's not impossible, you know," she returned. Coolness settled between them. And a slight prickling warmed up the back of her neck to the top of her head. *Not now. No weirdness now.*

"With Whitlock, it is." He spoke plainly, as if he were telling her how to log her time or fill out a work extension. Emotionless. "He would have to defy direct orders, and he doesn't do that sort of thing. He's watching you and is curious about you, but he won't go to them for you."

"What? I don't ..." Roxan pulled away. She couldn't breathe and the tingling intensified. He wasn't making sense. Deep in the pit of her stomach, a twisted feeling drained all the responsiveness from her arms and legs. The urge to run flooded her brain, but instead of throwing a wall up to his callous invasion, she opened the gate wide and gave the deluge full sway. "Why? What are you talking about? Defy what orders?"

"Why?" He leaned across the table. "You know why. You're a freak. They're watching you, waiting for you. They may have tampered with your eyes, but evidently, they're not sure they've taken care of the issue. And, even if they had, they'll never give consent to a match for someone who's been altered. Aberrations don't get perpetuated." He backed off and sat down.

The hum of the lights and the cooler filled the little room. Roxan couldn't bring herself to look at him. The prickles wouldn't stop. As if summoned by his tirade, the warmth washed through her head. A golden haze fell across the room. *No. I don't want this.*

Roxan focused on the table and pulled back the haze. The more she concentrated, the more the light faded until all went black for a flash, then the room looked normal again.

Jonas hadn't started writing or anything. He only sat there. "Roxan," he said hoarsely. For the first time since she'd met him, he sounded weak.

She stole a blurry glance at him, but couldn't see his face.

"Roxan, I shouldn't have. I'm …" As the door behind her beeped open, Jonas cleared his throat and leaned over to put papers into his satchel on the floor next to him, keeping his thought to himself.

"Hey there, you two. How goes it?" Whitlock's cheery voice filled the tiny room.

Jonas coughed and answered with his head still below the table, buried in his satchel. "Very well, sir." Roxan swallowed hard, wiping her nose on her sleeve. She kept her head down over the papers on the table.

"Great. Well, I came by to say that even my two hardest workers need a break. You two get out of here for a bit and get some fresh air, and that's an order." Whitlock's voice coated Roxan's nerves like a balm. His warm hand landed on her shoulder. If he felt her trembling, he didn't show it. She didn't look up.

Jonas made his way back to an upright position and pushed away from the table. "Why, thank you, sir. If you don't mind, I have a question or two about the project the new plebes turned in last roll. Do you have a minute now?"

"Sure, we could do that now." Whitlock's voice expressed his reluctance, even though his words didn't. Roxan felt his eyes on her. She wanted to look at him, but couldn't face him. "Let's go to my office. Roxan, get outside for a bit." He patted her shoulder before he turned to leave.

It felt like forever, sitting there in that artificially lit, humming prison cell. She sat there trying to block Jonas's words from her mind. But they kept bubbling back up.

"I can't do this." Slowly, she unclasped her hands and put them on the table, pushing herself out of the chair. "I won't do this." With one full sweep, she knocked all the papers into the floor. Let Jonas have it all. She'd ask for a transfer on the next roll of the sun.

CHAPTER 10

CHOICES

"Are you okay?" Someone touched Roxan's arm, stirring her senses back to the land of the living. A pounding ripped through her head as she sat up. "Lady, are you okay?"

She "uh-huhed" and nodded her head. As her eyes focused, a man leaned down.

"What happened to you?" He sounded more irritated than concerned.

The stranger smelled like cut grass. He wore work boots, a dark grey cover-up, and a grumpy, whiskered expression. He leaned on his shovel and stuck a broken twig in his mouth. Roxan rubbed her temples. Her eyes were puffy from crying. She hardly ever cried. But the floodgates had broken open.

"I must have fallen asleep." She pulled her satchel onto her lap from its place as her pillow.

"Well, you better get moving," he warned jiggling his head in the direction of two sentries. Roxan grabbed hold of his hand and scrambled to her feet. Swaying, she latched onto his arm and moaned. He pried her fingers from his arm. "Are you sure you're okay?" She grunted in the affirmative. "Well, then, I don't want any trouble." His boots squeaked as he walked away.

The guards stopped to talk to a delivery plebe who'd wheeled his cart onto the lawn. Still unsteady, Roxan willed herself away from them. "I don't need any trouble either," she whispered. She'd left the office without a word when Whitlock told her to take a break. Norwood had asked her where she was going, but Roxan had pretended not to hear her.

Sunlight brushed the top of the trees by the river. She must have slept for a while. A warm mid-roll can do that to a sad heart. And her heart was breaking in two. There would be no running away from her secrets, no avoiding them. If Jonas knew about her eyes, who else might?

Roxan pulled out Mullin's note and settled onto a bench in the sanctioned eating area. He should be round soon. When the first horn blew, she'd move to the trees beyond the pavilion. From the picture he had drawn, it looked like he wanted some privacy for their talk.

Another sentry came around from behind the structure, startling her. "Sorry, Miss." He didn't sound sorry though. He barked. Roxan pulled her braid around and wrapped it around her index finger.

"That's okay." She kept her head down. Who knew what her face looked like after all that crying? "I'm just looking for a place to eat." He grunted back at her and kept walking. The sentries with the delivery guy called out, and he jogged over to them. That delivery guy didn't want to move his cart.

Roxan pulled her mid-roll meal from her pack. The honey wafer tasted stale. As soon as the air hit those things, they practically turned soft and lost their crunch. Some lemon Vitawater washed the crumbs from the back of her throat. It still left a bad taste in her mouth, but that probably had more to do with Jonas's lingering words than with the wafer. Humming to drown out his meanness in her head, she jammed the opened packet of soggy wafers back into her satchel, took one more swig of water, and headed out into the sunlight.

Sparkles like a thousand moving diamonds twinkled off the river, as rays of bright goodness fell through the tree branches. Roxan dropped to her knees, drew in a fresh "by-the-river breath," and contemplated sticking her feet in. The water invited her.

Clear and shallow. It flowed peacefully by. Little fish shifted together as if they were trying to show her something. They split their ranks around three large, flat rocks, and then rejoined to continue on their way.

Something splashed about three meters up the river, and rings spread out from the disturbance. Roxan searched the current for the culprit, but he must have caught whatever he was after. It was beautiful out here. The water, the trees, the mysterious woods on the other side. It all made for a wonderful stroll and a blessed distraction from a very bad roll.

Jonas was horrible. Just thinking about him caused a heaviness to grip her chest. He was right, though. She was a freak, and evidently, nothing could change that. He didn't even know the half of it.

Roxan stretched away the kinks in her back from sleeping on the ground. Her arms were still in the air when she saw him. Standing across the river stood a boy. He wore an ivory cover-up, not an orange one. And a gold cord was tied around his waist. His pale skin shimmered in the sun, and his blonde hair stuck out. A smile spread across his face as their eyes met.

"Hey kid, what are you doing over there?" She loud-whispered. "You better get back. There are sentries all over the place." A mixture of fear and admiration filled her. This little guy had not only escaped from the raising home, but he'd made it through the woods. Impressive.

The boy moved closer, but didn't answer her. He waved at her as if he were just happening by and wanted to say hello. Then he pointed toward the rocks.

Roxan dismissed what she thought he was suggesting and took the lead. "How'd you get out there?" The boy's smile grew, but he didn't answer her. She motioned to the rocks and waved for *him* to jump across. He didn't move. Instead, he stood up straight, his smile fading into concentration. His smooth little face looked serious, more serious than a kid should look.

Roxan took a step forward. The world blurred. Gravity fell away, and the riverbank no longer supported her. She floated across the water. Below her, a school of fish darted back and forth covered by her shadow. The pavilion waited behind her. Gliding to a stop, she rested in front of the boy. His eyes shimmered like the jewels on Nanny Skelt's cover-up. A small scar ran along his jawbone to his ear where he wore a beautiful glass earring set in gold.

When he opened his mouth, she could almost hear him breathe, and then, instead of speaking, he blew out. A warm gust of air brushed across her cheeks. His breath smelled sweet. His eyes scanned back and forth as if he were reading her like a book, and then he smiled again.

He didn't move his lips, but his voice rang in her ears. "Come, follow me." It echoed in her mind. She closed her eyes, shook her head, and tried to extract herself from this weird dream. Her heart thudded. Something in her made her want to go, even though she had no idea what he meant, but everything she'd ever been taught pushed it aside and stirred her from the dream.

When she opened her eyes, the kid had gone, and she was back behind the Pavilion. Her satchel lay at her feet, and the other side of the river was distant and far away. Pieces of the golden haze fell from the air, and the tingling in the back of her head faded. She hadn't even been aware of its onset this time. But it must have been the cause of her weird vision.

"You're early."

Roxan jumped. Mullin leaned against the wooden wall.

"I … uh …" Roxan looked back across the river. Nothing but trees. "I'm having a very weird roll."

"Hmm. Those happen." He moved on. "It's beautiful over there, isn't it?" He waved his hand toward the other side, oblivious to what she'd seen.

"Yes, it's very beautiful. If only we were allowed to go over there." No sense in telling him about the kid. Mullin might be some sort of a far-thinker, but this story stretched things beyond the borders of reason.

"There are ways around that rule." The hint of a laugh followed his words. But Roxan didn't feel like laughing.

"Does anyone live out there?"

He grabbed her hand and pulled her to the bushes on the far side of the structure. "C'mon. There's a whole batch of new recruits here ready for their placement in sentry duty, and the new ones are always looking into things, trying to make an impression." He smelled more like sweat and less like jerky this roll, but the hint of cinnamon still accompanied his words.

He looked all around, even across the river. Little lines ran out from his eyes as he squinted. Such a light color, his eyebrows blended into his leathered face almost perfectly. The v-neck to his cover-up fell open, revealing the same blonde hair covering his tanned chest and a few bright pink spots.

"Okay, so yes, there are some people out there, Roxan. They're wild people, like animals. They're people who've been dissatisfied with things here and thought they could make a go of it out there, but they can't." He shot her a sideways glance and then continued. "It plays with their minds and makes them go crazy." He pulled his satchel off his shoulder and turned to face her. "Not that a run in the woods isn't good for some things."

A charged sensation ran up Roxan's back, but no tingling. Her cry from earlier forced its way into her throat. Too many things were colliding inside of her. She needed to get away and cry again. Quelling the urge to run, she tried to move things along. "Why did you want to meet with me?"

"What's bothering you? I thought we'd gotten past all that feisty stuff." His hurt tone pulled tears from her eyes. "Whoa. What is it?" He rested a hand on her shoulder. "What happened?" Concern and curiosity accompanied his words. Pulling away, she felt for the back wall of the pavilion and steadied herself.

"They know."

"Who?"

"Jonas, Whitlock, I'm not sure who else. They all know about me. They know there's something wrong with me." Roxan blurted it out in a rush of words and sobs. "I wasn't even sure I remembered it. It's all fuzzy, but Jonas knew. He knew they did something to my eyes. He called me a freak."

She turned toward the wall and huddled against the prickly wood. Quiet and still, Mullin pulled back from her. A silence roared between them, filled only with the quiet flow of the river. When he finally did speak, his words paralyzed her.

"I'd hoped we'd have more time. But they are forcing us to make a move." He turned her around to face him. "Roxan, you're special. I think you may be the one we've been waiting for. I wasn't supposed to talk to you about this, but I'm going to tell you because I trust you, and I think you can handle it." He paused, waiting for something, but Roxan wasn't sure where he was going, so she just nodded her head and wiped her face. "There's something about you. And they want it. Have you noticed anything strange? Unusual?"

"No." The lie came out smoothly. Roxan bit her lip. Telling anyone about her weird visions seemed like a bad move.

"I'll protect you Roxan, but you're gonna have to trust me. And, if this works out the way I hope, you'll never have to go back to Jonas or Whitlock. You'll be free." He closed the gap between them. "I know it's confusing. There's a lot you don't know about. But now that people like Jonas and Whitlock have made a move, I think it might be best for you to hide out for a while."

Roxan groped for words to express her questions, but she wasn't even sure what to ask.

Mullin caught her uncertainty. "Just for a bit. Once this is all worked out, you'll have your place and freedom."

A splinter cut into her palm as she grabbed again for the wood to steady herself. "What? I can't run away." It was hard to piece together what he was saying. This had jumped from people knowing her secret to her running away. "There's no hiding. Whitlock wouldn't hurt me. He's my friend. Jonas even said," she paused, unsure how much to share. Mullin pounced.

"You can't trust them, Roxan. Listen, there's more to it all. I haven't gotten to the bottom of it yet, but I will. I know what they did to you." He rested his calloused hand on her arm and stooped to look her in the eye. "I know, and you can pretend that it's no big deal, like it happens all of the time, but it doesn't. You're different."

He rubbed his whiskered chin as he stepped away. The pressure his words put on her drained the air from her chest, and she took shallow breaths.

The sliver of wood protruded from her palm, but she couldn't feel it.

"I don't know what you're talking about." An empty feeling filled her legs and crept up her body, stopping in her throat. Images of steel walls and people in white made their way from her memories. And a tear splashed onto her hand. She yanked out the splinter and tried to focus.

He whispered barely loud enough for her to hear, "I know about your eyes. I know they changed you. That's why you went to the Plateau. I'm just not sure why they did it." A calm, authority radiated from him as he turned around. Roxan stumbled forward. The packed reality of his words pried more images from the darkness—doctors talking with muffled tones and bandages on her eyes. Mullin steadied her, and she searched his face for more to the story.

"How do you know that?" The tears stopped, and fear crept into her gut. Fear mixed with anger. And a long-forgotten memory pried its way loose from a black place in her mind. It swept her back to a time when she was seven turns, obedient, and crying in the middle of Nanny Uric's headquarters.

"You're not like everyone else," the older nanny said. "And it's starting to hurt the others. You don't want to hurt the others. We work together for the good of all, you know. I know you won't put up a fuss. You have a good little heart. You will do the right thing. The guards will be here soon to take you to the Plateau, and they will take care of the matter there and then send you back here. And once you return, you can reintegrate with the other students. You will be fine. You won't even notice any difference. They'll take care of that." And the nanny had been right. There had been no obvious change, except the visions had stopped.

At the Plateau, they had taken her to a large room. Getting there was a blurry memory of blue sky and fresh air, a dream of a place she longed to be. The dream ended with her opening her eyes to a blinking red light and feeling a cold metal bed supporting her. Muffled voices came from beyond her head. They argued.

"This is the first one, and it happened naturally. We should study this, not destroy it." The words came from a woman. A man replied to her, but spoke so quietly Roxan couldn't make out his words. Both voices hushed as the door swooshed open.

"Lord Hyperion," the man addressed the visitor.

"Fix it." A deep, silky sound filled the room. No anger, just dominance. It almost seemed like he sang the order. An accent peppered his words. Other than Nanny Uric's slight twang, no one else had ever spoken differently. Hyperion was not like everyone else.

"I appreciate your interest in studying this rarity, but I assure you this is not something we want to have among us." An affirmative murmur came from those in the room, except for the first lady who had voiced her concern. She dared to question her master.

"Excuse me, sir. But could this be what you've been looking for. Perhaps the child is able to see something we cannot."

"We have not yet seen a modification that would be beneficial to the good of all. When we do, we will study it, explore it, and use it. But this is not the case here. Change her and send her back." He spoke with finality. The lady said not another word.

That was the last Roxan remembered of the Plateau. When she returned to the raising home, everything went right back to normal. No one knew where she'd been, or what had happened, except for Nanny Uric and the other head nannies. But evidently, they weren't the only ones to know after all.

"Jonas." Roxan glanced toward the work buildings, a scream building within her. "Jonas."

"What?" Mullin put his hands on her shoulders. "Calm down."

"You know about my problem. Jonas knows. How?" she questioned. "I don't even know what happened. How is it most of the Protectorate knows? How do you know?"

Mullin picked up her satchel. "It doesn't matter how I know it. It's true, isn't it?" Pulling out some of the papers in her bag, he filed through them.

"It does matter. It matters to me. Do you know what they did? How they *fixed* me?" She didn't bother to ask him why he was rifling through her things or to let him know that whatever they did was unfixed now.

"Yeah, I know what they did." He shoved the papers back in and let loose of the satchel. "But first, you have to do something for me," he growled. Roxan checked his eyes for anger, but he just looked serious.

He tossed her bag down and pulled his pack off his shoulder. The dirty leather bag smelled like jerky and cinnamon too. He pulled out a small scroll, tied with a red thread with faceted black stones on each end.

"Follow that path on the other side of the Goneer River. See it right there." He pointed across the stream with the scroll he held. "Follow the path until it forks and then go left. It will fork two more times. The first, go left, but the last, follow to the right. The path will wind through the trees to a clearing. On the opposite side of the clearing, you'll find a dilapidated cabin. There will be someone waiting for you there."

Roxan pushed away from the pavilion and stepped out from the shade into a warm stream of sunlight. "I can't do that. Are you crazy? If I get caught, I'll be locked up."

"It's up to you Roxan. If you want answers, you'll go." He joined her in the sunlight. And, I think when you get those answers, you're gonna want to join me. The choice is yours, though. You can walk away right now, and I won't bother you again. You can go back and take your chances with those imbeciles, Jonas and Whitlock. They don't see you, you know. They're just going to use you. But you do what you need to do. And I'll do what I need to do." Mullin's lips pressed together, but his eyes connected with hers warmly.

Life felt complicated. She walked to the bushes, plucked a leaf, and ripped it to shreds. "I don't know."

"Don't worry Roxan. I have friends in high places. If you get caught out there, which you won't, I can make sure you won't go to an underground cell."

"How can you be sure?"

"I just know. Take this." He pushed the scroll into her hands. "Go to the cabin. If you do this, you'll see how different you are." A fire lit up his eyes. "You're not like those two-dimensional morons walking around here every roll doing exactly what they're told and never questioning it. But I'd wager you're not like the others either."

"Others?"

"There are others. Others who do question it, but instead of joining the winning side, they choose to fight, lie, and do what they can to keep us all locked up in this prison world." His fire quieted to a smolder, but glowing embers of fury glinted in his constricted pupils. "Trust me, Roxan. And you will end up on the winning side."

She weighed her options. The events of the last few rolls darted through her head like a rubber ball flung into the metal walls of her raising home room. Less than seven rolls had passed since all she had to worry about was a nanny catching her sneaking another cup of Caftywater. This roll had started out so well. Now, she had to make a choice.

Mullin snapped her back with a different, almost-annoyed tone. "Do you have my note from earlier?" Roxan pulled the note from behind her belt. He took it, replacing it with the scroll.

"What about the wild people?"

His expression shifted from serious to light. "You will be fine, Roxan. I wouldn't put you in any danger. And, if there were any other way, I would do it, but we don't have time to waste. Things are moving quickly now, you do this for me, and I'll make sure you get the answers you need." He spoke in riddles. "He will meet you there or on your way. He will find you, and when he does tell him you need his help."

"Who?"

"I've got to go. Keep the scroll close and if a sentry catches you, give it to him. I'll meet you here at the next roll of the sun." And then he left.

The scroll fell to the ground. Roxan left it there. Going back was an option. Going back and shutting up. She could try for a transfer, but that might require explanations she didn't want to give. Jonas would leave her alone, if she didn't knock him off his pedestal. Whitlock wouldn't hurt her. She could do her work like everyone else and pretend nothing had ever happened. A mindless moron. Stuff it all back down; hide it away.

Across the stream, a path hidden slightly by the bushes invited her over. Rocks dotted through the water as if they were an arrow pointing the way. Going might force something to happen. Things don't change unless a person takes an action. The visions wouldn't just go away. Life would never be carefree and easy.

"I need answers," she mouthed the words.

A guard called from the other side of the pavilion. He shouted an order to someone farther down the river. Another sentry stepped toward the water, his eyes focused on the opposite bank of trees. Roxan grabbed the scroll, slipped around the bush, and inched her way down the incline to the first rock in the river. Being questioned by a sentry wasn't part of any plan.

The sentry by the river took off toward the pavilion and out of view. Something had them buzzing. The scroll might keep the sentries from locking her up, but it wouldn't supply any answers. Mullin had answers. But his bargain was high. This wasn't sneaking a drink or unlatching a hatch door to the surface.

Still, if she were careful, no one would ever find out, and she would know and maybe have a remedy to all the crazy visions. For ten turns of the sun, she had pretended the visions were a dream, but no more. As the lead guard shouted more orders from behind the pavilion wall, she sprang to her feet and jumped onto the first rock in the water.

CHAPTER 11

SPINNING

"Stupid girl." His indictment joined the hum of the lights and the buzz of the cooling box. Jonas stared blankly at Roxan's chair. His last words to her still bounced off the walls of the tiny office. Flexing his jaw, he fought the urge to feel sorry for her, to go and find her.

Neatly tucking the remains of his lunch into a small baggie, he put it away for later and took the last swig of his Vitawater. Pink light from Whitlock's huge windows flowed through the cracked door. The ending horn would sound soon. This roll of the sun had passed quickly. Being so engrossed in rewording the orders from the Plateau had been a welcomed distraction, but it hadn't given him any time to prepare for his meeting or work out how he would get there unnoticed.

Wortman had been reluctant to move up their meeting, but Jonas piqued his curiosity just enough. The overseer liked to have the inside track on things. He had a reputation for using the system and information in a profitable manner.

The folded red appointment card didn't have the meeting time on it. Jonas kept that in his head. A surge of adrenalin buzzed through his synapses. Playing by the rules had always been enough to stay ahead of everyone else, but not now. Now he needed more information than following orders would give him.

He put the card back in his pocket. Unlocking this door bothered him. But it had to be done. It wasn't about a promotion anymore. It was about keeping Roxan away from Whitlock and people who wanted to use her. That sentry wasn't going to leave all of this alone. And if in the end, it worked out for Whitlock to be adjusted and Roxan to pull herself together, then all the better. She could be a real asset in the office. She could be his next link in the chain, not Norwood.

Norwood worked hard and was completely devoted to the Plateau, but she possessed no real skill at motivating people toward a particular end. A good second in management, she could take over the perfunctory stuff. She was his robot, obeying orders perfectly. Roxan would be his muse, adding light to the edicts and guidelines sent from the Plateau. This office would shine.

A cloud covered his reverie, and he closed his eyes. Swinging around from some place he never knew he had, remorse squeezed his heart. Had he really called Roxan a freak? Her stunned eyes reflected every cruel word he'd said. Why did she have to make him say those things? If she jumped into the project, there would have been no need to put her in her place. But she had to challenge him. Perhaps muse was the wrong word. She was something different all right.

As Jonas left the conference room, the lights switched off automatically. His body moved slowly after sitting so long. Norwood had kept the plebes on task while he'd been huddled up. They feared her almost as much as him.

Patrolling the far side of office, she didn't notice him emerge from the cave. Obedient little drones, the staff finished their assignments in silence. The room was a perfect example of the Plateau's ideal. People working, following orders, and not asking questions.

Roxan hadn't quite gotten that part yet. She asked questions and had a hard time following orders. Stacks of paper and several Nutrivia wrappers cluttered her desk, but none of her stuff lay on the floor. When she was here, her satchel was usually on the floor next to her desk, causing people to trip. Catching Norwood's eye, Jonas motioned toward the mess. The tiny, gruff woman shrugged her shoulders and rolled her eyes. Her body art did nothing to help her curt demeanor.

"Where are you, Roxan," he sighed. Having a disorderly workstation and coming in a few clicks late from mid-meal might be tolerated. Not showing up to finish an assignment would get her in trouble with a Plateau underling. She didn't need that kind of trouble. The sentry from the other roll, Jasper, hadn't been back, since he had rifled through Whitlock's office, but something like this would definitely spark his curiosity.

Norwood marched to his side and handed him the roll overview. Everyone had been working hard. Almost everyone. Disappointment didn't belong in his cadre of emotions, so he fished through the familiar and pulled out anger. This whole thing was Whitlock's fault. He did this. If he hadn't been flirting with her, giving her lead on this project. What was he thinking? Did he want a matchment? The Guardians wouldn't sanction that.

Maybe they would though. Whitlock was their star. A genius. Why wouldn't they match him with someone bright like Roxan? Whatever was up with her eyes hadn't kept her from getting a work assignment. They had her marked for something. And they do like to breed the brightest with the best.

His anger morphed into enmity, and Jonas found himself full circle, hating his overseer and willing to do whatever he could to dethrone his master. Taking Whitlock's position wasn't going to be enough. The man needed to be completely discredited. Maybe that could be accomplished without Roxan. That was hard to predict.

"Jonas, get in here," Whitlock boomed from his office. "We have a problem."

Taking a deep breath, Jonas turned away from the workers and put his mask in place. He stopped off in the workroom first and gathered his things, but didn't delay too long.

The overseer's office met him with its usual grandeur, but Jonas stayed focused. Whitlock was the one with the problem. He was the one who needed to be deposed of. Step 1: disarm and acquire information.

"Sir, is Roxan with you?" He spoke first, ignoring that he'd just been summoned.

"Isn't she with you?" Whitlock's irritation escalated. "You have to keep up with these plebes, boy."

Jonas cringed, but kept his footing. "No sir. I haven't seen her since *you* sent us on a break."

"I'm sure she'll turn up. She's probably getting some air and enjoying what's left of the sunshine." He leaned back in his glorious chair, looking more tired than usual. The hint of dying honeysuckle circulated in the air. "We have a problem, though." His brown hair stuck out, and his cover-up top still held last roll's ink stains. Waving a small scroll in his hand, he cleared his throat. A large *P* was stamped in wax on the back of the paper. "The Plateau sent another order."

Jonas stepped closer. "What do they want? Are they changing the first one?" He knew he shouldn't sound annoyed, but he had done a lot of work already and wasting his time irritated him more than being rushed through a project.

"No, they're not changing it." Whitlock handed him the scroll. "They're just moving up the start of it all. Instead of three rolls of the sun, you have until the end of the next roll. They want all the orders out by then."

"The next roll of the sun. . .but what about All-In? Are they going to tolerate having a bunch of messengers out late delivering these things? What's the hurry?" Jonas unrolled the scroll and read over it, but it didn't offer much except for the change, no explanation or allowances.

"I don't know, but we do what we're told. It's for the good of all." Whitlock repeated the mantra, but his words couldn't deny his lack of sentiment. That was a shift in the master's politics. But how deep did his lack of devotion cut?

Altering his second-in-command mask to confidante, Jonas walked to the far side of the desk, away from the doorway, his cold hand running along the edge of the glossy desktop. "Do you think they know what they're doing on this? I mean, what are they looking for? They're looking for something…or someone. Don't you think? Why else would they be taking a Census of Souls?"

Jonas hadn't thought about the purpose of the edict before he made his suggestion. That wasn't his job, to think about the whys. Now, Roxan's earlier reluctance became obvious. This was the most intrusive missive to come from the Plateau. And the leadership wanted them to make it sound like they'd all been issued a holiday.

Whitlock had already gone there, though. His eyes gave him away. He grabbed the scroll. A different side of him emerged. Usually controlled and composed, he didn't seem to know what to do with his angst. He obviously had an opinion, but weighed his words carefully. "This isn't just a Census of Souls. They want to do more than count heads."

"Why?" A chill countered Jonas's hostility toward Whitlock. The man looked shaken and unsteady.

"My guess is they want someone," Whitlock yielded. "They're looking for someone, and *they're* not even sure who they're looking for. It could be any of us." He brought himself back from the edge of his unrest. "So every village will be scoured until they find the person." Balling up the scroll, he tossed it onto his desk. The material-like paper flopped back open.

Two thoughts hit Jonas. If Whitlock's distrust of their magnanimous leader was made known, he would be taken away and adjusted, probably demoted. But then concern over this invasion of personhood had merit. Without knowing exactly whom they wanted, no one was safe.

"Who are they looking for?" Jonas pressed. The question had to be asked. Maybe Whitlock had some idea.

"I don't know yet, but I have some people checking into it." He looked out across the workers. They were taking quick glances toward his office.

"That could earn you a free trip to the cells." Jonas prodded, clunking the desk with his knuckles. "I mean, you don't look into what's been ordered. That's as good as saying they don't know what they're doing."

Whitlock stood. "Is that concern for me I hear in your words?"

"Why of course, sir. What else would it be? I will obediently submit myself to your orders." Jonas lowered his head. "You are my overseer, and I trust you know a mistake when you see one, even one that comes from the Plateau."

"Hyperion doesn't make mistakes, does he?" He wasn't being led by Jonas's efforts to trap him in treason. "He only does what's for the good of all. We do what we're told, Jonas. We obey orders and work together, because it's for the good of all. Do you understand that?"

Jonas dropped his confidante mask and sized up the benefit of going on the offensive, but opted to stay silent.

"Just get it done, okay," Whitlock ordered. "Finish the project by the next roll. I want to see what you've done so far. On my desk before the horn blows, twig it? Now, get out of here." He sat back in his chair, waving his hand to dismiss him.

Heads jerked back to their papers as Jonas re-entered the workroom. Whitlock's orders made his stomach fume. Where's the Calciwater when you need it? *I can do this job twenty times better than he can. I'll get the work done. And I'll make it shine.* A quick head count told him he could get everyone on the project before they left for All-In, everyone except Roxan. She'd be on her own, if she didn't show up soon.

Hurrying down the hallway, Jonas called out for Norwood to follow him. Everyone should be formally obligated to do the work at his whim, and that called for an official notice. When he slammed it open, the door to the marker room hit the wall and bounced backward. Jonas stopped it with his hand and took a deep breath. Control. Calculation. Concentration. Giving into anger would handicap those essential tools.

He sensed Norwood standing behind him. "I need a marker for each plebe. Make it for the entire next roll. No excuses. They should report before the sun rolls up and be prepared to stay through All-In. Let's keep this roll as it is and put the start date on the next roll." Jonas picked out the metal markers for each of the plebes and stacked them on the worktable. "After you get them stamped, hand them out, but bring Roxan's to me. I'll deliver hers, myself." Norwood nodded her agreement and started preparing the stamps in silence. "I'll make the announcement." He pulled the door open more gently as he exited.

Jonas swelled at his dominion as he glanced at the work order wall. Twelve empty spaces clung to the magnetic board, each with a different plebe's name above it. These were his plebes. And he would have them all coming in early at the next roll of the sun and staying until their task was accomplished. The markers had only come out once before, to finish a project during one of Whitlock's absences. That project had been for the Plateau as well, and it had been completed without Whitlock's name anywhere on it.

"I need your attention, please," Jonas boomed. The new plebes froze. Older workers set their work aside and turned to face their guide. As if on cue, a gust of wind blew up some papers on the desks closest to the open windows. "We've received new orders from the Plateau. The assignment that I have been tirelessly pouring over this roll will need to be finished and ready for distribution by the end of the next roll." The absence of Roxan's name connected to the project was intentional. The older plebes grumbled. They knew this meant extra work. The new ones didn't move.

"You'll need to be here prior to the sun's ascent tomorrow and work indefinitely until the task is completed. I have a marker for each of you." The grumbling increased. Jonas took note of those complaining the loudest. He would deal with them and their attitude later. The new plebes still sat motionless.

"And for those of you who are new to our ranks, you will understand that once you are given a marker, it's a binding contract. You must complete the assignment on the marker or face discipline from the Plateau. Keep the marker with you at all times. It will give you some leeway with curfews and other guidelines which we may need to bend to get this job done." Panic blanketed the room. Several novice plebes began to whimper.

"Don't worry. I'm only giving out markers on this because it's *that* important to the Plateau. We will get this done, people, and we will do it well. For the good of all ..." Jonas waited, hungry for their reply and compliance.

"We give ourselves." Their half-hearted response sparked his already smoldering fury.

"What?" he roared. "You people work every roll with very little being demanded of you." No one would make eye contact, as he patrolled the aisles between the workstations. "You get asked to take part in a monumental action of the Plateau, and all you can do is complain? Do you have no idea what a privilege it is to serve our leaders in this way? You will not complain about this and you will get it done or I will personally escort you to the Plateau to be dealt with. Do I make myself clear?"

Silence.

Jonas inhaled their submission, as the weight of his words fell across them. "Let's try it again. For the good of all ..."

"We give ourselves!" the plebes rejoined.

"That's better," Jonas preened. There would be no question how he felt about the Plateau. Now every person in here could testify to that.

Another breeze blew past him as he ended his tour next to Roxan's desk. She had a good view of the Triangle from here. Three trails connected three clumps of trees on the edge of the grassy bowl. If she were anywhere, she'd be down there wandering around, feeling sorry for herself, and securing a trip to a detention cell.

Solar sticks along the main road began to glow in the dimming light. Jonas checked the fading sky. The horn would blow soon. Getting out of here early would be hard now. Everyone was sure to stay until after the first horn blew. Maybe asserting his authority could have waited until after he'd met with Wortman.

Norwood pulled him away from the window with the wave of an ink stained hand. The markers were ready. What she lacked in personality, she made up for with efficiency. Lifting the top marker from the stack, Jonas began calling out names. One by one, each plebe came forward and signed off for their marker.

Halfway through the roll call, Whitlock showed his sullen face. Standing in his doorway, he made no move to address the workers. He just stood there looking worn and weak. Did he sense that his end was near? If he didn't step up soon, he would be eclipsed. He had to know that. Maybe he didn't care. Maybe he was the one they're looking for.

Jonas ignored his superior, checking everyone he could off his list. Only two people were absent, Kain—who had missed the entire announcement somehow—and Roxan, who had evidently vanished. No one seemed to know where she'd gone or even when she had left. And since she hadn't been incredibly punctual since she'd arrived, no one even questioned why she might have disappeared.

Jonas gave the rest of the paperwork to Norwood. He had the excuse he needed. "I'll take care of these last two markers. You close things up here." Turning on his heel, he left the plebes to their cowering, breezed by Whitlock without a nod, and beeped the conference room door completely open.

Paper samples lay scattered on the floor, and Roxan's chair, still vacant, stirred up feelings he didn't want to think about. He diverted his attention to gathering his things. All roll, he'd been waiting for her to return, and now he hoped she wouldn't show her face. She'd given him the perfect excuse for an early dismissal. When he gave her the marker, he could throw an apology her way about what he'd said. She should be grateful he didn't throw her to the sentries for her infractions.

"Did you seriously think the markers were necessary?" Whitlock knocked the door shut. "I've never had to use that threat to get my workers on task. As daunting as this project is, I'm sure we can fulfill our obligation. It won't be a problem."

"I believe it was you who said we had a problem. And now it's no big deal? Make up your mind, Whitlock … sir." Jonas faced his overseer. Whitlock had a whole two inches of height on him, but Jonas ignored the difference.

"I'll take Roxan's." He held out his hand, but Jonas stuck the marker in his satchel and gathered his paperwork from the roll.

"I'll deliver her marker, myself," Whitlock reworded his demand.

Jonas panicked. No excuse came to mind. To defy his overseer's statement could mean getting a demerit. But without Roxan's marker to deliver, getting to his appointment would be impossible. He'd be saddled with spending the rest of the roll locked up with his workers. Maybe a request would work.

"If you don't mind, sir, I could use the fresh air. I've been inside all roll, and I think it's beginning to wear on me." This time his *sir* implied respect, not rebellion.

The beep and swoosh of the door interfered with their conversation. Norwood's plain face and gloomy body art had never looked so good. "Excuse me sirs, but Kain has returned. Would you like for me to deliver his marker?"

Jonas pulled it from his pack. "Here you go."

"And Master Whitlock," Norwood added. "There's a messenger in your office. Looks like another notice." Whitlock rushed by them both.

"Thanks, Norwood," Jonas grinned. "That was very good timing."

Norwood's face conveyed nothing but that she wasn't a robot.

"Sir."

"Yes, Norwood."

"Sir, did you want me to make a marker for Master Whitlock?" She said it so dryly that it could have come across as a brilliant joke, except she never joked. No one did. No one except Roxan. She was the only person who would actually take the time to think up a prank like that. "I wasn't sure if you wished to include him in the order," she pressed.

Including Whitlock in the order hadn't crossed his mind, but she was right. According to the guidelines, he could officially put a marker on his overseer in a situation like this. Jonas glanced at the darkening sky. No sense in spitting on that dying ember. Giving him a marker might fan a flame instead of smother it.

"No, Norwood. That won't be necessary. You're dismissed." She left without a sound.

The shutter to Whitlock's office had been closed. No more obstacles. And no secrets. Without another word, Jonas headed for his appointment. There was only one way to find out if Whitlock was planning to defy the Guardians. And there was only one way to keep him from requesting a matchment with Roxan.

CHAPTER 12

UNWELCOMED

"Altrist is going to meet us at Willow Way, right?" Abiga heard the kid's question over the boring conversations of the other Pocket-dwellers around her, and she picked up the pace so she could catch the answer.

She didn't know the kid's name, but he had been to Snowshoe once delivering a stash of staves. Younger than most of the Outcasts, he probably had an interesting story. He couldn't be a forest-born kid. He tripped over every rock and tree branch in the trail.

"We don't know where he will meet us." Grouper rumbled like thunder.

With a strange familiarity, the kid stumbled over a root in the pathway and, at the same time, whacked his head on a low-hanging branch. The event took two flashes and landed him smack into Grouper's back. The big man didn't say anything, and he didn't budge. The kid might have gotten more cushioning if he'd fallen into a tree.

Grouper reached around, pulled at the neck of the boy's cover-up, and steadied him. He lifted him off the ground, and placed him a few feet away. The look in Grouper's eyes said to leave it alone, but the kid didn't take the hint.

"How can you not know? What did he say?"

"We're fine, kid. Everything's right on schedule." Grouper waved his hand back as he spoke, nearly whapping the poor boy, but then he left it hovering over the kid's shoulder and eased the boy's fears with his calming gift.

That would work for a while, but the kid would be back asking questions again when the feelings of peace wore off. The boy turned and headed off to his friends, whistling as he walked by.

Abiga lagged behind Grouper, Jahn, and Thim, following close enough to hear what they were saying, but not close enough to be noticed. Normally, Thim would've been at her side, but he'd been keeping his distance ever since they left Snowshoe. That was fine. Dealing with his hurt feelings and the rejected matchment proposal weren't conducive to the kind of focus she needed to make peace with leaving everyone.

The trip into Pocket had been fast. The Outcasts there weren't ready either. So there had been a lot of packing to do. Abiga's muscles actually ached from the lifting. It felt good to be on their way finally and to not have to make small talk or ask for another job to do.

"Where do you think Altrist will meet up with us?" Thim's voice barely reached her. But she knew him well enough to piece together his question. The most practical of the three, he always wanted to have a plan and know what was coming.

Jahn sighed and gripped his walking stick tighter, jabbing it into the soft earth, causing little puffs of dirt to fly off the ground. He hadn't said much on their trip. And what he had said was filled with an exasperated undercurrent.

Grouper replied, "I don't know. You heard him. He doesn't even know."

"Well, what's that supposed to mean? He can't lead us to think he'll always be there and then desert us. We need him," Thim countered.

Grouper mumbled something, but Abiga couldn't make it out. Then he gave Jahn a pat on the back, but didn't leave his hand there. Not only could Grouper ease a person's feelings, but he could almost read their mind. He was acutely empathetic, which was completely uncharacteristic of an oversized, ex-sentry, who could wrestle a bear to the ground. Strong and sensitive.

It didn't take any special gift to tell that Jahn was holding back a fistful of anger. Grouper turned the conversation toward the stick-jabbing grump. "What do you think, Jahn?"

"How am I supposed to know? I don't get to know the comings and goings of the group."

Liza hadn't been at Pocket like they thought she would be. No one knew where she had disappeared to. And Jahn was always grumpy until he knew her whereabouts. "I know as much as you all do."

Something was up with Grouper. He wouldn't let the conversation drop. Lowering his voice, he still rumbled like thunder as he spoke. "This isn't going to get any easier. There are going to be more questions. I can feel restlessness among the group. Without Altrist shining the way, they will begin to wonder if we should go at all." No one answered him.

The sun beat down on them as they trekked up the trail heading over Obdon Bluff. Grouper kept silent, but mumbled something every few steps. Abiga wondered if he were trying to speak to the Leader. Altrist had told her to talk to their great Leader like she talked to him, but it felt silly and fake, like making a wish. She rubbed her sweaty palms on her cover-up. The smudge of her mark still glistened, barely visible.

She pulled her curls back with a string, then wiped the sweat from her temples. A cool stream would be nice about now or Snowshoe. Maybe they would delay leaving until Altrist returned. That would be good. It would give her more time to sort out this no-gift thing or to get a gift.

"Maybe we shouldn't go." Thim broke the silence. "Maybe we should wait. What if Altrist needs us? Or what if we need him? We have minds to think about all of this. Maybe we should examine all of our options before we go running off into a wall that's never been breached."

Finally, someone had braved the territory of questioning orders. Jahn was usually the one to buck the system, if you can call setting a few traps for sentries breaking the rules. It surprised Abiga that it was Thim who spoke up. His desire for more control seemed to be winning over his unswerving devotion to following the rules. Maybe he felt it too. Leaving everything behind would mean leaving possibilities, leaving the home of their hope.

Jahn smacked his walking stick into the ground so hard that it left a hole. "And do what? Stay? How can we stay when we know we're supposed to leave? That would blatantly be going against the Leader. No, we have to go, and we have to go with or without Altrist or Liza." He lingered over her name.

"What are you saying? You would leave her here?" Thim turned sideways and threw his arms up. Grouper walked silently next to them, listening and offering no help, not even a gentle wave of his hand to soften their moods.

"What choice do I have, Thim? This isn't about what I want, or what feels right, or anything that I can even understand. We go because he said to go. And if we go and there's nothing there, then so be it. After everything, I'm not going to start doing things my way now. The Leader made it clear. End of story." Jahn's voice cracked as he spoke. Grouper placed a hand on his shoulder, but Jahn pushed it off. "I don't need that, Grouper. I'll be fine. A little anger is good now and then."

"He made it clear?" Thim continued to question. "Maybe, but maybe not. I mean just because three different people had the same dream ... it could have been a coincidence. What proof is that? Maybe we should wait. People can come up with anything. How do we know for sure?"

Jahn shook his head. "Thim, three different people had a dream. Grouper saw the truth of it. Anna has always said we would eventually leave. Altrist agreed with it, and now, NOW is the time the wall will be broken. And don't ask me how. I don't know." Jahn grasped Thim's arm as if he were about to give him a hug. "My gut tells me it's right, but I can't always trust that. Maybe the point is that we're doing something that doesn't make any sense, and he'll work it out. Maybe it doesn't matter if we stay or we go; what matters is that we aren't staying the same. This is going to change all of us. If you don't think so, you don't have to go." His tone said the opposite though. Jahn choked out the last few words, his love for Thim pouring into each syllable. Turning, he yelled to the entire group. "We need to talk. Follow me."

Jahn guided the Outcasts off the trail and up a narrow pathway. Fallen leaves made the steep bank slippery, but everyone followed. Several older Outcasts needed help. With one foot wedged against a tree and the other in a rock crevice, Abiga stood off to the side and lent a steady hand to the less stable. She waved the last group of men on when they stopped to help her. One was the guy from earlier. He stumbled his way up in front of his more sure-footed friends.

The leafy path to the top leveled out to reveal a platform of rock jutting away from the mountaintop and a magnificent view. Amazing. The panorama took Abiga's breath away. Pocket and Snowshoe Falls were a ways off, but still it all looked like home. With the clear sky, the view stretched almost to the Balustrade. How could the Leader be calling them away from all of this? Why now? Why did he ask so much and withhold assurance? Didn't the Leader want them to know what his plan was?

Jahn marched to the edge of the bluff overlooking the valley and turned to face the group, motioning for them to sit down. No one else seemed to pay any attention to the vista. Jahn remained standing and steady.

"Okay, everybody, we're going to have a meeting," he yelled.

He waited for the group to quiet down. Abiga found a spot next to Thim, but still close enough so she could scoot to the edge if she wanted. Everyone faced Jahn except for Grouper, who sat to the side facing the group of Outcasts. His eyes searched the group for signs of discontent or unease. All he had to do was lift his hands, and he could calm them.

Jahn cleared his throat and leaned on his walking stick. Twice as old as Abiga's sixteen turns, he was still in good shape. The stick was more a companion than a crutch. "I know, we weren't supposed to have a meeting, but I also know some of you have questions—doubts. And we have to deal with that before we go on. Not that I'm going to be able to answer your questions or take away your doubts, but you need to deal with them. Because where we're going, you're going to need to be 100 percent committed. There's no turning back."

Murmurs spread through the group.

Jahn continued, "I'm not going to lie to you and tell you what you should be thinking about all of this. I'm not going to try to cheer you on or tell you that you're doing the right thing, because that wouldn't be any different than what the Protectorate does every roll. You believe what you want to. You can either keep on with the Leader or not. And you can go down to the village, if that's what you want. I don't really care. But whatever you decide, make sure you're all in, because half-hearted devotion is just apathy." Whispers of agreement rose above the nodding heads.

"We don't know what's going to happen. I don't know what's on the other side of that wall, but I'm going anyway. That's my decision." Jahn had their undivided attention. "You think long and hard about yours. But don't do it because that's where I'm going, or even because it's what Altrist says, or that's what Olivope wanted."

A sad quiet rested on them. Olivope hadn't come back to Pocket. Two rolls and no one had heard anything from her or the three Outcasts who'd been in her company.

Tears filled Jahn's eyes. "This isn't about Olivope or Altrist. Can you see that? You have the ability to know where you should be. I don't believe for a second that the Leader means for us to wander around guessing all the time. He may not be here, yelling out orders, but he hasn't left you defenseless. Use what you have and decide for yourself."

As he stopped talking, a gust of wind blew up from the valley, whipping through a pile of leaves and blowing them across the people sitting in the front. Jahn crossed over to Grouper and plopped down on a fallen birch tree. Almost every pair of eyes followed him, wanting more, but he'd said his peace. Leaning his head on his walking stick, he spoke silent words to the air now.

A low mumble of whispers started in the back where the boys sat. Abiga shifted to the edge of the bluff and looked out across the valley. An ache built inside of her. He doesn't want us guessing. Use what you have. Decide for yourself. Every prompt pointed toward the same decision. Separate from the Outcasts. Being with them constantly hurt. They had their gifts. Their assurance. Even if some decided to stay, it wouldn't be because they weren't sure of their place with the Leader. They knew. Their question wasn't one of belonging. But simply whether to leave their home or not. To fit like they did, to have their assurance of being wanted meant taking a different journey, and not stopping until the answers came. If the Leader really did find her once, then he would do it again, and then she would know.

Thim tapped Abiga's back and pointed toward one of the senior Pocket-dwellers just as she hollered from her spot in front of the boys.

"Not all of us have your fervor, Jahn." Older than Anna, Adora had lived in Pocket most of her life. "I know about the dreams and all, but I'm still not sure. Maybe I'm supposed to stay here. I don't *feel* like I'm supposed to go anywhere. I mean I would follow Altrist anywhere, but he's not even with us. Without him, I don't feel strongly either way. I want someone to tell me what to do." Adora's voice shook as she spoke, quiet tears streaming down her face. Others nodded their heads in agreement.

"Adora." Jahn spoke softly, but everyone was so quiet, he could have whispered and he still would have been heard. "You want someone to tell you what to do. But I say if it's not obvious then maybe that's your answer. You are looking with your eyes and your mind is seeing nothing. Is that how you came to be part of us? It's not, is it?"

Adora wagged her head looking down at her wrinkled hands.

"I don't know your story, Adora," Jahn continued. "I don't know a lot of your stories." He looked across the group. "And maybe it doesn't matter what your story is or how you came to be here. What matters is the Leader. Do you think he'll be our guide out of here? If you're not sure, then stay."

"What if you want to think he'll make it go right, but you're scared he won't?" The kid from earlier grumbled his question to himself, but Jahn answered him, anyway.

"Maybe that will be enough. Maybe that's part of this, not being sure, but going ahead, anyway, trusting him in the darkness. Do you doubt him? Do you doubt seeing him? Do you doubt that he loves you? That he cares? Because if you doubt, maybe you should start there, not on the other side of the wall." Jahn pushed up from his tree seat. He wasn't done with his speech.

"But don't think you have to have all the answers to still be part of this. Maybe it's enough to want to know the truth. You don't have to have it all figured out, or be perfect or have gifts." Jahn looked over at Abiga when he said that. "But you do need to know who we're following. It's not Altrist. It's definitely not me. You've met him, and if you haven't, well, I'm not going to tell you to stay. Because whether you've met him or not, he's still the only one we can completely trust in this whole messed up place."

Adora stood up, wobbling to get straight. She leaned on a thick, black walking cane with carvings running down the side. "I came here after my placement. They sent kids out earlier back then. I was only eleven turns when I left the raising home and I couldn't handle it. That happens sometimes. Kids can't adjust to the sky and outdoors. The sentries found me curled up on the floor of my shanty. I was weak and useless, and they said they had to follow orders. They sounded sad. I figured they would take me back to the raising home and fix me up. I wanted to go back, but that's not what they did. They dropped me outside the boundary, just took my little body and laid it under a tree."

Abiga felt her words. They'd all been touched by the cruelty of Hyperion.

"One of the guards said they should finish it. That would be the humane thing to do, but they left me there. Olivope found me, carried me to Pocket, and nursed me back." She paused and took a deep breath, closing her eyes. "I never chose to be here. This is the only place that would have me. I've never met the Leader or gone through the water. But I know he's real. I see him in your faces."

Abiga looked away, but kept her ears turned toward the woman's words.

"I don't want to go. It feels like I'm leaving the raising home all over again. But staying behind alone scares me more," Adora admitted.

"Don't let fear decide your fate, Adora," Grouper answered her misgivings. "Do what you need to do, no one will fault you with that, but do nothing motivated by fear."

Abiga felt the sting of his words, and couldn't help but look into her own heart. Some of the others around her cried softly. Some looked wild with fear. It danced in their eyes. They were scared to go and scared to stay. If fear had a scent, it would smell like this bluff, fresh thin air mixed with the hint of hot rock and dead leaves.

Thim left Abiga's side and made his way toward Adora. "How is it you've been with us for so long and haven't met the Leader? You believe? Right?"

That thought had crossed Abiga's mind too. One wonderful thing about these people is that they brought stuff out in the open. Thim was good at that. He never hid his feelings from her, and he assumed she hadn't hidden anything from him. They talked through problems, aired them, and then moved on. And never once did a disagreement end in someone getting their body bashed against a tree or catching a rock upside his head.

Another Pocket-dweller spoke for Adora. "We don't force anything on anyone. Olivope guided us to not press, but to accept whoever would be willing to live among us."

"So how many of you have never met the Leader?" Thim looked at Grouper and Jahn. They had already gotten to their feet.

Twenty-five Outcasts had joined them from Pocket, and they were to meet another twenty-two at Willow Way. Seven of the twenty-five raised their hands, the three boys in the back, Adora, two other women, and a man.

Jahn stepped forward. "We're not here to press either. It's your decision who you follow, but don't play games or be controlled by your fear, or think that you have all the time in the world to decide who your master is. Because not making a decision is making a decision. You either belong to the Leader or you are Hyperion's servant. There's no in between."

When he said Hyperion's name, they took their hands down quickly. No one wanted to follow him. Abiga knew each had been scarred in some way by his selfish reign.

"I can't believe Olivope didn't tell you this," Jahn pressed.

"She did tell us," called the boy from earlier. "We were to have a meeting, but she never came back. And we wanted her there."

"Make your choice now." Jahn lifted his walking stick. "I meant what I said. You don't have to be acquainted with the Leader to come with us. We will protect you. But we also need those of you who are ready." He meant their gifts. They would need everyone's gifts to make it through the woods. "You can't wait for Olivope or do this for show. Do it because it's what you believe. It's what you know to be true. This is your home. We are one body. Together. And we serve one master who will not let us down."

Abiga scooted to the edge of the bluff and dangled her legs over the edge. Those who had raised their hands had already stood up to be counted. Even Adora called out, "It is my time." From the sounds behind her, Abiga could tell they were going through the water. Splashes and cheers soaked up the top of the rock. Some of the spray carried on the breeze to her. It was the same when Altrist had visited one of the mini-camps. Water poured from an invisible spout and drenched the newly committed. She didn't need to look. They were meeting the Leader, getting their gifts, finding their assurance.

The valley stretched out before her. The river below sparkled as it wound its way through the tree-soaked terrain. The village that manufactured basic supplies, spread out to the right, and the edge of the Protectorate bordered her homeland on the left. Looking at it from up here made it all seem safe and beautiful.

Nothing was safe about that world below, though. Abiga let her mind float to a far off place and a different time. Closing her eyes, she heard the rasping of the sentry's last breath. In her hands, she felt his pulse fading away. Every cracking blow and smooth jab etched its way into her being. She would never be rid of it all. And no amount of water would wash it from her. Some things cannot be undone or forgotten.

The Leader had good reason to never give her a gift. What would she do with it? Sure, she had changed with the cycles at Snowshoe, but still the animal lived in her. The little girl raised by the crazies, enjoying the fight, killing for fun.

A tear escaped the corner of her eye. Being like these people would never be possible. Abiga wiped the betraying droplet away. Things that are done cannot be undone. There's a reason why there aren't many reformed Undesirables among the Outcasts. Changing a person from the inside is hard, even for someone like the Leader. And when he's silent and absent, it's probably impossible.

She traced the fading mark on her palm. Merely a smudge now, it made her mad. Why would he give her this and then take it away? Still, gratefulness tinged her anger. It was good to have been part of it for a few turns rather than to never have known it at all.

The others began to move behind her, but she stayed, palms up, her head bowed. They sounded happy. The water had stopped falling, and already some received their gifts. How nice it must be to immediately get your welcome.

"Abiga, we're leaving," Thim leaned over and whispered in her ear. His voice sent a tremor through her body. Happiness embodied him. Whatever doubts he'd had must have been cured by the events on the mountaintop. Part of her wanted to turn and wrap her arms around his neck, but instead she clasped her hands tightly and shook her head.

"I'm not coming." It seemed as if someone else were speaking.

He knelt beside her. "What? What are you talking about?" Panic shadowed his joy.

"I'm going to stay here through the roll. Jahn said for each of us to make our own choice, and I need to know for sure." She reached up and touched his pale face. "I've followed you everywhere. But I cannot go with you now. I don't belong with you. I know this is hard for you to understand. Just leave me here."

"But Abiga. . .I can't leave you. It's not that complicated. You've already made your choice. Remember? You know the truth. You belong with us."

She bit the inside of her jaw and looked deep into his eyes. She would miss those eyes. "I've done things that can never be undone. The Leader knows that. That's why I don't have a gift. He doesn't want me."

"How can you say that? He washed all that away. You're free from your past. I won't let you give up your future. And you know a gift isn't the stick you measure acceptance by. You're not some spoiled child, mad because she didn't get what she wanted. I don't have a gift. Maybe our gift is that we don't have these responsibilities to bear. Our assurance is in deeper things like hope and truth and love."

"This isn't your choice to make. And it's not just about the gift; you see that, I know you do. Maybe there are some things that hope can't breach, that truth only exposes more, and that love cannot heal." She looked away from his hurt eyes and let the silence echo her decision.

"Abiga, you can't stay here. It's not safe." Defeat colored his words. He knew she could take care of herself. That was part of the problem, wasn't it? She had already done so much bad *to take care of herself.* "And it's not like you have all of the time in the world," he tried again. "We don't even know how long the gap in the wall will last. You can think about it on the way. I mean, we all have questions. That's normal." He pulled at her arm, but she wrenched it quickly from his grasp.

"Thim, I've got to do this. I'll be fine." Her voice trembled. "I've been pretending I fit in, that I haven't done the things I've done, that I could belong. But I have no gift, no real assurance I am an Outcast. I need to know for sure that he wants *me.*"

"I want you." Thim leaned his face down and pulled her near to him. One last embrace before she said good-bye. His heart pounded in her ear. "Please," he whispered.

"Just go." She didn't look at him again, but she felt his hand hovering above her shoulder as he pulled away. The words *I love you* stuck in her throat. She should say them, but they should be said in a happy time with promise, not as a farewell with anguish as its companion. Thim left without another word.

They all left. The clearing was empty. They were back on the path to Willow Way. Abiga picked up a jagged stone, pitched it as far out as she could, and watched it fall to the trees below. The familiarity of being alone returned like an old friend. But something was different. The old friend had changed. His clothes were dark and foreboding. He lingered on the outskirts of her heart, as if he wasn't sure he was welcomed there.

CHAPTER 13

LOST

"I know he said to go this way." Roxan swatted a branch above her head. The woods stayed mostly quiet. Only a few toads croaked from the marsh to her right. "What was I thinking? I've only been here a few rolls of the sun and already I've violated a dozen rules. Maybe I should go back." But the thought of returning felt wrong too. "I must be crazy." She looked up through the treetops. The sun had already dipped below the horizon causing a dull purple-pink haze to reach across the darkening sky.

Beside the path, a fallen tree trunk offered up a place to sit. The mass of dirt clumps and moss dangling from its roots reached out like tentacles looking for something to grab. She checked the trunk for bugs, found a good spot, and settled down. The last of her Vitawater soothed her hot throat. Despite the cool late-roll air, it was still warm. And despite the rules forbidding them, the woods still captivated her. The boundaries, like everything else, kept people right where the Guardians wanted them. Maybe there really was no such thing as freedom.

Roxan adjusted her fancy footwear. Even though the new sandals hurt more than they helped, going barefoot in an unfamiliar place was never a good idea. That was a lesson learned in the recycling hall. She tucked napkin pieces between the sandal strap and her emerging blisters.

With a heavy sigh, she placed the empty Vitawater bottle into her sack and stood, stretching her back. One star poked its way into the sky. How beautiful! Perhaps the clouds would stay away. This would be the dark roll to find out. No need to worry about the All-In rule this roll of the sun. Besides, it would probably be best to wait until late to return so the sentries would have settled in and finished their rounds. Roxan headed deeper into the woods.

A horn sounded in the distance—the first warning horn releasing all who remained at their workstations. Roxan pictured herself finishing a normal roll. Right about now, she would be saying good-bye to Whitlock and ignoring Jonas. Then, she would skip down the steps, pretend to be interested in something besides the nosey receptionist, and fling open the heavy door, to be met by the cool evening air and the sounds of all the dark roll creatures waking up.

After a stroll around the Triangle, she would walk to her shanty using the back pathway between the shops and a grove of maple trees. Business owners would be setting out their trash for the Viand workers to take back to their village and pick through for useful items or things that could be recycled.

So far everything about the Protectorate had been predictable and pleasant, but a bit of a lie. How many notices had she swallowed with all their "for the good of all" rhetoric? How many other people had they "fixed"? It all looked good, but something lurked beneath the surface, some controlling force that didn't want to be seen.

A low-hanging branch smacked Roxan across the face. She yelped, hushing the closest crooning creatures. Darkness had quickly invaded the pathway. She pulled a small stave out of her bag and shook it. The slender stick glowed to life with its bluish hue. It didn't do much against the darkness, but at least she could see the pathway right in front of her and any stray branches reaching out to whap her in the face.

A second horn signaled All-In. Everyone would be to their homes by now. Roxan had been late once before, on an annoyingly cloudy dark roll, but she hadn't been caught. She wound her way between the trees and bushes behind her shanty and climbed through the back window as the final horn blew. Only sentries could be out after the final horn—sentries and disobedient girls who could see strange visions and dare to take unsanctioned adventures.

Trees, trees, trees lined the pathway to the top of the hill, trees stood by guarding the well-worn trail. "I love this," she whispered quietly to the darkness. Inhaling, she drew in the scent of the woods, fresh and green. And the sweet little beasties sang their songs robustly—so much better than the stale whir of the machinery running the air filters in the raising home and the scratchy complaints of a grumpy nanny.

At the top of the hill, the pathway opened into a clearing. From up here, Roxan could see the lights of the Protectorate glowing through the trees. And, on the opposite side down in a valley, a glittering line ran at the end of an open area. The gleaming streak disappeared into the tree line, but she could still see a twinkle from it through the foliage.

As she stared at the line, the valley before her filled up with a white light. A hazy glow spread across the whole area, a light-fog, eliminating the darkness and covering everything. She slid the light stave into her satchel.

The whiteness highlighted the world. Twirling, Roxan danced in the gray glow. It touched everything—her arms, her cover-up, everything. As if someone had turned a knob and booted up a massive battery light, the radiance fell across the trees, making them look white. It spread out to the village in the distance and lightened the sky with brilliance.

Her gaze drifted to the sky, and then she saw it. "Oh," she whispered her praise into the shimmering air. A magnificent white celestial body floated between two dark-gray clouds. The moon. *Finally.*

The world outside the raising home had awakened part of her already, but now, standing on the hill engulfed in light, she felt small. She hadn't been thinking big enough when she'd imagined this moment.

"Magnificent." She drank in the resplendence of it. Classes in science had lamely proclaimed this piece of rock hanging in the sky. Knowing how something came to be didn't quite explain the radiance of seeing it. And a part of her yearned for there to be more to the history of the world than a random occurrence in a nearby galaxy. How people in the old times believed stories and fables to explain all of this made more sense. Pictures had not conveyed the magnitude of the moon.

Large puffs veiled the sweet light as the wind blew them across the sky, but Roxan didn't care. The great reflecting ball had been revealed, and now she knew. This moment would be etched in her memory, homage to the moon. To make it official, she knelt down and bowed her head. It was a silly thing to do. But it was her statement, her acknowledgement of her tiny place in the huge world.

The tingling started as soon as she bowed her head. The prickles started slowly, but intensified as she stood. The moonlit world grew dark. Jagged, dead trees replaced the beautiful forest. Smoke rose from the landscape.

She dropped to her knees and tried to shake the images from her mind, but even closing her eyes didn't take them away. It made her want to cry. Her beautiful forest was gone. All was silent. There was no golden haze or streams of silver light this time. Darkness and death covered everything.

When Roxan opened her eyes, the same sweet moon greeted her, but a bit of its wonder was stained by the lingering dark images. "I don't want this curse. For all I know, they did this to me. They made me this way."

She pulled herself up, shook off the remnants of the vision, and marched down the hill into the valley. If a person wanted something, they had to go out and get it. She would get the answers she wanted. These blasted visions would stop.

* * * * *

Blood and puss oozed through the napkin onto the sandal strap, making it slick. Two blisters had come up under the front strap and made themselves known in a very dramatic and painful way. Tearing a strip from her cover-up, Roxan wrapped it around her foot. That eased the pain some, but her eyes watered with each step. Trying not to think about it, she shook the empty Vitawater bottle for another drop or two and finished off her wafers.

The forest had grown louder as dark roll settled in. Screeches and howls called through the darkness. But so far, nothing had crossed her path. For that matter, no path had crossed her path. It had been one lone trek, with no cross trails branching off. Mullin should've drawn a map or something. At this rate, there would be no making it back before sunrise.

She slowed to a shuffle as she came into a clearing. A massive wall, consisting of mirrored panels that were separated by white columns, reached up in front of her. It climbed up into the sky higher than the trees. Although the moon had disappeared behind a cloud, it still gave off enough light to see the long reflecting sides of the wall.

"The Balustrade." Roxan inched her way forward.

A soft humming came from the barrier. The panels reflected everything in front of them—including Roxan. If she weren't standing in front of the boundary between her world and a place of complete desolation, she might have taken the time to pull the leaves from her braid or wipe the dirt from her face. Reaching up, she meant to touch her reflection, but hesitated as the hum grew louder the closer her hand came to the wall.

"I wouldn't do that." The growl of a whisper came from behind her. A short man with stringy hair and a fur cover-up bobbed up and down as if he were exercising. "Its hurts." His tongue wagged, licking the sides of his open mouth. "The wall hurts." He waved his right hand and pointed at the nub of arm on his left side. "The wall's got a power all its own. Its'll blow yous clear back to the tree line if yous touch it. Here watch this."

He ran backwards, grabbed a rock, and launched it toward the wall. The rock hit the surface, stuck to it for a flash, then rebounded through the air, whizzing by Roxan's head and smacking into a tree about ten meters back.

"Oh, sorry. I guess I shoulda thrown its over there." He wagged his tongue up and down this time, keeping it within the confines of his open smile.

"Who are you?" Roxan pulled out her stave and held it up, although the moonlight reflecting off the wall gave plenty of light. Having something from home in her hand gave her a boost of confidence. "Where'd you come from?"

This time he actually hopped up off the ground before settling back into his bobbing up and down. "My name's Caton. Caton 14266. I got me a few good livin' spots. I move around mostly. Where're yous from?" He jumped up and down two times and then stood bobbing again.

Roxan hesitated. "Back there," she answered. He gave a number. He gave a call number. "I don't want any trouble." Other than the number, nothing about him suggested he came from a village.

"No trouble." He smiled again, but kept his tongue in its proper place. "Unless yous lookin' for trouble." The smile turned as his countenance changed to a glare.

Roxan stepped back. "I'm not looking for trouble." The path she'd travelled by was behind the little man. "I'm looking for a cabin. But I think I'm a little lost."

"Yous a spy, lady?" He eased forward, closing the gap between them. Even on his toes, he was a full head shorter than she was. But he was bulky and looked like he'd taken several hits in his lifetime.

His odor was his worst weapon so far. Roxan tilted her head up for fresh air. "No, I'm not a spy. I'm looking for a cabin."

"Why? Nobody comes out here just lookin' for that cabin. What yous really lookin' for?" His smile hadn't returned.

"Someone's supposed to meet me. They have some data I want." Little bits of information--never give more than you're asked. First rule from nanny interrogation protocol. "Do you know where the cabin is?" Second rule, put them in the question chair.

"Maybe." He knew protocol too. "What kind of data?"

Delivering answers without any promise never worked out well, so Roxan swallowed the pounding lump in her throat, and called back everything she'd learned from her bouts with Nanny Skelt. "I don't think you need to know that. And I don't have time for this. If you can't help me, I'll be on my way." The words came out with more confidence than she felt, and they fell well, softening the little man's grumpy face.

"Don't go yet. Maybe I can help yous. We could be ... friends." His lack of familiarity with the word *friends* didn't help him at all. "How's about I tell yous a shortcut to your cabin, and yous tell me who you've seen out here?"

Roxan couldn't tell from his face if he could deliver up on his promise of a shortcut, but she answered his question anyway. "I haven't seen anyone. You're the first."

"Yous seen anything weird out here?" That was two questions and no shortcut, but he was smart, and his eyes caught her shift. Roxan could tell she'd given herself away. Yes, she'd seen something weird out here, but it went along with all the other weird stuff she'd been seeing.

"Your eyes, deary." His words stopped her. "Your eyes give yous away."

She didn't reply.

"It's okay. I won't tell. Yous help me. I help yous. That's one rule we follow," he paused. "Sometimes." A crack sounded from the shadows, farther down the wall. "Oh, shikes! Not yet. Stupid rock. Think! Always got to give its away." As he rambled, Roxan took a step toward her path, but the crazy held his nub up. "Don't go that way. They're coming."

"Who?"

"The soldier guys. They'll get yous. Yous better hide, over there." He pointed with his nub toward a clump of bushes. "Those ain't the bad briars. Yous goes right there, and I'll fetch yous back. We still got our deal to work out. Now, go." His eyes bugged out, and she didn't ask questions. Men's voices echoed down the wall.

Taking three steps backward before turning, she darted for the thicket and slid to the ground between the briars and a sapling, just as the shouting started.

"You throwing rocks at the wall again, little freak?" Three sentries called from thirty meters down the wall. Caton could've taken off for the brush too, but he stood there waiting. He took every stinging comment they threw at him without replying. He had the protocol down.

Roxan scooted back into the brush. Several briars grabbed at her, jabbing into her right arm and leg. She pulled the intruders from her flesh and dabbed the injured spots with her spit. When she looked back, the sentries had surrounded the small man. He hopped up and down like a frog and kept his head down.

"Stop squirming, scrap." The shortest of the three pulled his scinter out and flicked it on. Caton settled down.

"You got anything for us?" This time the biggest one spoke. He had some gold on his cover-up top, but Roxan couldn't make out his face. "Anything new?"

Caton straightened up. "I got news. I got news." Waiting, the sentries took a step up wind of the little guy. "Theys on the move."

One sentry took lead on the interrogation. "Who?"

"Da ones yous after. Theys all headin' somewhere. Theys even takin' da sick ones."

"The boy with them?"

"I ain't seen da boy. Nobody sees da boy, and da girl's gone too." The sentries grinned at one another.

"Yeah, we know about the girl. Where're they going? You got people followin' 'em?"

"No. We stay away. Dem folks do weird things. We don't need dat. Theys leave us alone. We leave them alone."

"Well, you're going to follow 'em. You got that." He grabbed Caton by the neck. The little guy took his good hand and scratched at the sentry, but it didn't make any difference. "You're going to find them for us. Find out where they're going and report back. Understand?"

Roxan fumed. Those monsters. They think they can go around intimidating people. They're no better than the nannies, probably worse. They abuse their power and make threats. It isn't right.

She balled her fists and fought back the urge to run out there. Tingles pricked at the back of her head. Not now. Her vision changed quickly and instead of sentries, she saw men in black gowns, Caton just a shadow of a man. Turning away from the men, she became lightheaded as a shimmering blanket fell across the trees behind her. A silver cord wound its way out of sight, its path unobstructed and open.

Caton whimpered as the sentries punched at him to make their point. Roxan couldn't look back. Going to his defense had to wait until her eyes cleared. She shook her head, but the world still had a silver shroud covering it with a bright rope of light weaving around the trees.

He screamed out again for them to stop. Clear sight or not, she had to help him. As she got to her knees, Caton yelped out the one thing she wasn't prepared for.

"She's over there," he screamed. The guards immediately spotted her. They yelled for her to stop, but Roxan jumped to her feet and took off. The silver cord led her through the maze of trees.

Behind her, she could hear the growling shouts of the three guards as they smashed their way through the thickets. Curses and threats spewed from them. Running at top speed, Roxan trusted the cord to guide her through the unfamiliar terrain, but as she crested a hill, her sight returned to normal, stopping her dead, in plain view of the guards. Down below a creek wound its way through the valley. Roxan reached it before the fiends made it through the thickest part of the brush. With three leaps, she rock-hopped to the other side. At the top of the creek bank, a pathway opened up between the trees. That would be too easy.

Instead, she dashed around the trees and threaded her way along the ridge. Her lungs ached and her feet were numb. The men had reached the creek now. She rolled behind a tree and curled up close to its trunk as the sentries topped the bank.

They talked quietly, and looked as if they were planning to split up their search. Roxan leaned into the tree. She maybe had one strong sprint left in her, but it wouldn't be enough.

She grabbed the branch above her head, wedged her foot in a gap in the trunk, and pulled herself up. Three stair-stepped branches helped her farther up the tree. From her perch, she couldn't see the men, but heard them arguing. One called in her direction, and the other two cussed about the beating they'd taken following her through the briars. They wanted to head back.

As the lead guy ordered them to be silent, a scream ripped through the trees, and a rock zipped through the air. Another scream, then a group of people rampaged toward the guards. Some of the invaders wore cover-ups like Caton's, but others wore brown, green, even blue coverings, like the ones inside the boundary. They looked like people, but acted like animals.

Bursts of light energy flashed from the scinters, but the guard's weapons did nothing to protect them from a well-thrown rock. Roxan dropped down a branch to get a better view, but the injured retreated her way, so she climbed back up to her perch. Within a few flashes, the skirmish was over. The guards fled back toward the wall, and the crazies hooted about their victory.

After the last one had disappeared over the ridge, Roxan descended the tree and gave it a pat. "Thank you, dear friend," she whispered. Loneliness struck its chord in her. Trees for friends, frogs and crickets as companions, and no one to help her find her way. The world wasn't looking so adventurous any more. Ugly things lurked outside the boundary. Evil guards, crazy people, and a pathetic, little man. And none of it would help her to the cabin or to the answers she needed.

A warm breeze blew smoke up from the valley, and an echo of humanity held on to its scent. The crazies. They were celebrating. Roxan crept toward their screeches. She wanted one good look at them. She inched her way up the hill, crawling the last few meters. A leaf-covered crater sloped down from the hilltop, forming what looked like a large bowl of leaves. At the bottom in a clearing, a small fire glowed, and the crazy people danced and jumped around it.

One of the women wore a blue cover-up with a golden trim around the hem. Calling out, she pointed up the hill and grunted. Roxan ducked down. The partying stopped; they all looked, and then broke out in laughter. One of the men gave the woman a shove, and began hooting and hollering until the others joined in with him.

There was a fluency about them. They weren't animals. They were plebes, workers, and disillusioned members of society, evidently rejected and left to their own devices. Caton had a number. They all probably had numbers. They had to be at least twice her age, close to the time of attainment. Why would they throw that away to live out here? It didn't make sense.

A tap on her foot drew Roxan away from her thoughts. Crouched beside her was the boy she'd seen on the other side of the river. His white cover-up glowed in the moonlight. He had a finger to his lips and with his other hand motioned for her to follow him. She scooted back from the crest of the hill.

"What are you doing here?" Roxan jumped to her feet. "There are crazy people down there." She grabbed his arm and pulled him away from the ridge. "You should be in your raising home, kid."

The boy smiled and placed his hand on her shoulder. "Come with me. It's dangerous here."

"I know it's dangerous. That's what I'm telling you. This is no place for a child," she whispered.

He leaned forward, putting his lips right next to her ear. "I can take you to where you want to go. I have the answers to your questions." He looked past her as he stepped back. "We must go."

"Wait." Roxan turned and grabbed her satchel, locking eyes with the wild woman from below. They both screamed. The boy seized Roxan's hand and yanked her away. She didn't look back, but the mad screams roared after her.

The boy ran with precision around the trees and bushes, keeping his grip on her hand. He had answers, and he definitely seemed to know his way around. A rock struck a tree off to their right. And without warning, he stopped and turned to face her.

"Close your eyes." He smiled as he put his hands on her shoulders.

"What?"

"Just do it. Close your eyes."

The screams increased in volume, accompanied by the sound of a rampage through the woods. Roxan weighed her options. Leaving the kid wouldn't work, and this wasn't the time to argue. They couldn't take these lunatics on without any weapons. They needed to run.

"We need to get out of here," she insisted.

"I know," he countered strongly. "Close. Your. Eyes."

She closed them with a "fine." A tingling rushed through her body, and when she opened her eyes, everything was out of order. The screams were gone. Trees still surrounded them, but not in the same places. "What happened?"

"Don't worry," her little friend beamed. "You'll be safe now, but we still have a ways to go. And much to talk about."

CHAPTER 14

SMALL, INSIGNIFICANT, AND SPECIAL

Water tore over the edge of the cliff with a power that sent a surge of fear and admiration into Roxan's bones, while the roar drowned out everything around her. In the dark, the liquid sparkled, catching the light from the moon.

They had been walking for a while. And every time she asked the boy about the cabin, he had told her not to fret and to stay close.

Deftly, the boy wound his way down a narrow footpath, leading them closer to the crashing water. "Go slowly. It's slippery." He looked back and paused as he spoke, then took off practically skipping down the tapering pathway.

The boy didn't seem too concerned about getting her to the cabin. He was a kid on a mission, to take her to his hideout, maybe. Roxan wasn't sure, and she wasn't in a position to make any demands of him. This was crazy dangerous, though, and didn't hold any promise of getting safer.

"Wait," Roxan called, but the kid kept moving forward. Her foot slipped on the muddy path, and she steadied herself against the wet rocks protruding from the bank. When she looked up, the boy was gone. She'd only had her eyes off him for a flash, and now he was nowhere. "Hey, kid, are you there?" Her words fell silent in the roar of the waterfall. Had he fallen?

She hugged the side of the steep embankment and tried to think. Leaving the kid wasn't right, even if she could leave—the trail behind her had disappeared into the shadows, and the edge of the pathway met a ten-meter drop to rocks and whitewater. Crumpling to her knees, she panicked. Nothing in her knew how to handle this. They don't teach you about being lost, running from crazy people, or navigating narrow pathways next to certain death. The resolve that had driven her out here was replaced with defeat. But before she could wallow there, a sharp tingling shook her whole body. It came on quickly and spread into her neck, past her ears, through her cheeks, and pooled in her eyes. It hadn't happened like this before. She pressed her palms into her eyes, but the sensation wouldn't go away. When she lifted her hands, the pathway was outlined in silver strands that led to the sheer and brilliant cascade of water. Behind the silver spread, another light flickered and moved, as if carried by someone. Roxan covered her eyes again. "Stop. Please. Stop." This would be it. She would fall into the furious silver display and no one would ever know.

Bowing her head to the muddy ground, she pressed her arms to her ears to shut out the fury around her and the tingling within. Moments of her life flashed through her mind. A little girl on a nanny's lap. A tender kiss good bye. Steel corridors, stale air, and solitary confinement. The operation. And always being the last one chosen. Reprimands, arguments, punishments, and then freedom. The Protectorate, Whitlock, and Jonas. Mullin, secrets, and a search for answers. The tingling in her head faded into a dull throb, and she huddled tightly to the ground.

"Are you okay?" The boy grasped her shoulders as he spoke, lifting her up to meet his glowing face. A bright lumen sat behind him framing him in a bluish-white light. "You okay? I'm sorry. I shouldn't have left you. I wanted to get the lumen. Come; follow me. I've got you." He plucked her hand and pulled her to her feet.

The waterfall tore through the air above her head, but she kept her eyes on the boy. He clinched her hand with his iron grip. The torrent crashed into a slanted gray ledge and then tumbled over into inky blackness.

A few steps from where she'd had her vision, the bank gave way to an opening, and she crossed behind the cascade. A cave. Two burning torches revealed a home inside, complete with blankets, a shelf with supplies, and several boxes. "Wh ... where are we?" Adrenalin reeled through her body and her knees buckled.

The boy put a hand under her elbow and guided her away from the spray. Grabbing a blanket, he wrapped it around her and settled her into a large orange and black cushion under one of the torches.

"This is Snowshoe Falls. You'll be safe here." His singsong voice added to the irony of his statement. Safe? There's nothing safe about nearly falling ten meters onto jagged rocks in furious whitewater. The kid puttered about the cave gathering things.

First, he set up a short table next to her. Then he opened a large green box against a far wall. Almost half his size, the box nearly swallowed him when he reached inside to get something. Popping up, he held a leather jug and shook it.

"There you are!" When he smiled, his whole face got involved. His eyebrows went up, and his eyes twinkled. Even his ears perked up.

Roxan sunk farther into the cushion and watched him. Jumping up and down a few times, he popped the cork from the jug. "This is the good stuff. I hid it at the bottom so they wouldn't take it."

He reached into the box again, but not as far, and pulled out a cup that looked like a tree. He shook out the dirt, then he wiped it out with his sleeve. He poured a clear liquid from the jug into the cup, sniffed it, and smiled. "This will help."

Behind him stood a table laden with more cups like the one he held, several scrolls tied with leather cords, and two broken lumens. The cave continued back—into a darkness that ate up the light from the torch.

Spray from the waterfall hit her every time a breeze blew in. Pulling the blanket up, she wrapped herself tighter in its warmth. Her trembling slowed, but the feeling of dread and complete failure hunkered down inside of her.

Follow the path until it forks to the left, then go to the right. Mullin either didn't know his way around as well as he thought, or she'd completely missed the fork in the road. It didn't matter. There really was no going back anyway. Reaching up she pressed her hands to her aching eyes, but pulled them away quickly. Mud and grime covered her fingers.

"You can wipe them off on this." The boy held out a moist, warm towel, and then went back for a tray with the tree cup and a bowl filled with white chips. "We're the only ones here." He smiled and motioned toward the dark part of the cave. "The others have gone."

Roxan tried to sit up, but the cushion gave no support. "Who are you people? And what are you doing out here? You're just a kid." Her voice trembled as she spoke. "How did you get out of the raising home?"

The boy smiled again. He snatched the cup from the tray next to her and pulled over a blue and yellow cushion. Dropping into the softness, he spilled some of the liquid from the cup. "I've never been in a raising home." He crossed his legs and cradled the drink with both of his hands.

The smile stayed on his lips. His crazy blonde hair stuck out in all directions. Fair and clean, his cute nose and rosy cheeks glowed under the light of the torch. He didn't have a scar on his cheek or an earring like when she'd seen him by the river. The whiteness of his cover-up added to his innocent appearance, except that children only wore orange, never white, and never tied with a golden cord at the waist. Wearing white meant he'd been up to no good somewhere along the line. Probably stole it.

Roxan shook her head. The prickles started poking at her neck, cheeks, and eyes again, but she could tell nothing would come of it. Everything looked normal. That is if normal is sitting behind a waterfall in a cave—with a kid who claimed he never went to a raising home.

"Listen kid, I don't know what you're up to, but take it from someone who knows their way around the strictest nanny, you are going to be in huge trouble when they catch you."

The boy's expression never changed. He didn't seem to take her seriously.

"I'm not kidding. Why are you even out here? It's dangerous."

Still smiling, he lifted one hand. "Slow down. You're safe now. They won't find you here." He settled his hand back to cradle the cup. His sympathetic tone pricked her instead of helping her calm down. He talked as if he were taking care of her. "I'll make sure you stay safe."

The adrenalin went into gear again, and Roxan balled her hands into little fists. He could've gotten them killed bringing them down that path. *Stay safe.* The words made her boil.

"You're just a kid. And you don't know what's out there."

"I know what's out there.

"No, you don't. " You shouldn't even be out here. Those people who were after us are crazy. They ran away from the villages, and now they've gone mad. And the sentries. They'll throw us both in an underground cell for being out like this." The words poured out of her stifling the air.

"You need to calm down. Take a deep breath."

Roxan tried, but couldn't inhale. All the panic from the entire roll squeezed her lungs and sat on her chest. She shook her head back and forth. The whole world fell in on her.

Was it this roll she had gotten to work early? It felt like an eternity ago. The argument with Jonas, Mullin pushing the scroll into her hand, the beautiful moon. And she'd fled head-on into the forbidden to find answers. Answers about what? No one would be able to help her. Nothing could be done.

The tingling started again, but Roxan didn't care. She couldn't breathe. She pulled the blanket off and leaned forward, one hand on the cool dirt floor, the other clutching at her chest.

The boy set the cup aside, sprang to his knees, and half crawled, half walked to her. "It's going to be okay. Try to take deep, slow breaths. Come on." Settling in front of her, he took her hand from the dirt, and coaxed her back to breathing normally. She kept her eyes locked on his. They were blue, like the sky.

As she drew in a deep breath to fill her lungs, her eyes tingled sharply, and she saw the kid, radiant, beautiful, his face golden white, like a star. Then, all went black. When she came to, her head was on his lap.

"There. Slow down," he said. "It's a lot to take in all at once. I know. But you're not going to end up lost or abandoned. You're not going to be like those crazy people out there." He nodded toward the woods on the other side of the waterfall. "I won't let that happen. Besides they each made choices that led them to right where they are. You can make choices to keep you from that spot." His little voice soothed her.

He scooted up next to her and draped his skinny arm across her shoulder wrapping her with the blanket. That felt weird, but comforting, and Roxan let him stay like that until air flowed freely to her lungs again.

He must have seen something change, because he glided back to his cushion, content, his eyes glistening. Had he been crying? "You feeling better now?" He asked a question, but it seemed more like he was making a statement.

Roxan nodded her heavy head. "Yeah, I think so. That's never happened before." At least not the inability to breathe part. She held her hands in front of her to see if they were shaking like the rest of her. They barely moved.

"You're stronger than you think," he assured her. "That was a panic attack. You're fine."

Roxan didn't reply. She didn't feel fine. Lost and in trouble, not fine. What had she been thinking? Pulling her feet up on the cushion, she wrapped the blanket all around her so that only her head poked out. Had the kid noticed her vision? If he had, he didn't seem interested in finding out about it. He had to have noticed though. People usually notice when they're that close.

"I didn't escape from a raising home." He broke the silence with a matter-of-fact tone, as if he were telling her he hadn't eaten his morning meal. "Here." He lifted the cup toward Roxan.

Holding the blanket together at her neck, she snaked her other hand out from its cover to take the mug. Heat radiated from its contents. Still shivering under the blanket, she loosened her grip to grasp the mug with both hands and lifted it to her lips. It tasted like Calciwater, but was thicker and had honey in it. Taking another gulp, she closed her eyes and let the thick liquid slide down her throat and warm her.

"Do you like it?" The boy giggled out the words.

She licked her lips. "What is it?"

"Don't worry. It won't hurt you. It's called Ness. They don't have it in the villages. It's a combination of things." His eyes twinkled. "Let's start over, shall we? My name is Altrist." He stared at her waiting for a response.

"I'm Roxan 423B7." Roxan stirred the liquid with her finger.

Altrist curled up on his cushion and propped his elbows on his knees. "What's the number for?"

"It's my identity number. Everyone has one when they leave the *raising home*." She paused to make a point, but nothing seemed to register in the kid's curious eyes. "It tells my position."

Annoyance flickered through his expression. "Okay." He spoke slowly, with attitude. "What's your *position*?"

Roxan swallowed another gulp. This was better than the apple. The panicky feeling had evaporated, and now a warm, peace tingled up from her toes. Every sip of the Ness filtered through her veins, warming her. She held the cup close to her chest.

"I'm a replicator. I take messages and rulings from the Plateau—even the *Guardians*—and I reword them for the common people." She emphasized *Guardians* mostly out of habit. "You do know about the Plateau, don't you?"

His face went from placid to rigid. "Yes, I know of Hyperion." And then he leaned back in the cushion, turning away from her to face the sheets of water falling in front of them. "So do you like your job?"

The tone in his voice didn't match his superficial question, but Roxan ignored it and answered him.

"Yes ... I do. I haven't actually been at it very long, but I do. I'm not crazy about my guide. But my overseer's nice." She took another swig of the Ness and smiled at its goodness. They needed to get this stuff in the village.

Altrist turned back. "Did they send you out here?" His blue eyes were penetrating. "Or did you decide to take me up on my invitation?"

Roxan considered her answer carefully. Time for the protocol again. Even if he was a kid, he was after something. "No ... it was someone else." Lying would be fine here, but it was hard to tell what the best lie would be, and not knowing what he was fishing for left too many unknowns. She flashed him a smile and drained the rest of the Ness.

He wasn't going to let it drop. "Was it the guy by the river?"

This kid had shown up twice in one roll. "Why were *you* there?" With everything that had happened, there was a lot that didn't add up and questions that needed answers. With her strength returning, she felt more entitled to know what was going on with the kid and find out if he could help her. "You were looking for me, weren't you? Have you been following me?"

Altrist hesitated to reply, and held his hand up. But before she could demand an answer, he countered, "And I was going to ask if you were sent here to find me. Why are you out here, Roxan? What brings you to break the rules, defy your overseer, and put your future in jeopardy? What drove you to all of this treason?"

"What do you know about any of it?" She sat up straighter, but he didn't back off.

"Look at me," he demanded, in a tone that didn't suit a child. "You know I'm not some kid, a runaway. You know that already. You keep trying to convince yourself of a lie, but the truth is obvious to you. Things are not always as they seem. Are they?"

He glided to his feet as he spoke. "You are not just a girl sent into the woods on a simple errand either. Maybe those are the questions you should be asking." He extended his firm grip and helped her to her feet. Although she stood two hands taller than he, it was clear who was in control. "Why are you out here, Roxan?"

That question had already come to mind during the darkest part of the roll. And it always brought her back to one thing. "To get answers," she whispered.

"And what are the questions that demand to be answered?" His tender expression urged her to honesty.

She turned to the waterfall. "There's something wrong with me." Betraying tears jumped to their posts. "I have some kind of disorder, and I want to know why, where it came from, and how to get rid of it." She wiped her nose with her sleeve, and swallowed back her painful truth. "And I need to get to this cabin. Can you take me there?"

"Why? There's nothing at that cabin."

"He told me to go there, if I went, he would give me the answers I need."

"You made a deal?" His insinuation stung.

"It's not like that," she murmured. "He wants to help. He thinks I'm special, but I know the truth. You're right. I do know the truth." The monster of dread dismantled her armor. "I'm messed up, and I can't fix it."

Altrist wrapped his skinny arms around her. "You don't need to, Roxan. You don't need to fix anything." Pulling away, he wiped her tears from her face. "You're special, just the way you are."

He lost her when he said she didn't need to be fixed. The rest of his sentiment plunked against her wall. No one could make her stay like this. There had to be some way to fix it. "Will you take me to the cabin?" She checked the sky through the waterfall. The end of the roll was getting closer. "I haven't much time."

"Yeah, I'll take you there." His countenance dropped. "But not before I tell you that this is a very bad idea. You're making a mistake."

"Well, it's my mistake to make then. I didn't come all this way to not finish what I started." The dread had been locked away again. The more she pushed it to the back of her heart, the better she felt. Focusing on doing something helped. And thinking that something could be done gave her enough hope to push on. "I'm not going to be some freak. Either they tried to fix this and failed or they made this happen. I'm going to find out."

"You're forgetting something."

"What?"

"Maybe this is part of you. A gift given for a purpose."

She bent down and growled in his innocent face. "This is not a gift. It's a curse. And if you won't take me to the cabin, I'll find it myself."

He met her on level ground, just as fierce. "I'll take you, but you have to do something for me. You're used to making deals, right? This shouldn't be too hard for you."

"What?"

"Trust me." That caught her off her guard.

"What? How's that supposed to look?"

"You'll know when the time's right. I am not your enemy. But I think you know who is."

She would've asked him to explain, but a sound from the edge of the cave made her jump. Altrist eyes reflected surprise and a hint of anger. A young woman, with tangled blonde curls, black marks on her cheeks, and a huge grin on her face stood at the entrance by the waterfall.

"Abiga," Altrist growled.

CHAPTER 15

SILLY RHYMING WORDS

Jonas checked the pavilion, but found nothing. His search around the Triangle and Propagate building had produced no sign of Roxan either. Evidently, she hadn't been out getting fresh air, or—if she had—she had already moved on.

He checked the sky, then headed back into the building. The first warning bell would sound soon, and he had an appointment he couldn't miss. Delivering Roxan's marker would have to wait.

Avoiding the staircase to his workroom, he charged past the empty chair of the lobby attendant and pushed open a single door marked "Private." It was good timing to have arrived while that nosey receptionist was out. She would've asked a few questions, and made him use the main entrance to Wortman's department.

The heavy door snapped shut, grabbing the attention of Wortman's receptionist perched behind a large desk. She sat up in her seat, putting aside the temporary body paint and brush blade. Her big brown eyes, shiny dark hair, and stunning smile took him away from his purpose for a flash. He hadn't seen her before.

"May I help you?" She ran her hand through her silky hair and smiled. Her big brown eyes were vacant, like she might still be trying to decide what to paint on her hand. She wouldn't be chastising him for using the wrong door. More of a decoration than a guard, she tilted her head and smiled.

"I'm here to see Master Wortman. I'm Jonas 32107."

The girl pulled out a calendar from her front drawer and spent far too long looking over the empty spaces on the page.

Jonas shifted on his feet. "I have an appointment."

She didn't seem to be in any hurry. A plebe from the outer office brought a basket of papers over, but the girl never even looked up from her scrutiny of the calendar.

Finally finding what she was looking for, she glided from her chair to Wortman's door in one swift motion, her pale blue cover-up flowing behind her. There would never be any gold glistening on her trim. She might be cute, but cute only lands you a job sitting at a desk working for the smart people. Brains would always win out over beauty in Jonas's world.

"Jonas 32107 is here to see you, sir." The breathy words had a hard time making it past her plump lips. Had this girl even ranked in the raising home? She should spend time with Norwood. The idea of the pairing made him smile. Norwood didn't tolerate self-grooming on the job or anyone operating at an infuriatingly slow pace.

Unintelligible syllables rumbled from the other side of the door. At least Wortman hadn't taken off early. The overseer was known for coming in late and taking off without notice, and being lazy. He didn't bother to emerge from his stronghold.

His ornament of a receptionist closed the door and smiled her way back to her station. Once fully situated, every hair in place, and the paint top screwed back on, she looked up and smiled.

"You may go in." Giving him permission apparently made her happy. If she'd smiled any harder, she would've split a lip. The plebe with the papers still stood to the side, unnoticed and waiting. Maybe the figurine could only handle one thing at a time.

Holding back the urge to roll his eyes, Jonas entered the office with a fake smile on his face, prepared to wade through the pleasantries of conversation before getting to his point. But Wortman dismissed all formality and twigged it before Jonas could speak.

"There you are, boy. I was about to close up shop. I have an important trip to the Progenate in my future." Wortman's low voice filled the room, as did his stout form. He leaned back in his chair, balancing it on its back legs. It must have been stronger than it looked, because Wortman didn't seem concerned about snapping those thin sticks at all. "Have you made any trips back there, boy?"

"No sir. Haven't been there since I left my raising home." Heat rushed up his neck and Jonas tried hard to keep his face from flooding with red. "I'm hoping to soon, though." He hadn't even thought about it, at least not as much as most of the other males, anyway. There would be time for that after he had established himself.

"Yes, well, I'm sure you'll get to go soon enough, unless you're planning to follow your overseer's example. I hear he refuses any trips there. To each his own, I guess. But I'm certainly willing to do my part. For the good of all, you know." Wortman chuckled to himself. "Well, let's get right to business. I have to get moving soon. What's on your mind? I was surprised to get the text from you the last cycle requesting a meeting and even more when you requested to move up the appointment. I hear things are going well upstairs." Wortman motioned for Jonas to have a seat.

Two large brown leather chairs faced his desk. The dimly lit room felt like a cave and Wortman the bear inhabiting it. Jonas settled into the chair and took a deep breath. Time to bait the animal and hope for the best.

"I'm interested in what you're doing down here, sir. I mean I think I'm ready for something more—more than what Whitlock's doing for me, anyway. I think that if you check my record you'll find that I have a lot to offer." Jonas leaned forward. Having practiced this speech several times helped him ignore the quiver in his voice. "I'm looking for something to do on the side. You handle all of the personal notices and private texts. That's so different from what we do upstairs. I think I could be an asset to you." He finished his spiel and scooted back into the soft leather.

Wortman cocked his head and raised his bushy eyebrows into his chubby forehead. "How's that?"

Jonas hesitated, not sure how to answer. Wortman had to see the benefit of having someone from the replicating floor in his alliance.

"You boys from upstairs are all bound up with official business," he reviewed. Heck, you're like the Plateau's right arm. We have nothing to do with that stuff. What are you after, kid? Working for me would be a downgrade." Wortman settled his chair back to the floor.

Jonas could tell when he was being assessed. This wouldn't work if Wortman questioned his motives.

"No sir. It would be an opportunity." Looking directly at his superior, he treaded carefully. Some flattery should help. "You've got things to teach me that Whitlock can't. And, yeah, I know you don't handle the major stuff, but you," Jonas pointed straight at Wortman, never breaking eye contact, "you know things."

Wortman grinned and nodded his head. He seemed to know what Jonas was getting at. "Continue, young man."

"I'm asking for an apprenticeship. That's all." Relaxing, Jonas loosened his grip on the armrests and crossed his legs.

Wortman's eyes said he understood the use of "apprenticeship." He evidently was on familiar ground. So the rumors were true. Wortman wasn't lazy. He had his own sideline going on.

"Alright, 32107." His hefty hand slammed onto the desk causing stacks of paper to shift. But he kept his voice low. He wasn't going to give anything away. "I don't think you understand how things work around here. You can't go and decide you want to work with someone different. That's not how it goes. And even if I thought you were exactly what we need here, which I don't, I wouldn't be able to move you. All of that is decided at the Plateau. They're working with more information than we are. And you are going to have to trust their judgment on this one. They put you with Whitlock; they want you with Whitlock. There ain't nothing you can do to change that."

Jonas let the words settle in the room before he countered, "I'm not saying I want to leave Whitlock. I'm saying I could maybe be of service to you. Let's call it a hobby, an interest, not a job. The Plateau wouldn't even care, as long as I get my work done with Whitlock. Everyone wins." Wortman needed assurance he wouldn't be adjusted if the duplicity were uncovered. "Listen, you don't even need to give me wages. I want to do this for the experience and to learn from you. You have a knack with people." Stroking his ego couldn't hurt either. His gray eyes said he was weighing the advantages of having an ally from the replicating floor. Time to turn up the lumen and let him see how this could go for him. "Listen, sir. Our arrangement can be mutually beneficial." That sparked the scale.

"Beneficial?" His eyes were hungry for something.

Jonas weighed the tidbits he could throw the old guy's way, but only one held enough meat to keep him busy. "I'll give you this now," he disclosed, pulling his tongue from the roof of his mouth, "the Plateau has issued a census. They're going to interrogate every underling, plebe, guide, and overseer. No one will be overlooked. So it might be a good idea for you to get your affairs in order by the second roll from now."

Silence. It was the silence of not being able to undo something. A shocked quiet still trying to comprehend what had been done. He had just committed treason. He had stepped across a line that had always kept him one move ahead. No retreating now. Either he'd forged an alliance or found another enemy.

Wortman scowled. "Okay, kid. I'll give you one cycle to see where this goes. I'll do my part. I pay my debts." He screeched his tired chair back and pushed himself up from the desk. "I never liked Whitlock anyway."

Jonas found his footing and stood. Let him think this was about Whitlock and a preferment. "Thank you sir. I'll come on the next roll, then?"

Wortman hauled himself around the desk. "That's fine. Just look for the guide. He can help you. Stopping at the door, he rumbled a warning. "And if you double-cross me or word gets out about this, then it all falls on you. And I can make sure that happens. Okay?"

"Yes, sir." Jonas understood perfectly. "I'll hold up my end, and I know you will take care of yours." His eyes challenged Wortman's as he stretched out his hand to shake on their agreement. A hint of a smile crossed Wortman's round face, and he returned a firm grip, then nodded toward the door, dismissing Jonas.

"For the good of all," he grumbled.

"We give ourselves," Jonas responded as the door clicked shut behind him.

* * * * *

The warning bell rang as Jonas exited the building. Stopping off at a bench, he took a flash to let his new arrangement sink in. A lifetime of following rules and always coming out the better candidate left him feeling sick about his diversion into the seedier side of getting ahead. Maybe this could be considered proper use of the end justifying the means, though he never really condoned that excuse. If anything, this was Whitlock's fault. He had brought this on himself by his poor leadership.

That soothed his conscience. After all, Whitlock was being investigated as a possible traitor. If this arrangement with Wortman turned up anything, it would be to the Plateau's best interest. And when you're working for the higher ups, you're allowed to bend the rules a bit. And in the end, this could benefit Roxan too. If anyone were looking into her, he'd find out.

Three workers from his floor hurried by, casting him a quick glance. They clutched their markers in plain view, obviously not sure of how to use them. Jonas rummaged through his sack for the marker with Roxan's name on it. Might as well track her down and deliver it. And maybe apologize. That would depend on her behavior.

Jonas jogged along the backside of the small businesses lining the main thoroughfare and down the alley where four dilapidated shanties nestled into a thicket of trees. Roxan's stood the farthest back, right next to the wooded area. What a junk heap.

Jonas banged on the rickety door. Memories of his first visit here curled his mouth. Scared and trying to hide it, she had asked him for his number, looked him in the eye, and held her ground. She wasn't like other plebes.

"Roxan?" The old door creaked open as Jonas turned the handle. From the entryway, he could see the entire shanty except for the facilities. Several blue cover-ups lay strewn across the table and chair, along with various pieces of underwear. If she'd returned to her shanty, she hadn't done any cleaning.

Farther in, Jonas bumped into a metal can filled with ashes and singed pieces of orange cloth. Papers covered the unmade bed along with Nutrivia wrappers and a few bottles of Vitawater. She was a complete slob. No wonder they had held her back.

A breeze blew through her window rustling up the papers she had tacked to her windowsill. One of them caught his eye, and he plucked it down. It was his. She had added to his tree of wonderful words, filling up an entire landscape with her own thoughts and poems. Poetry. He hadn't let himself go there. Poetry's uselessness had been drilled into him, but now all of that fell away, and her words opened up a world he hadn't dared to see.

His feelings battled inside of him, and not a single one left him with a sense of control. Facts...facts give control. Solving problems, meeting deadlines, following orders, those are the things that work for the good of all. Not these crazy ideals, silly rhyming words. Still, no amount of data could do what a few well-placed rhymes could do. Roxan's poem brought his tree of words to life, awakening an unseen and forbidden reality.

He had tucked this word tree into his personal Guidebook—the one Nanny Skelt had given him when he graduated. He must have grabbed that Guidebook from his shelf instead of one of the others. And he'd given it to Roxan on that first roll when it appeared her own Guidebook was serving a different purpose.

Jonas shook his head and grinned. He should've known then that this girl would be trouble. And he should've reprimanded her for her ill use of their most important book. But he didn't. Why? Her bright brown eyes flashed through his mind.

She possessed an energy—a sight for the world—that made everything an adventure. And he had plunged a dagger into her happiness. He'd stepped into her world with his slanted facts. The look on her face when he'd called her a freak assaulted his sense of rightness.

Some things couldn't be undone. Anger and frustration moved in next to his joy, and he tucked the paper into his pocket. If she didn't show up soon, none of it would matter. Her discipline would be out of his hands, and his apology would reap nothing.

He moved her one chair in front of the doorway and set the marker on it. This would be the extent of his tracking. His heart couldn't take much more. She would have to find her own way back from wherever she was hiding..

Jonas pulled the door shut behind him and scanned the other huts and vacant path, hoping to see her mopey face puttering up the lane. A silhouette darted into the wooded area leading to the alleyway. The shadows gobbled it up before he could make it out. Most people, except for Roxan, had already made it to their huts and were tucked in for the dark roll. He almost called her name out, but decided to take a stealthier approach.

Acting as if he were preoccupied with his satchel, he slowed his pace as he approached the wooded area. The form slid farther back into the brush. The grove was too thick to see a face or even a body. Whoever it was definitely did not want to be seen.

"Hey, who's there?" Jonas paused hoping to hear Roxan's mousey reply. Instead, a man dressed in leather took a step out from the shadows.

"I think I'll ask the questions." The sentry moved into the dim light. He reached into his satchel, pulling out a small stave and shook it lighting up the twilight with beams of white light. That was one powerful stave. In the light, Jonas could clearly see the gold trim on the leather cover-up.

"What are you doing out here? This doesn't look to be your part of the village." The sentry nodded his head, eyeing Jonas's trimmed cover-up.

"I'm delivering a marker to one of my plebes, sir." Jonas's heart thudded in his chest. Although he knew he had every right to be out, he never felt comfortable dealing with sentries. And this sentry didn't act like the others.

"Which plebe?"

"Roxan 423B7, sir." Jonas took a step back and held in his desire to explain himself, waiting, instead, for the sentry to ask him questions.

No sense in giving out more information than was needed to get out of this predicament.

"423B7. And what is your business with her?" The sentry looked familiar. Jonas tried not to make eye contact, but took quick glances. Curly brown hair sat like a mop on his square head. This sentry ranked higher than most of the ones Jonas had ever met. The thick golden trim with one red stripe above it on his leather cover-up indicated he worked directly for the Guardians.

"I'm her guide. She's in my work station, sir." Jonas scanned the angry face for acquiescence, but saw none.

"Is she giving you trouble?" His voice cut the quiet. He sounded more familiar than he looked.

"Not exactly. We have a project for the Plateau and I needed to give her the orders."

"Did you give them to her?"

"I left the marker for her."

"And did she sign for it?" Annoyance filled his voice. "Good grief, man, don't make me ask you every little detail. We can do this here or you can come in with me and we can do it at the sector. It's your choice."

"No, she didn't sign for it. She's gone. I don't know where she is." Jonas filed through his options. Lying to a sentry was never a good idea, and so far, Roxan still fell under his jurisdiction. If she failed to show up on the next roll, the Plateau would be notified. But he could put that off until late-roll even.

"What do you mean you don't know where she is?"

"Just that." Jonas took a step back. "I haven't seen her since before mid-roll."

The sentry examined Jonas's face, but didn't say anything. He knew how it worked. As her guide, Jonas was responsible for her.

"I can handle her, sir," Jonas said. "And I will definitely report her if her behavior merits that."

The look in the guard's eye told him he wasn't going to let this go, but Jonas took advantage of his silence and made a bid to end the interrogation.

"For the good of all ..."

"We give ourselves." He didn't sound happy, but turned and dimmed his light. "You may go."

Jonas shifted backward, but paused for one last question. "And, sir, if I need to contact you about her, who should I ask for?"

"Jasper."

That was it. Jonas took a good look at the sentry while the scent of honeysuckle and the inside of Whitlock's cabinet attacked his memory. It was good to put a face with a name. "And your number, sir?"

Jasper sneered, but before he could answer, the bushes behind him started to shake and a yelp sounded from the middle of them.

"Who's there? Show yourself!" The sentry pulled out his scinter and it roared to life with a pale purplish glow. A quiet whimper came from the thick brush and then a woman's voice.

"I'm over here." A slender arm reached out of the thicket. Jasper shoved the stave into Jonas's hand and reached into the mess of thorns and leaves, pulling out a young woman.

She focused her attention on a briar vine wrapped around her right arm, still connecting her to the leafy prison. "Oh no, this isn't one of those bad briars, is it?" She hadn't even looked up at them yet. Framed by a leaf-filled mane of shiny black hair, her pale white skin glowed in the stave light.

"Liza?" Jasper's boldness deflated.

"Jasper!" She reached toward him, but the briar pulled her back. "Ouch. Oh, no." She cried at the vine.

"It's not that kind of bush. Those are only *out there*." He reached down and pulled the shrub loose with his bare hand. His countenance had shifted from angry guard to faint-hearted man. Once freed, she reached up and gave him a hug, but he pushed her away.

"What are you doing here?" He turned from Jonas and pulled her with him.

"Your guess is as good as mine! I just popped in. You know how that goes. I spent most of the roll sitting in a tree, watching sentries march in front of that hidden passage to the Plateau. And now here I am!" Though much smaller than the sentry, she had an energy about her that was full of life. "Oh, it's so good to see you. How long has it been?" She glanced back at Jonas still holding the stave. "And who is your friend?" The smile hadn't left her face since she recognized Jasper. Jonas lowered the light when she asked about him.

"He's not my friend." Jasper placed the scinter back in its holder and grabbed his stave from Jonas. "You're dismissed, boy. Get back to your shanty or workhouse, but get off the streets. Go!" Angry guard was back, but Jonas recognized that type of anger. It follows fear. This sentry had more secrets than breaking into someone else's files.

Jonas bowed his head and took three steps backward before turning to leave. After he rounded the corner, he doubled back cutting through the trees and brush. Jasper and the young woman had walked behind a line of bushes. His stave barely glowed. Jonas slipped closer. Their voices carried softly on the evening breeze.

"Jasper, don't talk that way," she pleaded.

"Stop it, Liza. You don't know what can happen here. It doesn't have to be like Altrist says. He tells you about many things you can't even see. But here, you don't have to wonder. You can walk right up to the Guardians and get your questions answered. Hyperion himself will meet with you."

"His answers are filled with lies. You know they are." Her black hair shimmered in the faint light. "And I doubt if anyone can walk right up to that monster." Jasper pulled out his scinter and raised it to her throat, but she didn't back off. "What? Are you going to slit my throat? Have I offended you?"

"Be careful, Liza." He lowered his weapon. "You're in my world now."

The girl mumbled something, but Jonas couldn't make it out.

Jasper walked around her, looking her over. "Why are you here?"

"I don't know. You know how it works. He sent me here, maybe for you."

He growled.

"Or maybe I'm here to help Altrist or the one he's trying to find."

Jasper stopped in front of her.

"Who?" Alarm filled his voice. "Altrist came *here*?"

"Oh, I don't know. I don't know where he is. But this person must be important. Altrist is planning to wait for her." Liza reached out to touch his arm, but pulled her hand back. Nothing about Jasper's demeanor had changed He still looked as if he were getting ready to pounce.

"You mean he can't leave without her, don't you." Leaning toward her, he lowered his voice.

Jonas bent over the prickly brush pile in front of him. With so much tension hovering between the sentry and his little friend, he didn't want to miss a single syllable.

Jasper's gritted words thudded into the quiet air. "I knew he would come after her. But I didn't think it would be this soon."

"There's no time. We're leaving. On the third roll of the sun, all of us are leaving." Sniffling, she wiped her nose with her cover-up.

Jasper exhaled. "You're not going anywhere. None of you are." He wrapped his hand around her forearm.

"Please Jasper. Reconsider. We are leaving. You can't stop us, but you can come with us." Making no effort to break free of his grasp, she reached up with her other hand and touched his cheek. "Please, you can still come."

"Is Jahn there?

She dropped her hand at his question, and tried to take a step back, but he kept his hold on her.

"Liza, you know you could stay here with me. What's going to happen to them will happen. There's no stopping that, but I can work things out for you. They make allowances for sentries. I will keep you safe." Jasper's voice was soft, entreating, but Jonas could hear a hint of ire beneath the words.

"Don't." She pulled at his grip, but he held her fast. "You know how I feel. Please don't make this about us. We all want you back. Even Jahn." Despite the quiver in her voice, her words soared like arrows, sure and strong, and the sentry deflected her plea with a low growl. She cried out, then doubling over, she fell to her knees and pulled out her own stave.

Jasper fumed over her, still holding her arm. "You're the one being stubborn. They're lies, all lies. Just a bunch of fairy tales and you're a fool if you think the master is going to let you go. He's going to put a stop to this. He's going to stop Altrist." She looked up at him, tears glistening in her eyes.

"You don't get it. You never did. You went through the waterfall. You met him, but you never would let yourself believe."

"I believed, and he let me down. Everybody gets gifts. Everybody fits into his neat little plan. Well, I didn't see me fitting into that. And I'm not taking my orders from a kid. It's all a bunch of lies. And that little freak probably made them all up." He snarled and lifted his other hand to hit her, but she wrenched free and fell back to the ground.

"No, Jasper." She scrambled to her knees. "You're wrong. We all love you. It's not a fairy tale. It's the most real thing in this world. I know you see that. You're being stubborn because you didn't get what you wanted. Things didn't work out how you hoped, so you ran away and what? You surrendered yourself to that monster? Why? You're throwing it all away. This is your choice, not the Leader's, not Altrist's. You're doing this to yourself. You know there's more."

"What do you mean, more? More lies?" He ignored her appeals.

She tilted her head back, defeated by his avoidance, but not surrendered. This phantom of a woman held her ground against his brutality. "There's more than what you see." Standing, she lifted her trembling hand from her stomach. "Jasper, look at me. I'm going. Is this a lie?" A light glowed from her mid-section and grew brighter.

Jasper brought his scinter to life and pulled her close. "I'm not going to let you go. They're all going to pay for this."

"You can't make me stay, and if you don't let go of me, you'll be coming too." He let loose of her arm as the light flashed, and then nothing. She vanished.

The only light came from the purple glow of the scinter. Jasper dropped it to the ground and gripped the air with his fist, yelling into the darkness. "No."

CHAPTER 16

UNDESIRABLE

Abiga scrambled down the limb to get a better view of Altrist and Roxan. He'd taken off toward the cabin right after he'd finished scolding her for thinking for herself. "You didn't have to isolate yourself to figure out the truth. Think about what you're going to do when everybody who loves you is gone." Everyone encouraged her to find her answers, but they wanted her to do it their way, on their timetable.

Altrist and Roxan stopped about ten meters from the trail at the top of the hill. Following him probably wasn't the smartest move, but lately following orders felt like being stuck inside a cage. Confining and empty. Answers would not come from sitting and waiting back at Snowshoe. It was ridiculous for him to tell her to stay anyway.

Straining, Abiga could only make out a few words here and there. From the looks of things, Roxan didn't like what Altrist was saying. She looked like every other village-raised sprout. They all had this air about them, like they had it all figured out. A patronizing air. She looked down on Altrist as if she were humoring him and ready to move on. If she only knew what he could do, who he was.

Altrist pointed out the way to the cabin. The shack was about one hundred meters past the trail. Barely standing, the cabin was the only evidence man had once lived beyond the village boundaries. It had a bad reputation with the Undesirables. People disappeared around it. Some went in, but never came out. And sometimes, a reddish glow could be seen through the windows.

A cool breeze blew through the trees. Inhaling the sweet air, Abiga filled her lungs with its freedom. Perhaps being a part of Altrist's stuffy, rule-following group had been a mistake from the beginning. Being out, tracking them like this, made her feel alive. Who needed one of the leader's gifts when she had skills of her own! Her eyes almost worked better in the dark. Trees were her guardians, and clouds were her cover. But there was something empty in it all too.

Abiga ignored the nagging blankness pecking at her heart and watched as Altrist let the girl go. Roxan pulled a second-rate stave from her bag and headed toward the trail. Had she even said thank you? Typical. They're all the same. They say they do everything for the good of all, but it's really for the good of that monster they follow. That girl didn't even realize what danger she'd put Altrist in. Maybe now that she was on her way, he'd get back to the group.

Abiga slid down the tree and leaned back against the trunk. The world felt lonely again. Not even the thrill of tracking in the dark could abate the questions and disquiet within her. No gift. No assurance. And what if Altrist returned to the Outcasts? She wouldn't be there. Nothing had changed for her. No answers had come.

When she'd found Altrist at Snowshoe, she'd thought that might be a sign. The Leader hadn't left her alone. He'd left a guide, but then that girl was there. And she was all Altrist cared about. But the only thing she cared about was getting to the cabin.

Roxan disappeared at the top of the hill, the dim stave she held bobbed in front of her as she hurried away. Altrist remained behind. His white tog billowed with the breeze like a ghost hovering in the moonlit air. He didn't appear to be in any hurry. He just stood there.

Abiga held her breath. The only thing worse than the scolding he gave her before he left would be the scolding he'd give her if he found out she hadn't stayed behind. Despite everything, his words still squeezed her heart. Pleasing him felt better than getting her way.

Altrist kept his back to her, though, and lifted his arms above his head. Without seeing his face, it was hard to tell what he was doing. But a soft, happy tune rose into the slumbering dark roll. And as he whistled, a ball of light appeared between his hands. It grew to melon size. As Altrist's song ended, tiny specks of light flickered to life inside of the ball.

He pumped his arms twice, and tossed the ball into the air. It flew up above the trees, then plummeted toward the ground, but before it hit, it split apart, and the pieces took off, darting through the woods. Buzzing little balls of light flew past Abiga and out of sight. They left more darkness in the forest than before.

Altrist didn't have the same glow about him. He looked small and sad—standing there, alone and quiet, almost as if he were defeated. Instead of compassion, anger heated Abiga's cheeks. Had Altrist felt sad like that when she told him she was going to leave? Maybe now would be the right time to get answers.

Before she could make a move, Altrist turned away from the trail to the cabin, took two steps, then became a hazy blur. He vanished, a spark of movement and then nothing.

"Oh, shikes!" Abiga pushed away from the tree. Altrist was going back to the falls. "Great, now all I'm gonna get from him is another lecture." Wrapping the laces to her boots tightly around her legs, she regretted not changing into Thim's old pants. Running was much easier in pants.

* * * * * *

The falls crashed against the slanted cliff with their normal brilliance. Abiga stood on the tip of the rock that formed the enormous shoe at the bottom of the falls. A calm pool of water surrounded the shoe. Behind the cascading water at the cliff's edge, a light flickered. Altrist awaited her.

Although fresh water abounded, her throat ached with more than physical thirst. Kneeling she scooped a few handfuls of cool hope to her mouth, but it didn't help. The Leader had forgotten her. The Outcasts had gone away from the bluff. She had been deserted twice now by these people she loved so much. To hear Altrist's rebuff would be the final shot hitting its mark and killing all confidence.

Asking for answers wasn't too much. Any truly great being would listen to questions, not deflect them. He would care that his followers knew his purpose. What did the Outcasts expect? For her to say, okay, and ignore who she really is. How could she possibly ever fit in with these people?

They lived in a bubble, pretending, untouched by the real world. And now they ran off to hide.

Abiga searched her palm for remnants of the Leader's touch. Hidden by a dirty smudge, it was still there. Filthy things have a way of tampering with goodness.. How could her life with the Outcasts be reconciled with all she'd done? Altrist said they wanted her, that the Leader loved her and had chosen her, but he denied her the evidence she needed. It didn't make sense.

The light in the cave grew brighter. "Okay, Altrist. You can chide me if you want, but you will answer my questions. She scrambled up the rocks to the pathway and followed her determination into the cave.

******

"I went for a walk," she lied. He knew it was a lie. His eyes registered it, but he didn't interrupt her story. "I needed to clear my head. I have a lot of questions, and there doesn't seem to be anybody with the answers." Abiga dropped on her orange and black cushion sending a cloud of dust into the air. "And you don't seem to be offering me any help. You'd prefer to gallivant around with an ignorant girl who still thinks the world exists inside those stupid villages. She's probably out there right now on some errand for the Guardians or even worse, for Hyperion."

Abiga hesitated when Altrist shot her a look, but then pressed on. "What? They follow him like we follow our Leader, and look where it's gotten them."

She waited for a response. Mentioning the Leader in the same sentence as his adversary would not sit well with Altrist, but these were her questions. If he couldn't answer them, what point was there in staying with the Outcasts? How were they any different from the Undesirables? Both groups were made up of people forgotten by the one who was supposed to protect and show them the way.

"The Leader has not left you alone, Abiga." Altrist's simple calm slowed her down. His liquid eyes entreated her. "Is this about your gift?"

Tears sprang into action. Blasted tears. She wiped her eyes with the back of her hand. "It's not just the gift, Altrist, or the lack of one. It's this alone feeling. I can't shake it. It envelopes me. It tells me I don't belong here. I'm not one of you people. But I'm not one of them either." She pelted the cushion with her fist. "Maybe we've all got it wrong."

"What do you mean?"

"Maybe there's not an absolute to any of this. That monster's right for them, the Leader for you—and for me, maybe there really is nothing. Maybe I am a misfit." The words caught in her throat. Following their predecessors, tears flowed down her cheeks, her own little waterfall. Altrist sat there, blurry and still. She slid off the cushion onto her knees. "Well, say something. Please, Altrist. I need answers."

He lifted his hands in surrender. "What should I say? What would make you believe the truth?" Then he knelt in front of her and took her hands in his. "You've seen many things. You've heard people's stories. You've felt our Leader's touch, yet you still refuse to believe. If you can reduce him to that fiend, you don't know him at all." Tired anger filled his words, and resignation. "What do you know of Hyperion? You've seen his work in the Undesirables, but that's all. He's just a story to you, someone who can't get enough power. The Leader will destroy him."

"I saw him in the woods. Hyperion. He's not a person; he's a monster. Scales and strength, flesh and blood. They worship him, as if he gave them life. They follow him. We listen to the Leader. They listen to him. The only difference is he's with them. They can talk to him when they want and get an answer. And we get none of that. We get dreams, feelings, and maybes. We get nothing."

"The only difference?" The blue in his eyes grew dark. "Do you seriously think that's the only difference? When did you see him? When you were with *them*?"

Abiga nodded her head. Regret filled her. Despite his contempt, kindness still carried each word.

"Abiga, you've seen so much. But what's happened in your past, doesn't have to determine your future. Would all of this have been different if he'd given you a gift?"

She shook her head. He was right. The gift wouldn't make a difference. These questions would keep haunting her. There didn't seem to be a solution. *What's the point?* She shifted off her knees and leaned to one side.

"Abiga?" Altrist ran his warm hand down her arm and whispered, "Your questions aren't bad things."

"How can you say that?" Anger bubbled from her despair. "Oh, I know. Because you know the answers. You know everything. I'm getting sick of it, Altrist. Honestly, it's like you're all part of an exclusive club and you have all these secrets. The Undesirables have that sort of thing, you know. It's called a pomper. It's a small group within the pack that has the power—they know stuff. Well, for once, I want to know stuff."

"What do you want to know? You already know more of the world than most of the Outcasts. What do you need? Here, ask me anything." Altrist crawled in front of her and sat up straight, waiting, his eyes wide and his lips pressed together in a smile.

He had to be bluffing. He wouldn't tell her whatever she wanted. Hundreds of questions had already met him unanswered, and he'd offer that stuff up now? Abiga doubted his sincerity, but tried anyway. "Okay, how 'bout you tell me what that thing was in the forest?"

"In the forest?" The confused look on his face was a good deflection, but not good enough.

"Oh, come on," she countered.

"Could you narrow it down a little? We're always in the forest. What did you see? Or should I say, what did you snoop?"

"You know I followed you. And I saw you with that glowing ball thing. What was that? Is that part of your many gifts?" Her teeth chattered, more the result of adrenalin than being cold.

"That was a drone pod. It's hard to explain."

"I bet it is," Abiga growled.

"Wait, I'll tell you more. Goodness, Abiga. I'm on your side, you know," he snapped. "The drone pod is a part of me. I send out the little lights, the drones, and they keep an eye on things. When they gather information, they bring it back and show me. It only works for a short time, not even a full roll of the sun. The drones will tell me if Roxan needs my help returning to the village, or if she changes her mind and decides to join us."

"And this drone pod thing is one of your gifts?"

"No, Abiga. You will be surprised to know that I actually don't have any gifts." His white skin reflected the warm glow of the torch. He looked sincere. "I don't have gifts. This is who I am, who I've always been. I'm nothing special. It's who I know that's special"

"I don't get it. You move incredibly fast, you have this ability to melt a chunk of ice with one touch, and you have that light thing. What do you mean you're not special? False humility does not become you." He didn't respond, so she proceeded, "You're not like all of us. Where did you come from?"

"Ah, now that's a good question. You know I'm not a boy. I'm quite old, actually. I was with the Leader, helping him. There were so many of us, we couldn't even be counted." He turned toward the water. "The Leader has sent me to many astonishing places, but I like this one best of all, because of you, all of you." He looked back and smiled. "But Hyperion was jealous. And powerful. None of us knew how strong he was, until he launched his attack. Most of my kind were destroyed."

Abiga crawled next to him, her empathy growing.

"You are special," he murmured. "We are supposed to protect you, help you not succumb to the liar's tricks. But there are only two of us within the barrier. We volunteered to come. We couldn't leave you here alone." He grabbed her arms. "It's just been the two of us."

"Olivope?"

"Yes, Olivope..." He released her arms. He wasn't saying something, but Abiga didn't know what question to ask to fish it out, so she sat letting the roar of the waterfall fill the space between them.

"Outside the Balustrade there are three more beings like Olivope and me." Altrist spoke the words into her mind. She shook her head. She hated it when he did that, but now wasn't the time to complain. He was filling in the gaps for her.

"And that's why the Outcasts are leaving to find the others? And then what?"

"I don't know. This world, the Oblate, is going to change. Hyperion is growing tired of his cage. It's not safe anymore."

"Why doesn't the Leader show himself and end all of this?"

"I don't know, Abiga. I don't know. He doesn't tell me everything. I have a connection with him, but only because I've been with him so long. But he doesn't tell me everything. He doesn't need to. I trust him, whatever happens. I trust him."

"How? How can you trust someone who has the power to change things, but stands by and does nothing?"

"He has a reason. If he ended things the way you say, you might have never heard of him. And there are others who need to hear. . .Roxan and, hopefully, more. I do what I'm told, and I wait. It's not for me to tell him what to do or how to fight his battle."

"What's special about Roxan? She doesn't even want to join us."

"She has a purpose, and I'm here to help her to that." This time he spoke aloud, leaving her space in her head to think.

"What's her purpose?"

Altrist shifted backwards. "I can't tell you that." He stood as he spoke.

"Why not?" Abiga followed him.

"Abiga, I can't tell you because it's none of your business. Roxan doesn't even understand her purpose yet. It's not for you to know it. It's not right for me to share *that* with you."

"What about my purpose? Can you tell me that?" She took a step closer to him. His face told her his answer would be no.

"I can't tell you your purpose. I probably would if I knew it—but I don't know yours. I don't exactly know Roxan's either. At least, I thought I did, but now I'm not sure." He started to pace. "What do you know about having a purpose anyway? What do any of us know about it? Is there only one purpose, and then you're done? Are there many purposes? And what if there isn't a purpose at all? What does that make a person?"

"Me."

"Abiga, stop feeling sorry for yourself. You have the same choices in front of you that all of us have." As he spoke, a flash of light darted through the water. It zipped around the cave and landed in the boy's hands.

He held the drone up, and it grew into a cherry-sized, glowing ball. It rolled and squeaked in his hand. Altrist nodded and then tossed the tiny orb in the air. It broke into pieces and died off like sparks from a fire.

"I've got to go, Abiga. Please stay out of trouble. The others will be to Willow Way by the end of the second roll. Go to them. This is not the place for you. I can tell you that. You'll all be much better off if you can get through the wall."

Altrist grabbed a small leather sack from the box in the cave and then bolted over to Abiga. Wrapping his arms around her, he stepped on her toes and kissed her cheek. "He loves you, Abiga. He will pursue you. He has done everything for you. Believe." He whispered the words into her ear, and then he stepped away and vanished.

CHAPTER 17

THE CABIN

Roxan stumbled over a root at the edge of the clearing. Her feet ached. Sweat stung the scratches on her arms and face, and the empty Vitawater bottle in her bag mocked her.

Altrist had offered her some cold Ness, but she'd declined it to get back out on the trail faster. It would be nice to take a couple swigs right now. The hike up from the falls had gone better than the one down, but navigating through the brush was still tricky.

Everything looked like Altrist had described it, every detail, all the way down to the three trees with the paper-like bark. He didn't seem to think much of her ability to follow directions, yet refused to accompany her to the cabin. His last words were warnings and another appeal for her to stay with him. At a different time, staying out here and living in the woods would've been a great adventure, but not now. Not with her eyes getting weird and the world being outlined with silver threads at the most inopportune times.

As she held up her stave and waved it toward the clearing, it flickered. "Oh c'mon." The poor little light-giver had about used itself up. But the moon cast an eerie glow across the meadow and illuminated an old house at the far tree line. It had to be the cabin. Finally. It had taken most of the roll, but she'd made it. So much had happened since she'd jumped across the rocks in the river. Now, she wanted this roll to be over.

Playing behind the clouds, the moon teased away the little bit of light it offered, but Roxan barely noticed. She kept her eyes on the cabin and jogged across the open field. Early roll dew had already formed on the tall grass. Somebody had better be over there.

Cool air blew at her back, sending loose strands of hair swirling around her face, and pushing her forward. The cabin leaned in front of her, defying a strong gust to bring it down. All the windows were broken out, and the front door hung on one hinge.

She stopped at the rickety steps leading to the porch and called out, "Hello, is anybody here? Mullin sent me. Hello?" Roxan lifted her stave above her head, but it offered no help. "Please, if you're there, come out. I need to get back." Her voice cracked and exhaustion summoned up despair. "Please, somebody be here. Please."

The door scraped across the boards on the porch and a man emerged. "Well, you're as spunky as they come, aren't you?" Mullin stepped out of the sagging shanty. Shadows darkened his face, but his voice gave him away. "It took you long enough to get here, didn't it?"

"Mullin!" Roxan stammered. Relief mixed with confusion swept through her. "I don't understand."

He creaked across the porch and descended the steps. "I know this wasn't easy." His arms wrapped around her. "You're safe now. I won't let anyone hurt you." No man had ever held her like that before.

She leaned into him. He felt strong and steady. Scenes from the roll flooded her mind, but she couldn't put any of them into words. "I want to go home." Sobs choked the rest of her words away.

"You will, I promise, but first things first." He stepped back, leaving her swaying and shaken. "We're not quite done out here yet."

She steadied herself and tried to concentrate. "Where's the person I'm supposed to meet?"

Mullin bristled and walked around her, as if he were a nanny on inspection day. "Ah, yes, well. Let's just say that this *someone* sent me instead." He smelled different. No jerky, no sweat, instead the fragrance of hot metal with a hint of cinnamon followed him when he moved. "Tell me, was the forest good to you?"

"*We* could have met in the Triangle, inside the safety of the Protectorate!" She ignored his shallow question and the slight tingle in the back of her head. "Do you know what I've been through? And what I'm facing when I get back? This isn't a game. I came out here for answers. Whitlock said you would be trouble." Anger dammed up her tears. "I shouldn't have come."

Mullin finished his orbit and grasped her arm. "Roxan, I can help you, but you have to trust me." His black eyes pulled her back from her tirade. "I care about you. I do, and I can help you find the answers you're looking for."

Exhaustion and uncertainty overtook her and she crumpled to her knees.

Mullin knelt and pulled her against him. "You'll be fine." Leaning back, he braced her with his hands and waited for her to look into his eyes. "I can tell you some of what you came here to find out, if you still want to hear it. Do you?" She nodded,

"There's a lot that will be hard to understand." He offered his hand and helped her to her feet, guiding her to the steps of the cabin. "Most of your memories have been wiped, so all you really have to go on is a vague recollection of a trip to the Plateau." He motioned for her to sit on the steps, then plunked down next to her. "Roxan, I'm going to be blunt. You're a modification."

She'd heard that term before—one of those things that she didn't really understand, but acted like she did, so no one would give her a long boring lecture. "A modification? What is that?"

"It's pretty rare. They tell you about it in training, but they only mention it." He took her hands in his. "It's when you have a special ability or power, or sometimes it's a physical aberration. In your case, it was both. A modification is supposed to be for the good of all, but so far, no one has been found with a useful one. That's why they changed you back, took it away, and cured you."

"My eyes. They fixed my eyes." The word "aberration" stuck in her mind. Roxan kept her visions to herself. They hadn't fixed them.

"Yes, your eyes. They glowed like silver orbs, not all the time, only occasionally, and you would see certain things."

"What things? What did I see? What did all of it mean?" She took her hands from his and scooted against the banister, so she could face him.

"I'm not sure, but whatever it was, it didn't help the people. It was seen as not beneficial. That's why they *fixed* you." He reached over and pushed a strand of hair out of the wetness on her cheek.

"How? How did they *fix* me?" She thought she knew the answer to this question. "How do you just change somebody's eyes?"

"Some sort of procedure. You'd be surprised at the things they can do in the heart of the Plateau. And then they gave you an amnesiospread, so you only remember what he wants you to know."

"He?" She knew the answer to that one too.

"Hyperion. He's marked you. It's in your file, coded as a *Clingman*—a danger to all. That's how Jonas knows about you, but he doesn't know the details. Or at least I'd wager he doesn't understand what it all means. And Whitlock. He may know more than you think. And, there are others." Mullin moved to her side and draped his arm across her shoulders. "I know this is all hard to hear, but I think you need to know it. You need to know who you can trust."

"What do you mean? Others?" She stood and retreated down the steps. "This is crazy. I wish I'd never come out here. I wish this would all go away."

"Roxan, there are others looking for you, bad people. They're liars, and they want to use you. They're in the midst of an all-out rebellion against the Guardians and Hyperion."

She didn't turn to see his face, but she felt him watching her, driving his words into her, calling on her fears.

"If they get to you, they'll lock you up and force you to help them. They think you still have these abilities." He ran his hand down her arm and whispered in her ear, "I won't let them get you, but I need to know everything."

"I've told you what I know." She hadn't though, and her lying was becoming less and less convincing. Somewhere inside of her, a bottom was falling out. She wasn't just a loner from the raising home who liked to take long walks, write poetry, and dance around her shanty. She was a modification. A failed modification who still carried with her the very thing they said would not be for the good of all. She didn't want to be this person that she was, but not even the great Hyperion could fix her.

Mullin walked around to face her. "Has your ability returned? Because if there's anything else, you should tell me. I can help you, but I need to know if the Outcasts know something we don't."

Taking out her stave, she shook it to life and held it between them. She gripped the little metal cylinder as if it were the secret she was hiding. Mullin looked different than he did in the village. He had changed cover-ups. Now, he wore a black one. It had a silver trim that sparkled in the light. He wasn't just some delivery guy from the Viand Clan. "Who are you?"

"You know who I am, and you can trust me." He put his hand over the fading light, shielding its sad rays. "Roxan, who did you see out here? What did they tell you?"

The cabin creaked behind them. The wind had picked up. It must have been blowing in the next roll, because there couldn't be much left of this one.

Roxan bit her lower lip. Things weren't adding up, and being on the receiving end of an interrogation never felt good. Mullin swung between trusted confidante and mysterious interviewer. For now, the scale fell to friend, but if he didn't lay off the questions soon, she'd rethink that.

"I saw those crazy people in the woods," she replied, maybe giving him a few answers would encourage him to take her home. "They were like animals, playing with fire and pawing at each other. They chased me. If it hadn't been for this boy, who knows what they would have done to me. And there was another man—Caton was his name. Do you know him? The sentries seemed to know him."

"Caton is an Undesirable, though he seems to be on the outs with his pack right now. They look scarier than they are. They wouldn't have hurt you. Maybe kept you as their little pet, but they're not the brightest bunch. Did the sentries see you?"

Roxan shook her head, not saying the lies aloud seemed to work.

Mullin continued with the questions. "Tell me about the boy."

"His name was Altrist. He knows the woods like you know the village. He brought me here."

Mullin looked around. "Is he still here?"

"No, he left me on the trail leading to the cabin road. I tried to get him to come. I thought maybe he could come back with me. But he wasn't interested. He wanted me to stay here." A foreboding vexed her, but she continued. She pointed in the direction of the road. "I suppose he went back to his cave."

"You know where he lives?" Mullin's steady demeanor offered no hint as to where he was going with this examination.

"He took me to a cave. Can't we talk about this when we get back?" Tired and depleted, Roxan reached for Mullin. His strong arm didn't flinch from her grasp. "I want to go home. Please."

"What did Altrist tell you?"

She let go of him. "I don't know. It didn't make sense." The apprehension she felt hit its mark. "He's not who you're talking about, is he? He was nice to me. He's just a boy."

"It's not him. It's who he follows," Mullin growled. "Did he tell you where the others are?"

"I can't remember. He was alone, except for a girl who came back. They're all going somewhere." Roxan turned toward the path she'd used before. "Can you take me home now? I want this all to be over."

"It's far from over, Roxan." Mullin pulled his satchel from his back and opened it. "Here." He handed her a small bottle of plain water. She took it and drank the whole thing in a few gulps.

Mullin looked like he wanted something, but instead he took a step toward the damp trail she'd made through the meadow. "I guess we better get you back."

Relief swept over her. Finally, this long horrible roll would be over.

He started back the way she had come without another word. Something was bothering him. She could feel it, an irritation eating at him, but she left it alone.

"The sun will be up soon. I hope you know a faster route than the one I came by." She found her footing next to his fast pace and nodded her head toward the tree line. Maybe conversation would ease the space between them.

"I know lots of routes faster than the one you followed," he assured her. His thoughts still seemed to be somewhere else. Roxan didn't reply, but focused on following him through the wet grass. They were almost to the tree line when he stopped and introduced what had been on his mind.

"I don't suppose you would be willing to make a little detour first, would you?"

"No, I want to go home."

"It's not really a detour. It's on the way."

"What?"

"I need to talk to the boy, Roxan. Maybe I can convince him to stop this craziness. You said he wouldn't come back with you, but maybe if I talked to him. . .I could help him. You want to help him, don't you?" That wasn't fair. He knew she wouldn't be able to ignore some kid who might need her. Before she could respond, he launched into his plan. "He's not going to willingly talk to me. He's scared of me, but if you introduced us…well, then maybe he'd give me a flash or two."

"That's all great, but I don't know how to find him,"

"I have an idea. You go back the way you came and wander around. I'll hide in the brush. I have a feeling your little friend will find you, and when he does, I'll try to talk to him. Maybe we can help him." He practically pushed her toward the road as he spoke.

"I don't know, Mullin. I want to go back. I don't want any trouble. Please, can you take me back?" She swatted his pushing hand away. "Please."

"I can't, Roxan. I wish I could, but I need to talk to that boy. You go on and I'll follow you from behind. If he doesn't show up soon, I'll take you back. I promise. Okay?" He rubbed her arm with his hand, but she pulled away and fished for the switch on her stave.

"Okay." Roxan flicked the weary light up to high beam, but it didn't make a difference. The little light had given about all it could. "I'm not going to get too far in the dark." Her complaint fell quietly on the breeze. Mullin was gone. He left no trace of which way he'd gone. Except for the curious wind, all was still.

"You were serious about hiding," she mumbled, then turned toward the opening in the woods. She passed the paper trees again, and quickly found the trail, but then had no idea which direction to go. All the trees looked the same, a bunch of silent guardians offering no help to get her home.

"This is useless." She called out, but Mullin didn't answer. "Did you hear me? I have no clue where I am or how to get back. Hello?"

"I think everyone can hear you. Are you always this loud?" Altrist's quiet voice came from the trees to her right.

Roxan turned to see his shining face and bad haircut just two meters away. The sight of him flooded her with relief and hope.

"I take it you are ready to go back now?" When he smiled, he gave her the same look the nannies used to give when they'd caught her trying to cut class.

"I am definitely ready to go back now." Roxan had nearly forgotten about Mullin. Returning to her shanty and ending this horrible roll was the goal now. "Will you help me?"

"Yep, I'll help you, but can you make me a promise?" Everyone wanted something. "I want to see you again."

"No way." Roxan shook her head. "I'm not coming back out here."

"That's okay. I'll come to you. Is it a deal?" Altrist held out his hand.

She shook it, immediately feeling a warmth flow up her arm. Gasping from the sensation, she pulled away. "Sure. Whatever. Just get me out of here."

"Is this your new friend?" Mullin came from the shadows. Altrist stiffened and took a step back.

"Altrist, this is Mullin." The clearing between the trees allowed enough light to make their faces plain to see. Neither of them smiled. "He thinks he can help you or that you can help us. You can trust him." The tension between them grew. It surged from each of them and collided with Roxan.

"You can't change anything. It's already started." Altrist kept his eyes on Mullin. Conviction carried his words through the air. He took two steps and grasped Roxan's hand. The tingling, warm sensation started all over again. "She gets to choose."

"She's made her choice. She's with us, and you can't change that, but you can change what happens to you, and to your friends. You have the power to do that." Mullin closed the gap between them. His black cover-up billowed as he walked and his right hand was hidden inside his satchel.

"She's not made her choice yet. And I won't force her to." Altrist loosened his grip on her hand.

"Oh come on, boy. She's of no use to you. He's fixed that. He just wants peace. You come with me now, and no one gets hurt." Mullin adjusted his grip on the satchel.

"Roxan." Altrist maintained his watch on Mullin. "You need to decide for yourself, but not this roll through the darkness. It's not the right time." He broke his gaze to look at her. His blue eyes entreated her.

Although his mouth didn't move, his words whispered into her mind. "When I say go, run to your right, and stay on the road. Abiga will guide you home. And remember ..." he turned back to Mullin, but she could still hear him in her head, "there is more. This isn't it. Now, go. Go!" He scream-whispered the last word, startling her.

She took a step back. It wasn't part of Mullin's plan for her to take off, but something inside of her made her run. As she left them there in the clearing, a crackling sound filled the air. She didn't look back. Instead, she picked up speed and tore down the only path she could make out.

"He wants me to take you back." The girl's voice came from right behind her.

Roxan slowed her pace. "Abiga?"

The wild girl waved and smiled as she kept in perfect step with Roxan's running.

"How did you find me?"

"I wasn't looking for *you*." Abiga rolled her eyes. "I've been following Altrist, which hasn't been easy the way he zips around. I thought he didn't know it, but I guess he did because he told me to take you home. He does that mind thing where he speaks thoughts into your head. He did it to you, right?" She didn't really wait for a response. "It's annoying, especially when you don't think he sees you. Anyway, I'll evidently be your guide through the wild woods." Abiga trotted ahead.

"Wild Woods. Is that what you people call it?" Roxan called after her.

"Oh, good grief. That's what *you* people call it." She turned around and ran backwards as she spoke. "No, sweetie, we call it *home*, and you're trespassing." Abiga mumbled something under her breath and twirled herself forward. "I have no idea what's so special about you."

"Neither do I," Roxan whispered and picked up her pace to stay close to Altrist's friend. A soft gray haze grew to the east. The last time that haze had filled the sky, Jonas was about to get bad news. That didn't go well. "How much farther?" Sunlight would make sneaking back to her shanty twice as difficult.

Abiga halted. "We're here." She waved her hand at the expanse of the Protectorate.

The Goneer River guarded the village just like Roxan had left it. Everything looked like a wonderful gift: the Pavilion, the Triangle, the rocks dotting their way through the water. Her relief nearly suppressed the tingling in the back of her head.

As Roxan blinked it all in, a golden haze fell across the scene. Bright beams of light marched over all the main paths and several back alleys. Taking a closer look, she could see how the beams of light outlined the sentries patrolling the village. For once, her vision served a purpose.

"You okay?"

"Uh… yeah." Roxan shook the world back to normal. "Would you like to have breakfast with me? I don't have much, but it would be something." Maybe Abiga could find a safe way around all those sentries. "Have you ever gotten by so many guards?"

Abiga patted her back. "Don't worry. I'm going to see you all the way home. I wouldn't get you this far to drop you into the fire pit."

She darted down the bank like a cat on the prowl. Roxan attempted to mimic her, but couldn't keep her speed or silence. The girl moved more like a mind-reading member of the patrol than a crazy person from the sticks. Her instincts guided her around the guards. She only spoke to give direction.

"Shhh. Go slowly or you're gonna get us both caught."

Once across the river, Roxan pointed Abiga in the direction of the shanty. Neither of them spoke. Sentries patrolled the entire main path all the way down to the river. Winding her way around to the back alleyway, Abiga ran from hiding spot to hiding spot until they arrived at the shanty.

Roxan slid the back window open enough for them to squeeze through. "Thank you." She collapsed onto her bed, knocking several empty bottles and some papers onto the floor. "Oh, it's good to be home. I'll never do that again."

Abiga stared at the tiny room. "Is this all yours?"

Roxan popped off the bed and glided around the room. "Isn't it wonderful? And the best part is there's no nanny around to make you clean up or force you to go to bed. It's freedom in small shanty form." She pulled her one chair toward the bed and offered it to her guest.

Abiga took something from the chair and shook it. "What's this?"

The heavy marker had Roxan's name stamped across the front, along with sign-in times and a job assignment. *When the sun makes itself known, there's no excuse for being late.* Roxan glanced at the hazy light streaming through her window. Jonas no doubt was already planning her discipline.

"I have to go." She grabbed the marker and tucked it in the front pocket of her dirty cover-up. "Sorry. Make yourself at home. You can stay for the roll, if you want." Roxan pulled the door shut before she finished speaking and hurried down the lane.

CHAPTER 18

THREATS

"She's not here, and I don't think she made it to her shanty before the last horn blew." Jonas plunked the finished template onto Whitlock's glossy, black desk and waited for the words to sink in.

The overseer had spent the last roll in his window-walled office, and his whiskered face showed it. He grabbed the template and glanced at the work floor. "How would you know that? Didn't you give her the marker before the horn blew?" He had to have noticed Roxan wasn't at her station. This kind of infraction couldn't be ignored, even if they wanted to. "You and your markers." He shook the template at Jonas. "Always looking for the power step, aren't you? And now we could lose the best replicator on the floor."

"Not if we find her before they find out." Jonas hated to admit it when he was wrong, but Whitlock was right. The marker did make it worse.

Whitlock waved him off. "It doesn't matter right now. We have to get this done, or we'll all be in trouble."

"But, sir." Groveling really felt out of character, but that sentry, Jasper, would undoubtedly be by to check on her whereabouts, and once that happened, there would be no keeping her here. "I think I should go look for her," Jonas suggested. "If I could get your permission, I'm sure I could figure out what's going on." He held back the information about Jasper. That might bring up questions he didn't want to answer. "I'll take a short look around."

"I'll do it." Whitlock pushed the template into Jonas's chest. "You take care of this. Get it to Norwood and oversee it. I have to go out on an errand, anyway. I'll check out the river benches and the willow tree, the whole blasted Triangle, if I need to." He stepped around Jonas and huffed out of the room.

On a normal roll, Whitlock would've already started the search for his favorite plebe. The first roll she was late he had three other plebes scouting out the Triangle. The latest order from the Plateau had him all lit up like a scinter.

Jonas looked over the template again. Reading it without thought, it proclaimed a great edict from the Plateau, one that would help everyone and further their world. But what it really said was that everyone would be interrogated, probed, and judged. They were looking for someone, and in two rolls they would find them.

"Sir?" Norwood eyed him from the doorway. "We're awaiting our orders."

The workers looked like a bunch of little ones waiting for their first assignment. Jonas handed the template to Norwood. "Take this, make five proofs, and get everyone on it. All six hundred and twelve copies need to be finished, rolled, and waxed before low sun."

Norwood slid the template from his hand and plowed into the workroom like a robot in overdrive, shouting orders and listing priorities, all in her droning monotone.

As the room came alive, Jonas made another check of Roxan's station. Even though she had only been working on the floor for a few rolls of the sun, her workstation looked like she'd been here for several cycles. There was an art to her mess, though, and it made him smile. The paper clips lined the front edge of the desk in a zigzag line. Little square notes had been folded into swans and bears. And her half-opened drawer revealed a hodgepodge of sticks, rocks, and leaves.

Normally such a messy desk would get him going on a good strong lecture about organization, but Roxan had her own little world and his lectures didn't amount to much in it. He lifted a page from her desk. Little doodles ran along its edge. Extravagant calligraphy, most of the markings didn't make sense, except at the bottom. Written with curly-cues decorating each of the letters, a phrase jumped out from the jumbled mess. "For the good of one, we give our eyes."

He shook his head at the words. *What happened to you, Roxan?* She probably didn't even know. Jonas pulled the inkpad from her desk, stamped across the markings, and tossed the blackened paper back onto the stack.

A cool breeze blew through the door to the workroom as it swished open. Jonas looked up, hoping to see Roxan come gliding through, but it was Kain. That guy seemed to hardly ever be sitting at his desk. *Where are you, Roxan?* Tired of waiting, Jonas moved toward the door.

"Norwood." He didn't look back, knowing she would take down every word. "Let me know when Roxan arrives and Whitlock returns. I'll be downstairs."

* * * * *

"Wortman's not here." The decorative receptionist turned a page in her Plantanate Planning Guidebook as she spoke, barely looking up. Jonas scowled. *Keep on planning, sweetheart. Your little brain will be put to better use planning parties and catching some sunshine.*

"That's fine. I came to see your guide." He emphasized the word guide, hoping to remind her she was at work and not passing the roll in a relaxation station. "Master Wortman didn't give me a name, but I think he will be expecting me."

Without looking up, she swooshed her dark hair off her shoulder, revealing the results of her body art endeavors yester-roll. Her entire neck was covered in curly cues and lacey designs. She pointed in the direction of an empty desk in front of a low-paneled wall to her right. "There's no one there." Jonas considered ripping the Planning Guidebook off her desk, but instead cleared his throat.

"Oh, well then, they're probably over there." She looked up, flashing her distracted eyes toward an archway leading farther back into the office suite, and then she went back to her book. Jonas poked his head through the archway. About a hundred small, numbered cubbies lined the three main walls of the room. Several workers chucked mail into the boxes, buzzing around the holes like bees on a honeycomb. One man stood near the center of the room, talking to three plebes. The gold trim on his cover-up gave him away. Noticing Jonas, he handed his papers to one of the workers, and then motioned for Jonas to come over.

"May I help you?" Silver peppered his black hair. He probably already had his Plantanate Planning Guidebook all filled out.

"Yes. I'm Jonas. I spoke with Master Wortman the last roll of the sun about possibly getting involved down here. I'm the guide upstairs." Jonas lingered over the last few words. "Has your overseer filled you in on the situation?" The older man bowed slightly and took a step forward.

"Why of course, Master Jonas. Overseer Wortman did mention you might be *helping* us here. I'm Guide Wessel. Where would you like to get started?" He didn't wait for an answer, but led Jonas to the side of the room nearest the reception area.

Jonas nodded toward the receptionist. She still had her head buried in the pages of her retirement planning. "She's a real keeper."

Wessel chuckled. "Yes, she's more like Overseer Wortman's pet. She's harmless. Say whatever you want in front of her. "If our conversation doesn't involve body art, shack decorating, or holiday spots, she won't be tuned in." A plebe handed him several sheets, and Wessel signed them as he continued the conversation. "Her job is to sit there and look pretty."

"Then I guess she's very good at her job." Jonas checked out the other workers. "And are your other workers as discreet as Wortman's trophy girl?" The other plebes zipped around the room like gears on a machine cranking out a product.

"For the most part, they all work hard. They have a lot to prove. Remember, Master Jonas, these are all the people who scored lowest in the class. You got the overachievers upstairs. But these guys get the job done and that's what matters."

He waved down a nearby plebe and handed off the signed papers. "And they know how to be subtle. We deal a lot with people's private messages here. Where you are all about getting the words out, we are all about keeping it quiet." He grinned and raised his eyebrows, pleased with himself. Wessel probably knew everyone's private business.

"You weren't at the bottom of your class, though, were you, Wessel?" Jonas purposely left out Wessel's title. That should remind him who had the higher ranking here. Wessel caught his gaze and straightened up.

"No sir, I wasn't," he mumbled. "But I know my place and what I want, and I can get things done."

"What kind of things?"

"That depends ..." Wessel didn't finish his sentence, but Jonas understood.

Reaching into the hidden pocket in his cover-up, Jonas pulled out three service cards. *These should help him decide what he can and can't do.* Wessel took the cards, glanced at them, and then tucked them away. His crooked lips carved their way through his whiskers.

"I think we can work together well," Wessel assured him. This evidently hadn't been the first time Wortman's guide had helped someone out. He seemed to know his way around this sort of thing.

A combination of body odor and ink washed over Jonas as Wessel leaned around him to bark a few orders to his plebes. The acid in his stomach tried to crawl its way out. Subversive activities didn't settle well. His chest tightened. If he didn't get out of here soon, he'd be gasping and puking. Taking a deep breath, he held his resolve while Wessel finished strutting the sad hold he had on his office. Before the little man could address him again, Jonas took the lead.

"I would like to monitor the memos of Master Whitlock and a plebe on my floor, Roxan 423B7." Fighting the urge to spin a story to justify his spying, Jonas kept it simple. "Can you do that?"

Wessel nodded his head. "No problem, but to let you know, Master Whitlock is quick to get his memos." He cast a glance at a redheaded plebe off to the side. "That's the one assigned to deliver his memos, and he has her do so directly upon their arrival. And he usually delivers outgoing messages himself." Wessel took a step back and the faint whiff of mildew flew off his cover-up.

Jonas turned his head slightly and ignored his churning insides. "So, is there a problem?" To spy on an overseer would be difficult. He knew that, and it carried with it major disciplinary action. That's why the right balance of blackmail and trust needed to be communicated without actually being spoken. "Will she cooperate?" His throat burned.

"Yes sir, this is nothing I can't handle. They do all report to me, after all." The smile on the man's face was beginning to look more like a smirk. "Is that all?"

Jonas hesitated. Was Wessel trying to be dismissive? Taking in a gulp of the inky air, he considered his words. "Well, actually there's one more thing." This next request might stretch the new arrangement. "Can you also monitor the memos of a head sentry named Jasper? I don't have his number, but I'm pretty sure there can't be too many head sentries named Jasper out there."

"I can't monitor the memos of a sentry. It's against Plateau orders. We don't get 'em here, no copies, nothing. It all goes through their system. The sentries are a direct arm of the Plateau. They're like you guys. They get direct orders, and nobody else gets to see 'em."

One more question and then he'd drop it. "What about their personal stuff? That doesn't go through the sentry offices."

Wessel ran his chubby hand through his thinning hair and huffed out a laugh. "Personal stuff?" At least now he didn't seem as dark and serious. "Sentries have no personal stuff. They do what they're told. They don't even have their own shanties. They live and breathe Plateau. If you've got problems with a sentry, you better watch out." He poked a stubby finger up at Jonas's face. "They don't give second chances, and our great master doesn't take kindly to people who spy on his servants."

"Thanks for the advice. You keep up your end of things, and I'll take care of myself." Locking eyes with his new informant, he checked the traitor for where he would fall on all of this. Wessel's eyes only conveyed compliance with maybe a hint of admiration. "I think it will be good working with you, Wessel." Jonas offered him his hand with another service card stuck to his palm. "You seem like a man who can get things done, and I like that."

Wessel bowed his head, breaking eye contact, as he took the card and tucked it away with the others.

Jonas straightened. "For the good of all."

Snapping up as if someone had pulled a string at the top of his balding head, Wessel practically yelled back the response, quieting the room with his raspy voice. Then he turned and shouted orders to the plebes buzzing around the little cubbies.

Jonas bolted for the door, holding his breath and feeling himself fall farther away from the man he wanted to be.

CHAPTER 19

FAMOUS

Roxan's heart thudded at her chest when she saw the sentry talking to Mullin. Keeping her head down, she glanced at the deliveryman. A bandage covered his right forearm. He had changed back to his green cover-up and made no indication that he'd noticed her.

Gripping her marker tightly in her hands, she forced herself not to look at them again and pushed open the heavy entry door. The perfectly annoying receptionist lifted her chin and narrowed her eyes. She wasn't really a receptionist, more like the building snitch. Roxan glanced away from the vulture's eyes and growled a warning. No snippy comments or provoking questions, thank you.

After jumping the steps by twos, she stopped at the top. Whitlock's voice echoed off the shiny hardwood of the balcony. Ducking into the supplies closet, she cracked the door enough to see Norwood glide out of the main office and match Whitlock's huffy pace. The two grunted at one another as they slowed to a stop to the left of the staircase and looked through some papers. Roxan slipped from the closet and didn't look back.

No one noticed her smooth entrance. An alarming quiet blanketed the room. Roxan zipped back to her station and started arranging the stacks of paper littering her workspace. All the other plebes sat in the same position, all of them writing quietly, hunched over and oblivious.

"Hey, psst," Roxan whispered to the girl sitting to her right. They'd been in the same class, but Roxan never got her name. The only other plebe's name she knew on their floor was Kain's, and that was only because he had already received three demerits for his poor work. When the girl glanced back, tears rolled down her red face.

"What's wrong?" Roxan slid from her seat and kneeled next to her coworker. "Are you okay?"

The girl shook her head and looked back to her work. Everyone was doing the same thing. Copying and stamping and copying some more.

"Here, give me part of your stack." Roxan didn't wait for her to agree, but slid half the blank pages from her, snatching one finished product to copy from.

"You'll get in trouble. The guide is already fixed to a pitch about you." The girl reached limply for the stack of pages.

"Oh, he won't even notice me doing your work," Roxan grinned. "He'll be too busy yelling at me for being late." The girl's wet eyes brightened and she turned back to her drudgery. Roxan settled into her seat and went to work. Mindless copying always gave her a chance to think out a plan.

* * * * * * *

Jonas squinted as he walked into the bright, sunlit main foyer. Sitting behind the elevated counter to the right of the staircase, the young curious-eyed brunette glanced up as he breezed by. She hadn't been there when he had entered Wortman's office. A carrier boy approached her, looking lost and in need of directions. Jonas scurried around him and jumped on the first step. Maybe Roxan would be in by now.

A flash to his left caught his attention. A sentry had drawn a scinter. Obscured by the shrubbery, a guard had cornered someone against the side of the building. Jonas leaned over the railing, but couldn't make out any faces. Three workers from Wortman's office hovered near the window whispering and trying to get a better view of the commotion too.

"Okay, you guys. My guess is that doesn't concern you. Get back to work." The three sulked back to their workroom, giving Jonas a better line of sight, but the bushes gave nothing away except the hint of a leather cover-up and an occasional flash of light. A familiar grumbling pulled him back to the staircase.

Whitlock snatched a stack of papers from Norwood and barreled down the steps. Jonas waited for him to pass. He never even noticed him. The overseer bolted by, his eyes fixed on a mission that didn't seem to involve helping Norwood with her paperwork.

"Master Jonas." Norwood's monotone fell flat in the massive room. She waited for him at the top of the stairway. "You said to notify you when Master Whitlock returned."

"You're a little late on that, don't you think?" Jonas looked over the balcony, but Whitlock had disappeared. "How about Roxan? Has she shown up yet?"

His trusted subordinate wagged her head. "No sir. There has been no word from 423B7. Shall I issue a warrant?" Norwood always stood at the ready with her Guideline Book. Jonas waved her off, though.

"Whitlock wants to handle this. We'll let him take responsibility for it." Jonas began to step around her, but she held up her hand, her expression focused behind him, stern and compliant.

"Sir, I think there's someone to talk with you." She bowed her head, took two steps back, and then turned for the office. The scent of leather warned him. He forced a smile, then turned to face Jasper. The glare on the guard's face put him on the defensive.

"Yes? Can I help you?" A dozen spins flooded his mind as Jonas tried to figure out the best way to handle what he'd witnessed last roll.

Without speaking, Jasper nodded toward a room directly across from the top of the stairs and led the way. Jonas quietly followed.

"Has your plebe shown up?"

"What plebe?" Playing dumb wouldn't work, but Jonas needed to think. Whitlock needed to be taken out, not Roxan. The sentry rested his hand on his weapon, giving Jonas an incentive to answer the question. "Do you mean the one from last roll?" Jonas ignored the sentry's growl. "Master Whitlock is out dealing with her right now." That wasn't true, but it would work. "He wants to take care of this himself. I thought that was strange, but I don't get to monitor the decisions of an overseer."

Jasper stepped closer. His muscular form dwarfed Jonas even though they stood eye to eye. "Don't play with me," he challenged. "Have you seen the girl?"

"No sir. She's not arrived as of yet." Taking a step toward the door, Jonas deflected the sentry's glare. "She's just an undisciplined plebe."

"And have you issued the warrant on her?" He wasn't going to let it drop.

"No, sir. Master Whitlock wanted to handle this in-house. She's still learning her way around the Guidelines."

"And Whitlock's with her now? Where?"

"I don't know. I think he went to her shanty." Evidently the more lies you tell the easier it gets. "He just left maybe you can catch him." The only bad part of this lie would be if Roxan really were in her shanty. "She's new. And she comes with skills. Really, you should speak with Master Whitlock. He seems to have taken a particular interest in the girl."

"I'll take a company by her shanty and see what we find." He smiled but it looked more evil than reassuring.

Jonas stayed between him and the door. "I'd like to speak with her…if you find her. She dropped off on a major project and I'd like a flash of my own to pull a few answers out of her." He met the guard's cold glare. This wasn't the time to bring up the girl from last roll, but the knowledge was there, waiting for when he needed leverage. "If that would be okay with you, sir."

"I'll give you one shot at her before we follow protocol and lock her up for two rolls of the sun." Leather, sweat, and the hot threatening odor of a warmed scinter stayed behind after the guard left. Jonas collapsed into a chair, took a deep breath, and evaluated his next best move.

****

"Roxan." Norwood stood beside the desk with a stack of work in her hands.

Where had she come from? Roxan finished the last paper from the other plebe's stack, then looked up. "Yes, Norwood?"

"These need to be copied, then taken to the rollers. We've stationed them in the workroom." Norwood set the stack on the desk and walked away. She seemed like an emotionless shell of a human being—all work and conformity without a thought for herself. But at least she didn't ask any questions.

Roxan pulled her chair closer to the desk and skimmed the main copy. Jonas had spun quite the story about the census. Throwing in words like "duty" and "privilege," he made it sound like a reward to spill out every detail of your life to the powers at the Plateau.

Roxan shook her head. She would do the copies, but she didn't have to like it. Pulling out the flyers she'd already finished, she tossed them onto the girl's desk. "Here ya go. I'm Roxan, by the way."

"I know. We all know who you are." The girl had stopped crying. "I'm Lidya." She glanced at the stack Norwood had left and turned away.

"Roxan." Norwood stood at the doorway with Mullin.

He looked over at her as the walking Guideline pointed. Grinning with annoying confidence, he held a small box up and made his way back. "Delivery for Roxan 423B7." He chucked the box on to her desk and pulled a sheet of paper from his satchel.

"Mullin, what are you doing here?" Roxan kept her eyes on the square, brown package as she spoke. Her new friend, Lidya, glanced back at them.

"I wanted to make sure you got back safely. That's all," he whispered, handing her the paper. She stared at it, unable to focus. Mullin put a pen in her hand and pointed to the lined sheet. "Please sign this."

"No thanks to you, I'm fine." Now wasn't the time to ply him with questions or to be questioned. And part of her wanted to pretend everything was fine.

For a small fraction, while page after copied page had landed in the finished pile, everything had almost seemed routine. Like she wasn't in violation of a marker, like she hadn't broken twenty different guidelines and discovered a whole other world beyond the boundary, like she was almost normal. And now Mullin stood there, causing words like Clingman and modification to rattle around her head.

"Yeah, you look fine." He directed his nod to her dirty cover-up and pulled a stray leaf from her hair. "We need to talk. Meet me in the Triangle at the first horn."

"No. I'm done with this. You don't have any answers. Nobody does. No one can help me. And I don't want to be a part of whatever it is you're doing. I want to do my job, and that's it." She pushed the signed paper toward him.

"You're wrong, Roxan. There are answers." His gentle tone caused her heart to tremble. "And you're already part of this. You can't change that. But what you can do is choose your side. Join us." He leaned down and whispered in her ear. "We can help you and everyone else they've changed. This isn't just about you. It goes farther than that. Think about all those poor kids stuck underground. We have the power to change those things, but we need your help."

Tears splashed across her signature.

Mullin settled his hand on hers. "We need the boy." He spoke so softly Roxan wasn't sure she had heard him correctly. Stepping back, he put the paper away and scanned the buried heads of the other plebes. "Things are not what they seem, Roxan. You've been to his cave. We need you take us there." He spoke as if he were talking about a trail along the Triangle, but his light demeanor only masked his urgency. "Do the right thing."

Before she could reply, he turned away. He didn't look back. It was as if he already knew she'd meet him. She'd do what he asked, even though all she wanted was to be left alone now.

She watched him leave, and her eyes were still staring blankly on the doorway when Whitlock entered the room. He pointed toward his office and tilted his head for her to follow. Roxan put the small package from Mullin into her drawer and braced herself for the worst. He waited for her at the doorway and closed the large wooden door after her.

"Roxan, we need to talk." Motioning for her to sit, he closed the shutters blocking out the outer office. He'd never done that before. "I'm not sure how to bring this up, so I'm going to be direct."

"What is it?" Any color left in her face must have drained into her stomach. He was going to send her for an adjustment. The look on his face said everything. He knew, and any hope there had been for a matchment was destroyed. "What are you going to do?" She couldn't bring her voice above a whisper.

"I know I'm taking a risk here, but I think we're on the same page. The Census we're working on isn't for informational purposes."

His words hung in the air. The intense look on his face kept her from letting out a sigh of relief. Whatever was bothering him was serious, and thankfully distracting him away from her wayward behavior. "What do you mean?" Maybe no one would ever know about her escapade. Ignoring Mullin wouldn't be hard if she had Whitlock's eyes to light her way.

"They're looking for someone or a group of someones. And I don't want to be part of it. I don't think you do, either. It's all going to change. They'll find who they're looking for one way or another, but I won't help them anymore."

He slammed his hand on the glossy desk and leaned toward her, wanting a response. Two thoughts collided in her head: he was even more striking all riled up, and his words were beginning to sound more and more like treason. Was he really entertaining the idea of defying the Guardians?

"Why are you telling me this?"

"I know you don't know me, Roxan. We haven't even been together a full cycle yet, barely a few rolls really. But I want you to know I've been watching out for you–keeping Jonas in check and letting you get outside when I can." He slid into his chair.

"Remember that first roll when we stopped to talk? I rallied all my arguments to convince you that the blessed Guardians know what's best for us all, that Hyperion himself is our great protector. But I knew it then. I think I've known it for a while, I've tried to believe their lie." His voice trailed off and his mind went somewhere else. The silence pelted away at Roxan's reality while the echo of his contempt swirled through her head. He snapped back with a whisper. "They're after you."

Was this the same man who'd told her repeatedly to read the Guidelines, who handed her that horrible edict last roll, and encouraged her to paint the Plateau in a good light? Plenty of questions poured through her, but none made their way to her lips.

"Do you remember that first roll? You asked me why they would be watching you. I'd hoped you assumed they watched all the new plebes. But they don't. Not like they're watching you. You're marked. Clingman. Bonded. Honestly, I don't even know why you're still here. It's as if they're waiting for you to do something."

"What is Clingman?" Out of everything he'd said, that was the only question that made its way through her fog.

"It means that you're a danger to others, or you were." Kindness coated his words. "I think it has something to do with your eyes. That was in your file too."

"No," she murmured. He couldn't be right. She pushed her reality wall back into place. "You can't be right about this. Maybe they're concerned about my eyes and maybe they're going too far with that edict, but I don't think they're after me. I don't think they're watching me."

"They've watched your every move since you arrived. And that edict is nothing more than a flat out effort to search every shanty, every mind, and every heart to find whoever they're looking for. Somehow you're connected to that."

"No, you're wrong. They're not watching me."

"I know it's hard, but try to see it," he pleaded.

"I know you're wrong because if they were watching me," she paused, "if they were watching me, they'd know I went outside the boundary last roll." She watched his eyes for a hint of his heart. Making a confession hadn't been in the plan, but he was in desperate need of convincing. He didn't fly off at her, but the warmth in his eyes faded a bit.

"That's where you've been?" She nodded a reply. His composure only slipped a little. "Roxan, what possessed you to go out there? You could've been killed."

"I wanted answers. He said someone could tell me what had happened to my eyes. I wanted to know what they did to me, what was wrong with me, why I'm like this."

"Don't think that way. There's nothing wrong with you. It's them. They control everything about us, and if one person doesn't serve their purpose, they expel them or modify them. It's not you."

Roxan wiped the tears from her cheeks and pinched her hand. Pinching helped distract from the pain inside and kept the tears away. But Whitlock rounded his desk and took her hands in his. "It's going to be okay, Rox."

She wanted him to hold her like Mullin had at the cabin, but she pulled her hands away and went to the window. "Sometimes you can't go back, can you? You find something out, and you can't go back to pretending like you don't know."

"What would be the good in that? You have a purpose. You're special. And I'm not the only one who sees that." His words thudded off her wall. "Who told you that you could find answers out there anyway?"

She turned to see his expression as she answered him, "Mullin."

Red blotches of anger dotted his white skin. "Mullin? The delivery guy?" He ran his hand through his hair leaving his bangs unsure of where to go. "Did you get the answers you were looking for?"

Roxan shook her head. Exhaustion was beginning to hit.

"He could've gotten you killed. There are crazy people out there." He knew more about the woods than she'd thought.

"And kind ones too."

He nodded. That was no surprise to him either. "It used to just be stories, you know. And then someone would break a guideline and get caught on the other side of the river. They'd come back talking about the crazies with rocks and sticks. There were other stories too, of another kind of people, people free from Hyperion and beyond his reach."

"We'll never be free of Hyperion's reach. Mullin thinks we can change things, get them all to see, but I'm starting to think that nothing can ever really change."

"That might be up to you."

She questioned him with her eyes.

"I'm saying you have a choice in the matter. You made a choice last roll to listen to that delivery guy, to risk being caught by sentries and being adjusted. You did all of that because you know something's wrong here. You have a choice now. We can make it out there. Come with me."

"No. I'm done with that. I want to go back to the way things were and pretend none of this has happened."

"You can't do that. They're not going to let you. The Guardians are going to send someone. They have their reasons for not detaining you already. You have something they want or else they'd have already dragged you in."

"You're wrong. Nobody knows but you and Mullin. No one needs to know. I won't go there again." Air drained from her lungs. *Not another panic attack. Stay calm. Breathe.* Whitlock's eyes brought her back. Despite his warnings, his eyes soothed her.

"I know this is hard to hear, but the sentries are going to come for you."

"Let 'em come." Roxan reached into her pocket and pulled out the scroll Mullin had given her. "I'll give them this."

Whitlock crossed the space between them in two steps, put his hand over hers, and looked at the seal on the parchment. The two jewels still hung from the red thread that encircled the rolled-up notice. "Mullin gave this to you?" His eyes flashed from hers to the scroll.

"Yes, he said to give it to the sentries if they questioned me."

The office door clicked open and Jonas stepped into the room. The sight of him shook her like a charge of electricity. The last time she'd seen him he'd called her a freak. Now he stood there, looking like he'd been socked in the chest. Surprise danced in his eyes.

"Master Whitlock." His voice cracked and he bowed his head, clearing his throat. "I didn't know you had gotten back."

Whitlock tightened his grip on Roxan's hand and pushed it to her pocket, mouthing the words "hide it" before he turned to face Jonas. "Jonas, we need to talk." He took off for the door. "Roxan, stay here. You may NOT leave this office." The overseer plowed by Jonas and headed toward the conference room.

Jonas paused. "Roxan, you're back. I need to talk to you." He cast a glance at the conference room. "But I don't think there's time right now. Don't leave the office before you talk to me. Okay?"

Roxan shook her head; Jonas was the least of her problems now. There was no way she'd be waiting around to hear anything he had to say unless it was an apology. Jonas closed the door as Whitlock yelled his name.

The breeze from the open windows hinted at another warm roll. But it didn't bring a smile to Roxan's face. Even the promise of more sweet sunshine couldn't shake away the feeling that something very bad was about to happen.

For the first time since she had left her raising home, she missed it. Life was simple there. It was routine, shielded, and predictable. The worst trouble was staying up past curfew and sneaking a peak through a hatch door. Now everything was changing.

People milled about below, running errands and following orders. Happy and full of life, ignorant and free. "Is it freedom if you never know you're in bondage?" Roxan touched one of the closed windowpanes. The heat from the sun on the glass warmed her cold fingers.

"Master Whitlock?" Norwood's detached drone filled the office. "Oh, Roxan. Where is Master Whitlock?"

"I don't know. He left with Jonas. Uh, the conference room." She moved back to the chair. "He told me to wait here until he returned."

"Well, you can set the box by the desk. I'll sign for it." A delivery boy entered the office wheeling in a crate. His little cart creaked with the load. Behind him, grinning from ear to ear, walked Altrist.

Roxan double blinked and started to speak, but Altrist raised his finger to his lips. His white robe stood out against their blue and green cover-ups, but neither Norwood nor the delivery boy noticed the little intruder. While the plebe lugged the crate from his cart, Altrist padded his way to the window. Norwood only watched the worker struggle. The delivery guy barely waited for the crate to hit the floor before he made his way to the door. Norwood chided him to be more careful as she followed him out of the office, closing the door behind her.

Altrist stepped away from the window. "Hi, Roxan."

CHAPTER 20

UNFORGIVEN

Abiga slid a blue cover-up out of Roxan's cubby in the wall, causing the entire stack to fall out. She left them scattered on the floor and swung the lovely garment in the air. Inhaling its new scent, she caressed her face with the soft material. What a perfect piece of fabric—tons softer than that rag from the Undesirables. Did they give these things to everybody?

She nudged the four or five cover-ups lying on the floor. Nobody needs that many clothes. Roxan probably wouldn't miss one of these. Ripping off her old robe, she pulled the clean cover-up over her head.

The two layers were connected at the shoulder, but twisted at the top, not leaving enough space for her arm to make its way into the sleeve. She reached around with her right arm and gave a jerk to the top layer, tearing it free. No one outside the boundary wore two layers. Some didn't even have one to cover themselves.

Abiga found the mirror on the wall next to the facility, then ran her hands down the front of her new outfit and twirled around. The spin didn't help the image staring back at her, though. Her skin was covered in dirt, and her blonde curls were more like little nests. Grabbing a rag at the water basin, she wiped the grime off. The hair was a different story. No amount of combing was going to fix that, so she fished through Roxan's things to find something sharp enough to cut away the tangles. But Roxan had nothing, not even a knife. Bunching the tangles back with a tie helped. She almost looked like she belonged inside the boundary.

Roxan's bed was littered with a bunch of junk that would have to be moved if Abiga wanted to rest. Her mind still buzzed too much to settle down anyway. Sleep could come later, after breakfast.

The food area didn't look much better than the bed. How could one person make such a mess? Abiga found the Nutrivia bars and Vitawater.

So this was village life. A place to stay, food, clothes, and all you had to do was your job. That wasn't so bad, if people left you alone and you got time to do your own stuff.

Abiga tucked the Nutrivia wrapper in her pocket, a memento of her tour inside of enemy lines. Despite all these conveniences, she could never be part of a place that threw its sick and old out to die. This place belonged to Hyperion. And Hyperion only lived to destroy everything the Leader loved. Who could bear to be part of such a place?

Altrist had told her to go to Willow Way—that the Leader wanted her. But there was no proof. Some sort of sign would be good. If he didn't think her good enough for a precious gift, then maybe a sign to tell her he hadn't abandoned her. Something to tell her the past could be forgotten.

She held up her palm. Smudges were all that remained of her mark. That wasn't enough anymore. You can't tell someone you love her and that you want her and then ignore her when she calls for you.

"I'm trying to believe," she mouthed the words to the empty room. No reply came, but her memory brought back things she didn't want to think about. Maybe he can't ignore some things. Maybe he thought he could at first, but then he realized that it wouldn't work. That no one with a past like hers could ever really be one of them.

A man's voice interrupted her thoughts. Abiga crouched beside the table and raised her head to the bottom of the shutter, cracking open a wooden slat. Sentries, at least half a dozen, marched up the path to the shanty. The one in the lead told the others to wait outside while he dealt with the girl. Abiga sprang from the window and pushed the table in front of the door as the handle turned. She sprinted through the tiny shack and dove head first through the open window, landing on her hands and turning a somersault to put her on her feet.

"She's out the window. Go to the back."

Abiga didn't look back. She didn't want them to get a good look at her. Branches smacked at her as she ran into the brush. There wasn't a path, just trees, shrubs, and briar patches. *How'd they know I was there?* The late morning sun offered no help. With darkness, those stupid guards wouldn't even have a clue, but in the light of the roll, on their land, they had the upper hand.

A line of thick brush and trees created a wall ahead of her. Not knowing the terrain kept her from paralleling the barrier. Inside something returned, an instinct, and she ran up the side of the big maple. As her forward momentum failed, her hands grabbed a branch jutting out. Swinging up, she climbed from limb to limb until the only thing below her was grass and pathway.

The sentries would be at the tree in a flash. On the other side of the thick brush, village-dwellers—sprouts—went about their roll oblivious to the chase. Abiga crouched above them weighing her options.

Wearing blue, green, and brown cover-ups, the sprouts made their way to whatever mindless jobs gave them meaning. Doing a disappearing act among them wouldn't be as easy as hiding out in the woods beyond the boundary, but it was the only option. As she dropped down the tree, a flash of white caught her eye. "Altrist." The paths were crowded, but no one looked like that kid. It had to be him.

Pushing through the lousy sprouts, she kept her eye on the white tog. He walked out in plain view, right behind a guy with a cart. He would rescue her. He always knew where she was, what she was up to. A wealth of thanksgiving bubbled up inside of her. The Leader had sent Altrist to get her out of here.

She zigzagged around the people traffic, following Altrist, and listening for his voice in her head. Could this be the sign that the Leader cared?

"Not so fast, girl." A sentry gripped her arm and jerked her back.

Altrist disappeared into a building. He never looked back.

"We have some questions for you." The golden trim on the guard's cover-up glistened in the sunlight.

Abiga took a deep breath. Altrist hadn't come to rescue her. He hadn't even noticed her. Cast aside, that's what she was. The Leader didn't want her after all. In the half a flash she stood there, she doused the remnants of longing. Unwanted, that's what she was. Every fear found its way back, and she recalled her darkness. Maybe that's all that could help her now.

As the sentry moved to pin her hands behind her back, she wrenched free and slid his scinter from its place. Flicking it to life, she grabbed the nearest sprout, and held the weapon to the squirming girl's throat.

"I'm leaving here, and you're not going to stop me." The girl froze beneath Abiga's grip, her chin turned away from the scinter.

"We'll see about that." Four more sentries ran up behind their leader, but he waved them down. "Are you really going to hurt her? Will you go that far?"

"I'll do what it takes. I don't belong here." He was trying to call her bluff, but her eyes must have given her away because his tone shifted.

"I guess you will won't you. Go ahead. Killing her will get you nowhere." He snapped his fingers, and the guards behind him drew their weapons. Then he smiled a challenge.

Sprouts ran off in every direction. Abiga measured the distance to the river. Dragging the girl there wouldn't be easy, but once in the woods, the guards would be at a loss.

The sentry followed her thoughts. "We're not going to let that happen."

"I'll kill her," Abiga growled.

The sentry leaned forward, "So will we."

She knew he would. Their value for life was less than that of the Undesirables. He would kill that innocent sprout to prevent her from escaping.

Abiga stared into his cold eyes. "You make me sick." Before she'd even fully released her hostage, the other guards had grabbed the girl, showing her less mercy than Abiga had.

The commanding sentry jerked Abiga's arms behind her back. "What were you doing in Roxan's shanty? Where is she?"

Abiga pulled at his hold.

"I asked you a question, plebe." He wrenched her wrists with the cuffs and turned her around. "I must say you surprised me. I've never seen a plebe move like that." He walked around her. Two other guards stood at the ready.

Abiga spit at his boots.

"Where'd a plebe who sits behind a desk all roll get the idea she could treat a sentry with such little respect? I'm your master. You will give me my due." He motioned to the other guards, and they forced her to her knees.

She kept her eyes on his and didn't react. He wanted to subdue her with his inflated sense of power. But that wasn't going to work. His arrogance kept him from being a real adversary. Anyone who so quickly dismissed his opponent would have other weaknesses that would be easy enough to expose with a few words and a stiff lip.

"You will talk, girl. One way or another. You will tell us where that freak is and everything you know."

"You are used to being disappointed, aren't you? I mean you must be," Abiga stated matter-of-factly, as if she were standing eye-to-eye with him. "Look at where you are." She looked around, unafraid. "I actually feel sorry for you. You have no idea what you're up against. You live in oblivion, chasing a fantasy. You do what you're told, another mindless pawn of the monster. You are weak, and you will not win. I'll stop you myself." A new kind of rage found its place inside of her. Different from old power struggles, this anger found a resting place on truth.

The guard snarled and swung his fist upside Abiga's head.

CHAPTER 21

FORETOLD

"How did you do that?" Roxan looked back and forth from the door to Altrist. "Why didn't they see you?"

"Oh, that's nothing. I walked through the entire village from the river." Altrist slid onto the edge of Whitlock's desk, moving the vase of honeysuckle to the middle. "People, for the most part, see what they want to see. You're all selectively blind."

Roxan didn't buy it. No amount of credits would get her to believe he could walk around in plain view without being seen. The kid was wearing white. How could they not see him?

He noticed her disbelief. "Look, it's not that big of a stretch. How many people go through their lives without being noticed? Lots of them. You've done it." That made sense, but that was different. "Well, take it a little bit farther."

He was practically glowing. The whole room lightened when he came in. Roxan pulled her legs up into the chair and hugged her knees. Talk about freaky. None of this would lead to forgetting everything and trying to be normal.

"They're all busy in their thoughts with what they know and what's out there. If something very different crosses their path, they don't tend to notice it. It's like. . .a monarch butterfly. Do you know what a monarch butterfly is?" She shot him a look. That was a stupid question. Every little one could identify a butterfly. "Okay, so you know about butterflies. Well, say you were on your way here to your station, and you were thinking about going to work and all the stuff you have to do, and a monarch butterfly flew right in front of your face. You probably wouldn't even notice it. To you, it would be something you needed to go around in order to get on with your own plans. It's kind of like that."

He held up his hands like scales. "It works one of two ways. On the one hand, some see me, but it doesn't register in their mind that I'm out of place. Their minds replace me with what they ought to see because it's easier for them." He shook his other hand. "Or, their minds are so preoccupied with whatever it is that keeps you people busy that they don't notice me. It's not magic. It's more like a science of the mind."

Science was more of a friend than mind tricks. "No one can see you?" Roxan poked his knee.

"I'm not invisible. The more still a person is the more likely they'll notice me, but as long as they prance around with their minds all occupied on this or that, I'm pretty safe. The sentries are the worst. They're sort of on the lookout, so I have to be careful around them. Most of them miss me, though. And they're easily distracted, a sound behind them draws them away quick enough."

"And if someone doesn't miss you or get distracted, what would you do then?"

"Well, let's try not to find that out. If someone comes in, don't draw attention to me. Okay?" He smiled, and the room grew brighter like the sun coming out from behind a cloud. "And I'll try to stay out of the way."

"Why are you here, anyway?" Roxan let her legs back down and fiddled with her hands. Whitlock would be back soon. It would be good to think through his appeal. He wanted to leave? Mullin wanted the boy? Everybody wanted something, even the kid. "What do *you* want?"

Altrist jumped down from the desk and moved the vase back to its place. "I've come to see you, of course! I trust Abiga helped you get back safely?"

"Oh, Abiga!" The girl hadn't crossed her mind. "I left her in my shanty. I was late for work."

"She came all the way into the village with you?" Altrist's little mouth twisted to the side, and he used that grown-up tone.

"She said I wouldn't make it back in without getting caught," Roxan defended her. "She helped me get around the sentries."

"Yes, well, if anyone can take care of herself, it's Abiga. That girl has a knack for getting into trouble and then back out of it again. She's pretty stubborn." Altrist took Roxan's freezing hand in his. Warmth washed up her arm as if she'd plunged her body into a hot spring, hand first. "Roxan, I'm sorry to push you, but I don't think you have much time."

"So you do want something?" It was hard to look into his sincere face and call him out. "Everybody seems to have plans for me."

He released her hand and settled back on his knees next to her chair. Now he looked like a little one waiting to hear a story. But he wasn't a little one. That had become very apparent.

"I do need something from you. I won't lie to you, but I also care about you. I care about what's going to happen to you."

"You don't even know me."

"I know someone who does. Roxan, you're special and you have a gift, a very important gift." He stood and took his glow with him. "We need your help, and we want to help you."

"No one can help me. They've already tried." The truth of her situation was making its home inside of her: She had an aberration that couldn't be modified. She was a danger to others. "There's something wrong with me."

Maybe if the kid knew the truth, he would leave her alone.

"People keep telling me I'm special and I have something, but the truth is I'm messed up and broken, and now all I want is to be left alone, to be normal and unnoticed."

His eyes glistened with sadness. "There's nothing wrong with you Roxan. What you have is a gift, a very special gift."

"It's not a gift. It's a curse. And it can hurt people. I hurt people." Whitlock's desperation came to mind and Mullin's plea. She had set something in motion that couldn't be stopped.

"No, the Leader only gives good gifts. It's a gift."

Roxan didn't let his words penetrate her resolve. "I want to be left alone." Her voice cracked. "I want to pretend like none of this has happened, and I want make it stop. Can you help me with that?"

His eyes told her no or that he wouldn't. She let a few tears slip out, but then rubbed them away, balling her hands up at her eyes.

The boy pulled her fists from her face. "It will go dormant, if you want it to." A touch of rose kissed his white cheeks, and his blue eyes sparkled with sincerity. "It can be stifled. The Leader would never force anything on you. It will never totally go away though, not even Hyperion can do that. It's a part of who you are. But if you ignore the gift long enough, if you push it aside, don't ever develop it, it will eventually stop knocking at your head."

Although he gave her good news, the emptiness inside didn't go away. "I want to be normal. I wish I'd never tried to figure it all out."

Altrist went to the window. As his words took root inside of her, her strength returned. She could be free of all of this. The visions could be stopped. Joining him at the window, she worked her way past her own hurts to her curiosity.

"How do you know all of this?" She watched his face for clues.

"The Leader told me."

"The Leader? You're not talking about our master Hyperion. Who do you follow?" She looked at the world below. A few people bustled down the main path.

"He's greater than a name. No name can contain him. And he is the master of all, even that beast, Hyperion."

She ignored his rebellious rhetoric. "Why have I never heard of him if he's so powerful? Is he good? Does he work for the good of all or only himself?"

"He is only good. He is love."

Roxan shook her head. "Love? I've heard about love. They taught us about it in the raising home—stories of people falling in love, and friends standing up for one another, and even whole groups of people being led in the name of love."

She paused; anger replaced her curiosity. "But that thing that you call love divides people, even destroys them. I might not like how the Guardians control everything, and they might not be getting it right all of the time, but I think they're right about this. Hyperion saved us all from people who destroyed the world in the name of love. He's the one we should follow. Besides, if your leader made me this way, then you should seriously rethink whom you're following. No one should ever be made into a freak."

Altrist closed his eyes. A tear escaped down his pale cheek. "Hyperion is not who you think he is." He pulled her from the window. "If he had known your abilities, he would never have let you go. He thinks he cured you long ago."

Roxan guarded her mind from his treacherous talk, and turned her head.

"That's the only reason he let you wander into the woods. If he knew the truth, he would have locked you up and forced you to destroy the one thing that keeps his evil from getting free. But he didn't know. And now he's using you as bait. He's trying to capture me." That part was true.

"I know about you, about all of this," he recalled her question, "because you were foretold. I never knew your name, or even what you looked like, though. I just happened upon you by the river." A gentle smile replaced his grim expression. "There aren't many like me, Roxan, just one other inside the wall. But we've all been told about you, about how you can see things, how the destroyer will try to take away your gift and fail, about what you can do, and how you are the one who can open the Balustrade door."

"What door? What can I see?" Her defenses threw up her hedge to his propaganda. "I can't see anything. I'm no one."

"That's not true. You do see things, even without your visions, you see something in the world that others miss. You see beauty, art, poetry, and nature." Insistence highlighted his words, and he probed on. "What happens to you when your eyes turn silver?" He *had* seen her eyes in the cave that roll.

"Nothing. I see nothing."

"That's a lie. You see something. You don't understand what you're seeing, but with time, you can develop this. You can learn how to use it."

"No." She backed away from him.

"It's your choice. We won't force you to do anything. Hyperion won't be as kind. He's looking for you. He knows we're on the move, planning to leave, so he knows we have a way to escape. If he figures out it's you, he will use you. There will be no choice. And if he gets free, he will kill, steal, and destroy everything in his path. He only has one goal, one ambition, and that is to hurt the Leader as much as he can before his time is over."

Roxan collapsed into her chair. This was too much to digest. "I want to be left alone."

"We need your help Roxan. If there were another way, I would do it, but you are the only one who can see the way out."

"Who needs my help? A bunch of rebels, crazy people living beyond the boundary?" She wiped the tears away with the back of her sleeve.

"Where do you think those crazy people in the forest came from? They used to live here, work here, but now they're retired, the undesirable refuse of your world."

"No, those people ran off. Some people do that. Mullin told me about them. They rebel and go outside the boundaries." Her heart pounded. "When people retire, they go to the Plantanate. Everyone goes there to live and rest at the end. I've seen pictures. And I don't care what you say— the Plantanate is not out there in those woods."

"Well, call it whatever you want. That is where every one of you ends up, thrown out and tossed aside. Most die off quickly, either killed by the stronger ones or hunted down by a sentry patrol for sport. Some make it, and some even join us." He spoke the horrible truth. "We're the Outcasts. We live together, work together, love one another, and live by the goodness that is our Leader."

The boy had no reason to lie. It made sense, and all of the pictures and stories about the Plantanate were spun by a replicator, like her, telling the world what it needed to hear to stay in line. Hadn't she already done that sort of thing? Painted a lie to look like reality?

"I'm sorry Roxan. I wish things were different too, but it's not that easy." He read her thoughts. "No amount of tweaking will fix this. This place was never meant to be a paradise. There's no middle ground. In the end, we will all choose whose side we're on—and the Guardians won't even be there. This fight is between Hyperion and the Leader."

"I don't get it." She rose on shaky legs. "We owe everything to Hyperion. He saved us. Where would we all be, if it weren't for him?"

Altrist didn't respond.

"We'd be lost. He put up the Balustrade. He sealed us in and created the Oblate. If it weren't for Hyperion, we would have died out long ago, after the great conflict—a conflict brought about from zealots claiming their way was the only way." She walked over to Altrist. "I know it's not perfect here. They get some things wrong, but we owe Hyperion our allegiance."

Altrist didn't back down. "You say that even after you know what they do with the ones who retire, how they deprive children of the world and crush their ability to think for themselves, after what they've done to you?"

"You make him out to be the enemy, but I think if we talk to him, he will listen. He'll explain to me what they did." Roxan groped for a footing. "Things can change here. Following some man who professes to be the new Leader is not the answer. It's rebellion, and it will only hurt people."

"He's not some man, Roxan." Altrist gently gripped her arms. His little white face and crazy hair inches away. "This all belongs to the Leader. It was his before, and it will be his again. Who do you think stole it from him? Who do you think was behind the great conflict? Your precious Hyperion, the Tatief. He had everything, but it wasn't enough for him. He refused to be second, and he saw it coming. He saw it. The Leader meant to make this world a paradise, and you would all be free, but Hyperion wanted it for himself. He doesn't care about you. He envies and hates you. He only wants to destroy you."

Roxan held her hand up. "Stop." Her body trembled.

"I'm sorry Roxan. I know it's all you've ever known. But I'm telling you there's more. There is another. And he's coming back. You're going to need to make a choice, Hyperion or the Leader."

Altrist finished and backed away.

She couldn't stop shaking. His words numbed her, except for a hot feeling snaking around the back of her head. "How do I know that any of what you say is true?" She ignored the golden haze starting to edge its way across her vision. Taking a deep breath, she pushed it back with her will. It receded. "I hate this. When I hear Mullin speak, he strikes a chord in me, but your words touch something inside too. How can I tell who's right?"

"Come with me," he urged. "And if you want to come back, I'll let you go. It's your choice whether you stay or come with us all the way. But at least meet the others. Let them tell you their stories." He paused and took her hands in his. "Please, Roxan. We need you. That part's true, but we won't force you to stay. I'll bring you back myself, and I'll take you straight to Hyperion, if that's what you choose. Give us one roll of the sun to show you the truth. Please." When he smiled, his perfectly straight teeth lined up, outlined by light pink lips.

She wanted to trust him. There was something right about him. But what he said was overwhelming. It drained her. "Maybe ..." Before she could finish her thought, Altrist raised his finger to his lips and motioned toward the chair, while he slid into the corner next to a large cabinet. Someone was at the door.

CHAPTER 22

COUNTER-OFFENSIVE

Whitlock's lips were moving, but Jonas heard nothing. Roxan was back, and she looked scared and little. She hadn't said anything when he'd told her he wanted to talk. But at least she didn't look like she hated him. The only way to know for sure was to talk to her, but Whitlock blocked the doorway.

Jonas caught the last sentence and reeled back to focus on his overseer. "You're leaving?" Whitlock was planning a trip. He never took trips that lasted longer than a few rolls of the sun. "Did you say a tour?" What he was suggesting meant he'd be gone for an entire season.

Whitlock held up another scroll from the Plateau. "While you're working on this new project, I'll be doing a follow-up tour covering the Census of the Souls." He shook the scroll. "Here, and I will be taking Roxan with me." He turned toward his office. Evidently, it wasn't up for discussion.

Jonas flew at him pulling him back." What?" He held back the urge to slam his overseer into the wall.

Whitlock knocked his hand away and stepped back out of view of the workroom. Too late, though, everyone was watching.

"Sir, when did you decide this? I thought these sorts of trips took a minicycle to confirm." The Plateau hadn't approved this trip. Whitlock was up to something and he was going to take Roxan with him. "I don't think this is a good idea, sir. I mean, in regard to Roxan, this could be seen as a reward and might cause discord with the other plebes. Perhaps Norwood would be a better option."

"This isn't up for discussion. Do you need to be reminded who's the overseer here?" Whitlock waited, but Jonas wasn't ready to concede. "Jonas, you've put her danger, using the markers. If she goes with me, the entire matter will dissipate and become history."

"But, sir…" Jonas searched for a counter-offensive. "Don't you think you're overreacting? If the sentries want her, they'll get her, whether she's here or travelling around with you. I think it would be safer to return her to a normal schedule and downplay the entire episode."

"Do you?" Whitlock growled in his face. "Because, the way I see it, you should be handled as well. How is it that one of *your* plebes could take off in the middle roll of the sun and not be seen until the middle of the next roll, and you not even know where she was? Did you even deliver a marker to her? Watch your step, Jonas. I'll handle this." He pushed by Jonas and called out to Norwood.

Jonas pulled out a chair and plopped down. That hadn't gone well. Roxan sat on the other side of the closed shutters, and Whitlock guarded her like a nanny. He knew something. Maybe he'd already found out about the sentry looking for her and investigating him. Maybe he was trying to escape and wanted to have her with him. Whatever, Whitlock definitely had an agenda that didn't involve promoting the Census of the Souls. And he was scared, desperate, and dangerous.

Jonas leaned forward and rubbed his temples with his fingers—time to regroup. Roxan wasn't gone yet. There was still time to urge her not to get involved with whatever Whitlock had planned and to offer his apology.

"Excuse me, sir." Norwood stood in the doorway.

"What?" Jonas didn't bother to look up, anticipating her commentary on Whitlock's upcoming trip. Certainly, he had given her orders to cover in his absence.

"I'm sorry, sir, but there's someone here to see you." She waited for him to follow, then led him out of the workroom to the balcony. Two guards stood at attention outside of the conference room at the top of the staircase.

Norwood offered a worried smile and retreated to her domain. Jonas tried to hide his concern, but his infractions knocked out reasons why guards would want to see him. The deal with Wessel. Roxan. His encounter with Jasper. Slipping on his strong face, he ignored the guards and plowed into the room.

"What's going on here?" Jonas held back his attack mode. He hadn't been prepared for the scene in front of him. The guards hadn't come for Roxan or to question him about his arrangement with Wortman. It was something else entirely. "Jasper, what is this?"

"Roxan wasn't in her shanty, but we found this. How many insurgents do you have working for you here? You want to tell me how many of your other workers are looking to cause trouble?"

Jasper nodded his head toward a girl. Her hands were clamped behind her back, but that didn't make her appear subdued. She leaned against the wall, her hazel eyes cutting down the sentry. A reddish lump glowed over her cheekbone.

"Who is this girl? What does she have to do with me?"

"We caught her running from Roxan's shanty." Jasper rounded the conference table and pulled her to her toes by the neckline of her blue cover-up. "She's one of your plebes."

"I don't know this girl. She's an imposter. She's not with our building. Maybe all you've done is caught yourself a thief, not a rebel."

Jasper picked the girl up and slammed her against the wall like a rag doll. "Who are you? You will talk. What were you doing in Roxan's shanty? What do you know?" With every question, he pulled her out then pinned her to the wall again.

"I don't know anything. I'm a stupid Undesirable. You self-serving pig." She spat the words out, and Jasper met them by laying the back of his hand across her face. She fell to the floor, her hands struggling to be free of the clamp.

"Uh, maybe you should take this to your headquarters or something. This girl has nothing to do with us. I don't even know what she's talking about." Jonas turned the doorknob, but Jasper flew around, slamming his hand against the door.

"You're the fool, little guide. This girl has everything to do with your Roxan, and if I were you, I would wait to find out what she has to say." Turning back, he hauled her off the floor and set her on her feet again.

"Isn't that right, trash? What game are the Undesirables playing now?"

"Undesirable? What's that? What village is she from? She's not one of us. How'd she get one of our cover-ups?" Jonas moved away from the door, but stayed out of kicking distance.

"Undesirables live outside the village." Jasper gritted his teeth as he spoke.

Jonas shook his head. The sentry wasn't interested in answering questions, just getting answers.

Jasper turned back to the girl. "She's not an Undesirable, though, are you sweetie? No, you're far too healthy-looking and smart for that. And you're not one of them, because your gifts are a little different. So what's your story?"

"Wait a minute." Jonas moved closer. "Are you telling me there are people living out there? How do they survive? It's forbidden."

The girl laughed. "You've got to be kidding me." Shaking her head, she rolled her eyes. Her tongue poked out of her tiny mouth and licked the red spot on her swelling lip. "No wonder most of you die when you get dumped."

"Shut up girl." Jasper motioned for Jonas to move back. "The people living beyond the boundaries are from the Plantanate. Don't ask me why, but once people retire, sometimes they wander off, and the place beyond the boundaries does things to them. It changes them. They turn into animals. But this one." He grabbed her blonde ponytail. "This one's too healthy and strong. She's not one of them."

"You're as stupid as he is." The girl nodded her head from Jasper to Jonas. "You don't get it, none of you do." Standing straight, she was almost as tall as both of them. "You're right. I'm not an Undesirable. I left them after they killed my mother. But I was born there, and we're not the animals. It's you. You're the sick ones, hunting them, throwing them out like trash. You should be ashamed."

"Oh how sad. What a story. They killed your mother, and I suppose you were raised by wolves," Jasper mocked.

"I made it okay." Her steady voice and cold stare made her more like a soldier than a girl. "I can't say the same about those murderers. They got what was coming to them. And so did the sentries who tried to hunt down the pack." She leaned back against the wall.

Jasper snarled, "You will die for killing a sentry. Who are you? What were you doing in Roxan's shanty?" When she ignored him, he tore out his scinter and brought it to life. "You can die here."

Jonas jumped between them. "Give her a chance. There's no need to get extreme." The girl's eyes softened. "Can you tell us anything that might help Roxan? Anything at all?"

"I helped her. That's all. Is there a crime against helping someone?"

"How did you help her?" Jonas searched her face. There was something different about her, besides her feisty death wish.

"She couldn't find her way back. I led her home."

The acid in Jonas's stomach burned. "Roxan couldn't find her way back from where?"

Jasper put his weapon away and grunted, "She was out there, wasn't she?" He seemed to know what was going on.

"Yeah." The girl lowered her head.

"Out where?" This time Jonas directed his question to Jasper.

"She was outside the boundary. It seems your little Roxan took a trip outside the boundary last roll, and her new friend, here, brought her back." Jasper rested his hand on the girl's shoulder. "Now, why would Roxan be wandering around out there with a bunch of animals?"

The girl shrugged her shoulders. "They don't tell me anything. You know how it is." She looked at Jonas.

The air in the room had gone stale. Jonas leaned on the table. What had Roxan done? He hadn't seen this coming at all.

"Why was Roxan out there?" He hoped for something to vindicate her.

The girl shook her head. "I don't know. I don't know. She was with a man, someone from here. That's all I know. We didn't really have time to chat."

An uncomfortable silence filled the room. Jasper started pacing. Something was eating at him. Jonas took a gulp of singed air. The scinter had sucked away the fresh oxygen.

In one swift motion, the girl brought her hands from around her back and propelled Jonas to the floor out of the way. Then she lunged for Jasper, but he laid his fist upside her head before she could get his weapon from its holder. Jumping on top of her, he punched her. She brought her arms up to cover her face. Grabbing the back of the sentry, Jonas pulled him off and shoved him into the table. The guard wrangled free, but kept his distance. The girl huddled up on the floor covering her head.

"What are you doing?" Jonas yelled at Jasper.

"Stay out of it. This is outside your jurisdiction."

"You can't kill her. She needs to go to the Guardians. They can deal with her. You can't kill her." Jonas backed away from them. The sentry smirked, power and arrogance balled in his hands.

Jonas glanced at the closed door. Now would be the time to leave. But he couldn't. He couldn't let this animal get a hold of Roxan, so he pulled his own threat.

"Roxan's not the only person with friends outside the boundary," Jonas blurted out. "Is she?" That got his attention. "Who was that girl last roll? What was her name, Liza? She wasn't from here either, was she?" Jasper's countenance told him his jab had found its mark.

"You don't want to do this guide," Jasper warned.

"Liza?" The girl struggled to her feet. "Where is she? What have you done with her?"

"She zipped away. But you aren't going to be that lucky, are you?" The sentry wiped blood from a scratch over his eye. "And you, Jonas, you need to watch your step. Don't throw an apple at a hornet's nest unless you have a very good exit strategy."

Jonas ignored him and took a good look at the girl. "What's your name?"

Her sad eyes met his. "Abiga."

A guard cracked the door as she spoke. "Sir, the guide has a visitor." Norwood stood behind him. Her plain face fixed blankly forward.

"What is it?" Jonas pushed the door open.

"Guide Wessel said I was to bring this directly to you." She held out a small sheet of paper marked private. "He says you might find it interesting." Jonas snatched the paper and dismissed her.

"You can go back out there. I don't need you anymore." Jasper sneered and pressed a button on his belt. Two large sentries stepped forward from the sides of the doorway, nearly knocking Jonas over. "You're dismissed," he chided, and the guards escorted Jonas back to the workroom.

The shutters to Whitlock's office blocked Roxan from view. Whitlock must be with her making his plans. Did he know? Did he know she had broken the boundary? He had to know something. Maybe he was the one behind it all, leading Roxan astray.

The plebes moved back and forth from their stations to the office across from Whitlock's. They had all been working at a steady clip. Jonas dodged their glances and slipped into the marker room. His churning stomach had moved aside for the tension surging through his veins. His whole body shook. Jasper was going to kill that girl, and Roxan could be next. No amount of spinning or blaming could fix this. They couldn't go back now. Everything had gotten out of his control in a flash.

Opening the note from Wessel, Jonas expected to find a resignation from their arrangement, but the note wasn't from Wessel. The words didn't make any sense, but the handwriting was unmistakable. Five words pointed straight to Whitlock.

CHAPTER 23

UNWANTED

Abiga winced as Jasper ran the dormant scinter up her arm. His threats weren't working. Altrist may have turned his back on her, but she wouldn't do that to him. She wouldn't ignore him when he needed her.

"I don't understand why you're protecting him." Jasper put the scinter away and shoved her into a chair. "You're not like them," he grunted. "I guess that's part of the problem, isn't it? If you were like them, you'd already have spilled your merits. No, you're not like them at all." He was getting closer to her thoughts, but she kept her mouth shut.

"Let me tell you a story, Abiga." He slid into the chair opposite her. Abiga examined every scratch, cut, and line on his hardened face. His thick brown curls brushed the neckline of his leather cover-up top. Despite all the hair, there was no mistaking him for anything but masculine and mean.

Even though he had turned down the anger, an undercurrent of loathing coated his words. "There once was a young sentry ready to graduate from his class with honors. Idealistic and strong, he went up against his final test with bravado. Some guards hated it, but not him. A trip beyond the boundary, surviving in the forest, it excited him."

"The trip was supposed to be one turn. You go in, make camp, and fight off the crazies. But instead of one turn, it lasted for five turns. Halfway through the first turn, he was attacked by a band of Undesirables. They came at him from behind, stripped him of his gear, and nearly beat him to death. They probably would've finished him off, but then this man came out of nowhere, beat them all down, and scared them off. His name was Jahn."

Abiga tried to hide her surprise, but Jasper caught the look in her eyes and grinned.

"Yeah, you know him, don't you? He took me to the others, and they welcomed me as if I were a treasure they'd been searching for. I'd never had anyone treat me like that."

He hesitated. Abiga kept her guard up. Anyone worth a fight knew how to play to their opponent's weaknesses. And becoming emotionally entangled in someone's sad story was most definitely a weakness.

"They're different. I'll give you that. But that doesn't mean that they have it figured out. I spent five turns with them. Have you been with them that long?" He didn't wait for her to answer. "I know you haven't. You didn't learn the things you know from them. They're against that kind of violence. Love." He shuddered. "It's that love that gets us, isn't it?"

The fan kicked on above her head and blew cool air down her back. Abiga leaned forward and closed her eyes. He knew her Outcasts; he'd lived with them. Something had obviously gone wrong.

When she opened her eyes, he continued. "We all desperately think we need to be loved, to belong, but the truth is no one ever really loves. It's all a play for control. I learned that the hard way. I fell in love, but it didn't matter. Liza. She loved me too." The brown in his eyes grew darker. "But she loved someone else more. That's when it all clicked. If she could love me and yet cast me aside, then so could the Leader, so could Altrist, so could all of them. They just use you. They string you along until they don't need you anymore, and then they reject you."

He stopped again, smug and sure of himself. His words troubled her, like thunder rumbling through the quiet sky. Something bad was coming. He wasn't opening up his life so they could be buddies. He had something else, and he was waiting for her to bite. Abiga kept her questions to herself.

"I know. You don't want to think they could do any wrong. I didn't either. I believed all of it. Have you been through the water?" He waited for a response. Abiga nodded. "So have I. Did you see the Leader?"

"Yes," she whispered.

"So did I. Look he gave me a mark." He held up his hand. The remnants of a distant impression were left there, not a mark, more like the kind of wrinkles you get on your face when you sleep on straw. "It's not actually a mark anymore. It's all but faded away."

Abiga lifted her hand. He acknowledged their shared sign with a smile.

"But you know what I never got." Pushing away from the table, he raised his voice. "I never got the one thing I really wanted. I talked with him about it. I pleaded, and you know what I got? Silence. Nothing. Abandoned. Altrist said the Leader had other plans for me, but he didn't know. They treat that kid like some kind of prophet, but he barely knows what he's doing most of the time. I knew what I wanted. There was nothing clearer to me. But she didn't want me."

He stood and turned away. Abiga glanced at the door. One hard push to the table would slow him and she could get out, but then there'd be more sentries and a hard sprint to the river. Maybe the safest course would be to play his game.

"So you came back here?" It was probably best not to comment on how spoiled he was sounding. "Then what happened?"

"I moved on. At least I thought I'd moved on, until I saw her last roll. She appeared out of nowhere. I never thought I'd see her again." He turned and leaned into her face. "I need to find them. I need to find her, Liza. I didn't get a chance to apologize. I never meant to hurt her. Can you take me to her?"

Abiga swallowed his lies and let them swim around in the acid of her gut. He was good. It takes an artist to weave the truth in with a bunch of bunk and make it sound real and heart wrenching. His little yarn would probably have worked on anyone else.

"I can't help you. I don't know where they are." Keep it simple. She didn't trust herself not to give away something.

"You've got to have some idea. Someone like you knows the woods far better than any pack of them put together. I'm surprised they let you out of their sight. How'd they make it through the infidel pockets without your expertise?" His tone sharpened. "Oh, I forgot. They have all of those gifts. Well, Liza and Anna can fix the sick or injured ones, and Jahn can sing 'em a pretty song. Altrist can't do much, except disappear when you need him." He caught the look in her eyes and took off. "Yeah, you know how that is, don't you? He does what he wants, and if that doesn't include you, he has no problem leaving you to fight for yourself."

Abiga lowered her head breaking his examination of her. The eyes. The eyes always give her way. Tears were threatening to take over again. Altrist had left her. He'd walked away. He didn't sense her presence, her need. He kept going, and now she was here alone and fighting for herself.

"The Leader's no better." Jasper squatted next to her chair. "Think about it. He just leaves us here. Sure, we can talk to him, but what good is that? A few words thrown into the empty air? I can't help but wonder if what happened in the water really happened at all. Maybe it's some mind trick Altrist plays on us. Where's Altrist?" His question caught her off guard, and she hesitated.

"I don't know." That was the truth. Jasper didn't need to know she'd seen Altrist within the village.

"Why are you protecting them, Abiga? They've done nothing for you."

She pushed away from the table and stood. He followed.

"You will never be part of their little club, no matter how much you want to be."

That did it. Tears pushed their way to the surface.

"You aren't ever going to be good enough. Look at how you've lived. What you've had to do to survive." He turned her around. "What are you sixteen, seventeen turns? And you've already lived a lifetime. No one grows up like you did without carrying that world with them." He pulled her hands out and flipped the palms up. "What have these hands done? What have they had to do to survive? Those people can't understand that. They can't accept it."

Tears slipped silently out. Treasonous droplets.

"Where are they Abiga?"

She checked his eyes for his heart, but he'd hidden it well. His motive didn't show. "I can't," she sputtered.

"If you tell us, we can help you. You can be safe and in a place that knows your gifts and accepts you. I won't turn my back on you. They are going to get hurt if they keep going. If you want to save them, you need to tell us where they're going. Where's the boy?"

She crumpled to the floor. Despair choked the truth out of her, "In the village."

Those three words sent him into action. "Where?" He pinned her against the wall again, his forearm pressed against her neck, his scinter already buzzing to life. This was the sentry she knew. "You cooperate and you live, I promise."

"Go to Hyperion with your promises," she sobbed.

Before Jasper could respond, the door beeped open and Jonas paraded into the room. Jasper grunted and stepped away from her.

"You guys are about at the same place that I left you. I need to ask the girl a question."

Jasper released her neck but grabbed her by the arm and pushed her forward. "Ask away. She's just starting to warm up now."

"Anna." He said the name then stood there, waiting. Abiga stiffened, and he noticed. "Abiga, do you know Anna?" He read her easily. Tears flowed down. The whole world was coming down.

"What is this about, guide?" Jasper shoved Jonas back a step. "How do you know that name?"

Jonas ignored the sentry. "You know her, don't you Abiga? She's one of your people. A guide maybe?" He was fishing. But it was enough. Abiga stopped pulling from Jasper's grip and stared blankly forward. It was all about to end. And she would forever be alone, left out, lost.

Clearing his throat, Jonas shifted his attention to Jasper . "I want Roxan to stay here. It's Whitlock you're after." He unfolded a piece of paper and held it up. Abiga glanced at the words. Nothing made sense anymore.

Anna, leaving at dusk, Whitlock

CHAPTER 24

CAPTURED

The honeysuckle quaked as Whitlock slammed the door. Roxan stole a look at Altrist. He ignored all the commotion and enjoyed the view from the window again.

"Whitlock." Roxan reached across the desk to slow his hands from throwing things into the satchel. "Are you okay?'

He took her hands in his. "We have to go Roxan. There are sentries in the building and from what Norwood says, they're holding someone in the district conference room. I don't know how much time we have." Her hands trembled under his.

"You will come with me, won't you?" he pleaded. "There's nothing for you here. The Census, Mullin—they're all part of some plan, and you're mixed up in it somehow."

She pulled her hands from his. He was flying at a pace she couldn't comprehend. Everything was going fast.

He bolted to her nearly knocking the vase over. "Please, please come with me." Urgency accompanied his plea, his hazel eyes hardly blinked. Fear propelled him, a sense of responsibility. He hadn't mentioned anything about a matchment. He was talking about running away, escaping everything.

Roxan covered her face with her hands. Just for a flash, the whole world needed to stay out of her head. Whitlock, Altrist, Mullin. Everyone kept telling her what to do. No one cared about what she needed.

"I want things to go back to the way they were," she whispered. "You and I and the replicating and the walks in the Triangle and a picnic by the Willow. My perfect little shanty. I don't want to leave it all. And I don't want you to go either."

Whitlock pulled her hands away from her face and kept them in his. "I know. I know it's hard. I've been thinking about this for a while, and then you came here and the world grew lighter. My dreams to explore more than the Protectorate started to seem too risky." Flecks of green and gold lit up his eyes. "Things will never go back to the way they were. Believe me. I wish they could. I had some plans." He grinned. "But what's already started can't be stopped. They won't forgive your trip into the woods. They will come for you." His grip on her hands tightened. "Will you come with me?"

She nodded her head, and he pulled her into a hug. Wrapping her arms around him felt like the safest thing she'd ever done. Then he let her loose and went back to packing his satchel.

"Our biggest problem now," he said, "is getting out of here without anybody noticing. They're watching, and with guards in the building, it isn't likely we'll get out of here without someone following us."

"Perhaps I can help with that," Altrist chirped from the window. Roxan had almost forgotten he was there. "Now that everyone's set on leaving this charade." He glanced at Roxan. "I believe I can help you make a clean getaway."

Whitlock hardly flinched. Instead he held out his arms as if he were about to hug the kid. "You're Altrist, aren't you?"

"You know him? How do you know this stuff?"

"My friend told me about him. He can do things, and he helps people." Next to Altrist's childlike form, Whitlock looked like a starved giant.

Altrist didn't miss a beat. "Who's your friend?"

"Anna. She's more than a friend. She's my mother."

The kid beamed like a new star. "She's been looking for you. She's—"

"Your mother?" Roxan interrupted. "How do you even know who your mother is? No one knows who their seed parents are."

A twinge of jealousy raced through her as she thought about how many times she'd wondered who her parents were. Fraternizing with parents directly violated the Plateau Guidelines. Whitlock wasn't as great about following the Guidebook as he pretended to be.

"She found me." A peaceful smile curved Whitlock's lips. "Right before she left. She was scheduled to go to the Plantanate, but she had heard stories, stories of another world." He caught Roxan's eyes. "I didn't believe her, but I let her go. I didn't report her treason. I couldn't turn her in. She sent me a message later, telling me she had found a home, and asking me to come. I ignored all her pleas, but every turn she still sent one pleading with me to leave all of this."

A bell rang under Whitlock's desk, and he snapped back from his happy place. "That's Norwood. The sentries are on their way."

"Take my hands." Altrist grabbed Whitlock and headed for Roxan as the door swung open.

Jonas tore into the office followed by two guards. "There he is, take him," he said as he pulled Roxan to his side. "Are you okay? I won't let him hurt you." Nothing about the words he said or the look in his eyes registered. She stepped away, but he gently guided her to the side of the desk. "Let the guards do what they need to. He's not going to pull you in to whatever trouble he's in. I'll vouch for you."

"Have you gone mad?" She yanked her arm free. "What are you doing?" The guards hadn't noticed Altrist, but they had Whitlock by each arm. Roxan raged. "Are you insane? Whitlock hasn't done anything. It was me. I broke the rules, not him." She blurted out her indiscretions openly, then pushed away from Jonas and ran to Whitlock's side.

Jonas hushed her as another man's voice boomed into the room. "Well, well, well, and I thought we'd get some nonconforming overseer, but it looks as if we're getting the real trophy. Hello, Altrist."

Ignoring his unveiling, Altrist laid a hand on Whitlock's back and drew Roxan closer with his other. "Let's get out of here." A sparkly glow emanated from his chest, and warmth crept up Roxan's arm from where he held her hand.

"I wouldn't do that if I were you." The sentry reached outside the doorway and pulled a girl into the room, holding her by her hair. "You wouldn't want to leave this one behind."

Altrist let go and took a step forward.

"Abiga. What are you doing here?"

The room filled with guards and the heavy scent of leather and sweat. Abiga stumbled forward, but Jasper kept a firm grasp on her arm. She kept her eyes down. One was pretty swollen, and her lip was puffed out with a cut running through it.

Altrist glided forward, but the monster holding Abiga pulled out his scinter and held it to her throat. Putting his hands up, Altrist halted. "Calm down, Jasper." He spoke with unruffled sureness. "You've made your choice. Now let us make ours."

"It doesn't work that way," the head sentry boomed. "You know that. Your rolls of making choices and meddling with the choices of others are over."

"Let her go, Jasper." Altrist knew this guy. And he wasn't about to back down.

"I'll let her go. I'm not worried about her. She's got her own issues of abandonment to deal with." Jasper shoved Abiga to the floor, then stepped into the office. "*He* wants to see you, Altrist."

"Well, I'm busy." Altrist gritted his teeth.

"Take them," Jasper ordered. One of the sentries next to Whitlock grabbed Roxan.

Altrist took a step back. "What business do you have with them?"

"It seems the girl has been running around beyond the boundary. And her overseer pal here is planning an escape to see Anna."

Altrist pulled the lever to the shutters. "You can't prove any of that. And you can't drag them off. Bad press, you know. I dare say there are at least ten or so plebes out there ready to start asking some questions." He knew how the world worked. Lidya and Kain stood by their stations. Everyone else sat frozen, their eyes fixed on the scene.

"Well, this wild thing," Jasper nodded his head toward Abiga, "says she brought the girl back from the woods. I'm guessing she was there to see you. Did you send her a note, lure her outside the safety of our boundaries? How did you hear about her? One of your spies?" He rattled off the questions, not waiting for any answers. "Evidently, she didn't believe any of your lies, though. Have you lost your powers of persuasion?"

"I didn't lure her. One of your goons sent her out there. She could have been killed. And that would've been on you. Hyperion won't be too happy with how you've handled any of this."

Jasper ignored Altrist's jab and turned his rage on Roxan. "Who? Who sent you out, girl?" She took a step on wobbly legs. Altrist reached out to steady her, but Jasper drew his scinter between Roxan and the boy.

She yanked away from the guards and sat down in a chair. "Mullin." Her dry throat nearly choked on the word. "He told me to go out there. He wanted me to meet someone. Altrist helped me. He saved me. Mullin was the one who sent me into the woods."

The energy in the room evaporated as she spoke. Ice ran into her veins, except for a warm sensation creeping up the back of her neck. The tingling ripped through head. Now was not the time for her aberration to display itself.

Altrist caught her worried eyes and spoke into her mind. "Breath Roxan, slowly. You can control it." Closing her eyes, she willed it back, pushing the heat into her freezing body. A growling roar filled the room, and rage rained down on Jasper. Grabbing the vase of honeysuckle from the desk, he brought it above his head then slammed it into a thousand pieces on the floor. Glass and water sprayed across the office.

"Mullin." The guard stepped away from his tantrum and directed his anger toward Roxan. "I don't believe you. He had strict orders to leave you alone."

"I can prove it." Roxan met his rage. The box from earlier was in her desk. That would show his contact.

"Roxan, no!" Whitlock tore away from the guards and reached over to her, but they were fast with their scinters and shot him in the side, crumpling him to the floor. Roxan grabbed his hand, but the heat of a scinter made her let go and move back. Jonas stepped out of his corner, but said nothing.

Steadying herself, she stood. "Please, no one else needs to get hurt. Mullin brought me a package this morning. It's in my desk drawer. You'll see."

"Get it." Jasper looked at Jonas. Slithering out the doorway, Jonas obeyed and returned in a flash holding the box. Grabbing it, Jasper ripped off the outer layer, and then turned the box upside down. "It's empty. Nice try, but you could have at least put his name in it. This isn't proof." He tossed the package to the floor.

"What about this?" Roxan reached into her pocket and pulled out the scroll with the two jewels on it. Whitlock moaned and lifted a limp hand. The sentry still hovered over him, scinter at the ready. Roxan denied the urge to fall at his side and hold him. Keeping her eyes on Jasper, she held up the scroll. "He gave me this too."

Disbelief and loathing contorted Jasper's face. He took two huge steps and yanked the scroll from her hand.

"Where'd you get this?" He turned it over to reveal the seal on the other side.

"I told you, Mullin gave it to me. He said to give it to the guards if I were found. It would save me."

Jasper untied the string with the jewels and broke the seal. "This is your ticket to the Guardians, my dear, and it says here that all surrounding the individual with the scroll must also be taken to the Plateau, as well. I don't know who gave this to you, but whoever it was, he wasn't a friend."

Dread swept across Roxan, and she dropped to the floor. Jasper raised the scroll into the air and gloated.

"This works out nicely for me. End of argument. You're all coming. And, Altrist, if you try any tricks, I kill her." He waved his scinter toward Abiga. Then shouted orders to the other guards. "Whatever you do, don't let them near the boy. Take them to the cells."

CHAPTER 25

THE ONE TO BLAME

Water dripped from a pipe above. Roxan watched as the droplets splashed into a puddle on the dirt floor of the cell. As soon as Jasper gave the order, the guards had dragged everyone except Jonas from the office. All the plebes and Norwood stood by and watched as they hauled them off to the underground sentry holding cells where they were separated from one another.

Jasper warned the guards to especially keep the others away from Altrist. Jasper had hit him with a high bolt from his scinter before they'd even left the office. The poor little guy dropped to his knees at the jolt, but he didn't go all the way down. It took the guards a few flashes to grab him. They were all a little scared of the boy who could withstand a hit like that.

An orb from the hallway flickered through the bars at the top of Roxan's door, casting an eerie bluish tint to the cell. The sheet of rock creating the back wall glistened. Cutting through the browns of the wall, a bright orange streak zigzagged down the middle. Roxan waited. No one had been by since they'd thrown her in here. No food, no water, nothing. Occasionally, the grumbling of guards drifted through the barred window, but not enough to be understood.

A rat scampered along the sidewall and disappeared into a crack at the base where the stones were split. Roxan welcomed the visitor. She unfolded the blanket she'd used as a pillow, pulled it around her shoulders, and sorted out all that had happened. Not knowing anything was maddening. And until the rat, guilt had been the only thing keeping her company. She had caused this. If she'd ignored the visions or told someone about them, she'd be the only one going to the Plateau. No one else would've gotten hurt.

Movement in the hallway cast shadows in the blue light. Five beeps and the steel door slid open. A sentry shoved someone through the doorway then beeped it shut again. The girl fell into a heap. It was Abiga.

"What have they done to you?" Roxan crossed the space between them on her hands and knees, scooping Abiga into her arms. "I'm sorry. Are you okay? You'll be okay." Abiga shivered, but said nothing.

Roxan stroked her back. "I'm sorry Abiga. This is my fault."

Abiga pushed away, gasping and coughing. Blood stained the front of the blue cover-up she wore. She braced herself up with her arms.

"I need your help, Roxan." Wiping her mouth with her sleeve, she sat up.

"What? What can I do?"

Abiga leaned forward, "They said they'd kill me unless you told them what you know." She glanced around as if she expected to find someone else in the cell, and then she fixed her serious eyes on Roxan.

Roxan held back her secrets. "I can't. I don't know anything," she murmured. The words came out hollow, obviously untrue. Jasper had already asked her where the Outcasts were. Altrist may have mentioned it, but Roxan didn't remember. Besides that was all stuff Abiga should know. "Abiga, are you okay? Do you know where Altrist is? Whitlock?" Time to steer things away from the stuff she didn't want to say.

Abiga shook her head. "No. They took your friend to a questioning chamber, and I don't know where the kid is. I didn't watch. Please Roxan, Altrist had to have told you something. What did he want you to do? What's your purpose with them?" Her voice was steady, not scared.

Roxan thought about the wall, but remembered Altrist's warning not to let Hyperion find out that she was the one he'd been looking for. The visions were still a secret. The boy wouldn't tell. That was the one bit of information that might help them, and he wouldn't tell.

Abiga continued, "Please, if you don't tell them, they're going to kill me."

"I don't know Abiga," Roxan whispered. "I don't want them to hurt you. I don't want them to hurt anyone, but I don't think I know much that's going to help." Something about Abiga put Roxan on edge. "Are you okay? Did they hurt you?" That was obvious from her swollen lip and bruises, but Roxan wanted to say something that would show she cared and that she was sorry.

"Think, Roxan. You have to know something. What did Altrist tell you? Do you know how they're going to get through the wall?" There wasn't any fear in Abiga's eyes. Anger flickered there.

Roxan shook her head. "I can't. What will they do to your people if they find out where they are and what they're doing?"

Abiga sat up. "They're not *my* people," she growled. "They didn't want me. They wanted you." Jasper had broken down her alliance.

"What have you done, Abiga?"

"I'm doing what I have to do to survive. And it's not me," she sneered. "You did this. You. You brought Altrist here, and now they have him. This is your fault. You were out there—and Altrist came to your rescue, but what did you do? You wanted to go to that stupid cabin. If it weren't for you, none of this would've happened."

Roxan fought back tears. She couldn't argue. The entire world had shifted, and somehow she was the cause.

"You have nothing to say?" Abiga stood. "You can still fix this. If you tell them what they want to know, they'll let us go. Tell them."

"Even Altrist? They'll let Altrist go?"

Abiga didn't answer.

Roxan shook her head. "No," she cried. "It's not fair. It's not his fault."

"Yeah, you're right. It's not his fault. It's yours," Abiga blamed. "And if you want to fix this, you'll tell them whatever you know."

"I don't know anything."

"That's not true. What did Altrist tell you? What were you supposed to do?" Despite her injuries, Abiga looked more like a lion than a wounded lamb.

Roxan held on to her guilt, but refused to accept all the blame for Altrist's imprisonment. "I know this is my fault. Don't you think I've already thought of all of that? Of what I should have done? What I could have done that would have kept everyone out of this? I know that. But it's not *all* my fault, you know."

"How's that? He wasn't about to turn his back on *you*. You're his precious prize, whatever that is. What makes you so special? Why did he need to get you out of here?" Abiga's venom tainted the room.

Roxan pulled away. Something else motivated Abiga. It hid in her eyes. It hovered behind her large pupils. It carved the downward turn in her lips. Her body slumped from it. Sadness. Profound loss. She was hurting. Her anger flowed from grief.

Exchanging her offense for compassion, Roxan spoke softly, "He wouldn't leave you, Abiga. He wouldn't turn his back on you."

She stiffened. "Well, then you don't know him very well." Tears choked her words. "He'd already walked away from me, left me alone. And he did it because of you."

Roxan crawled toward her. "That's not true. He stayed because of you." She reached for Abiga's hand, but the girl backed away. "You know he could've gotten away, and if he only wanted me, then he had his chance in the office. I felt it. He put his hand on me and the world started to fade, and then he saw you, and he stopped. He couldn't leave you."

The truth registered in Abiga's eyes. Dropping to the floor, she cried into her hands. Roxan turned away. It was true. Altrist wouldn't have left any of them. If there really was such a thing as love, he made a good show of it. He had already risked himself repeatedly for her.

Tiny prickles warmed the back of Roxan's head, and she pushed them away. Not now. She didn't hate the vision this time, but she wasn't ready to share her secret with anyone else.

Abiga had stopped crying, but before Roxan could turn to check on her, the wild girl pounced on her back and pushed her to the ground, pinning her face against the dirt.

"Listen to me," Abiga whispered in her ear. "They sent me here to get information out of you. They're desperate. We've got to give them something." Leaning back, she put her knee in Roxan's side and yelled, "Tell me what he said."

"Nothing," Roxan sputtered into the dirt. Abiga flipped her over and waited. Her eyes expressed sorrow, not anger. She mouthed the words, "Make something up," and glanced toward a box on the wall. They were watching.

Roxan coughed, "He told me to leave. Someone else would show me what to do. I don't know anything else."

Releasing her, Abiga scooted against the opposite wall. Silent. Roxan brushed the dirt from her cover-up. Poor Abiga. They'd put her up to this.

A tiny red light flashed from the box on the wall. Roxan hadn't even noticed it before. What else hadn't she noticed? Sweaty pipes ran along the ceiling. Two of the walls to the cell were steel and smooth, one was solid rock, and the one with the door was made of hewn stones.

Two buckets sat in the corner, one with water, one empty. They'd been watching her this whole time. Despair snaked its way into her heart as a hot, tingling ripple crawled up her neck. The haze started across the room, and she glanced at the box. They couldn't find out about her visions. That was one thing Altrist had made clear.

"Abiga," she whispered.

Abiga wiped the tears from her eyes. "What?"

Roxan took deep breaths and tried to push the feeling back, but it wasn't going to go away. "Help me."

Abiga grabbed the blanket from the floor and tossed it over the box, then descended on Roxan. "Make it stop."

"I can't."

"If they see you ... you've got to make it stop. This is it, isn't it? Your gift." She barely spoke the word aloud. "I'm sorry to do this Roxan, but we can't give them what they want." Pulling her fist back, she whispered another apology then punched Roxan upside the head. Everything went black.

When Roxan came to, Abiga was sitting next to her nursing a fresh cut across her forehead. "Hey there." She helped Roxan sit up. The box was uncovered, and the blanket was gone. "I got in trouble for beating you up. We're supposed to be friends now," she whispered. "You okay?"

Roxan smacked her hand away and crawled toward the rock wall. "Leave me alone."

"Hey, think of it as an initiation. I didn't mean any harm. Seriously, it was for your own good."

Roxan ran her fingers over her bruised cheek. "Yeah," Roxan groaned. "Thanks, but I don't really care for your methods."

"I'm willing to let the past stay in the past." Abiga held her hand out again, but Roxan ignored it. "Fine, but I think you might want me on your side."

Roxan cut her eyes toward the box, and Abiga caught her question. "Listen, I'm sorry I punched you, but you made me mad. Now it's out of my system, and I'm willing to move on." She met Roxan's eyes with assurance. They hadn't seen anything. Her secret was still safe.

"Fine."

Abiga scooted next to her on the wall. "How much longer do you think we'll be in here?"

Roxan shrugged.

"Don't give up yet, Roxan."

"This is hopeless," she murmured.

Abiga swiveled in front of her and whispered, "Not yet, Roxan. Don't give up yet. There's always a way out. If you're as important as they say you are, then the Leader himself will come set you free. Don't give up." She moved back to her spot on the wall. Her confidence was back. "And I don't care if they do hear me."

Abiga stood up and marched in front of the little red light. "Hear me Jasper. You almost got me there. You and your lies. I'm not going to help you. You make me sick." She spit on the floor. "And you know what else?

I'm sure you've heard this, right? Your side loses. So you keep pouting about how you didn't get what you wanted. And I'm gonna move on. I can take responsibility for what I've done." She threw a handful of dirt at the box and settled into her spot next to Roxan.

"Feel better?"

Abiga smiled and nodded. "A little."

Five beeps dinged, and the door slid open.

CHAPTER 26

ATTACKED

Jonas tossed the bag of garbage into the heap. Getting into the compound wasn't as easy as he'd thought. Turns out sentries can't be bought. Janitors, however, don't have as many scruples and have keys to everything.

The plans the janitor gave him showed a courtyard on the other side of the disposal bins beyond the end building. The entrance to the underground holding cell was in the middle of the courtyard.

The dark part of the roll still held the sun at bay and lumens lit the empty alley. As Jonas crept along the side of the building toward the courtyard, the ground rumbled beneath his feet. Dropping to the dirt, Jonas peeked into the courtyard. Smoke poured from the edges of two large black doors to a subterranean transport station. Guards and sentries scrambled toward the opening.

Jasper appeared from the middle of the commotion and yelled that the engines in the transport car had blown. A guard sprinted away from Jasper and out of the compound.

Gray smoke rose into the air as the sentries opened the black doors. Evidently, there were still men down there. Two medics set up a station for the injured. Within a few flashes, Jasper was in command in a fortified gazebo in the middle of the courtyard. He leaned over a table, his eyes fixed on a spread of maps.

Left of the gazebo, two massive sentries stood guard at the entrance to the holding cells. A yellow light glowed from the opening. It was now or not at all. Jasper wouldn't wait for the roll to warm up for his travel.

Jonas brushed off his cover-up and marched toward Jasper. Two guards intercepted him, but Jonas assured them he was there on Plateau orders. They didn't stand down, but escorted him to their master.

"Jasper," Jonas waited for Jasper to look up. "I know it must have been an oversight that I wasn't given clearance to accompany you and the prisoners to the Plateau."

"Get him out of here." Jasper went back to his map.

The guards took Jonas by the arm, but he yanked free and stood his ground. "I *am* coming. You can't stop me without disobeying orders."

"What are you talking about? I enforce the orders." Jasper kept his eyes on the map, but he was listening.

"The order Roxan held said that *everyone* in the room must be taken to the Plateau. That would include me." The guards released his arms, but stayed close.

Jasper rubbed his chin and pressed his skinny lips together. "Fine," he growled. "But you will follow my orders, stay quiet, and have no contact with the prisoners." His eyes looked black in the artificial light.

"Yes, sir." Jonas took a step back. There would be time to work on that "no contact" condition. For now, he would wait. They had a journey ahead of them. An opportunity to talk to Roxan would present itself.

The head sentry waved a dismissal, and Jonas pushed by the guards and found a bench with a good view of the cell corridor. Roxan was down their somewhere. She had swallowed whatever story Whitlock was feeding her, probably with matchment papers in her eyes. Poor girl. Despite the trouble she'd caused him, she didn't deserve this.

Stars still hung in the velvet sky. Stifling a yawn, Jonas dug through his pack for a Caftywater. The bitter energy drink helped keep the adrenalin pumping. No sense in giving Jasper a reason to leave him behind. Falling asleep would be his ticket to nowhere.

Officers pulled supplies from the smoky hole. It reminded Jonas of sitting in a lecture hall. No one was really lecturing, but the commotion held all of his attention. Every sentry walked or ran with the same sort of hop to their step. And evidently, they only had one volume. Loud.

"Sir, the transport is inoperable." The guard yelled his news to Jasper.

"Fine. I've already sent officers to commandeer the Progenate transport. We'll move the prisoners once we get the go ahead." The loud guard bowed and backed away.

A buzzing alarm sounded from the stairway to the underground cells. The two mammoths posted at the top didn't even flinch as another guard bolted into the courtyard carrying a black box. "Sir," the sentry called to Jasper. "Sir, the prisoner isn't cooperating. You should hear this."

The guard slammed the box onto Jasper's maps. Jonas leaned forward, perking his ears up. A girl's voice came from the box. It had to be a surveillance machine. The voice coming from it didn't sound like Roxan...maybe Abiga.

As the girl finished her tirade, Jasper slammed his fist into the monitor. "Prepare them for transport. Put this one in heavy chains." The guard gathered the pieces of the box and ran-hopped back to the cells.

Rising from the east, a soft gray haze invaded the sky. Jonas welcomed it. They would bring the prisoners out soon. Roxan hadn't looked at him before she was taken away, and he didn't get an opportunity to explain anything or reason with her. Maybe being locked up had brought her to her senses. Cooperating would get her farther than arguing. Maybe even land her back at her station, once they realized she wasn't a threat. It was Whitlock who had been tainting her mind, exploiting her.

Two sentries bounced into the courtyard, stopping in front of Jasper. Despite their yelling, Jonas could only hear bits and pieces of their report.

Jasper wasn't happy with whatever news they brought. The business in the courtyard slowed down when Jasper yelled. "What do you mean, he wasn't there?" Did you go to the cabin in the woods?" The younger sentry nodded his head. "Alright, well, there's nothing we can do about it. Put out an alert and report to Clary. He will be in charge while I'm at the Plateau." Jasper waved a dismissal, but they didn't budge. "Well, you can go now." The guards remained, and the second one offered up the next bit of offensive news.

"What? When?" Jasper fumed. The guard replied and stepped back, leaving the younger one within Jasper's striking range. Their leader growled and slammed his fists on the table, then raged toward his officers. "Get out of my sight." Retreating, they didn't turn their backs until they were out of Jasper's reach.

Another guard, larger than the other two, and evidently more of an equal to Jasper approached the gazebo fortress where Jasper paced.

"Sir, what would you like us to do?" His voice carried around the open area, and the other soldiers stopped and listened.

Jasper composed himself and answered, "Stinnett, prepare the prisoners to walk. We'll go on foot to Spring Stop."

Grumbles and protests shot through the sentries surrounding the gazebo. "What? Are you all such babies you can't take a walk through the woods? We will be to Spring Stop before the sun reaches the middle of the sky, and we'll wait there for the next transport.

Stinnett turned and marched toward the cell, calling four other sentries to join him. "Wait for me to give you the signal before you retrieve the boy," Jasper added. "The less time he has with the others the better, and keep a blindfold and gag on him. He sees nothing and says even less."

Stinnett turned and saluted. "Yes, sir." The large guard roared out his response and headed back down the stairway to the underground cells.

"You still want to come, little guide man?" Jasper called Jonas out. The guards closest snickered.

Jonas stood. "I'll be fine."

"You could stay here, not waste a trip. This doesn't concern you." He stepped out of the gazebo.

"I won't defy Plateau orders," Jonas retorted. "I will accompany the prisoners."

"You'll have nothing to do with the prisoners. You pick up the rear." Laughter spread among the guards, and Jasper went back to his maps.

Jonas retreated to his bench and ignored them. Jasper was the type of sentry that made everyone else distrust and hate the sworn protectors of the Oblate. He was small-minded and ignorant. None of the sentries had much of an ability to strategize. And the ones who did went straight to the Plateau. Jasper didn't make the cut.

The most worrisome thing about Jasper was his loose temper. His position and physical strength combined with his temper made him an adversary not to underestimate. But Jonas wasn't planning to do battle with him. He only wanted to get Roxan back.

A flashing red light blinked from the stairwell to the cells, and the two men standing guard drew their scinters. Jasper breezed by Jonas and waited by the guards. With wrists and ankles cuffed, Roxan was the first to appear.

Despite the restraints, the same spark glowed in her eyes, and her little chin was pushed out. She didn't look at Jonas, but shuffled behind a guard who led her to a spot near the other side of the gazebo.

Abiga came up next. Before she could pass by Jasper, he stopped the guards and walked around her. Her eyes ignored him, but the corners of her mouth found their way into a smirk. Jasper noticed her inappropriate demeanor and smacked her bruised face with the back of his hand knocking her to the ground. The guards pulled her to her feet again.

"You made a poor choice girl," Jasper raged. Something had stirred his anger again. "I could've made this easy for you. You could've been one of us."

Abiga looked away and didn't engage with him.

"Put her in line."

As Whitlock emerged, Roxan turned from her spot and gasped. The overseer had a gash from his cheek to his ear. Blood stained his cover-up in long dark streaks, and he looked like he hadn't slept all roll. Jonas looked away. It was hard to see Whitlock as the enemy when he looked so crushed.

Jasper shouted for the guards to surround the three twice. It took twenty sentries to create the buffer. Once they were in position, he called for the boy to be brought out. Jonas hadn't given the kid much thought. That was the strangest part of all of this. The kid seemed to be the real culprit, the one they were after. It didn't make sense. Runaways get in trouble, but not the kind of trouble that leads to the Plateau.

A black hood covered the boy's face. The cuffs on his wrists and feet were different from the other prisoners', and three sentries surrounded him with their weapons glowing. It looked ridiculous.

"Attention, company!" Jasper yelled. "We make it to Spring Stop before mid-roll, or you're all on detail. No one drops out of formation, no one. One troop in front with the three prisoners and another in the back with the boy. And you," he called to Jonas, "you walk in between. I won't guarantee your safety, so keep up. Are we clear?" The company of sentries barked out a "yea-yea" and did a little hop.

Suddenly, Abiga let out three piercing shrieks followed by a deep bark. The guard nearest hit her across the back, but she kept her balance and shut her mouth. Jasper yelled for them to proceed, and they took off with a steady walk-hop. Jonas jumped into his position and followed. Getting to Roxan wouldn't be easy.

****

By the time the sun was above them, they still hadn't made it out of the woods. Jonas took in every sight and sound of the forbidden world. Paths wound around trees, into valleys, by creeks. It was beautiful, fresh, and clean. Whitlock's plan to run away out here made more sense. This pastoral paradise had no rules, no sentries, and no curfew. But it wasn't without worries.

The sentries covered the terrain with familiarity and skill. And they kept their weapons at the ready. Jonas felt their tension. Stories about the crazy people in the woods couldn't all be made up. There was a reason for the boundary line. And there was still a stretch to go before they crossed over into the security of the Viand territory.

Jonas stayed close to the line of three guards in front of him.

Sunlight filtered through the canopy of trees that crowded the steep banks on each side of the pathway. As Jonas leaned over to pick up a long stick from the wayside, a scream broke through the sound of marching feet followed by a shower of sticks, rocks, and arrows aimed at the caravan.

Sentries lit up their scinters, but their weapons were useless at a distance. Yells and screams came from every direction. Jonas ran forward, pushing his way toward the prisoners. Whitlock and Abiga had already made it to the brush on the left embankment. Jonas grabbed Roxan's arm and jerked her back as she kicked her chains to the side.

"Roxan, get down." He shoved her to the ground and shielded her with his body.

She pushed him away. "What are you doing? Get off of me."

He loosed his grip, but didn't let go of her arm. "You can't run off. They'll hunt you down. It'll make things worse."

"I'm not staying here." She ducked as a box of supplies shattered right behind her. "

"If you run off now, you'll ruin any chance you have of going back to your life." She yanked her arm free. Jonas jumped to his feet and followed as she headed toward the brush. "Are you crazy? You're giving up everything. You go out there and they'll kill you. I can protect you. I have something on that lead sentry. He'll have to let you go."

Roxan paused and met his eyes, but all she said was a quiet, "No."

Jonas reached for her arm again, but Abiga intervened. "She said no." Before Jonas could argue, Abiga hit him with a charge from a scinter and knocked him back. When he got to his feet, they were gone.

CHAPTER 27

FORGIVEN

Abiga shot Altrist a look. He had appeared beside Whitlock as soon as they had gotten through the thick brush and into the forest. The grin on his face did not suit their circumstances.

"We're not out of this yet," she barked. Crazy kid, he loved this sort of thing as much as she did. If only the stakes weren't so high. "You should've stayed out of the village."

He ignored her correction. "Stay with us," he chimed. At least he wasn't assuming anything. "You belong with us, sweet Abiga. We can all make it beyond the wall and into an even greater adventure!"

"It's not that simple." As she whispered, Altrist ran to her side, but she didn't look at him. "I can't." She balled her marked hand into a fist. Whitlock and Roxan lagged behind, clumsy, out-of- shape sprouts.

"You're making it harder than it needs to be," Altrist treaded on unwelcomed ground.

"You don't know. So stay out of it."

"I know I care about you, and I don't want to leave you alone here."

Abiga jumped across a tiny creek and waited for the others to catch up. "Come on, move it," she ordered.

Battle cries from the fray behind them had died down. The Undesirables would be giving up soon. They were no real match for a band of sentries who could call in reinforcements. They had served their purpose.

As soon as Jasper had announced they'd be traveling through the woods, Abiga had known they had a chance. Her screams in the compound were a battle cry, alerting the Undesirable outposts of sentry movement. They loved a fight. She knew they'd be ready.

Jasper's decision to travel in the back with Altrist sealed their fate. He knew the woods— and what to look for. If he'd been up front, he would have suspected the attack. The Undesirables had been easy enough to spot, but the sentries missed every single scout.

"Where are we going?" Whitlock asked as he helped Roxan across the creek.

"Snowshoe," Altrist chirped.

Abiga looped back to them from where she'd been pacing. "You should go on to Willow Way. There's not a lot of time."

"We can't." Altrist motioned for them to get moving again. The commotion behind them had quieted. The guards were regrouping and would be tracking them soon. "It's too dangerous. I can't risk giving everybody away. We'll go to Snowshoe first and rest, then head out later."

"That won't give you enough time. You can't make it there on foot, at least not with the way they travel." She glanced back at the sprouts.

"The Leader will work it out."

Abiga growled, "Some things you don't leave to chance."

"It's not chance," Altrist whispered into her head.

Abiga swung around and gripped Altrist's arm. "Stay out of my head."

The shouts of the approaching guards were getting closer.

"You better go."

Altrist hugged her tightly. "Not without you."

Peeling his arms away, she distanced herself. "I'm not going with you. I told you. I wouldn't leave until the Leader made it clear to me."

"Abiga," Altrist pleaded.

"I'm not like any of you. I've done things that can't be undone. It's part of me. I can't ignore how I feel, and he shouldn't expect me to."

Roxan let go of Whitlock and wrapped her arms around Abiga's neck.

"Thank you," she whispered.

Abiga stifled tears and returned the kindness. "You do the right thing."

Altrist pulled Whitlock and Roxan close, then looked back at Abiga as he began to glow. "We will be at Snowshoe until dark, if you change your mind." He kept his eyes on her until he—and Roxan and Whitlock—faded away. A golden haze hovered in the spot where they'd been.

"There, a light! I see one of them," a sentry shouted. Abiga dashed down the other side of the embankment. The chase was on. They wouldn't give up, not with Jasper's prize Altrist set free. They'd find something to bring back to their master.

Abiga sprinted on familiar ground now, confidence and experience guiding her through the thick woods. The chase wouldn't be easy for them. Sentries weren't trackers, as soon as she was out of sight, they'd be fools to keep going.

Taxar bushes lined the drop to the creek below. She headed for a gap between the thorns. Guards avoid the deadly bush. Halfway through, a briar snagged her leg and pain shot from her calf to her shoulder. Pulling herself the rest of the way through, she steadied herself above the creek. Just a nick, but it was enough to paralyze her right side with agony.

"Burn it," a sentry ordered from the other side, and the whoosh of fire hitting the thicket propelled her down the bank. A few flashes in the heat and the thorns would lose their power.

Abiga crawled into the coolness, but the water didn't ease the hurt. A blurry blanket fell across the world, and two arms scooped her from the flow.

"Get up," a man growled in her ear and pulled her down the creek. Abiga leaned against him, fighting the urge to pass out. She jerked away once to vomit, but he showed no mercy, pushing her on. The sentries were cutting through the bushes behind them.

"Here." He pulled away branches that hid a recess under a rock overhang in the bank. There was enough space for them to lie down. "Take this." He handed her a canteen. "It'll help; drink it."

Lifting the canteen to her lips, she only managed a sip before everything started to go black. The man grabbed her hair and tilted her head back, placing the canteen to her lips, and forcing her to drink. Two big gulps brought relief and revived her. One more and the knives in her side dulled to a constant throb.

He took the canteen and screwed the top back on. "You can have more later. Let this do its best first." His blue eyes met her with confidence. "You're either crazy or brave," he muttered.

Body art on his arm suggested he was from a village, but he wore half a brown tog and torn pants, not normal garments for a sprout. His face was shaved, but his black hair was long. Smart, strong, healthy, but not one of them.

Abiga didn't ask any of her questions, and he didn't introduce himself. She put her head down and closed her eyes.

A tapping on her arm stirred her. The man covered her mouth and pointed to the creek below. Jasper. He stood on a rock in the middle of the water. He was alone. Her new alliance pulled a tiny crossbow out and smiled, pointing it at the head sentry.

"I could take him out, and he'd never know what hit him."

Jasper turned toward them, providing a clear shot to his cold heart. Abiga hated him. He'd made her turn traitor, gotten her to help him. If Roxan hadn't been able to see through it all, all of the Outcasts might be his by now. Just one shot would put him in his place.

Propping himself up, the stranger took aim. "What do you think?"

Abiga pulled the bow to the side. "No."

He questioned her with his eyes, but kept his mouth shut.

She prodded him. "Are you a cold-blooded killer?"

"I could be," he smirked.

"I won't be. Leave him alone. He'll get what's coming to him."

"You leave him alone now, and you might come to regret it."

"If I let you shoot him now, I know I'll regret that."

"Fair enough." He put the crossbow aside, and they watched as Jasper waded to the other side of the creek.

Two guards jogged toward him. The shorter one called out, "Sir, there's no sign of her."

"Fall back. Men, fall back!" Jasper boomed, his temper showing. "We regroup, and then we'll go out. I have a few ideas of where they might be."

The outsider removed the covering from the cave after the soldiers left. "You think you can walk?"

Abiga grunted and crawled out. "I'll try."

"My camp is west of here. You can stay with me until your scratch heals," he grinned. "You're lucky you didn't really get stuck with one of those taxar briars."

"Yeah, I know." Abiga took another swig from the canteen. The liquid went down her throat directly to her throbbing side. "What is this stuff?"

"That's my secret recipe." He was all smiles. "So, you made some sentries mad, did you?"

"Aren't sentries always mad about something?" She replied.

"True." He put the canteen in his pack, pulled a walking stick from the cave, and pointed toward the crest of creek bank. "Shall we?"

Abiga hesitated, but limped her way up the bank. He loaned her his walking stick and let her lean on his arm. He smelled like sassafras and fresh air. "What's your story, guy?"

He stretched. "My story is I just saved your life."

"Why?" Abiga let loose of his arm and used a tree limb to pull herself the rest of the way up the bank. Undesirables don't put themselves in danger for others. Sprouts don't know how, and a sentry wouldn't have threatened Jasper. The only other option was Outcast. "Who are you?"

"I'm passing through." He smiled again. "Who are you? Where are you headed?"

"I don't know," Abiga mumbled.

"You don't?" He made his own trail, and she followed. "How's that?

"I'm not sure what to do now."

He slowed, held his hand up, and listened. A red bird chased its mate through the bushes chirping wildly, but nothing else was out of order. The sentries had moved on. Picking up his pace, he started in with the questions again. "So you're completely on your own? No pomper, no parent, no principal?"

"Something like that." Too many questions. "I tried to be part of something, but the principal didn't want me."

"You didn't make the cut?"

"No. I was part of the group."

"He cut you back?" Whoever he was, he knew how Undesirables worked. Hardly any of the Outcasts knew about cutting back, even the one's who'd come from the packs.

"No, he took me in, even gave me a mark." She flashed her palm. "It's about gone now."

"What happened? He kick you out?"

"Why all the questions mystery man? I don't hear you offering up your life's story."

"Sorry, I don't get it. Why'd you leave?"

"He didn't want me."

He stopped walking. "Okay, I'll drop it, just one more thing. How'd you know he didn't want you? I mean you were part of the group, he didn't cut you back, and he didn't kick you out, what happened?"

"Nothing. I'm not good enough for them." He stood there, not convinced. "I didn't get a gift. Most people get gifts, and I didn't get one because I'm not good enough. He knows it. I know it. So there, back off."

He started walking again. He had successfully pried her story out of her and given her nothing about himself.

"How far is it?" Abiga asked.

"Your leg hurting?" His concern was genuine. Abiga shook her head. She didn't really need the walking stick anymore. She offered it back, but he waved her off and answered her question. "It's not too far. We can be there before the dark." They hiked off the normal trails, but the stranger moved with confidence.

Abiga tried to read him, but he was still all smiles and humming. "What's your story?" she asked again, then added, "I'm Abiga."

"Melkin, you can call me Mel. And we don't have enough trail left for my story," he teased. "I've been around."

"You don't run with a pack?" He shot her a knowing look. She knew he wasn't with a pack, but there weren't too many options. "Okay, you're not a sprout. That's clear. You're not an Outcast or you wouldn't be here." She paused, took a breath and forced the question out, "Are you with Hyperion?"

His humming came to an abrupt stop, and he faced her with a carefree confidence. "No, I don't follow him."

"Then who? No one lasts out here alone. I know. I've tried."

"I didn't say I was alone." He flicked a pesky butterfly from the top of his walking stick. "Now I have another question for you." He waited for her assent and proceeded with her nod. "You said you weren't good enough for these people, but they had already accepted you. Didn't they know about your past, about who you really are before they chose you? I mean you're not that hard to figure out. No offense. It wouldn't take an expert to see you've been around a little too."

Abiga broke away from his eyes, but he tipped her chin up, so she could look into his blue eyes. "You need to go back, Abiga," he whispered.

She shook her head. "I can't."

"And that is your choice. Don't blame him for it. He loves you." He wiped the tears from her face and smiled again. "You can go back too. You can forgive yourself for all of it, move on, and embrace all that's ahead of you. You're the only one who's saying you aren't good enough."

"But the gift ..." That was the briar pricking her hope away. No gift had been given. Nothing, not even a peace, like Thim had.

His smile didn't change. "Is the gift really the problem? You think he's not giving you a gift because you don't deserve it, but you don't know the whole picture, do you? There are more paths and more people and they all intertwine. Yours is only one path. Don't get me wrong. It's a very special one, but your getting a gift doesn't affect just you."

Abiga ran her hand down the smooth walking stick. Melkin's name was carved above a knot in the wood, and above his name some numbers and letters. Under the knot, an *X* was etched next to an *A*.

His arguments made sense. She hadn't forgiven herself. She had kept her past close. She wanted answers to questions that had already been answered. They were answered the flash she stepped through the water. That wasn't a lie.

He must have read her thoughts. "Now don't go to feeling guilty about this little journey either. Nothing is lost. It's all good." His words took root in her heart. "You can have the stick, if you want." He pushed it toward her.

"I can't. It's yours." She sent it back his way.

"You take it," he grinned. "And look..." He pressed a notch and a blade shot out the end. "It's a weapon too." His eyebrows brought a laugh out of her. Black, like his hair, they took his excitement into his forehead. "I want you to have it. Think of it as a gift preview." She looked away. But he brought her back. "I know it's not what you meant, but please take it."

She pulled the stick close to her side. "Thank you." In no more than a flash, he had saved her life and guided her back to home. Thank you wasn't exactly the right thing to say, but when emotions run deep, there aren't words good enough to express them.

"You are very welcome." He seemed to understand. His eyes sparkled with appreciation of the moment.

"Who are you?"

He gave her a knowing look. "You know, don't you? You know whose order I follow."

Some things didn't need to be put into words, to be pulled out into plain view. Some things stayed secret, but were still true. She did know who had sent him to her, and that truth both stopped her and gave her the courage to go on.

He took her hand and led her up a hill. "See the top of that pine peeking out over there?" He motioned until she saw it. "Walk toward that and you'll find Stony Way Path. You know how to find your way from there?" She nodded. Altrist and the others were at Snowshoe. She could be there before the sun let up.

Holding back the urge to give the stranger a hug, Abiga met his blue eyes one last time, then turned toward home. The pain in her leg had completely vanished, so she jogged off. Stopping part way, she turned to wave one more time, but Melkin was gone.

CHAPTER 28

REBORN

Roxan slid across the dirt floor. Cold, damp air blew her hair back and a muted roar of water surrounded her. No light, nothing.

"Is anyone there?" A hand grabbed at her leg, and she kicked.

"Ow." Whitlock let go. "I'm here. It's me."

"Whitlock." Roxan ran her hand through the dirt until she found him. "Where are we?"

A light flickered behind them revealing rock walls and Whitlock's worried face. "You okay?"

"Yeah," she replied. "Where are we?"

Altrist lit another fixture and hung it on a hook fastened into the rock. "We're at Snowshoe Falls. Welcome back!"

Roxan didn't recognize the cave. "Where's the waterfall?"

Altrist pointed toward the blackness. "Down that corridor. We're in a back chamber. I thought we could hide out here for a bit, and then leave when the sun sets."

Whitlock stood and brushed the dirt off. "How'd we get here? What happened? We were in the woods."

"Yeah, sorry about that," Altrist replied then pried open a box with an *A* painted on the side. "Drastic times call for whatever we've got, and I've got a few things I can do." He lifted his hand, and a warm light glowed from his palm. It spread across his body, and then he vanished. "I'm back here."

He glowed in the archway of another tunnel on the other side of the cavern. "I would have snatched you from the office, but I couldn't leave

Abiga there. Anyway, we're safe for now. I don't think the sentries will come here. At least, I hope they'll go back to the village and let things be."

Whitlock met Altrist at the box and showered him with questions, but Roxan stayed back. It was too much to process. Two rolls ago she had gotten in to work early and been appointed lead on a project, and now she was a fugitive, in the company of a strange boy who had abilities beyond the laws of science. Life spiraled out of control with no good end in sight.

"This is Anna's pallet," Altrist said, pointing to a woven mat by the far wall. Whitlock launched into more questions about his mother. Roxan looked down the corridor to the falls. Going back now wasn't an option. Jonas had been right. The sentries wouldn't just let her go.

She stared at the blackness. Mullin knew what he wanted. Whitlock knew he didn't belong in the Protectorate. Altrist didn't have questions. Even Abiga was sure about what she was doing. And they all had clear ideas about Roxan too. "We need you." "There's nothing here for you." Why wasn't some of that clarity coming her way?

"Why don't you take us there now?" Whitlock held up his hand like Altrist had done. "You know, with that light thing you do."

"Yeah, I would if I could, but I can't go that far with two people. At least, not and be accurate, and I don't want to risk landing somewhere we don't want to be, like with the Undesirables or along the path of a sentry patrol." Altrist fastened the lid back on the box. "Hyperion might be able to sense us too, if I use that kind of energy. And I can't take that chance. We'll wait until the sun goes down. The others won't go to the Balustrade until the next roll of the sun. We have time." Altrist lifted his hand, and the light glowed again. "Be right back." He vanished.

Whitlock shook his head and came back to Roxan. "It's amazing, isn't it? I think I knew somewhere down inside of me that there was more. It's hard to believe, hard to let go when you've been told one thing all your life." His eyes danced with excitement in the flickering light. "You okay?"

"I'm not sure about all of this." Roxan kept her questions to herself, but let a little of her heart show. "It's all hard to take in."

Whitlock agreed, "I know. It was more than I could have hoped for." That wasn't exactly the direction she was going. "My mother lived here. These people are free. Really free."

"What if they're wrong?" There she said it.

"What if they aren't?" Whitlock shot back. "Just because we haven't known this world doesn't mean it isn't real. Does a little one growing up in the raising home and never seeing the sun, never feeling its heat, mean that the sun isn't there? Now we've discovered the sun again. And we can leave Hyperion's dark world behind."

"Why do we have to be part of either world? Why do we have to choose sides?" Roxan's eyes searched Whitlock's face. "We could start over out here and make our own freedom. I can ignore my curse until it fades away—you can meet up with your mother, but we don't have to join their society. We can make our own."

Whitlock didn't respond, and Roxan couldn't read his expression.

A light flashed, and Altrist appeared next to them. He had a red scarf around his neck and lugged the black and orange cushion behind him. "Sorry, I went to get my scarf! Abiga thought I shouldn't have it on, but now I guess it doesn't matter, and I like it!" He pulled the cushion around. "And this might be more comfortable than the dirt." It took him a flash to notice Whitlock's serious expression. "Is something wrong?"

"Roxan has some doubts about joining you." Whitlock didn't sound as sure anymore.

"Mmmm. Well, I won't force you to leave with us, Roxan. It must be your choice."

Roxan didn't look into the boy's sweet blue eyes or at Whitlock, but she felt them both looking at her.

A man's voice echoed from the outer room of the cave. Altrist clapped his hands together, and the two lights went out. "Stay here," he whispered. Roxan scooted closer to Whitlock. Altrist didn't do his little trick and flash away, but padded down the corridor on foot.

Roxan strained to see, but all was black. "Should we let him go alone?"

"That's no little boy. I think he can take care of himself." Whitlock hid his fear, but Roxan could see it, even in the darkness. She could see his heart had already promised itself to this new world. Anything that would threaten that would be his enemy.

The two sat in the dark, listening and waiting. Muffled sounds of men talking echoed down the walls. And Altrist's little voice was right there with them. Sounds of joy, not danger. Flickering light announced their coming and laughter boomed into the cavern as Altrist appeared with his little arm wrapped around a very large man with a whiskered face.

"Here they are," Altrist announced, clapping the lights back on. Another man filed in behind them. Both men wore brown cover-ups and carried small packs. "Roxan and Whitlock, I'd like to introduce you to two of my dear friends, Grouper and Thim." Thim peaked out from behind Grouper. The narrow passageway barely provided enough room for Grouper to fit through. "Anna sent them." Altrist pointed to Whitlock. "Whitlock, here, is Anna's son." The two men pulled Whitlock to his feet and hugged him.

"She's going to be happy to see you." Everything Grouper said bounced off the walls. The whiskers on his face had almost made a beard, but his smile was plain to see. Despite his muscles and size, nothing about him was intimidating or rough. "I'm guessing he's the one she was hoping would make it out with us." Altrist smiled and nodded. "And this little lady? Is she the one you were hoping to find?" Altrist smiled again. "Welcome! We're glad you're coming with us." He pulled her from the dirt and set her on her feet.

"Where's Abiga?" Thim looked around. Clean-shaven and trimmed, he could be Whitlock's little brother. Although much smaller in stature than Grouper, his arms rippled with muscles too. "We hoped she'd be with you."

"No. She left us." Altrist touched Thim's arm. "But I'm hopeful she will still find her way to us." Thim turned away, but Roxan saw the tears.

An uncomfortable silence swept through the corridor. Roxan barely noticed the muted waterfall, but the silence was loud and put her on edge.

These people had their own secrets and struggles. Their world wasn't perfect either. Out of nowhere, a sweet peace swept over her. The cadence of the falling water played across the open space, and she could see colors falling on the walls like rain drops on a window pain.

"Stop it, Grouper," Thim broke the roaring silence, and took two steps back, shaking his head and growling. "I'm fine. I don't need you trying to fix things."

"I'm trying to help, buddy." Grouper shrugged his shoulders.

"Well, stop," he warned. "Being sad and hurt and confused aren't bad things. Let me be. I'll work through this on my own. You keep that sweet-feelin' gift of yours in its holster."

Grouper nodded his understanding, and Thim turned toward Altrist. "What's the plan?" he questioned. "Should we head back to Willow Way now? Everyone's going to be happy to see you. We were all starting to wonder how we'd get through the wall."

"We'll wait. " Altrist ordered. "But you two go on ahead. A group of five will be easier to track than three. Take the short cut through the Protectorate. Grouper can navigate that, and we'll use the narrow passage through the bluffs."

"You can't make it there in one roll. It's too far," Grouper disputed.

"We won't go the whole way on foot," the kid replied. "I'll transport them when I think it's safe." Grouper backed down, and Altrist continued as the one in charge. "Have you seen Liza? Was she at Pocket?"

"No. Jahn's pretty bent out of shape about it. He doesn't want to leave without her, even though he says he will," Thim answered, his own pain still showing.

"It seems we're all being tested." The two men nodded in sad agreement, and Altrist addressed Roxan, "You have a decision to make too. If you plan to head back to your village, you should go in the light of the roll. It will be safer for you. Grouper can take you to the boundary line." His directness took Roxan off-guard. There hadn't been any time to think all of this through.

Thim jumped between them. "What? Why would you want to go back?" He barely looked at her, and started grilling Altrist, "You're going to let her go? How can you do that? We need her. Right? We can't make it through the wall without her. That's what you said. That's why you went after her."

Altrist pulled Thim away, and Roxan withdrew out of the fray, grabbed a light fixture, and headed toward the tunnel at the back of the cave. Everyone knew exactly what she should do except for her.

The tunnel opened up to a smaller cavern room, which contained a long table and seven chairs. Grouper had joined the conversation with Altrist and Thim. Their voices carried through the tunnel, and Roxan heard what she wanted to escape. They argued because of her. They were on the run because of her. They were in peril because she had some aberration that was a danger to others.

"I didn't want any of this," she whispered to the echo of arguing. "I only wanted to know what was wrong with me. I wasn't looking for another world, another person to follow. Hyperion was fine. Life was fine." She refused to let tears cloud her eyes. "I never wanted any of this."

The fixture cast an eerie glow on the smooth cavern walls and revealed a huge mural reaching from the dirt floor to where the prickly ceiling interrupted it. Roxan followed the picture around the room. It must have taken cycles to finish. Amazing. It started small and grew into a full-height picture.

At the beginning of the mural, a hand reached out of darkness touching a bluish orb, and from there pictures of canyons, waterfalls, animals, and landscapes filled the gray stone. The hand appeared again midway around the picture—this time emerging through a wall of water. Rays of light shot from each fingertip and connected with drawings of five people. Three of these she recognized: Grouper, Thim, and Abiga. Below that group, five smaller figures reached up with their hands outstretched, sending light up to the hand from the waterfall. Or, was it the other way around?

Another group of people filled the last wall. They were dark and sad. Their heads poked out of a sack attached to a dark figure with red slits for eyes. Roxan shifted uneasily. The eyes followed her. This was more than simple art. This was their story.

A tingle pulsated up the back of Roxan's head. She closed her eyes and pushed at the aberration that was causing her so much trouble. Curiosity slowed her, though. And for the first time, she let the vision come, welcomed it, and watched.

The golden haze filled up the room with brilliant light, and the drawings of Abiga and the others smiled and danced in the brilliance. Darkness lapped at the edges of the light chipping it away. And in a whoosh of fire, a monster appeared behind the red eyes and lunged toward Roxan. She screamed, and jumping back knocked the light fixture over. The room went black. Whitlock and the others came running, a flurry of light and men.

"I'm fine." Roxan pushed away from Whitlock's half-embrace. "What's wrong with you?" She pulled at his soppy cover-up top. "You're soaking wet."

"I did it." Whitlock threw his hands in the air. "I did it."

"What?" Roxan glanced at the others. Smiles decorated each of them.

"I joined them. I'm officially an Outcast. And I met him." Happy tears sparkled in his eyes.

"What are you talking about? Who did you meet?" That uneasy feeling returned to her stomach.

"The Leader. I met him." Whitlock scooped Roxan up and flung her around.

"Put me down." She smacked him with her hand, and he plopped her back onto her feet. "Where is he? You actually saw him?"

"Yes, I went through the waterfall. He took my hand and led me through." Whitlock carefully took Roxan's hand. "It was like something clicked into place inside of me, and when it did, I felt it."

"What?" Roxan doubted the craziness, but kept quiet.

"I felt loved." He grabbed her other hand and made her look him in the eyes. "Roxan, you have to believe. Please. I know it sounds strange. Love. Who ever thought that concept could be real? Just some crazy emotion, right?" He smiled at her, but kept on talking. "And here I thought we were going to be escaping from something. I never dreamed we would actually be coming to something." Roxan pulled her hands loose from his, and Whitlock reached for her. "Roxan, please."

"Let's give her some time." Altrist stepped between them. "It's a lot to take in."

"We don't have time." Whitlock grabbed her hand and pulled her toward the tunnel to the outer part of the cave. "Roxan you have to do it too. Step under the waterfall." She pulled at his hand, but he had a firm grasp.

Grouper blocked him. "Slow down there, fella. You can't force this on anyone. It has to be their choice."

Roxan pulled free and stepped back as Altrist glided to her side. "He's right, Whitlock," Altrist affirmed. "If Roxan chooses to join us, it can happen anywhere. It doesn't have to be here. Just because this is where your experience happened, doesn't mean it has to be where hers takes place."

"But I thought the waterfall was like a doorway or something." More and more crazy-talk spewed from the overseer.

"No, it's only a waterfall. Don't make it more than that. The Leader will meet Roxan wherever she is, whenever she's ready." Altrist lightly grasped Roxan's hand. "Roxan, you have such a kind heart, quick to return caring with compliance, but this decision must be yours alone. You must choose for yourself whether you will be a child of the Leader or one of Hyperion's offspring."

"I thought a child couldn't choose who its parents are." Roxan ignored the others and looked at Altrist. "If a choice is to be made, why must it only be between these two? Is the world so narrow that there's only one standing in the name of good and one in the name of bad?" The faces on the wall seemed to stare at her in disbelief, as did Thim and Grouper. They all kept telling her she had a choice to make, but she reached beyond them.

"What do you think?" Altrist returned.

"I think we should get to choose for neither. Let them have their fight for power. Neither should demand our allegiance. We don't need either one. In the Protectorate, we have no father or mother; we're raised by nannies. We are our own leaders." Her words echoed into the darkness.

Thim intruded. "That's not true. You bow to that monster. You may think you are on your own, living out in merry oblivion, but whether you realize it or not, you are Hyperion's servant, his slave."

Roxan met his challenge. "Well, maybe that's the thing that needs to change. Maybe we can see the way to our own destinies without either one manipulating us."

"You do get to choose which road you follow," Altrist declared. "As much as we want you with us, we won't make you join us. We won't even make you go to the wall with us. And we will love you no matter what."

Grouper and Thim stiffened, and Altrist addressed them. "That is love. The Leader has shown us that. He loved you through the darkness, how can we do less?" He turned back to Roxan. "I will warn you, though. You can see things others cannot. But sometimes the truth takes a closer look to see, and sometimes even our own hearts betray us. But the Leader will never betray us. If you trust him, he will show you the way."

"Well, that depends on where you're standing, now doesn't it?" Jasper's venom spewed into the cavern. A hoard of scinters lit up the passageway behind him. "So your prized possession is asking some hard questions. I bet our Lord Hyperion can help her find the truth."

"Jasper." Grouper held up his hand.

"I wouldn't try that either, Grouper. No mushy feelings of love and peace are going to dissuade me from my purpose here. I've come for Altrist."

"You know I can't let you do that." Grouper took two steps and stood in front of the boy. "You can't take him there. We need him."

"I can, and I will." Jasper didn't hesitate, but jabbed Grouper with the scinter sending the gentle colossus to his knees. Other sentries filled the cramped room, and Altrist closed his eyes and let them take him away.

CHAPTER 29

GIFTED

Late-roll light filtered through the tall pines. Abiga knelt on the ledge overlooking Snowshoe Falls. This was home. It looked strange from this height. From here, Snowshoe was even more beautiful and dangerous. A deer waded into the river in the shallows before the falls; several others lingered at the tree line, timid and unsure.

How could the Outcasts leave this behind? In another roll, they'd all be gone, and this place would only be a precious memory. Maybe beyond the wall there would be a new life, a world free from hiding and scavenging. Maybe all the stories about a vast wasteland were part of Hyperion's lies.

"Maybe," Abiga whispered and grabbed her walking stick. She took one last look at the world she loved. It was better to have had a little while here than to never have known it at all.

Altrist would be proud to see her being grateful and not whining. Abiga searched the falls for a sign of Altrist. If he didn't do that transporting thing with Whitlock and Roxan, he would take the path and cross down river, instead of climbing up here. On this side of the falls, the only way up from the cave was to climb the rocks. No way Roxan was gonna do that.

On the other side of the river, a light flickered to life midway down the path to the cave. Abiga dropped back to her knees. Trees blocked the trail, but something was there. The slim route was the only way in and out on that side. More lights broke through the leaves. Scinters. Their blue, purple, and pink luminosity pulsated with enthusiasm. Sentries. Jasper knew about the cave? That monster. Did he hate them all that much?

A squadron of at least twenty soldiers filed slowly along the narrow path and slipped one by one behind the sheet of water. Abiga popped up as the last one disappeared, and she scrambled toward the plucky deer. The animal zigzagged through the shallows before finding her sense and diving for the woods. This would be the best place to cross the river.

Three large boulders led away from the little beach. Abiga judged the distance carefully. From the last rock, she would have to swim about five meters until she could have any hope of touching the bottom. The strong current pulled everything in the deep water toward the falls, but there was plenty of brush on the other side offering assistance. Hiking down and crossing below would take too long and be too vulnerable. This was the only option.

She fastened Mel's stick to her back, waded into the shallows, and climbed onto the first boulder. She whispered a plea to the Leader before leaping to the second and third.

At the last boulder, the black water ribboned its way through the gap between the rock and the bank. "One, two, three," she counted, took a gulp of air, and dove into the smooth fury. The current grabbed her, pulling her toward the falls. Pumping her legs, she fought the force of gravity's quarrel with water, keeping her eyes on the brush and not on the drop.

Exposed roots reached out from the bank lending their slippery curves, and she heaved herself up into the prickly arms of the brush. The path down to the cave was still a solid run. A run that would need to be made on light feet. Jasper would be watching this time. He would have guards on the lookout.

Cutting back, she stayed off the easy route and ran flat out until she got to the pines. One guard paced at the head of the cave path. From the scars on his bulky arms, he had seen his share of fights.

A man yelled from below, and the guard stopped his pacing. Abiga held her breath. Altrist could have transported Roxan and Whitlock, if he'd had any notice about the surprise attack. For that matter, he could put that traitor in his place. No scinter could subdue the kid. The only thing that would hinder Altrist would be leaving somebody behind. He wouldn't do that.

A guard emerged from the hidden path. "We move fast when we hit the road. Master Jasper doesn't want to take any chances."

"And the other troop?" The scarred sentry kept looking around. Did he sense he was being watched?

"Master Jasper wants them to meet us at the Gold Horizon. From there, we take the Plateau transport. Stinnett's waiting. Go." He yanked his arm toward the trail and waited for the lookout to leave his post. Then, he marched back down into shadows.

"The Gold Horizon." The words put a bitter taste in her mouth. Of all the misnamed places in this world, that was the worst. The last hilltop overlooking the wasteland of the Plateau, it was fortified with traps. There was nothing trustworthy about it. It promised only lies and death.

"Impossible." Abiga sank onto the bed of pine needles. "There's no way." Her skills would not be enough to take down twenty-some sentries. And the Undesirables weren't gonna come anywhere close to the Gold Horizon. Everybody would be trapped. All of them.

Another guard crested the top of the trail. His scinter's pink glow lit up the shadows. A lookout. He scanned the woods and listened to every creaking limb and feisty bird. Abiga waited for him to turn toward the falls, before she scooted behind the tree. He flashed his stave three times and then stood at the ready.

More sentries emerged from the curve of the path. Abiga counted them as they passed. Ten guards led the way, and then Roxan came around the bend, followed by Whitlock. More guards trailed them. Altrist wasn't there. Instead, Grouper trudged into view, and then Thim. Abiga shot up. "No," she whispered. How did they get here?

Jasper followed. Altrist plodded along behind him, a black hood over his little head. Five more soldiers brought up the rear. Abiga tracked them from the side, keeping an even pace with Altrist. Five prisoners. Twenty-five sentries. Not good odds. But Grouper's presence leveled out the scale a bit.

A deep red flushed Thim's cheeks. His eyes bore into the guard in front of him. Abiga willed him to look at her, but he kept his focus on the guards. A rescue attempt would be dangerous for him. He had little experience fighting.

Jasper growled and swung toward Altrist. "Stay out of my head. I will not discuss this with you." He poked Altrist in the chest. "I mean it," Jasper raged and held his scinter near Altrist's hood. The entire company stopped. "I have to deliver you. You don't have to be in one piece for me to do that."

The boy didn't respond, and Jasper paced down the line taking his anger out on the entire troop. Abiga let out a quiet birdcall. With Jasper shouting, the lookouts wouldn't notice, but she watched Altrist. His hood tilted, and she whistled again.

"Abiga?" The faint sound came to her on the breeze.

"Here, Altrist, I'm here," she whispered. "What can I do?"

He bowed his head and spoke louder, connecting with her mind. "Sweet Abiga. I knew you would come back. You must go to Willow Way. Tell the others what has happened. Perhaps the Leader will make a way through this for all of us."

"I can't leave you. They're going to kill you and Thim and …" She couldn't say any more.

"If we fight out-numbered, someone will definitely die. We must wait. Don't be deceived. Our Leader goes before us. This is not news to him. He knew. We must trust."

Abiga gripped her walking stick. This kind of following was what had driven her away. Not knowing or understanding why something's happening, but still abiding in some unfounded hope that everything would work out. They needed a plan. They needed more than hope. Jasper spewed out his anger and waved his scinter in their faces, and they just stood there. It wasn't fair.

Altrist stepped forward. "Thim, no," he screamed. Abiga jumped up as Thim smashed his bound hands into Jasper's back, knocking the sentry into the guards in front of him. A light shot from Altrist's palm connecting with the chains of all the other prisoners, except Grouper, who had already broken free.

The unsettling buzz of hot scinters filled the air. Abiga sprinted toward the front of the line. Two guards held Roxan, and three others had pounced on Whitlock. Altrist knocked guards away with streams of light pouring from him. Grouper tossed sentries back as if they were chunks of firewood.

As Abiga disarmed the guards holding Roxan, a scream cut above the chaos. Thim. She knocked the second guard out and turned to see Thim fall. A young sentry stood above him holding his brutal scinter.

"Thim." She ran to his side. Grouper and Altrist stopped their assault. "What have you done?" Abiga screamed at the guard.

The guard lowered his weapon and stepped away, keeping his head down.

Jasper patted him on the back. "What would you expect? We're not nannies taking you to task. He brought this on himself. Back in line, everybody." The injured sentries had already helped one another up and were eyeing Grouper.

"Jasper, you can't do this." Grouper stood next to Altrist. "Thim's your friend. He'll die. Let him go. He has a chance, if you let us take him to Anna."

"Forget it. All of you are going to the Plateau. I'll send guards to collect his body."

Thim groaned. The gash from the scinter crossed his arm and cut into the mid-part of his chest. No blood, but internally, he'd been severed. Abiga checked Altrist and Grouper for hope. "We've got to do something." They shook their heads. Even if they could get him to Anna, his injuries were severe. "Please. Please don't do this," she pleaded with Jasper. "You're one of us, right? You know the Leader. How can you do this?" Anger heated her tears.

"I am not one of you." Jasper leaned forward, his black eyes ignoring Thim. "I was never one of you."

Abiga grabbed his hand and flipped it open, revealing the pale mark from the Leader. "You are his. You've met him." She held up her hand, but the mark on her palm only looked like a smudge. "How can you do this? Please. Please. There's nothing more right in the whole world. You've heard it all. You know him."

"Knowing him and being part of his special little group are two different things. He doesn't want me. And I don't want him. I've found my place." Jasper walked back toward the line. "Altrist, this is your fault. Control them, or they won't make it to the Plateau."

Abiga stroked Thim's face. His red cheeks paled, and he took shallow breaths. Wrapping her arms around him, she shifted him into her lap. His familiar scent drew her in, and she kissed his forehead. A pain shot through her stomach forcing her to let go, and she let out a yelp. The air fled from her lungs, as a fire filled her body.

"Altrist," she whimpered, "what's happening to me?" Every eye was fixed on her. Altrist grinned and cut his eyes toward Grouper.

Grouper had knocked free from the sentries and scooped her and Thim into his arms. "The Leader has great timing," he whispered.

Jasper's livid shriek echoed across the blackness in front of her, and she fell into oblivion.

CHAPTER 30

SEEING

At the top of the mountain, a golden glow silhouetted the trees, causing them to appear black against the blaze from whatever was on the other side. After losing two eager guards at the front of the caravan, sentries were pausing now every few meters to unhinge wires and cover the deep pits along the trail with sturdy limbs. Evidently, walking on the trail to the Gold Horizon was deadlier than wandering off of it. Roxan plopped down and kicked her sandals off. Her throbbing feet won out over the threat of some unseen trap.

"You okay?" Whitlock crouched next to her. He hadn't said anything since they'd be taken. When Thim started the commotion, Whitlock had jumped into the fray, but three guards had tackled him to the ground and hit him with a jolt from that stupid weapon.

Roxan nodded. "I guess I have to be." She closed her eyes. Ever since the fight, the back of her head had been tingling. It lingered there threatening to take over her vision. "This is my fault. I've been so stupid. If I'd followed the rules, never left the boundary, none of this would be happening."

"That's not true. Hyperion was planning the Census. He wasn't going to let you live quietly. And I wasn't going to stay." Whitlock turned her face toward his. "Open your eyes. Don't keep them closed when you need to use them the most."

"Get up," a guard barked. "Get back in line." Whitlock tapped her shoulder then stepped back. The guard nudged her with his hard boot. "You too, freak. Get back in line."

As the path became steeper, a wide staircase took over and led the rest of the way up the incline. Two bowls filled with flames licking at the darkening sky sat perched on steel columns that rose above the crest of the hill. A hot, gaseous stench blew over Roxan as she took the creaky, wooden steps slowly.

The stairs ended at a railed platform. Every guard paused at the zenith and nodded to the two sentries who stood there, then disappeared down the other side.

As Roxan neared the platform, the familiar tingling throbbed its way through her brain. She pressed her fingers up the back of her neck and into her hair. Every step increased the pulse. Tired and weak, she didn't even try to fight it.

The curse took over as she stepped onto the platform and took in the scene below. A black mist fell across the wooden stairs leading down the incline on the other side.

At the end of the oversized steps, a pathway led to the opening of the underground transit tunnel. The pathway bisected an expansive ring of ruby-colored columns, each topped with glowing brass bowls of fire. More fire-topped columns paralleled each side of the path all the way up the steps and to the platform. Between the columns, a sheer, red haze hung like a fence panel. From where Roxan stood, the columns stretched out creating a massive fiery ring about three kilometers in circumference.

Roxan could see the land both beyond and within the hazy, red panels. Inside the ring, brown creatures with some sort of ribbed, black armor covered the ground. Their eyes reflected the glow of the flames, and their faces had a strange human-like quality to them. Shooting rays of blue light out of their scaly front appendages, they aimed at one another, at the sky, and vainly at everything beyond the columns. Whatever the red haze was, it held them back. The buggy creatures never crossed beyond the columns.

"A ruby balustrade," Roxan whispered as she looked out across the plateau.

A guard pressed his unlit scinter into the small of her back. Roxan shook her head, and the tingling faded. The world returned to its weird normal. Filled with sharp silhouettes of dead plants and broken trees, a black marsh replaced the creatures on the inside of the ring of fire-topped columns—now steel, without any red haze. Golden light flickered across the guard in front of her, as an oppressive gust bent the flames in the fire bowls, carrying with it the smell of rotten eggs. Gripping the banister, she shuffled down each wooden step, trying not to breathe and daring not to tempt the tingling to return. The scinter was still at her back.

Sentries lined the pathway, their backs to her, they faced the steel columns and the barren wasteland and swamp. Jasper waited at the entryway to the underground transport. Roxan took sluggish steps and focused on Jasper's feet. She noticed flickers of movement beyond the columns, but she didn't look away from the black boots of her captor.

"You're almost there, freak." Jasper's steel-toes met her bare feet. "I guess you're something special after all," he smirked.

His words, the sound of his voice pricked a memory, and Roxan recognized something in his black eyes. "It was you," she accused. He tilted his head, as if to affirm her. "You were the one that first roll, looking through my window."

"What can I say? They said you were special," he whispered into her face with hot minty breath. "But we both know you're not. You're a freak modification and very effective bait."

His provocation pushed her recollection. The vision from that first roll danced in her mind. The waterfall, the joy, the woman crying, the darkness. He had been one of them. An Outcast. The pictures fit together like a puzzle. He had embraced them. Loved them, but turned on them.

"You had it all," she answered his cruelty.

Jasper stepped back, but Roxan continued, "You met him. The one Altrist talks about and you were happy. The happiest you've ever been in your life. You fell in love." She taunted him with his past. "But it wasn't enough for you. You wanted something else. And when you couldn't get it. You ran away, angry and sulking, like a child. You had something real, and you threw it away because you didn't get exactly what you wanted."

Rage flooded Jasper's being, but Roxan's gift took hold, and she saw exactly what he was going to do. Before he could lay his hand upside her head, she met his forearm with hers, knocking it away. Her defense took him by surprise, and she was practically out of his reach when he grabbed her hair and pulled her back.

"You're going to die," he growled in her ear. "If Hyperion doesn't do it. I'll do it myself. All of them are going to die. And there's nothing you can do to change that." He shoved her through the doorway, and she caught herself from falling down the shaft to the tracks below.

The transport hummed at the ready. Roxan followed the sentry in front of her and sat where he pointed. Despite Jasper's threat, a peace took root inside of her. It was good to see the truth and understand it for a change.

CHAPTER 31

ANOTHER WORLD

Jonas shoved the chair in front of him and paced the room. Nothing. No sentries, no Guardians, nothing. After the attack, a small troop of sentries had loaded him onto the transport and dumped him into this gaudy chamber without a word. So far, the Plateau had been only a series of dark tunnels leading to hallways, leading to this fancy prison cell. The guards wouldn't say anything. They were tracking the others down, and weren't about to give him a report.

Two Plateau sentries had responded when he beat at the door, but only to hit him with a low dose from their flat-edged scinters. They didn't say a word, just glided into the room in their black cover-ups, held him down, and shocked the protests away. Then they were gone.

Jonas plopped onto the red sofa at the far end of the room. A tray of wafers and fresh fruit lay untouched on the marble-topped table. He hadn't even inspected the cooler in the corner. Nothing made sense. The glorious Plateau wasn't the gleaming city of hope from his dreams. And if all of this was for the good of all then they needed to rethink their definition of good. Roxan couldn't have done anything to merit this extreme action. And Whitlock. Why not throw him in a cell or adjust him? And the most baffling part of all was the kid. He was the one they wanted. But why?

The door swung open and a black-draped sentry stomped into the room. All the plateau sentries had black hair and white skin, and their eyes were darker than brown. A familiar grunt catapulted Jonas from his seat.

"Roxan," he gasped as another guard shoved her into the room. Jonas stepped between her and the sentries and led her toward the sofa. "Are you okay? I didn't think I was going to see you again. I guess they found you, eh."

She pulled away from his arm and faced him. "Why are you here?" Her tangled brown hair curved around her set jaw.

His voice cracked as he answered, "I demanded to come." Her eyes questioned him, so he cleared his throat and continued. "I couldn't let you have all the fun. You know how competitive I am." He paused. It might be now or never. "I'm sorry Roxan. I said some horrible things to you, and I'm sorry."

She turned away from him. "You came all this way to tell me you're sorry? That's the least of our worries, isn't it?" The words thudded against his heart.

"Probably. But I wanted to tell you. You deserved better than that. You're not a freak. I was stupid and jealous, and thought I knew exactly how things should be."

"And you don't now?" Her voice softened.

He shook his head. "I don't know anything. I don't understand all of this. I thought I could get here and tell them what I know about Jasper and explain that none of this is your fault, that Whitlock was using you, and that you're innocent, but no one will listen to me."

"Whitlock's our friend."

"How can you say that? He was running away, and he was trying to take you with him. He made this a thousand times worse. I know you think he's wonderful and that maybe some matchment can happen, but if he really cared he wouldn't have gotten you mixed up in all of this."

Roxan stiffened, but didn't argue.

"This isn't our fight. Whatever trouble Hyperion has with the boy and Whitlock. It's not our problem. They should let us go back to the Protectorate and do what we were trained to do. You and me. You're no threat to them. They have to know that."

She moved away and didn't respond. Blood and dirt covered her feet. Her "blue-like-the-sky" cover-up wasn't so blue anymore. A tear made its way through the dirt on her cheek.

"I'm doing it again, aren't I? I'm sorry." Jonas settled onto the couch and pressed his palms to his eyes. Not having a plan to fix all of this tore at his confidence.

Roxan ran her hand along the side table and stopped at the red and black upholstered chair. The furniture was strange. Fancy and different. She sat down and pulled her injured feet onto the velvety material. "It's hard to know who to trust, what to do," she murmured. "I'd like to have your conviction, your clarity. I hate this. I hear you speak, and that makes sense to me, even though I know you're wrong. Still, going back, pretending like none of this happened, that would be nice."

Jonas clasped his hands together and held back the urge to scoop her into his arms and tell her everything would be okay. Instead, he let her talk.

"I wanted to know," she declared. "I wanted to know why I was a freak. Why this was happening to me. Mullin tried to help. Altrist told me something else. And Whitlock warned me that I couldn't stay. And now you. Everybody knows what I should do better than I do. I want to be left alone. But how can we go back?" She met his eyes. "How can I go back after what I've seen? I don't know what to do."

They shared the silence together. Jonas fell into her deep eyes, but said nothing. For now, they had no choices. They would be at the mercy of Hyperion.

The door flew open and Whitlock stumbled in. Roxan ran to his side and steadied him. Several patches of red dotted his arms, neck, and face. Scinter marks. Jonas ran his hand over the one on his arm.

The overseer wrapped his arms around Roxan. "I didn't think they were going to let us see each other. How ya holding up?" He ignored Jonas.

Roxan shrugged. "I've been better. Where'd they take you?"

"They had some questions for me. They want to know about the others."

Jonas couldn't take it anymore. "What others?"

Whitlock let loose of Roxan and charged at Jonas. "Why are you here? You? You had to keep at it. What were you doing? Reading my mail?"

Roxan pulled Whitlock away, and Jonas retreated to the sofa.

"Leave him alone, Whitlock. We're all prisoners here." Roxan challenged her overseer as if he were her equal. "Have you seen Altrist?"

A worried expression crossed his face. "No. They took him."

"Why doesn't he leave? He could get away." Tears filled her eyes.

Whitlock took her hand. "He doesn't leave because of you, Roxan. He won't leave you behind. They need you."

"That doesn't make any sense. He doesn't need me. Maybe he thinks he does, but I don't have anything that's going to help them."

"He cares about you too. He wants you to understand the truth like I do. The Leader loves you. Why can't you see that?" Whitlock's words opened the gates holding back her tears. Jonas wanted to intervene, but stayed put. Roxan did have choices to make. Hard choices.

"I know you've seen him," Whitlock pressed. "Think about it Roxan. Haven't you known he was there all along? Look at how you love the sky, the trees, and the adventure in life. That has been his invitation to you. You just need to believe."

Jonas stood. Whitlock's rant had pushed Roxan into a corner.

"Leave her alone," Jonas warned.

Her little jaw was set again and stained with tears. Whitlock backed away. Jonas gave her space too and kept his questions inside. The world he'd known had just become a lot bigger. It wasn't only villages, rules, and following Hyperion. It wasn't him trying to get ahead and make the most of life. There was something more.

When the door slid open again, Roxan was scrunched up in the chair and Whitlock had made his way to the food. A sentry shoved someone onto the floor and slammed the door shut.

Roxan ran to the injured man. "Mullin, are you okay?"

CHAPTER 32

SILENT ANSWERS

When the world came back into focus, Abiga pushed free from Grouper. He held Thim up with his other arm. Grass surrounded them and a creek fussed off to their right. Huge willow trees towered into the fading pinks of twilight. Their black billows hinted at an evening breeze.

"Where are we?" Abiga turned in a circle. Behind her, rows of taxar bushes lined up walling them in. "That ain't good."

"What the—" Grouper hollered, and Abiga swiveled and pulled out Mel's stick ready to fight. The largest group of Outcasts she'd ever seen stared at her through a widening hole in the landscape in front of her. Two men pulled at the sides as if they were opening the flaps on a tent, and the grass, willows and sky folded back like a canvas being rolled up. Jahn and Anna broke through the group, and Abiga remembered Thim.

"Anna, help him," she cried.

Picking Thim up in his arms, Grouper barreled through the entrance following Anna toward a large white tent. Anna shouted orders to three Pocket Outcasts and then motioned for Grouper to lay Thim inside the tent. The three helpers dashed away and then were back in a flash, each toting something. Grouper emerged as the last one entered the tent.

"Well, it looks like someone got their gift, finally! You transported us!" Grouper scooped Abiga up and swung her around. "And just in time. I guess our Leader knows about timing." Setting her down, he met her concern for Thim with a smile. "He'll be okay, Abiga. Anna's seen worse. And don't think the Leader whisked us away so Thim could die here instead of there."

"Impressive." Jahn wrapped his arms around Abiga. "It's good to have you home." He let her loose and motioned for them to follow. The fellows near the entrance were closing the flaps to their camouflaged area. From the inside, a sheer film separated them from the willows and taxar bushes. "Pretty cool, isn't it?" Jahn gestured toward the barrier. It went over their heads too. "The camouflage was a gift from two of the nomad Outcasts. If you walk into the covering from the outside, you move directly through and pop out over there." He pointed toward the willows. "It's only a shield, though. Sentries could get in if they wanted. But this makes us harder to find."

Grouper bear-hugged Jahn and launched into recounting all that had happened since he and Thim had left. Abiga glanced around. Tents peppered the small clearing between the willow trees on one side, and a dense line of taxar bushes on the other. Two or three small fires burned, with something different cooking on each.

"Is that rabbit I smell?" She licked her lips. "I'm starved."

"Not too upset to eat, eh?" Grouper punched her lightly in the arm and smiled.

"He'll be okay." She reassured herself. "Anna knows her stuff. But I'm not sure about the rest of us. How're we gonna get through there, anyway?" The taxar bushes blocked the way to the Balustrade. "That's a good reason right there for us to put down stakes, let your new friends do their shield thing, and we all stay here."

"Oh, you have to see this." Jahn grabbed her hand and dragged her toward one of the fire pits. Four of the Pocket Outcasts circled the flames, with two rabbits hanging from a spit. Two others sat huddled next to each other. "Abiga, I'd like to introduce you to Jun and Ixon." Jun tossed her brown hair back and smiled, but the man next to her gave a nod and never took his eyes off the fire. Jahn mouthed the words, "They're quiet," and then cleared his throat and motioned toward the bushes. "Would you mind showing her?"

Fair-skinned and beautiful, Jun kissed Ixon on the cheek and glided to her feet. He held her hand until she stepped away then he let her go. Jun floated by them, her tiny, silver-sandaled feet hardly touching the ground.

"She's one of us," Jahn answered Abiga's question before she could ask it. "Jun was born in Pocket. Olivope raised her."

"She looks like a spirit or something," Abiga whispered.

Jun's lavender cover-up had a lacey coverlet over it that billowed as she moved. Her skin didn't glow like Altrist's but she carried the same peaceful, assurance with her. The two fellows from earlier peeled their shroud back, and Jun ducked through it and stopped in front of the taxars. She held her hands up and rubbed them together, slowly at first and then so quickly they became a blur. In one swift motion, she whipped her palms toward the bush, moving her hands apart. As the gap between her hands widened, so did the bushes. Soon, a passageway big enough for Grouper to squeeze through had formed. It stayed there as long as her hands stayed up, but when she lowered them, the bushes fell back into place.

"Whoa," Abiga murmured.

"Yeah, I know. Isn't it cool? The Outcasts at Pocket have many different gifts to share. Altrist was right about us needing one another. Together, we're stronger than when we were apart." Jahn's confidence had returned. "I'm not sure what the point was in us living that far apart. It seems like we should've always been together."

"Maybe, but not when you've got sentries hunting you down, and Hyperion scanning the woods. He's not without his own powers, you know. I wouldn't call them gifts, but warped, mutated powers." Antipathy colored Grouper's words.

Jahn agreed, "Yeah, there was a reason to keep us apart, and there is a reason to bring us together now. The next roll we go through the Balustrade."

"Is that how we're getting through the barrier?" Abiga asked as Jun tossed them a happy nod and returned to her spot next to Ixon. He whispered something to her that made her giggle. "Can she do that to the big wall?"

"No, the wall's impenetrable as far as we know," Jahn answered. "There aren't any gifts here that can help with that. But there's the girl—"He didn't finish.

"I don't understand why Altrist hasn't taken her and gone. He could get away from those sentries any time he wanted. What's he waiting for?"

Abiga searched their faces, but neither had an answer. "This is crazy. She can't decide what she believes. She doesn't even know what she can do. What? Is he going to let them take her all the way to Hyperion? He should leave her there."

Jahn agreed, but Grouper threw out a rebuttal. "He's not going to leave her, like he wouldn't leave Thim and me. And now he's watching over that other sprout too."

"Who?" Jahn's annoyance grew.

"Whitlock," Grouper answered. "He's Anna's son."

"Oh," Jahn conceded. "Well, we have to do something. If they don't show up, we're all trapped. And if they get all the way to Hyperion, Altrist won't stand a chance."

Jahn whistled, motioning to the other Outcasts. "We're going to have to act fast. You said they were going to transport from the Gold Horizon?"

Grouper held up his hand to slow him down. "Hold up there, little buddy. We can't do that."

A circle of ten Outcasts had formed around them. Six were from Pocket, but the other four didn't look familiar. Abiga read their faces. All of them knew how to fight. Some had scars to show it. All of them had that familiar look in their eye. They formed a strong core, and if they had gifts, even better.

"It ain't going to work that way," Grouper protested the posse. "We're going to have to let him handle this on his own. You know Altrist. He's got more gifts than all of us put together. Escaping the sentries will be easy. That's not the problem." Everyone waited for him to explain. "The thing is, Altrist won't leave the girl. He's determined to stay with her until she makes her choice, and as far as I know, she hasn't yet. When she does, he'll get them all out of there. Our going there won't do any good."

"Can't she make her choice out here?" Jahn swatted Grouper's hand down. "This isn't the time to make us feel better. We can't let them take Altrist to Hyperion." Pink blotches on his neck and face punctuated his anger.

"Altrist can handle Hyperion. The Leader will see to that." Grouper's voice wasn't as convincing as his words.

"No, Grouper," Jahn contended. "You're wrong. There's a lot we didn't know, that he didn't tell us." The circle of Outcasts mumbled agreement, and Jahn continued, "Altrist is no match for Hyperion. Only the Leader is going to be able to take him down. If they get Altrist inside the confines of the Plateau, he'll be the one who suffers, and the girl will be lost, no matter what her choice becomes."

"What are you talking about?" Grouper's soothing hand balled into a fist. "Tell us what you know." The circle of Outcasts around them opened up, and they all looked toward a grey tent situated close to an old willow tree. Jahn walked through the circle toward the tent, and Grouper and Abiga followed.

"We found Olivope," Jahn stopped at the front of the tent and faced them. "She's like Altrist. Little, strong, not like us." The torch outside the tent flickered in the breeze. "She had gone out to gather any who might come with us. You know, every once and a while an Undesirable will split off from the group or a new sprout will be dumped some place different." The whole camp quieted as he spoke.

"She found that monster, Hyperion, near the Viand Village, on the far side of where Pocket is. There were three Outcasts with her when they found him. Jun, Ixon, and Chas. Hyperion pretended to be a lost sprout. After a few moments, Olivope knew things weren't as they seemed, but instead of making a run for it, she faced him. She told the others to leave, but they stayed. It was a battle—a horrible, bloody battle."

"Hyperion?" Abiga mumbled. "Why? He's not done that before. He's desperate, isn't he?" No one answered her. "What does he want? Isn't it enough that he holds all of them hostage with his lies? Why does he have to come after us?"

Tears filled Jahn's eyes. "Who knows? Hate? Greed? We stand with his enemy, and he can't take that. What difference does it make? He killed Chas and would've killed Jun and Ixon, if Olivope hadn't been there."

Abiga shook her head and caught Grouper's eye. "It's not right. What did Hyperion want from Olivope?"

"Jun and Ixon haven't said much, and no one's been able to heal her wounds." Jahn pulled back the tent flap. A small figure, ghostly white, covered with a load of blankets stared vacantly through ice-blue eyes. Two female Outcasts sat next to Olivope, guarding her. They scolded Jahn to close the curtain. He let the flap drop.

"She's not dead. Hyperion didn't kill her, but he could have. We've always thought Altrist and Olivope could defend us, but we were wrong. The only one who can destroy Hyperion is the Leader, and he's not here."

"You're wrong." Abiga jammed Mel's stick into the soft grass. "No principal leaves his adversary alive unless he has to. Hyperion's after something, and until he gets it, he's not going to risk killing anybody. I say we form a pack and go get him."

"Abiga," Anna called from Thim's tent. "Abiga, he wants you."

Abiga pushed through the circle and ran to Anna. "Anna, is he okay?"

The older Outcast took Abiga's trembling hands. "Oh dear, Abiga. He's bad. I don't know if he can make the trip."

Grouper came to the tent. "I can carry him. It's no problem."

"Maybe not for you, Grouper. But Thim's very weak. Under any normal circumstance, I'd have him in bed for three rolls, at least. He has internal injuries, and my gift isn't enough."

"But your gift is healing. I thought you could fix him with a touch." Abiga pulled away.

"Well, I've been able to do that in the past, but for tough cases, I've always needed. . ." Her voice trailed off, but Jahn came forward and finished her sentence.

"Liza. The two of you together could do it?"

Anna nodded and looked down. "He wants to see you Abiga."

Abiga shook her head. "No, I won't tell him good bye. I can't." Tears rolled down her cheeks. "It's not fair. Where's Liza? Why hasn't she come back?" She screamed at the Leader. "Why? It doesn't make any sense. It's not fair. I came back. I believed, and now this—"

"Go talk to him," Anna urged. "He needs your strength right now."

Grouper settled her emotions with his gift, and Abiga wiped her tears away. Good men shouldn't die, but they do. Pulling the tent flap back, she left the others and went to Thim.

CHAPTER 33

UNDERSTANDING

Roxan helped Mullin sit up. Dried blood stained the side of his face and turned his sandy hair black. He coughed and braced himself with one arm, holding onto to Roxan with the other.

"Roxan, I didn't know what they'd done to you." He pulled her to him.

"Mullin, are you okay? How did they get you?" His arms held her tightly. "I gave them the scroll, like you told me to." There was a hint of accusation in her words.

"I know. I had no idea this would happen. When they found me on my route, I realized I'd been tricked." He sat back. "Are you okay?"

"I'm fine. I'm not the only one they took, though." She nodded her head toward Whitlock. He hadn't moved. Jonas came to her side.

"I think I can get us out of here." Mullin rose to his feet. "They're not really after us anyway. I told you that boy was trouble. They want his people, but he won't say anything."

"I don't understand." Roxan caught Whitlock's eyes. "Those people aren't bad. They want to live out there. They haven't hurt anyone." Whitlock nodded. He was one of them now. "The only people I've seen causing trouble have been the sentries."

Mullin should understand that. He wanted to change things here, make them better.

"They don't care about anyone," Roxan continued. "And if they're acting on Hyperion's orders then maybe he's forgotten what's for the good of all."

Mullin crossed between her and Whitlock. "That's not true Roxan. Those people living out there. That boy. They're trying to break through the

Balustrade," he paused. "Do you know what that means? It means we're all in danger. It would be one thing if they wanted to live out there and keep to themselves, but they don't. They're after a way to open up the wall. They need to be stopped."

"I don't know," she lied. "I don't know anything about all of that."

"Think Roxan," he pushed. "Maybe the kid said something or that girl, or one of the others. Think. How do they plan to get it open?"

Jonas came to her defense. "She said she didn't know, alright? Leave her alone."

"Stay out of this," Mullin returned. "This has nothing to do with you."

Jonas stepped in front of Roxan. "I know you," he countered. "You're friends with him." He nodded toward the exit. "That sentry, Jasper. You're lying."

Mullin ignored him and pulled Roxan toward the door. "Listen, you might be willing to let them destroy what we have, but I'm not. Tell me what you know, please Roxan."

Before she could answer, Jonas turned Mullin around. "Leave her alone. She doesn't know anything."

Mullin rammed him backwards into the wall. "Listen, you worm," he pressed his forearm into Jonas's throat. "You stay out of this, and you can go back to your little office. This isn't your fight. You know that. She's not worth it. You've got a good situation, don't throw it out." He let go, and Jonas dropped to the floor gasping. "What's it going to be Roxan?" She backed away, but he came at her. "Please tell me you're not siding with these people." He grabbed her wrists and pinned her to the door. "They're using you. They think you can help them, but the Master fixed that. Now you're nothing but a modified freak, so tell me what you know. I'll get you out of here."

"I don't know anything," she cried. A pulse of tingles shot up her neck to the back of her head, and she closed her eyes. Not now.

Mullin leaned close, his mouth next to her ear. "I think you might be telling the truth." He yanked her from the door, wrapped his arm around her neck, and pulled a scinter from beneath his cover-up holding it close to her face. It buzzed in her ear, and the metallic burning gagged her. "What about you, Whitlock? Do you know where they are?"

With Mullin holding her from behind, she opened her eyes. The warmth washed through her brain. It flooded her and spread through the room with brilliance. This modified freak still had her ability. Whitlock glowed, a golden light pulsating from him. It outlined him and filled him up. As he took a step forward, a different kind of radiance washed down from the ceiling, covering him with sparkles of silver and blue.

Jonas clambered to his feet. "Roxan, what's happening?" When his eyes met hers, she could see his fear and affection. She recognized the emotions as if they were a tree or a cloud. He could see her curse. She held up her hand to stop him from saying anything more. A slender cord of blue, green, and yellow floated between them connecting her to him.

Mullin whispered to her from behind, oblivious to the wonder she saw, "You better talk some sense into your friends Roxan or they're not going to make it out of here." The vision faded from her eyes, and she blinked back tears.

Whitlock had changed. He looked the same, but something had happened. "Let her go," he challenged. A new resolve held him in place.

Mullin pulled Roxan's head back exposing her neck to the scinter. "Shall we make a deal, Overseer? I have something you want. And you have something I want. I won't slit her throat as long as you tell me what I need to know. How are they going to get out?"

"You can't fight us both," Jonas warned and moved to Whitlock's side. "Let her go."

"Don't try me." Mullin's jaw flexed. Gasping for air, Roxan ignored her racing heart. He'd been scheming all along. Even that first roll, he knew. He knew what to say, what she needed to hear. It had all been lies. He wasn't trying to help people. He wasn't trying to change things. He was after Altrist and the others; he was after their escape route.

Heat from the scinter glowed hot on her neck. She pulled in a fresh gulp of air, and pushed away the panic. Her purpose wasn't to die here. She felt the shift in the room. Calm washed over her, and she waited.

Whitlock sensed it too. "Mullin, you're going to lose this battle." Assurance carried his words.

"You think? I'm not going to ask again." He pulled at her hair, but before he could slide the scinter through her neck, Whitlock ripped it from his hand and shattered it against the wall. The overseer had carried Roxan to the couch and returned to pin Mullin to the floor faster than a flash. When he let Mullin go, the traitor scrambled toward the door yelling for the sentries. It slid open, and three Plateau sentries rushed into the room.

"No. Leave them." Mullin yelled orders as he limped into the hallway and the sentries retreated. "Notify Hyperion. The overseer has a gift, and the girl knows nothing." The door slid shut.

CHAPTER 34

TRUSTING

"You came back." Thim reached for Abiga's face.

A smile crowded out her worry. "I came back." She swallowed back her tears. "There's no other place for me."

"How?" He wanted more of her transformation.

"I don't know." She scooted closer to his mat. "It came down to me choosing. I was mad and hurt and feeling like nobody could ever love me. I've done terrible things. I have no right to be a part of this group. But no one ever pushed me away. No one ever told me I couldn't be here. He put a mark on my hand, and told me he loved me, and all I did was complain that I wasn't like everyone else."

Dull light glowed in Thim's eyes. His chest moved with shallow breaths. He blinked slowly and waited for her to go on.

"I ran away. And he waited. You waited. No one's ever loved me like this." She turned away and wiped her eyes. "You don't make people be a certain way. You take them as they are. I can do that with all of you. That part wasn't hard. It was believing that you all could take me as I am that I couldn't trust." The lumen dimmed and then came back. "But he knows it all. Altrist knows too. And somehow, it's okay. I'm forgiven."

"Yes." The pain left his face for a moment. "No gift?"

Abiga shook her head. "I got my gift. It came the moment I realized nothing I could do would keep him from loving me, from wanting me to come back. That was all I needed. That was really all I ever needed." She took his hand. "But I'm doubly favored. Despite my whining and complaining, he also gifted me. I can transport."

Surprise spread across Thim's pale face.

"That's how you got here." She squeezed his hand. "The Leader brought you here." A tear escaped down the side of her cheek.

"It will be okay," he whispered. "You came back." He winced. He hurt, and Abiga couldn't help him. Anna couldn't help him, and Liza wasn't here. Abiga fought her anger. The familiarity of not getting what she wanted mocked her, and she rested her head against his heart. It beat faintly, and he stroked her curls.

She met his sweet eyes. "I love you Thim. I've loved you from the first time you came and sat next to me. You know me like no one else ever will. I love you with all my heart. Please don't leave me." She kissed him once and felt a hand on her shoulder.

"He needs to rest," Anna intervened. "Let him sleep." He had already drifted into unconsciousness.

Abiga left without looking back. Grouper met her as she emerged from the tent and engulfed her in his strong arms. No words. Just his gift intermingling peace with her grief. "Some things can't be taken away," he whispered and he let her go. "All feelings serve some purpose."

"Save it," Abiga snapped back. Now wasn't the time for a teachable moment. "Are we going after Altrist?"

Jahn came up from behind her. "He's already to the transport."

"You can't know that for sure," she protested. It felt good to growl at someone. "For all we know another band of Undesirables took a shot at them."

"No, we know," Jahn countered and motioned to two fellows. A short, scrawny guy practically hopped over while his counterpart took two tries to push up from the rock he was sitting on. The skinny one had to have been picked from the Undesirables, somebody's unwanted kid. From his looks, he didn't care much for personal hygiene. And the other guy looked older, but it was hard to tell, since he hadn't stopped gnawing at a rabbit leg since he left his rock.

Those two would never have made it on their own in the woods.

"This is Eldem and Bru." Jahn walked between the two, draping his arms over their shoulders. "Eldem's been with Olivope since she joined the Outcasts—she practically raised him after he and his twin brother were dumped by the Undesirables. And Bru has a very different kind of gift. Bru, well … you better show her, Bru." Jahn stepped back. Raising his chubby arm into the air, Bru spread his greasy fingers apart as light beams shot out of each fingertip. In the light shafts, Abiga could see faces.

"Altrist," she whispered. Altrist's little face lit up one of the light beams. His shaft of light shot up in the air and disappeared in the direction of the Plateau. From Bru's pinky, a light ray snaked its way toward Olivope's tent. Her little face laughed at the pinky tip. "The light points to them?"

"That's the best we can figure." Jahn stepped forward and plucked a fabric map from Bru's pocket. When he unfolded it, two pinpricks of light glowed—one at Willow Way, and one flickered at the Plateau. "He's already there."

Abiga lifted the map. "What's this?" She pointed to additional faint dots of light on the edges of the map.

"We think others like Altrist and Olivope are beyond the Balustrade. If we can get Olivope out of the Oblate, we might be able to find someone who can help her."

"And Altrist?" Abiga questioned what they all knew. "We're just gonna leave him?" They couldn't hold her glare. "How can you even consider that? He wouldn't do that to us. You said it yourself." She jabbed Grouper's arm. "He won't leave the girl. How can we not follow his example, and stay for him."

Jahn met her anger. "I know what you mean. I'm not ready to leave here not knowing where Liza is. I've said that I will leave without her, but the truth is, I'm not sure I can. We're supposed to go where we think he wants us to go and do what we think he wants us to do."

"But sometimes it doesn't seem right," she finished his thought. "How can he ask us to do things that we don't understand? Shouldn't we follow our hearts? Shouldn't we do what we think is right?"

"That's all fine, until someone thinks the right thing is to dictate a world and throw people away like they're trash." Grouper referred to Hyperion. "I know we wouldn't do that. We're different, but so were some of those people. The Leader made it clear that we're to leave."

"Well then maybe he can make it clear exactly how that's the right thing to do when the one person who means something to all of us is going to be slaughtered by that monster. How can that be right?" The entire camp stared at Abiga, even Ixon who'd moved from the fire to the base of a willow tree.

Jun left his side and ambled over. "Don't you think the Leader loves your Altrist?" Her voice had a wispy quality, as if the breeze had formed words. She didn't wait for an answer. "He loves Olivope, and yet she's dying. He brought your Thim here, and yet Anna cannot heal him. Altrist is at the mercy of Hyperion. And the only one who's promised to lead us out of here chooses not to join us. His ways are not our ways." She glanced at Ixon and smiled. "We have our own pains. Our own struggles that teach us and make us into new people. If you trust him, let him work it out. And if he needs you, he will use you. Be certain of these things you hope for and sure of him in whom you trust." She glided back to Ixon's side and pulled his arm around her shoulder.

Abiga waited for everyone to start back to their business then locked eyes with Jahn. "I say we fight."

Jahn chuckled. "You're the fighter, aren't you? We weren't all raised in the wild, dear one. Besides, the battles we need to fight won't be done with our fists. They're against forces that can't be seen so easily. If you engage in some fight that isn't yours to battle, you could lose, and in the process hurt a lot of other people." He motioned toward the others. "The Leader will destroy Hyperion. That's been foretold. And maybe Altrist will survive this. And maybe Liza will be waiting on the other side of the wall. We don't know, do we?"

Abiga pulled her walking stick from the strap on her back. "I'm going for a walk." They were done listening. None of them knew how to fight. But all of them knew how to follow. What if they did get through the

Balustrade? Without Altrist, they'd all flounder. Not even one of them could lead a group like this.

The silver shroud kept her from wandering too far. As she marched around the perimeter, the weight of the roll hit. No food, no sleep. There wasn't much left to fuel her struggle.

Grouper called to her and held up some roasted rabbit. Her stomach growled and she met him half way.

"Thanks."

"Yeah, I could hear your stomach growling from over there."

She gobbled down the entire chunk of meat and drained Grouper's canteen.

"You get enough?" He grinned. Abiga looked into his happy face, but couldn't say anything. The tingling in her stomach sent shockwaves through her body and sucked the air from her lungs. This time, she knew what was happening—a transport—and she braced herself as the darkness swallowed her up.

* * * *

Abiga landed in darkness, on a cold, stone floor. When her eyes adjusted, she realized she was on a balcony overlooking a large room. Muffled voices spiked her defenses and she crawled to the railing and looked below. Two dark figures lit miniature cauldrons along a red carpet that led to a platform on the main floor. This wasn't a village. Wood and metal were the building blocks of the villages. This place was made of marble and gold.

Both men wore black robes and carried weapons at their side. Scooting behind a column on the balcony, she surveyed the room through the railing. Two huge doors, plated with silver towered at one end. A red-carpeted platform graced the other side. Tapestries hung behind the platform, and a throne-like chair and a table sat on it. The men worked their way toward the doors lighting the golden cauldrons with their torches.

A short, stocky man trailed two huge sentries through the doorway. The sentries stepped to the side, letting the man examine the room. "It looks perfect." He clapped his hands and smiled. "The aroma is much better. Our master will be pleased." Abiga took a whiff of the cold air, but only smelled a hint of whatever oil they were burning to light the room.

One of the sentries started toward the doorway, and the little man gave him a schedule of how the roll would go. Just as Abiga found a better spot to watch the action, sentries began pouring in from openings under the balcony. Each strutted to his post around the room.

"When the guests arrive, we will need to help keep them in order." The stocky man commanded the sentries as if he were their overseer. Abiga sized the plump, little guy up. There was no way that out of shape dope had ever served in a legion of sentries. "They'll want to participate, but the master only wants them to observe. They are to be witnesses of his generosity to these traitors. Make sure they do not crowd the prisoners. When you are ready, you may let the observers in. Start with the Guardians first."

Abiga jumped back. Guardians. Her heart pounded in her ears. The Plateau? The Leader had landed her in the heart of the Plateau.

CHAPTER 35

A NEW LIFE

As the door slid open, Jonas's heart broke. A sentry backed away from Roxan, leaving her limp body to swing from the chains cuffed around her wrists. The black-clad sentry put away his fading scinter and joined his counterpart next to Jonas. Their white faces were dead and emotionless. Without a word, they left, and Jonas flew to Roxan's side.

The cuffs unlatched easily, and he scooped her into his arms and carried her to a rug near the table by the wall. Nothing could make this right. She was only a girl, an undisciplined plebe, not a traitor.

He brushed her chestnut hair from her face. The braid was long gone. "Roxan, are you okay? What did they do to you?"

Roxan winced as she sat up. "Whitlock?"

"They took him," Jonas replied. The rest of the answer stuck in his throat. Whitlock wasn't the enemy anymore. He could've escaped, but before the sentries came to take him from the room, they had warned him over an intercom that they wouldn't hesitate to discipline Roxan for his missteps. After that, he went with them without any use of his new gift.

Roxan pressed her hands to her face and cried. Her sobs took him by surprise. He hadn't seen her cry once since all of this had started. Even when he called her a freak, she had held it together.

He pulled her shivering body into his arms. "Don't give up yet, Rox."

"This is my fault." She pushed away. "All of it. None of us would be here if it weren't for me."

"That's not true." He held his hand up waving off her self-deprecation. "You can't take the blame for all of this. Whatever's going on here started long before you and I got here. This isn't even Whitlock's fault, as much as I was determined to think it was."

"You don't understand. It's me."

Jonas scanned the room. The sentries had left, but they were still listening. They wanted this, for her to confide and share what she knows. He wanted it too, something to connect them, but he shushed her, and pointed at his ears and then to the room. She understood.

Silence settled between them, accompanied only by the hum of the lights and the whir of the air filtering in. Jonas weighed his options. There was little they could talk about that wouldn't feed those monsters' curiosity. Every question that came to him had to be something they wanted to know too.

Roxan broke the silence, "I thought you would be thrilled to be here." She had her own picture of him, and it made him sad. "This is the mighty Plateau."

"Yeah, five rolls ago I would've, but things are different now."

"How? How have things changed for you?" The strong cut to her jaw gave away her drive. Even sad and broken, her face quietly revealed the depths inside of her. She would never be a hollow shell laced with shallow compliments and tedious reminders. Norwood crossed his mind.

"Oh, I know how things have changed," she prodded. "You're now destined for that overseer position and a top notch replicating floor that falls at your feet and trembles when you pass by."

All she knew were his orders and arrogance, his cruelty. He searched for the words to explain the change in his heart. He deserved everything she said. He'd not shown her one ounce of who he really was. He had to take a chance. He pulled a paper from his pocket and unfolded it as he watched her eyes. Recognition settled there and a hint of anger.

"I know. I went through your things," he conceded. "But technically this was mine to begin with." He grinned, and her eyes warmed. "I have changed, Roxan. Somewhere between the 'you're-a-freak' speech and watching Whitlock stay when he could run, I changed." His throat tightened. "You changed me."

She bit her lower lip and looked away. "I'm nobody, a freak." Her use of his words reduced him, but he stayed focused on her and caught her brilliant eyes flashing with anger and determination.

"You're not a freak," he paused to let it sink in. "I'm the freak. I'm the one who was jealous and thought all there was to life were promotions and accolades. I stifled and condemned the part of me that wanted to embrace life." He pointed to the picture he'd written with words. "You reminded me of that. You showed me things I was having trouble seeing. You see things no one else sees."

His hand moved to her poem. "Look what you did. You wrote a silly, beautiful poem. And you brought out my words and gave them life, because you could see what I really meant. I didn't even see it. I just put it down. But you saw the hidden meaning and helped me to see it too. You see things." He didn't mention what had happened in the other room and her silver eyes. *They* hadn't found this out yet.

She grunted. "And that's my curse."

"Or a gift."

She folded her arms and jerked her defiant chin a little higher, so he let it go. To keep going might reveal more than the listening ears needed to know.

He turned the conversation, "Who's the boy?" These people knew who he was. Whitlock had somehow joined whatever faction the kid was leading, but no one had explained the importance of the child. "You don't have to tell me. I seem to be the only one around here who doesn't know who this kid is."

Roxan glanced around the room. "He's part of a group, the Outcasts. They live beyond the boundary. They talk about freedom and goodness and love."

"Love?" Jonas was becoming more and more familiar with that concept. "Does the kid lead them?"

"Sort of, I guess. He seems to be the one throwing out the orders, but he says they follow someone called the Leader, but that guy isn't around much."

"So, it's some revolution against Hyperion? What do they plan to do?" Skepticism punctuated his questions. "Fight?"

"No, they're planning to leave." She had regained her strength now and was looking more and more like the hot-blooded plebe he knew.

"Leave?"

"Through the Balustrade. They have a way out."

"How?"

She stopped. "That's what *they* want to know." Her face told him she knew more, but he let it drop.

"That's crazy." He couldn't tell from her face if she agreed with him. "That's suicide."

A buzzer sounded, and the door slid open. A thin man in a red and black checkered cover-up entered the room. Two sentries stood outside the doorway.

"Please rise," the skinny guy commanded, sounding more like a nasally little one than a grown man.

Jonas helped Roxan to her feet.

"Our Overseer Hillton wishes to prep you." He stepped to the wall, and a short, chubby man strutted in.

"Good. You both are fairly ready," he stopped in the middle of the room, the cuffs dangling over his balding head. "The girls will come in and clean you up a bit. They have fresh clothes too, if you wish to change." He scrutinized Roxan. "*You* will need to change. No one sees the master looking like that." His smug grin made him more irritating. "You," he addressed Jonas, "can wait in the anteroom." He pointed to the wall, and a hidden door popped open.

Jonas squeezed Roxan's hand, and he hesitated to leave her.

"You should not look so glum," the horrible little man continued. "Happy faces, people. You are about to meet the Master Hyperion. It is an honor that few live to experience. You *will* show him the reverence he deserves, or you *will* be detained until you do." He spun on the high heel of his shoe and marched out. Four women flooded the room carrying baskets of supplies and water jars. A man followed pulling a tub.

One of the sentries crossed to the anteroom doorway and glared at Jonas.

"It will be okay," Jonas whispered as he left her side. She didn't respond, but when he glanced back, her sweet eyes met his.

CHAPTER 36

BELOVED

Roxan lagged behind the two plebes who led her down the narrow corridor. The tube-like walkway opened up to reveal a tall domed ceiling of golden swirls. Four other walkways emptied into the foyer, and all led to a set of tall, silver doors with gold-plated knobs and golden vines etched around their edges. Jasper waited in front of the doors, sentries on each side of him.

Overseer Hillton's plebes had cleaned her up well. Despite its lack of color, the cover-up they gave her felt clean and soft, and the little cloth slippers matched the silky black clothes perfectly. Black ribbons intertwined with the curls in her hair, and the human decorators had even applied some color to her lips and cheeks and swirls of ebony body art to her neck and arm. All for their master, Hyperion.

Jasper held up his hand and halted the entourage. "Wait here until the guide arrives." He circled the trio inspecting Roxan and flicked one of her curls. "Well, freak. It's time you made some choices." She didn't look at him, but he whispered in her ear, "You really are nothing special, you know. You have one last chance to get this right. Don't be an idiot." He marched back to the doors and nodded to the plebes. A gust of cold air blew by them as they pushed the ornate doors open.

A wide strip of red carpet paved the way from the doorway into a large room. At least a hundred people sat, craning from their chairs, watching the doorway. The two plebes stepped into the room, but stopped, and Roxan didn't budge. So far, the Plateau had been one mystery after another. And the spectacle in front of her didn't offer any answers.

A hand tapped her shoulder, and Jonas stood at her side.

"It'll be okay," he whispered, but she could tell his smile was put on. "It looks like we're part of their festivities."

Her dry mouth made it hard to speak, but she forced her words out. "Or part of the show." She gazed at the grand room. "Can you see it? It's all for show. Just like what we do." He nodded, and she went on. "We take what they say and make it look good, make it look like what the people need, but it's lies."

Jasper cleared his throat and motioned to the sentries, who then gave Jonas and Roxan a shove onto the carpet. Roxan searched the faces. Curious eyes looked back at her. These were the best of the best. Master Hyperion's special servants who kept their world in order.

The sentries paraded Jonas and Roxan to the front of the grand room and an area evidently reserved for them: a square section of black marble flooring bordered with maroon tiles. The stage—emblazoned in black and gold and glowing in the light of two large cauldrons—was directly in front of this uncarpeted area.

As the guards positioned Roxan and Jonas there, another troop of sentries marched down a side aisle, drawing everyone's attention away. When the sentries stepped aside, Whitlock fell to the floor. Roxan gasped and took a step toward him, but a sentry blocked her, and Jonas pulled her back.

Jasper growled at Whitlock, "Get up. You can bow when *he* comes in, but for now, you stand." The overseer pushed himself up and met Jasper's eyes. The spectators gawked and whispered. Some of them knew Jasper's name, and a few even mentioned Whitlock.

The mumbling died down as more sentries entered on the opposite side of the room. A band of five armed men entered first, followed by two lines of four sentries. They carried a clear box with Altrist standing inside. The boy kept his eyes on Roxan. She couldn't return his gaze, though. His innocent eyes triggered her guilt. This was her fault. He stayed for her. He was captured because of her.

A woman ascended the steps to the platform and addressed the assembly. "Ladies and gentlemen, distinguished guests, Guardians of the Most High, thank you for coming to this unusual council. Our master shall explain everything. Now will you please rise and bow for your leader." She paused and lifted her arms, and shouted above their cheers, "Hyperion."

Her voice didn't match her eyes. Not once did she look away from Roxan, a sadness colored her countenance, but her announcement rang like a bell, filled with awe and wonder.

As Hyperion swept onto the stage, the guards forced Roxan to her knees. The onlookers also descended to one knee, even the largest sentry. Hyperion commanded them all, and their cheers quieted into reverent submission. The entire room belonged to him.

"Please everyone, be seated." He smiled as he spoke, but the crowd was slow to move. "Eveleen," he called to the woman who'd made the announcement, and she addressed the throng again.

"Our master wishes for your comfort. Please be seated." She cast another sad look Roxan's way then scurried down the steps and through a door to the side of the platform.

"My friends," Hyperion charmed the crowd, "I've asked you all here because I want you to know what's going on. I am not a despot who wishes to keep you in the dark. I am your friend, who desires that we would live for the good of all."

The spectators cheered back, "We give ourselves."

Hyperion held them captive. Roxan watched his every move. He paced across the platform as if he were gliding, and every word floated to their ears with his energy and charm.

His handsome face clouded with concern. "But there are some, my friends, who do not wish to be tolerant and free like us. They demand to have their own way. They require their own leader be followed." Protests filtered through the room. "They believe theirs to be the only road to happiness. But we know this is not the truth," he continued. "We know that true freedom lies when we tolerate each other's differences, when we do not push our own agenda on those who have a mind of their own, and when we live for the good of all."

The crowd chanted back the mantra again. "We give ourselves." And then broke out in cheers.

"I do not demand your allegiance. I do not ask you to do anything, but what your job would require. You are all free." Applause erupted around the room. "This world I've built has been for you. So you can live and enjoy all that it offers. The Progenate, the Protectorate, the Viand, and the oasis that is the Plantanate."

Whitlock grumbled, and a guard poked him with an unlit scinter. Roxan glanced around the room. No one even questioned what Hyperion said. Why should they? Five rolls ago she would've believed it all too.

Hyperion ignored his captives and kept his fiery eyes on the crowd. "All of these are for you, for your growth, your protection, your needs, and your reward."

He walked to the edge of the platform and pointed toward Altrist. "But there are some who wish to destroy all of that." A mixture of anger and alarm rose from the audience. "This boy is one of them. He wishes to destroy what we have here. He wishes to take it all away and break through the Balustrade." The protests quieted. "Yes, that's right. He wants to open the wall. He has found a way to go through. His leader tells him that there's hope on the other side, but I have seen that world, and it holds nothing but death. If the wall is opened, we will all die."

His words echoed around the quiet room. No one moved. Roxan bowed her head and closed her eyes. A faint tingling began in her neck.

"You okay?" Jonas whispered. She nodded and kept her head down. She'd almost forgotten he was next to her.

Hyperion launched into another speech explaining how it was his duty and honor to protect their world. His words ran together as Roxan concentrated on pushing away the warmth that was spreading through her head to her eyes.

Jonas tapped her arm. "You don't look okay."

"Thanks," she growled. "It's my eyes again. Stupid curse."

"Can't you stop it?"

Before she could answer, Jasper pushed Jonas from the marble square back onto the red carpet. The marble started to shake, and Roxan fell to her knees. The floor beneath her jolted and rose. When the section of floor stopped rising, she stood level with Hyperion.

Reflections of the flames danced in his black eyes. He offered a passing scan of Roxan and returned his attention to the audience. "None of you know what I've done to secure our safety. It's a constant battle against those who only wish to destroy. Why even nature itself sometimes is against us. Allow me to share with you a story."

He stepped onto Roxan's platform and walked around her. She kept her head down, but followed the golden hem of his black robe with her fickle eyes. The spectators sat in rapt silence, breathing his words as if they were air.

"Seventeen turns ago, a child was born. Her genetics had been carefully planned, and by all accounts, she showed great promise. From her earliest turns, she had scored highly and advanced quickly. However, by her sixth turn a modification was discovered." Understanding filtered through the listeners.

Roxan squeezed her eyes shut and swallowed back her urge to cry. This wasn't the time to be a baby. He was about to display her life for them all to see. She gritted her teeth and faced him. Let him reduce her to a story that doesn't end so well. It wouldn't change a thing. Her story was not finished yet.

"This child," he continued, "had a special kind of vision. A true aberration. At first, we thought it might prove useful, helpful even, but no good use for it was found. Nothing good at all. We handled her case differently than others, though, and we operated, offering her a cure to her abnormality. She, of course, was happy to receive the reprieve and has proven to be a strong and effective worker."

Gliding around, he settled in front of Roxan, and kept his eyes on her as he continued. "There's more to this story though. Some people think this girl can change things, that she is the key to their freedom." He pointed at Altrist. "They want to use her. They believe her defect to be some sort of saving gift that would reveal the truths they so blindly believe. However, what they didn't know is that we delivered her from her deviation. We removed it."

He stepped back to his platform. Roxan stole a glance at Altrist. A peaceful smile crossed his lips, and his blue eyes conveyed only concern. He had been nothing but honest, pure, and kind. In his world, people cared for each other, watched out for one another, and told the truth. They loved.

Hyperion raised his voice and grabbed her attention back, "And this girl, my friends, has served her purpose well, and I believe she will rise to the challenge before her, and be our savior from their madness."

The room erupted in cheers, but Roxan could only focus on what he'd said. *She had served her purpose well.* Had she always been a part of some demented plan? Had her whole life only been to serve as bait in some trap to stop the Outcasts and capture Altrist?

A man climbed the steps to the platform and joined Hyperion. Mullin. Clean-shaven and robed in black, gold, and red, he bowed before Hyperion and then turned toward the assembly.

Hyperion snapped his fingers and two of the fire bowls by the platform grew brighter. "My friends, I would like to introduce you to my very special servant. It is because of him we have these prisoners. It is because of him, we have the hope of freedom and victory. This, my friends, is Mullin, the Chief Guardian, second only to me."

A roar pounded the room. Mullin welcomed their applause. Rage, despair, and disbelief filled Roxan and the tingling rallied in the back of her head. Soon it would spread, and they would see how they'd failed at repairing her modification. Then it would all be over. They had used her and manipulated her. They would completely unravel her—and she could do nothing about it.

Hyperion calmed the people's frenzied roar. "There is one last matter we must settle." His charisma turned to domination, and he addressed Roxan, "You, my child, have a choice to make. You have been thrust in the middle of a battle that is not your own, and for that I wish to express regret. However, you may end this now. You can return to your little shanty in the Protectorate and work for your new overseer." He motioned toward Jonas. "And live out your dreams, but first we ask simply for your help once more. Will you stop their madness? Will you stop these people who push their own agenda, and do nothing for the good of all?"

The crowd barely responded, "We give ourselves." Every eye rested on Roxan.

"Roxan, you have the power to save the boy and Whitlock. *You* can do that. They can be spared for their treason," he paused.

Roxan pinched her hands and looked to her friends. Whitlock's head was down. They had dressed him in black too, but had done nothing for his wounds. Altrist glowed still, a calm peace on his little face. No anger, no blame. He looked at her with kindness in his eyes. Jonas stayed near her, different, changed by what he'd seen.

Hyperion softened, "My child, tell us what you know. How do they hope to open the wall? What is their secret weapon that will bring about our destruction? Help us stop them. We urge you." Raising his arms, he led the throng in calls for her acquiescence.

The roar grew. It pounded at her, and with its rhythmic chant, she closed her eyes and looked into her heart. All she had seen, the life she had enjoyed, her pursuit for freedom, all of it had been pointing to one thing. Love. Love kept Altrist from hating her for causing his capture. Love kept Whitlock from forcing her to make a choice she wasn't ready to make. Love changed Jonas. Love knocked at her heart. Love had chosen her to help, not hurt. It had called her to see, not ignore. It waited. The Leader waited.

She whispered her revelation to the deafening crowd, "Love."

Hyperion heard her and demanded quiet. She looked to Altrist with her question settled, "He loves me." Altrist smiled and nodded, and a peace rushed across her blowing away her indecision. She turned and stepped toward the gaping crowd. "No more lies. No more. There is another. He is the way. He does not deceive. He gives life. He loves, and I believe."

The Leader whispered in her ear, "I love you Roxan. I will help you. Open your eyes and see the truth."

She tilted her head back and droplets of water splashed on her face. Joy burst into her and staked its claim. And real love rained down, soaking her through.

"No," Hyperion thundered, and the crowd stirred again.

Warmth surged through Roxan's head forcing her eyes open. The crowd below sat bound together in black chains. Clamps attached them to the shackles, and the sentries each held huge rings that connected the chains. The Plateau sentries weren't men, but beasts, scaly and green with black drool dripping from their mouths, their eyes red with rage.

Hyperion growled behind her. Smoke snaked from his nostrils, and brown scales replaced his olive skin. Red gashes scarred the scales. Sheer now, his black robes revealed two massive legs like a horse's and silver armor that covered his chest. He pounded his claw-like fists against the armor and let out a deafening roar.

Roxan jumped back and fell from the platform. Everything went black. Arms plucked her from the darkness, and Whitlock whispered in her ear. "I've got you." He held her close to his chest, and she felt his heart pounding. "Now, I think we should probably be leaving." But before he could move, a jolt shot through him and into Roxan.

He grunted and dropped to his knees, keeping her close. Jasper waved his scinter toward Roxan. "Maybe I'll hit her full force next time." Whitlock flexed, but a line of sentries had already surrounded them. "You want to try it, overseer?" Jasper taunted. "There's no way out from here. You can't run fast enough to get through walls," he jeered. "And, I dare say, you don't move at the speed of light. But you give it a try, and I will kill you both."

The sentries moved closer, and Jasper motioned for Whitlock and Roxan to stand.

"Master," Jasper addressed Hyperion, "where would you like the traitors?"

A small sentry stepped forward from the line and removed her hood. "Why don't I take them? I can move pretty fast." Abiga grinned and wrapped her arms around them sending a rush of heat down Roxan's back. As the warmth spread into her legs and arms, colors danced on a blanket of light. But a scream invaded the swarming array, and Roxan felt Abiga move away. The colors gave way to darkness, and cool air killed the warmth, just as Roxan hit the floor.

CHAPTER 37

LOVE HURTS

Pain tore up Abiga's arm, as she rolled over.

Whitlock pushed her leg off his chest and sat up. "What happened?"

Rows of corn reached toward the blue sky. Abiga crawled onto the dirt path between the stalks and sat up. "I rescued you." She spat corn silks out of her mouth. "Where's Roxan?" Corn rustled several rows over, and a man groaned. Abiga jumped up. "Oh, no."

"What?" Whitlock made it to his feet.

"Jasper." She pointed toward a moving body on the ground several rows over. Whitlock came to her side. "Jasper came, not Roxan," she whispered.

The corn stalks swayed again, and Abiga tore between the rows and pounced on Jasper's back, kicking his scinter out of reach. She shoved his face into the dirt, and pulled his right arm behind him, calling him a few angry names.

Whitlock grabbed the scinter and lit it up. "Where are we?" Confusion still clouded his judgment.

"Where do you think? I'll give you three guesses, and this ain't the Plantanate." Abiga growled, grabbing her captive's curly brown locks.

Whitlock turned around. "The Viand? Why'd you bring us to the Viand?"

She gritted her teeth. Another slow sprout to babysit. "I don't exactly have a lot of control over it yet." Jasper grumbled, and she pushed his face into the dirt. "What should we do with him?"

"Get off me, trash," Jasper growled.

Abiga settled her knee against his neck. "No way, fiend. You're not going anywhere." Despite their predicament, it felt good to knock the miserable sentry off his post.

"Where's Roxan?" Whitlock was still figuring out the scene.

"To be so fast, your brain's about five clicks behind," she replied. "Roxan's still at the Plateau. This moron must have knocked her away and taken her place when I transported us."

"You left her with *him*?" Whitlock complained. "We have to go back."

"I don't think that's going to happen." Her knee slipped off Jasper's squirming shoulder, and he flipped over knocking her off balance.

She scrambled backwards, but he pounced and punched her in the gut. As he cocked back for another punch, she kicked and started crawling, trying to get to her feet, but he grabbed her and dragged her back.

"Where ya goin', trash?" Kicking her over, he stomped his boot into her wrist and pinned her to the ground. "Time for you to get what you deserve." Abiga punched at his foot, but it wouldn't budge. He pulled a blade from his belt and leaned toward her, but before he could find his mark, his body shook and he dropped to his knees. Abiga swiped the knife and pushed away as he fell face down in the cornrow.

Whitlock stepped over him and waved the scinter close to his head. "Doesn't feel so great, does it?" Jasper moaned and rolled over.

"Turn it up and hit him again." Abiga tossed the knife into the field. "I don't think he understands his predicament yet."

"Do you understand our predicament?" Whitlock turned on her. "We have to go back for Roxan."

"Listen, you don't get it. I can't choose where I go. If the Leader wants us to go back for her, then he'll send us, otherwise my instructions are to meet the others." The fact that she was simply letting things fall into the Leader's hands didn't escape her. One roll ago she would've been complaining about the situation too, but now she knew to carry on, to do what she could and leave the rest. It wasn't her problem. If the Leader wanted Roxan out, he'd get her out. If he wanted Thim to make it another roll, then he would live. Some things you don't get to know ahead of time. It's walking and trusting, with a healthy dose of hope.

Still fighting off the scinter effects, Jasper got to his feet. "Yeah, you keep waiting on that Leader of yours to come and help." He sucked in some air and glared at Whitlock who waved the glowing stick at him. "Just keep waiting, and let's see how that works out for ya."

"You know Jasper, our dear Leader guides us with power and truth and love," she replied. "Not evil, lies and borrowed time."

"Love," he smirked. "That's special."

"Yeah, I thought you'd say that." She circled him and met his cold eyes. "Love is misunderstood I think. It's not some gooey emotion and a bunch of silly sentiments. Sometimes—" She pulled her arm back and threw her body into a punch that landed upside his jaw. Jasper fell back unconscious. "Sometimes love hurts."

"What are you doing? Are you crazy?" Whitlock lowered the scinter.

"Are you? That guy's nothing but trouble. He deserved it." She rubbed her hand. "Besides, you're the one who shocked him with a scinter. Don't judge me. Now help me tie him up."

She pulled the top layer of her black cover-up off, used it to wipe the grime from her face, and then tore the soft fabric into strips. Whitlock helped her tie Jasper's wrists and ankles. The irony of sweet justice made her smile. A sentry being bound with a Plateau cover-up.

"How'd you get this?" Whitlock tossed the unused pieces of cloth next to Jasper.

"Let's just say there's one mousey Plateau plebe wearing a dirty blue cover-up."

Whitlock shook his head.

"What?" She responded. "At least I put my old one on her. That wasn't easy either. She was out cold." Abiga walked down the row and jumped three times. "All I can see is corn. Which way to the boundary?"

"I don't know. I've been in the Protectorate or underground for the last twenty turns." He nodded toward Jasper. "I bet he'd know the way out of here."

Abiga rolled her eyes. Jasper wasn't going to help them get anywhere. Even if he were conscious, he wouldn't help them. "We've got to get to Willow Way."

"Why? Whose instructions are you following anyway? Do they know that Altrist and Roxan are still trapped by Hyperion?" he challenged. "Because I think if they knew they'd want us to go back for them."

She ignored his questions. "Let's go south. Willow Way is south of Viand…somewhere."

"Your friends at Willow Way aren't going anywhere without Roxan. We have to go back."

Abiga shook her head. He wasn't going to take orders from her. Just like a sprout. He had no idea where he was or what he was up against out here, but he still thought he was the one in charge. Tall and lanky, he was one of the few men who stood a good head over her. But he wouldn't have much of a chance on his own out here. He might be able to move fast, but that wouldn't be enough to keep him alive.

"Who gave you your instructions?" Whitlock demanded.

"Altrist." Her answer softened his expression, so she offered more. "He spoke to me at the Plateau. It wasn't easy letting him know I was there. Though I think he sensed something. When that monster took off on his tirade explaining Roxan's life story, I made my way through the crowd until the kid noticed me. After that, it was all orders and urgency in my head. He said to get you both out of there and meet the others at Willow Way."

Whitlock eyed Jasper. A red patch had formed on the sentry's jaw, and he was still out.

"You're not considering staying here, are you?" Abiga challenged. "He's not going to help you. The only way he'll take you back to the Plateau is in chains. Besides, my orders aren't just for me. They go for you too, you know. You're one of us now. You can't run off doing whatever you think is best."

He took several flashes before he spoke. "You know your definition of love needs some serious work." He nudged Jasper with his foot.

Relief flooded through Abiga. If he'd wanted to stay, she would've left him, but it wouldn't have been easy. She took his changing the subject as a good sign and followed his lead. "Oh, I know all about love, don't you worry about me."

He shot her a wide-eyed, disagreeing look, but she smiled it off. The joy of being loved and wanted by the Outcasts and the Leader hadn't faded any since she'd left Melkin in the forest. It was part of her blood now. It coursed through her, adding fullness to life and thankfulness to hardship. The farther along she went, the deeper it took root.

"You, however," she kidded, "may need some remedial help and a special course in not freaking out."

"I'm not freaking out."

She didn't bother replying, better to not bring up his wanting to go straight back into the heart of evil. "If we're lucky, I'll figure out where we are before we go too far, and we can make it to Willow Way before the sun lets up."

"What about him?"

"Let's leave the moron here. He can find his own way out."

"Yeah, you have *love* down, just perfectly."

"What? You think we should treat him like an equal. He doesn't deserve that."

"Yeah, well, let's hope none of us get what we deserve."

Abiga bit her lip. Stupid sprout. Now wasn't the time for a lecture on her moral depravity. And Jasper wasn't the right person to be on the receiving end of any kindness. He had caused nothing but trouble.

As they came out of the rows of corn, Abiga headed for the road that ran alongside the ridge above the fields. It wound its way up a hill, and hopefully to a better vantage point. Whitlock jogged patiently by her side. He could've beaten her to the top, but he took his time.

More fields spread out toward the east, but the tree line on the west looked promising. "We should go that way." She pointed toward the trees.

"How you figure that?" Whitlock surveyed the whole area, even the cornfields. He really was clueless out here.

"Well, there's not going to be a boundary line that way." The fields stretched into the horizon. "At least not a close one. I say we take a gamble and head for the trees."

Whitlock looked around as if he were calculating something in his head. "You're the boss," he finally replied.

"Yes, I am," she said, poking her index finger at his chest.

CHAPTER 38

A LITTLE BIT FARTHER

Jonas knelt by an unconscious Roxan. She had fallen when Hyperion shot a stream of fire at Abiga. It had happened fast. Dressed in a black robe with a hood, the wild girl had stepped from the crowd and wrapped her arms around Roxan and Whitlock. Lunging into the trio, Jasper had knocked Roxan away as a bright light engulfed them, and Hyperion's spray of fire whooshed through empty space hitting the front row of the audience. Then Jasper, Whitlock, and Abiga were gone.

Hyperion paced the platform in a frenzied rage. Scanning the room, Jonas looked for the closest exit. Spectators in the front were patting fires out from the seats and on one another's clothing. No one seemed to understand what had happened. How could they? Three people had completely disappeared. Roxan had turned on them with her glowing eyes talking about love, and their great master had shot fire from his fingertips.

Growls came from the front again, and Hyperion turned on Mullin, "How did she hide this from you? Look at her. She hasn't been modified. How is it that you didn't know that? I thought she confided in you?" He stormed at the deliveryman and picked him up by his neck. "Who did this? Who disobeyed me? Was it you?"

Mullin attempted to shake his head, but his face was turning red, and holding back Hyperion's grip was about all he could manage.

"It's been her all along, you fool," Hyperion ranted. "She's the one. That's why he's here." He pointed toward Altrist. "That's why he didn't leave her." Mullin squirmed against the monster's other hand. "She is the key to open the door. Go." He tossed Mullin onto the red carpet. "Go to them. You know what to do."

Mullin scrambled to his feet, whistled, and led a group of sentries through a doorway under the balcony. Jonas tried to get Roxan up, but she wouldn't come to. Despite the frenzy around her, a look of contentment and peace rested on her unconscious face.

A red glow formed between Hyperion's hands as if he meant to throw more fire at someone. Jonas dropped to his knees and covered Roxan's still body. She moaned, but didn't move. Fireballs whooshed from the platform as Hyperion brought his arms down.

People screamed and ran, as the fire rained down on them like heated hailstones. Jonas scooped up Roxan and huddled behind one of the golden cauldrons until the spray died away. Injured people staggered around, as they cried and smacked at the flames on their burning clothes.

Hyperion turned his fury on Altrist. "You miserable slave. You are nothing. You're nothing to him. He uses you like he uses everyone else. I could give you real power." Crazed, Hyperion fumed like a rabid animal. The veins in his forehead bulged. Even his hair spiked up in anger. "But you come in here holding your piety up like a shield. Do you realize who I am?"

Altrist pressed his hand to the front wall of his clear prison, but didn't respond.

Roxan groaned, "He loves me," and rested her head against Jonas's chest. "Wake up Roxan," Jonas blew in her face. "C'mon. I need you to wake up."

Her eyes fluttered open, normal again, no glowing weirdness.

"Jonas?"

Before Jonas could respond, Hyperion screamed—a guttural howl that chilled to the bone. "You. You dare not answer me? This is my kingdom. You will bow to me, or I will end you." He jumped from the platform to Altrist's box. "I drained Olivope. I will take from you as well." With a flick of his wrist, the walls to the box fell away and Hyperion lifted Altrist into the air and flung him toward the balcony.

Roxan screamed as Altrist crashed into the railing and fell to the floor.

Controlling the room, Hyperion waited for the boy to get to his feet before he hit him again, pounding orange glowing orbs of power into the kid's chest. "How does it feel, little Altrist? How does it feel to know that the very thing you've been trying to shield and protect is now in my hands?" He leered at Roxan. "She will never show them. But she will help me," he crowed. "She will take me right to where I want to go, and you won't be able to stop any of it." He pranced back to his platform, as Altrist crawled toward Roxan.

Jonas held her back from running to the kid. "No, you can't. You can't help him."

"Please," she pleaded.

But Jonas blocked her. Instinct drove him, and the kid met him there. "Keep her away. Keep her safe." Jonas shook the voice from his head, but understood and gripped her tighter.

Hyperion bounded through the air and landed between Jonas and Altrist. An evil laugh accompanied the ball of energy forming between his hands. "No, my little friend. You have not even begun to feel my fury yet."

"Nor you mine," Altrist returned with force. Something had changed with him. A shield of light flew up in front of him and he rose off the floor. His bright body hovered over the beast. "I'll destroy you, Tatief. You take things that don't belong to you. I won't let it happen. You will let the girl go."

Hyperion made for the balcony, but Altrist waved his hand and the great leader thudded onto the platform, his arrogance replaced by fear. He shielded himself with a wall of fire. "You are out of bounds. There are rules," he shook. "You cross this line, you can't go back. You will belong to me."

"Never," Altrist raged. "I'll never be yours. You have no dominion over me." Altrist took slow, deliberate steps through the air toward the platform. "You have no idea what I can do." He blew a gust of air, and Hyperion's wall disintegrated.

"What are you doing, boy?"

"I'm doing what should have been done long ago." The glow around Altrist grew brighter.

"You are violating his rules, *his* order." Panic replaced Hyperion's confidence.

"Am I?" Filled with fury, Altrist kept his blue eyes fixed on the monster. "Tatief, you will die. Justice will have its way with you." He lifted his hands above his head. Pulsating, an orb of white light expanded between his palms like a ball being inflated.

Hyperion stumbled backwards. "And you, Altrist. You're the one to administer this justice? You're going too far."

"Not yet."

"You do this, then you will take my place. Is that what you want? To be *his* enemy?"

"Never. It will end now."

"It's not yours to end," the monster quivered. "Justice will have its way with you, as well. And the girl still will be lost. All of them will be. Their great ambassador will have betrayed their confidence and stolen an honor that was not his to take." He barely spoke the words aloud.

Altrist shook his head and lowered his hands. His rage evaporated and he dropped to the carpet.

A roaring wind blew around the room, and all but one of the flaming bowls went dark. Crumpled on the floor, Altrist barely glowed, and Hyperion got to his feet.

"You're more like me than you thought, aren't you?" The monster smirked. "Don't look so sad, Altrist. We can't all be so merciful and right and pathetic all the time. You've shown great promise with your power. You should be proud. We are brothers now."

Altrist met Hyperion's dark eyes. "I'll never be like you," he whispered.

Roxan broke free of Jonas's arms and ran toward the boy, but he stopped her. An invisible force from his hand kept her from getting to him. He didn't speak aloud, but Roxan responded.

"No, I can't. I need you. They need you," she begged. "Don't do this. I don't know what to do."

The boy yelled into Jonas's mind. "Get her out of here. Go now. Get her to the girl." Jonas turned, and a woman with long black hair touched his arm. It was Liza—the girl he'd seen with Jasper in the Protectorate. Without hesitation, he wrenched Roxan away and joined hands with the mysterious girl.

Hyperion roared, but the sound faded into a whoosh of static as light flooded the room, and the world fell away.

* * * * * *

Searing pain burned up Jonas's leg, and the sky and trees spun around until he found the perfect face of a beautiful, angelic woman. She smiled and held her hands above her head. The lavender sleeves of her cover-up blew in the late-roll breeze.

As she stood next to his head, she hummed, grinned, and kept her arms in the air. Jonas tried to speak, but the pain burned through to his lungs. A black haze framed the woman's creamy, perfect face and inched its way inward.

"Tell Anna to hurry. He doesn't have much time." Her plump, cherry lips opened to let her breathy sweetness form words.

Strong hands pulled Jonas backwards across the grass, and the lady brought her arms to her sides. Every breath increased his agony. Hyperion, the boy, the Plateau. Nothing made sense—and where was Roxan? The darkness swallowed a field and trees and a group of strangers.

"Oh, look at the poor thing," an older woman murmured as she came close.

"I know. Isn't it terrible?" Liza spoke, her voice recognizable and happy despite what she said. She lifted his head into her lap. "I never know where I'll end up. I feel terrible." She leaned above his face. He felt her breathing. "Oh, I'm so sorry, dear." She nodded toward an older woman, "This is Anna, and we're going to fix you right up. Hang in there."

"Liza, here put your hands here," Anna ordered. Warmth surged through Jonas's chest as she touched him, flowing into his arms and legs, and to his eyes. Now, only his legs throbbed with sharp pricks of pain.

The blackness receded, and the world came back into focus. The angelic lady with the cherry lips had vanished, replaced by these two mouthy worker bees—Liza and Anna. They touched Jonas's legs with their hot hands, and within two flashes, the pain withdrew. Another three flashes and it entirely vanished.

"Feeling better?" Anna asked. "You should be back to normal in a bit. It might take some time for you to walk on it, though."

Jonas pushed himself up. His right leg was completely numb and the left one tingled, but it didn't bother him. Everything was brighter than before. Joy buoyed his heart, and he took it all in. Willow trees swayed with the breeze dancing to freedom. Then he looked at his legs. His pants were torn in shreds and covered in blood, and his shoes were missing from his feet.

"What happened?" he asked.

Liza lifted a cup to his lips. "I'm afraid this was my fault, sort of. I really haven't figured out how to control any of this." She blew some unruly strands of hair away from her eyes. The silky black tresses contrasted with her white skin. More like a doll than a young woman, she did everything with a smile. "But I guess on the bright side, you're out of that horrible place." Her little lips framed her perfect teeth. Everything she said had a happy lilt to it.

"Liza, Anna, if he's better, we need you to see to Thim," a man called from behind them.

Liza smiled and gave Jonas a strong hug, then ran toward a tent.

"Welcome, Jonas." Anna took his hand. "It's so good to have you here. You know my son, don't you? Roxan said you worked together." Her smile brought out her turns. "It's all a wonderful miracle. The first of many." She winked then followed Liza's tracks.

"Roxan," Jonas whispered. Getting to his feet proved to be too much for him, and the angel from earlier floated to his side and braced him up.

"Careful," she whispered. "That taxar bush you landed in nearly killed you. You may be healed, but there are still consequences to be had."

A large fellow wedged his way between them and helped Jonas to the base of a willow tree where several men were talking. Then, without a word, the man whisked the angel into his arms and carried her back toward the brush.

"Where's Roxan?" Jonas broke into the conversation. "Do you know? I have to get to her."

"She's in the main tent with Grouper and Jahn," a young boy responded. "They're preparing to go through the Balustrade.

The wall. Jonas leaned against the tree. At least fifty people milled about between the taxar bushes and the willow trees. Most of them carried their packs with them or had their belongings close by. These were Abiga's people. The ones who followed Hyperion's enemy. They were leaving.

"You're a sprout," the boy interrupted Jonas's thoughts. "Me too. I'm Huzzah. They call me Huzz." He held his hand out and nodded at the other guys who had taken their conversation closer to the bushes.

"A sprout?"

The kid had a firm handshake and made good eye contact. "That's what they call us, people from the villages." Huzz picked at a broken willow twig. "You look like somebody pretty important." He eyed the black cover-up from the Plateau.

Jonas shook his head. "No, I'm not one of them." That part was clear. The desire to be noticed and recommended by the Plateau vanished when he saw Roxan hanging from those cuffs. "I used to work in the Protectorate."

"I was supposed to go there. Work for some guy called," he paused. "Workman or something."

"Wortman?"

"Yeah, maybe." Tripping over a root, Huzz plopped down next to Jonas.

"How'd you end up out here?"

"When I got to fifteen turns and was about to be advanced, I got sick. They said it was something wrong with my blood. I thought I was going to the doctors at the Plateau . . ." he shook his head. "But I guess they figured I wasn't worth fixing or whatever. The sentries dumped me beyond the boundary, wished me luck, and left me to die. Olivope found me and took me to Anna. She fixed me up, and here I am."

The kid flicked a spindly branch and leaned back against the tree. Dread, hurt and anger collided inside of Jonas. The world got worse and worse. Everything he'd known had been a lie.

"For the good of all," he muttered.

"Yeah, I know." Huzz understood. "I was pretty angry at first, but how could I stay mad knowing that if they hadn't done what they did, I'd have never ended up out here. I would have gone to work for that guy and lived out one of their lives, for the good of all, never knowing what I was missing."

Jonas surveyed the camp again. The group of men who'd been near the tree were gathering supplies and strapping them on. As the angelic woman from earlier and the man who'd carried her away approached the bushes, a hush fell across the camp.

"I guess it's about time." Huzz scrambled to his feet and dusted off his brown pants.

"Time?" Jonas asked.

"It's time to head to the Balustrade," he scowled. "I'm not so crazy about the idea myself. I liked it here. But the Leader said to go, so we go."

"The Leader?" Jonas looked around. No one appeared to be giving any orders.

Huzz offered his hand and pulled Jonas to his feet. "You won't see him here." He lifted Jonas's arm around his neck and helped him balance.

Feeling had returned to the left leg, but the right one was mostly useless. "The Leader isn't here. Some think maybe he's beyond the wall. But we don't really know. He comes and goes as he pleases."

"So you've never even seen him?"

"Nope. I've not seen him, but I do think I've met him."

"How's that?" Jonas hobbled forward. The boy's shorter frame served well as a crutch.

"I see him in these people. The way they care for each other. It's different." He adjusted his grasp on Jonas and lowered his voice. "And they have these gifts too. Like Jun and Ixon over there." He pointed toward the angelic woman in lavender and the big guy who'd sat him by the tree. "Watch 'em. They're going to make an opening in the taxar brush by lifting their hands in the air."

A flash later, a passageway had formed through the prickly plants, and Jun and Ixon were smiling at one another with their arms lifted high. People lined up to go through the opening. About ten men went first, and next the women and children started through.

"I guess you should go with this group." Huzz nodded toward Jonas's leg. "Not to make you out to be a girl or anything, but they're trying to keep everybody safe." He started toward the brush, but Jonas didn't budge.

"You are coming, aren't you?" Huzz handed him a stick to help him balance. When Jonas looked back toward the main tent, Huzz caught his worry. "She's coming. She's the knob to open the doorway. If she doesn't go, none of us do."

Rays of sunlight streamed through the willows and fell across the emptying camp. Silent and motionless, the main tent offered no sign of Roxan. Holding his ground, Jonas weighed his options. As of yet, he'd broken no guideline. He could return, have Whitlock's position, and live out the life he'd been planning. But could he? Could he live out that life and ignore all that he's seen?

"C'mon," Huzz urged. "You need to make up your mind."

The last of the women and children had slipped into the passageway through the thorny bush. Jonas glanced at the main tent and then swiveled toward the taxars, "I'll go a little farther," he decided.

CHAPTER 39

A NEW KIND OF SEEING

Reddish bruises marked her wrists. Roxan couldn't stop fiddling with her hands. To stay mentally engaged with Grouper's coaxing was too much. He hadn't stopped telling her how important she was to them since the tent flap closed.

Immediately after she'd fallen to the grass, he had scooped her up. It was as if he was expecting her. He didn't even tell her where she was or what had happened. And he wouldn't listen when she told him they needed to go back for Altrist.

"They're almost through," the other guy, Jahn, poked his head into the tent and pushed more. "You got this?" He looked at Grouper.

The big guy shrugged.

"What's the problem?" Jahn stepped into the white fabric room, a hint of anger in his eyes.

"She wants to go back for Altrist," Grouper answered.

Jahn pulled Roxan to her feet. "Altrist wants *you* to take us through the wall," he said. "I don't understand what the problem is. There are seventy-two people out there depending on you. Can you get outside of your little world for a flash and help us?" Grouper lifted his hand, but Jahn waved him off. "No, Grouper. She needs to hear this. He put himself in danger, so she could be here. She's not going to waste that."

They hovered over her and waited. Roxan kept seeing Altrist lying on the carpet, telling her to stop. He wouldn't let her get near him. As he spoke into her mind, she'd felt the world fall away. He ordered her to leave, to go help the Outcasts get through the Balustrade. He told *her* to lead them.

"This is crazy," she mumbled. "I'm nobody. I can't do this."

"The Leader chose you," Grouper returned. "He gave *you* the gift. He could've given it to any one of us, but he picked you."

"I'm only seventeen," she countered. "All I ever wanted was to see the sky and be free. I didn't ask for any of this." She gained her footing. "And look what I've done. Altrist fell because of me. I don't even know what I'm seeing half the time. How am I supposed to lead anybody?"

"Altrist knew what he was doing," Jahn joined in. "He's responsible for his own actions, as you will be."

"I want to help him." She clenched her fists. "We can't leave him there alone. We have to go back."

Grouper pulled her out of the tent. The last of the Outcasts were filing through a corridor in the bushes. "There isn't a single person here who wouldn't want to help Altrist, but we can't stay. The Leader will take care of him. You'll have to trust that." He made her face him. "We need you. You can see the doorway. You can lead us out. And don't worry about whether or not they'll listen to you. I'll make sure they listen."

She shook her head and choked on her fears. "I don't think I can do this."

"Well, you definitely can't do it if you're standing here waffling back and forth, waiting for a surge of confidence or courage. Sometimes you have to walk into it," Grouper rumbled. "The courage comes, the way grows clearer. You do have the gift, right? You can see things."

She nodded her head and her curtain of hair fell across the right side of her face. There would be no hiding behind it anymore. Decisions needed to be made.

Grouper continued, "It's your choice, but to not use your gift, to not help all of these people because you don't *feel* like you can do it or because you're scared you might mess up, isn't good enough. What kind of person do you want to be Roxan? Do you wanna just get by, sit to the side, and hide behind your hair?" He tucked her hair behind her ear and smiled. "Or do you want to take a chance and see what might happen?"

Jahn stepped to her side. "You can do this." Determination glowed from him. "We need to get through the Balustrade with some light left in the sky. We don't know what's on the other side, but whatever it is, we don't want to face it in the dark."

Roxan watched as the final Outcast entered the opening, and the woman in lavender stepped in after him. The bushes fell in about a meter. A large man, with arms the size of logs, looked their way. His tree-trunk appendages were lifted in the air, and he nodded toward the brush.

Without a word, Roxan followed the others with Grouper and Jahn close behind.

"Don't touch the bush," Jahn warned. "We don't need to be slowed down any more than we already have.

As she came out the other side of the thicket, warmth spread through her head and lit up her eyes. The Balustrade was less than ten meters away. The mirrored panels between the tall white columns reflected the group.

People stood back from the huge wall. The barrier seemed taller than when she'd seen it on her first visit beyond the boundary. As Roxan looked into the faces of the Outcasts, they began to radiate. They were beautiful. Glistening like diamonds, rubies, and sapphires, they sparkled, uniquely exquisite. A few of them didn't glow, but were still cloaked in light.

The glow from the Outcasts flickered as they talked to one another. They were scared of the wall, and so was she. Nothing from the scene in front of her explained how they would escape. Fear raged through her and made her body shake. Seeing a bunch of pretty lights wasn't going to help anyone.

As the Outcasts noticed Roxan, their objections died away, and they waited. The silence urged her to address them, but no words came to mind. No words that would help them, anyway. The only thing she could think of was how stupid and weak, and useless she was.

She looked at Grouper and Jahn. Grouper glistened like a diamond with prisms of light glinting from the facets that formed his body. He pointed toward their obstacle. Ribbons of color ran through Jahn and moved constantly as if dancing to some rhythm in his soul. Both men stepped to her side and waited.

Her gift took full possession of her sight, and she examined the wall. It no longer reflected anything. Constant movement covered it like bees on a hive. Instead of the mirrored Balustrade, the black panels crawled with thousands of creatures. They bit and tore at one another. And fell over each another as they stretched to inflict their venom on the Outcasts. They couldn't get free of the wall though—they were trapped within its panels.

They were the same insect-like fiends Roxan had seen at the Gold Horizon. They shot little puffs of blue energy from their claws, but the wisps dissipated before hitting anyone. Some of them zapped each other. The blue tufts seared and opened gashes oozing with sticky red sludge.

Moving constantly, they roamed the panels trying to break free. White columns, about ten meters tall, separated each panel and were linked at the top by a glowing rail that shot blue light into the sky.

Roxan scanned the wall. Three panels down, one of the columns was clear. She walked toward it, and the crowd of glowing people followed her in silence. Through the transparent column, a beautiful countryside spread out. A red sun, inching toward the horizon, poured its warm light across a field, a forest, and a river. This was it, right in plain view. This single column was the doorway.

The scaly little beasts flocked to the edge of the panels adjacent to the doorway. They jumped and contorted, and an Outcast to Roxan's side covered her ears and dropped to the ground.

"You hear them?" Roxan addressed the girl.

She nodded her pink glowing head. "Make it stop," she pleaded.

"I can't, but it will be okay. They can't hurt you." Roxan stepped toward the opening. The creatures cowered backward the closer she got. They turned away as if they were embarrassed by their hideous appearance.

Roxan pounded her fist on the clear column of the Balustrade—transparent and hard, it was freezing cold. This was the way, but that was all she could see. Getting it open wasn't something she could do.

An emerald handle ran along the bottom of the doorway. Roxan pulled at it, but it wouldn't budge either. It glistened and twinkled like the lights coming from the Outcasts. A deep green ray stretched out from the handle toward a huddle of people in the back.

Roxan followed the green light through the crowd. The colorful people separated like a rainbow breaking apart. Growing brighter, the handle's pulsing beam nearly hurt her eyes. It engulfed a man sitting next to Liza, the girl who'd helped them escape the Plateau. The light linked him to the door handle.

Roxan shut her eyes and pushed the tingling away. As the world returned to normal, their escape fell into place in her mind. And she felt a confidence surge through her that made her feet sure and her voice strong. It's a different kind of seeing to *understand* what you've seen.

"That man can open the door." She pointed toward the sickly fellow on the ground.

"Thim?" Jahn asked. "I thought *you* were going to lead us through the Balustrade." Whispers spread through the crowd with a growing unrest.

"I can take you to the doorway, but he will have to open it." She turned back toward the column. It was white again and the panels were mirrored.

Next to Thim, other groups of injured people rested. Three women crowded around a child on a stretcher. Then a familiar cover-up top caught her eye, and Jonas met her with a smile. He couldn't stand on his own. Blood stained his pants. Her heart cheered at the sight of his warm eyes.

"How can he open something, he can't even see?" Jahn called her back. Thim had gotten to his feet and was walking toward the wall. Jahn followed. "Ya see anything, man?"

"I see the same thing you see," Thim replied and turned to Roxan for answers.

Disquiet snaked through the group. Closing her eyes, Roxan inhaled and focused on her gift. If she could push it away at times, then she could bring it back too. The warmth and tingling flooded across her with exuberance, and it all came back to her.

The girl who'd been covering her ears stepped next to Grouper and shoved a boy toward Roxan. "He can you help you," she said. The boy had a frown on his pearl-like face. "He can help you show everybody what you see. Do it." She gave him a gentle push. He jerked his shoulder from her and then moped past Grouper.

As he laced his fingers with Roxan's, his eyes lit up, and he shouted a little whoop. The girl grabbed his hand and Grouper's, then motioned for all of them to join hands. One by one each of their eyes were opened. Somehow, the boy connected them all, and Roxan's gift flowed through him. They could all see through her eyes.

Within a flash, Thim let go and rushed to the clear column. The green of the handle exploded into lines of brilliant color as he pulled the door open. A gust of fresh, sweet air blew across them. It was as if all the air of the Protectorate had been tainted and sick, an imitation of goodness. Out there, beyond the wall, nothing dampened the breeze. Crisp, it blew in the scent of a new life.

The Outcasts stood in awe, staring at the new world beyond the Balustrade. No one moved.

"You must go through the doorway now," Roxan ordered. They flashed their twinkling faces at her, and she pointed toward the sky behind them. A dark cloud approached from the North. "Hyperion is coming."

CHAPTER 40

A SPECIAL KIND OF LOVE

Abiga sliced the last taxar limb away as the sky turned black.

"We can't make it," Whitlock said what she didn't want to hear.

As they edged their way past the last thorny clump, a crack of thunder pounded the sky. Thirty meters off, Thim, supported by Anna, stood in the Balustrade, his arm holding the column open as the last of the Outcasts went through. Beyond him, a countryside opened up. Freedom. Love and freedom stood right next to each other.

Hyperion's fury descended from the sky behind them. As he landed, he comprehended the scene and flew toward the doorway, but Thim let his arms down and the doorway fell shut. The monster hurled Thim onto the grass, unconscious. Anna ran to him, and Hyperion screamed and clawed at the wall.

Abiga didn't need to say anything. Whitlock took off and grabbed Thim and Anna, zipping back before the sentries caught up with their master. The guards ran-hopped down the wall, a line of ten at a time. Their ridiculous formation would've made Abiga laugh, if so much danger didn't surround it. As they approached Hyperion, he erupted into a mad frenzy and picked up sentry after sentry tossing them toward the wall. They screamed in agony as they hit. Their bodies ripped apart.

Whitlock hauled Thim over his shoulder back through the bushes while Abiga led them. He took turns carrying Thim and Anna, doubling back to help the one left behind catch up. By the time they made it to the river, Abiga's lungs burned. Thim had regained consciousness, but he needed help walking.

Anna patted his back. "You've had quite the roll." Thim collapsed next to the water, and she ran her hands along his back, helping him with her gift.

"Whitlock, are you sure you can carry him the rest of the way?" Abiga called.

Whitlock nodded and stepped forward. He hadn't fully recovered from the beating he took at the Plateau. Two of the cuts on his chest had begun to bleed through his cover-up. But Abiga didn't argue. They needed his speed.

Anna left Thim and attended her son's wounds. Within a flash, she'd stopped the bleeding, but she was weak and tired too. "I'm afraid my gift is only as strong as I am." Whitlock watched her with admiration and love in his eyes.

"We need to keep moving. Our best bet is to get to Snowshoe," Abiga ordered.

Thim rolled over and rejoined them. "There's no way we can make it to Snowshoe before the roll turns dark," he warned. "I think we should find a good spot to hide." Whitlock and Anna looked to Abiga, but she turned away and faced the busy water.

Evening pinks decorated the sky. Driving the tip of her walking stick into the soft ground, Abiga weighed their options. Thim was right. Even alone, she couldn't make it to Snowshoe before the next roll. It would be impossible for all four of them to even make it half way.

"I could take you," Whitlock suggested.

Abiga shrugged off his offer. "You can't carry all three of us."

"But I can do one at a time."

"You're not in the best shape, you know." Abiga met Whitlock's determined eyes. During their run to the wall from the Viand, he hadn't had a problem keeping up his speed, but carrying someone else twenty-five kilometers was asking for trouble. Abiga knew he'd do what she told him. Despite his position in the village, he let her lead him out here.

Thim watched her for an answer too. He'd already offered his advice. Abiga stared at Melvin's carvings on the walking stick and tried to think like her old survivor self. In the pack, it would have been everybody fending for himself. With the Outcasts, it was always staying together and watching out for one another. Neither option gave them all very good odds.

"What if you can't make it?" She met Whitlock's determination with the question that needed to be answered.

"I'll make it. Twice." He glanced down at Anna. He meant to carry her to Snowshoe too.

"Well, I guess that's our best bet. And who knows, maybe my stupid gift will click in and we can beat you there."

Anna chimed in, "Well, he should take you first. I'll stay back and take care of Thim."

Shaking her head, Abiga shoved Anna into Whitlock. "No, take Anna. She can show you the way, and I'll stay with Thim." Anna started to protest, but Abiga explained. "That way Thim's never alone, I'll stay with him now, and you'll be at Snowshoe when Whitlock delivers him. He's gonna need a nurse after riding on this guy's back."

"Hey," Whitlock protested and grinned. "I'm smooth."

"You're a sprout who has a tendency to stumble over every little stick on the trail," Abiga retorted.

He knew it was true. "Sounds about right, I guess." He held his hand out and his mother slipped her healing fingers into his. "Shall we go, Mum?" Pulling her close, he swept her off her feet and zipped away.

"I hope Anna doesn't get her directions mixed up." Abiga settled next to Thim. "You comfortable?"

He nodded. Something was on his mind. He kept looking away and flexing his jaw. Stubble covered his handsome, tan face. They hadn't talked since she'd seen him at Willow Way near death. A lot had happened since then.

Abiga waited. If he wanted to talk he'd come around soon enough, and she felt complete sitting by his side. He had been a step away from making it through the Balustrade. His sacrifice ensured the Outcast's safety, but also locked the four of them inside with Hyperion. Having Thim close made everything bearable, though.

He reached over and took her hand. His rough fingers caressed her palm. The mark was gone. She didn't need it anymore. "So you got a gift," he started.

She laughed. "Some gift. I can't seem to use it when I need it or else we'd be out of here already." She swiped a happy curl from her eyes, undid the tie in her hair, and let the rest of the curls take over. "I don't get it."

"What?"

"I don't get the gift thing. What's the point if we can't use it when we need to?"

"It got you away from the sentries. It got you out of the Plateau. That's pretty useful."

"I guess," she agreed. "But I can't make it work now."

"Well, maybe right now," he whispered and put his arm around her, "is a gift all in itself. A gift that gives us some time alone."

She smiled, and his face lightened. Resting her hand on his knee, she leaned into his side and let him hold her. He was alive, and they were together.

"I was really worried about you." She looked up into his clear, brown eyes. He nodded his head. "I couldn't have made it without you," she whispered.

He held her close, but stayed silent.

Abiga chewed her lower lip. Maybe this wasn't the time for him to ask for a matchment or for them to even think about that, but she longed for some affirmation of his feelings. Maybe, after everything, he'd changed his mind.

"I don't know what I would've done." The words caught in his throat. "I was standing there, and I wasn't sure."

Abiga pulled away so she could see his face better.

"I wasn't sure if I could do it." He took her hands in his.

"Do what?"

"Leave without you." He swallowed and shook his head. "Even knowing it's what the Leader wanted, I hesitated. How could I leave you behind? I hesitated, and I'm here."

She smiled and touched his cheek. "I can never be sad that you're with me."

He leaned forward and kissed her for the very first time. Abiga melted inside and became a pool of curly goo in his arms. When he pulled back, a huge smile fixed his serious face.

"Wow," he beamed.

She settled back next to him. "Well, I totally didn't see that coming."

"Yeah, I figured I needed to get one in before you took off again."

She pulled his arm around her. "I'm not going anywhere without you."

"That sounds about right."

The river sparkled by in front of them and the messed up world paused to let their love make its official entrance. Abiga let the sweetness of the moment dull her senses. It wouldn't be bad to take a flash in the middle of their flight to revel in the precious gift of love, but the absence of Altrist kept the wonder of the moment from taking full hold.

"I'm worried about him." She brought it up. Despite their joy, there was one huge gap in their world. Thim hadn't mentioned him, nor had Anna. They had to be wondering though. If Altrist wasn't here, if he didn't go through the wall, something terrible must have happened.

"Me too," Thim mumbled.

"I guess there's nothing we can do to help him."

"Just send a message to the Leader and wait. If Hyperion still has him, we can get him back."

Abiga nodded. Thim wasn't one to fight, but he wouldn't shy away from it, if it were needed. She liked that about him, how he would do the right thing even if it weren't something he liked. Squeezing his hand, she let the quiet settle between them and tried not worry about where Whitlock might be.

The pinks in the sky gave way to dusky grays by the time Whitlock's heavy steps crunched off the trail behind them. They heard him coming long before he made it into view. Abiga picked him out through the trees before he even realized how close he was. He might be super-fast, but he was also super noisy. It was a good thing all the sentries were occupied at the wall.

"There you are," Whitlock sputtered. "I kind of got lost on my way back."

Abiga gave Thim's knee a squeeze then got to her feet. "You know that doesn't really surprise me," she chided.

"Looks like you two are getting along well." Whitlock grinned.

"I take it you found Snowshoe okay." Abiga steered things to a more appropriate place. Whitlock really hadn't earned enough friend points to be commenting on anyone's love life.

Whitlock helped Thim to his feet. "Yeah, and you'll never guess who was there."

"Who?" Abiga and Thim chimed together.

"Altrist."

CHAPTER 41

THE NEW GUIDE

The Outcasts ignored the paradise they'd crossed into and watched the last of the men tote supplies through the open door in the Balustrade. They were a knot of little ones corralled by some unseen, scary nanny, waiting for directions to proceed.

Jonas paused to take in the great Balustrade from the outside. What had been a wall of mirrors connected by white columns was now a solid, clear barrier with pearly columns. One doorway in the single column appeared to be the only exit, and the Outcast, Thim, the only one who could keep it from closing. Everything on this side of the wall sparkled. The greens were greener, the sky more blue. It almost distracted Jonas from his most recent concern. He was sure he'd seen Hyperion's second-in-command come through the doorway.

Mullin had cut in front of Huzz and helped an older lady cross over. They chatted for a flash, and then he disappeared into the crowd. Even though he wasn't wearing black or even his normal green, it had to be him. Jonas limped around the huddled Outcasts and searched their faces—but not one of them looked like Mullin.

At the Plateau, Hyperion had sent Mullin out to do something. Was it to come here, infiltrate the Outcasts and destroy from within? With the different groups of Outcasts uniting, an imposter could easily blend in and not be recognized.

A collective gasp from the group drowned out the gentle breeze, as a skinny man pushed a loaded cart into the open field. Thim and Anna were all that remained inside the wall. Within a flash, the sky beyond the wall went from fading blue to a hazy darkness, and Hyperion fell from the black clouds. Dark green scales covered his face and arms. Silver armor covered his chest, and his legs were like an animal's. When he landed, Thim let the doorway fall shut. The monster threw Thim to the ground, then turned and ranted along the wall, pawing at it and howling.

Roxan tore away from the two men she'd been standing with and ran to the passageway screaming, "No, no."

Tossing sentries at the wall, Hyperion raged on, untouched by the men's screams of agony as the hideous creatures gobbled at them. Thim and Anna disappeared, but the monster didn't seem to notice. He slowed his tantrum and faced Roxan.

"Release me," he growled.

Roxan wiped her eyes. Tiny and frail opposite Hyperion's hideous frame, she stood straight and unflinching.

Limping closer, Jonas stopped next to the men—Grouper and Jahn—who'd been talking with Roxan. They kept their distance from the wall, letting her confront their enemy alone.

"Let me go, and I will free the boy." Hyperion's silky voice had a smile in it, though his black lips stayed straight. Smoke followed the words from his fanged mouth. His face was a mixture of man, beast, and reptile.

Roxan challenged him on sure feet. "I will never show you the way out. The door's already changed," she responded to his pawing at the balustrade. "When it shuts, it moves." Her words provoked him and he threw fireballs at the wall, but she didn't back down. "You will never go free. He will destroy you." She drew her prediction out. And a few brave souls behind her applauded.

Hyperion reared his head and shook the ground with his roar.

As the earth quaked beneath him, Jonas steadied himself with his walking stick and looked at the barrier with new understanding. It had never been to protect the people from a world of destruction. It was *Hyperion's* prison. It restrained him, and he hated it. The Census of Souls had been his effort to find the person who could help him escape. He never meant to stop people from leaving, but to leave himself. He wanted out into this paradise. He wanted to be free.

"I will kill the boy." The venom from Hyperion's words hit its mark on Roxan. She took a step back, but he kept on. "And it will be your fault. You brought him to me." His snout turned up into a twisted smile. "You did this."

"Please, let him go. He's the only thing good in your world," she pleaded.

"Good?" he questioned. "You say he's good, but he violated one of his own laws. He will have to pay for that."

Roxan dropped to her knees, as the beast patrolled the wall. His sentry lackeys were keeping their distance. Jonas limped three steps toward her when Grouper stopped him.

"Let her be," he grumbled.

Jahn came up on the other side. "You can't help her right now. Leave her alone." Tears filled his eyes too.

Jonas shook his head. They might be able to stand by and let her face that monster alone, but he wouldn't. Before Jonas could respond, Hyperion stopped his pacing tirade and looked past them. His red-black eyes fixed on the tree line and a smile curved on his lips. Turning just in time, Jonas saw him—Mullin, dressed like an Outcast, but holding a scinter. He looked back at the wall, nodded to his master, and then disappeared into the forest.

"Mullin's here," Jonas sputtered.

Grouper jerked him back. "What did you say?"

"He came through the wall with the group," Jonas replied. "I thought I'd seen him. He's Hyperion's—"

"We know who he is," Jahn growled. "Where? Where is he?"

"He went into the forest over there. He has a scinter." Jonas pointed, trying to discern what facts needed to be told first. "He was right here with us the whole time."

"Jahn," Grouper addressed his friend. "We can't let him find them."

"Who?" Jonas leaned in. Wasn't everybody here?

Jahn ignored his question. "Well, we can't go after him, not yet anyway. Besides Mullin doesn't have the gifts we do. With Bru and Elder, we should have the edge."

Grouper agreed.

Jonas leaned into their conversation. "I want to help." He was part of these people now, and he would do all that he could to stop Hyperion, the monster who'd used Roxan so thoroughly.

"You can help," Jahn took the lead. "You're a guide? Right? You know how to get people to do something, don't you?"

Jonas nodded. All he'd ever done was get people to do what he wanted.

"Then get them organized." Jahn nodded toward the jumble of Outcasts watching the wall and milling about the field. "As soon as she's ready," he pointed toward Roxan, "we'll go. If they're grouped, it will be easier to tell if anything's amiss. Don't tell them about Mullin, but make sure they know to watch out for their own and alert us to any stragglers."

Jonas grabbed hold of the order. This was what he could do. This was familiar. In a place where everything had shifted, this one thing felt right to him.

He glanced at Roxan. She had gotten to her feet and was looking through the wall. Tears streamed down her face. The sight of her grabbed his heart. He moved toward her, but Jahn held him back.

"Let her alone. You have a job to do, and so does she. Go," he said.

Grouper stepped toward the group. "I'll make sure they know you have the authority to do this. And you can take it from there." He waited for Jonas to follow him.

Still clumped together, the Outcasts had the same sad faces Grouper and Jahn had worn earlier. Some of the women were crying, and the men stood back resting on the supply boxes and waiting. Several young ones had made their way to the river and were tossing rocks and sticks into the busy water. Jonas followed Grouper to the middle of the group.

"Listen up," Grouper called. He didn't need to yell. His voice carried fine. "I want you to listen to—" He turned to Jonas and whispered, though everybody could still hear him. "What's your name again?"

"Jonas." Jonas smiled and nodded toward the kind faces.

"I want you to listen to Jonas, here," he continued. "He's going to help get us ready to move on."

"Move on where?" one of the younger guys with Huzz questioned and looked around. "Where are we going to go from here? Out there?" He pointed to the thick trees. "Through that?" His other hand motioned toward the river.

Grouper lifted his arms, and the restlessness faded away. "We take this a step at a time. When we tell you the next step, you need to be ready to move. Jonas is going to help us with that. Listen to him."

Everyone aimed their growing worry at Jonas, and a sense of responsibility surged up within him. Never before had he led people with any thought to *their* needs. His agenda had been all that mattered. But these people, these strangers and rebels, needed him. It was up to him to look out for them, to act in their best interest, and to pull them together. He met their anxious eyes and stepped up to be their guide.

CHAPTER 42

GIFTED AND LOVED AND LEADING

A sparkling ball of white light buzzed behind Hyperion's head like a hummingbird, flitting back and forth—Altrist? Roxan watched it dart back to the tree line and then up to the wall. Finally, it hovered on the other side of the panel. "Roxan, my dear friend," Altrist chimed into her mind. "You did it. You got them out. How can I ever thank you?"

All she could do was shake her head; no words would come. She was the reason Altrist wasn't free. Because of her, he was trapped inside the Balustrade. He could've gotten away, but he stayed to help her.

"Look at them." The light flitted down the wall and darted back. "They're waiting for you."

She trembled and forced the words past her constricted throat. "I'm sorry. I'm so sorry." Altrist wouldn't blame her, but that didn't mean she wasn't to blame.

"Let it go Roxan," he addressed her pain. "This isn't your fault. I made my own choices. I stepped across a line I wasn't supposed to cross, and that is not your fault." He paused. She could almost hear him breathing. "I will face my consequences. I know that I am loved. Nothing changes that. Nothing changes who he is." The fondness in his tone pointed her toward their Leader. "I might not have been so faithful to his orders, but he is faithful to me, and will not leave me to that beast."

The light danced over Hyperion's head. The monster had called his Guardians and soldiers to him, and they were taking down every order. None of them had noticed the sphere.

"Things are about to change here, but we are not alone, and neither are you. You must go, Roxan. Take them. Show them the way. Lead them."

She held her hand up to the wall and touched the smooth surface. "I can't do this. They need you, not me," she whispered.

Altrist smiled. She could hear it in the way his breathing changed and his words tilted upward. "No, Roxan. I was never meant to lead them on this journey. It's always been you."

"I'm nothing. I can't lead them." She took her hand away from the panel.

"You must. They need you." The light flickered. "Just start the journey; you will find your way as you go. You're not alone in this. The Leader will help you. Trust. You need to trust." His voice weakened. "I must rest now. Anna is by my side, and Thim, Abiga, and Whitlock are coming. We'll do our part here. You must go for now. I will see you again. Peace, my friend." Before she could respond, the light grew small and zipped away.

Hyperion withdrew to his troops, looking more like a man again, though some of the scales remained from his ears down the sides of his neck. Roxan took one last look at her homeland through the wall. The trees were sticks, charred and black. Over the top of the Balustrade, where the sky grew pink from the sunset, a blue shroud of energy reached out from the rail that capped the wall. Her world had been—and was—a prison for a terrible beast.

Turning, she faced the Outcasts. They stood in groups of eight, waiting. Grouper and Jahn were where she'd left them. Grouper nodded to her, his kind encouragement. Jahn kept his serious face on.

Jonas hobbled in the back of the crowd guiding some stragglers to another pod of misfits. Joy flooded her heart at the sight of him. One old friend, if she could call him that. He'd come through the Balustrade, and never hesitated to leave it all behind.

Streaks of red stretched across the sky ending the light roll. It would be dark soon and there wouldn't be enough staves to guide them through the woods.

As if he were reading her mind, an older man stepped away from his group. A breeze whipped up the few strands of hair on top of his head. He smiled, then held up his hands. Beams shot from his palms up into the sky. Roxan grinned and nodded. The gifts. They all had some way they could help. Together they could make it, maybe.

The Outcasts stared at her, still waiting. Some in the back whispered, but mostly they stood there wide-eyed and expectant. Roxan glanced at Grouper, but he had the same hopeful expression. He wasn't looking to be their overseer. He expected that of her.

A crack came from the wall, and Roxan turned. A group of sentries rammed the closed passageway with a log. Panic took root in her stomach. Altrist's words were crazy. "Lead them. It's always been you." How could he think that a girl could show them the way?

Keeping her back to the Outcasts, she glanced at her sore feet and twisted her hands in front of her. "I'm weak. I'm nothing," she whispered. Was it fear or reality countering Altrist's push for her to lead these people? They'd made it through the Balustrade, but now what? Not even one of them knew what was supposed to happen next, especially not her.

A warm gust blew her hair away from her face. She stared at the wall. There was no going back and no clue about how to go forward. Is this really how their Leader wanted it? Some inexperienced girl leading his chosen few? His words came to her. "I will help you." Relief and panic collided, and she retreated into her feelings.

"That's great, but I don't want to do this," she muttered. "Let someone else lead them. Why don't you come here and do it?" Following someone who hardly showed his face was almost as crazy as thinking your world's a paradise when it's actually a prison.

The words echoed back again, "I will help you." The Leader had his reasons for keeping his distance. But even that wasn't true. He wasn't distant. He was equipping the Outcasts and giving them legs to stand on, letting them know true freedom—the mixture of total dependence and well-found independence.

Calm untied the knot in her stomach, and she drew in a deep breath of free air. It would be one step at a time, and if she failed, the Leader would be there. And it wasn't only her. They were in this together. Behind her, the Outcasts waited.

Jonas watched Roxan with the same expectant expression as the others, although his had that sweet little twitch to it. She searched each face. They wanted her to tell them what to do. Her dream to live a normal life, unnoticed, and breathing Protectorate air under a blue sky melted away. Need and commission replaced it.

"Okay, we'll do it your way. I'll do what you want, and we shall see," she whispered to their invisible Leader and stepped forward. "This freaky girl will be their guide." Jasper had gotten it wrong that first roll. She was someone special, and she was loved. Taking a long blink to settle her heart, she opened her eyes to the familiar tingling of her blessed gift. More welcome now than ever before.

The Outcasts lit up the meadow with a bejeweled glow. Peace took over the last visages of panic inside of her, and Roxan scanned the free world. Where the trees and bushes lined either side of the field, shadows hovered, dark patches lurking and snaking their way through the forest. Glints of red flickered between the trees, and a chill shivered down her spine.

The river flowed brilliantly behind the Outcasts, sparkles of rainbow color bounced on its ripples. A silver path wound its way from the Balustrade, through the water and up on to the bank on the other side. In the distance, a strobe of light shot up into the sky. Roxan rejoiced in the scene. All along, her gift had been showing her things. She hadn't understood what she was seeing. Now it was clear. A path unfolded in front of her. A path. A road map for them to follow.

"We go that way," she pointed toward the water. The groups parted and she led them to the river. "We will go through here." Before the murmuring took over, she found Jun and Ixon in the crowd, "You two, come. You can clear the way for us."

Jun glided forward and bowed her head before meeting Roxan's glowing eyes. "I don't think we can do that. It's never worked on water." Her wispy voice wasn't defiant, just frank.

"And you've tried your gift with water?" Roxan asked.

"No, not exactly," Jun responded. "We've never really had a need for that."

"Well, we have a need now." Roxan stepped aside. "Please, we need to move out of here before the darkness settles."

Jun lifted her arms and the river frothed, but nothing more. Ixon came to her side, grinned down at Roxan, and thrust his arms into the air. Like a gale had hit it, the water blew back, creating a clear path through.

"Please everyone," Roxan addressed the crowd. "We must go now." Without much hesitation, the different groups stepped forward and made their way into the muddy river bottom. Roxan waited for them all to get through.

Grouper, Jahn, and Jonas came alongside her. "You seem more certain of yourself," Grouper pressed his hand to the small of her back. "And you're not in any need of encouragement, I see."

"Well, don't go too far away," she grinned. "This 'leaning into things' isn't for the faint."

Jahn didn't look her in the eye. "This is the way?" He couldn't hide his fears.

Roxan met him there. Her eyes had faded back to their normal brown. "Yes, Jahn. I'm sure. We go through the water, yet again. And we will find a whole new life waiting for us on the other side."

Liza broke away from one of the small groups and joined them, lacing her fingers with Jahn's. She looked back at the Balustrade with concern in her dark eyes.

Jahn followed her gaze to Hyperion, still visible through the wall. "And him?"

"He stays here," Roxan eyed their Leader's adversary. He'd given up on escaping, and was shouting orders to his devoted troops. "That is his judgment for now." No one would be getting out of there without someone to see the door.

"What about the kid?" Jonas said what was on all of their minds. "And the others? What's going to happen to them?"

Roxan yearned to see their faces again, but moved on to logic. "Altrist will be okay. He has a job to do there, with Anna, Thim, Abiga, and Whitlock." Saying Whitlock's name made it final. Would she see him—or the others— again? "And I suppose we have a job to do out here."

Jahn nodded. "We do." He reviewed their very rough plan to help Olivope, but Roxan stopped listening and let the moment slow down. She held it like a photograph to go on a page in the scrapbook of her tingling mind. This was it. They were casting off a lie that had held them captive, and would follow the way of the truth that had set them free. There was no turning back now.

She skirted the others and stepped into the mud. "I suppose dear Ixon can't hold back the waters forever. Shall we go into the great unknown?"

Grouper nodded his head and led the way past her, and the others followed. If they weren't sure, they didn't show it. Not even Jonas.

Roxan glanced back at the closed Balustrade, and then turned to follow Grouper. Threads of light streamed down from above, causing the Outcasts to look up and point to the array. There between them danced a gossamer haze of sapphire, amber, and emerald. Reaching out, Roxan touched each color and then held her palm up as the gauzy lights came together to rest in her hand. Grouper's hand came under hers, and the colors danced in his eyes. One by one, they each settled a hand under Roxan's until they were all united in the vision of light.

Roxan trembled. This was beyond all of them. "You can see the ribbons of light?"

"Yeah," Jonas said touching the amber strand with his other hand. "How are you doing that?"

"The Leader's wonders seem to have no end," Liza chimed, before Roxan could say that it wasn't her doing it.

Grouper pushed up on Roxan's hand making the colors ripple. "To freedom," he hollered.

And in a burst from the bottom, Jahn shoved their hands into the air and cheered, "To our Leader, the hope for us all." The gossamer ribbons exploded into the air and a warm breeze blew the lights into the darkening sky.

Acknowledgments

Writing this novel was a journey for me. It began in 2007 when someone showed me unconditional love, and it travelled on from there exploring new places and meeting new faces. This entire book would have been cast aside except for the encouragement of Michelle Medlock Adams who sought me out at the Blue Ridge Mountains Christian Writers' conference to tell me she thought I had something with my little Balustrade book and that I should keep writing. Vonda Skelton, another teacher at the conference, helped me realize how writing in third person omniscient might not be the way to go, and that starting with a flashback and mostly back story really didn't help the reader connect with dear Roxan. The next year at the BRMCWC, I entered my little novel in a contest with Sonfire Media and won second place. Sam Bartlett, Larry Van Hoose, and Vie Herlocker remembered me a year later and called me up to offer me the opportunity of a lifetime. Their encouragement and expertise has made the journey a wonderful expedition led by experts who know the terrain and what it takes to get to the other side.

I didn't go through all of this alone. I've had wonderful, loving friends who have encouraged me, pushed me, and believed in me even when I figured the best I could do was write in my journal. Thank you, Karen, for your love and confidence. Thank you, Whitney Cole, for calling me unexpectedly and telling me not to give up. That was perfect timing. Thank you, Amy, for meeting me for coffee and listening to me dream, and for all the strength you've shown in how to live a life. Thank you, Alicia, for our afternoon meetings, your way with words, and all your tireless editing. Thank you, Elizabeth W., for being the one to point out that Roxan fiddles with her hair too much, and Mullin needs to not seem so fresh. Thank you, Debbie, for walking with me through the pit, holding me up, and telling me you loved this story. Thank you, Catherine, for sneaking a read-through and loving the book. Thank you, June, for always being my friend and for reminding me of what kind of person I want to be. Thank you, Tammie, Lori, and Cynthia for offering me your editing and proofing expertise, and for propping me up when I couldn't do it myself. Thank you sweet Light Brigade for praying for me and being my faithful companions on this road.

I should probably thank all the Mullins and Jaspers out there who've made life hard. Certainly there are better ways to learn these lessons, but I'm grateful for how God brought me through trials so I could get to a place of forgiveness, love, and a better world.

And finally, I need to say thank you to my family. Thank you, mom and dad, for being two of the smartest and most creative people I know. Thank you, Fran and Ron, for telling me I could do it. Thank you, Elizabeth, for being my first fan and for drawing the map—you drew out my words so everyone else might know what this little world looked like. Thank you, Julia, for giving me constant encouragement and hope—your way with words helped me write mine out. And thank you, Cameron, for showing me the depths love will go and for helping me become the person I'm meant to be—you are my matchment.

And thank you, Father. You are my Leader, the King of Kings, and Lord of Lords. You are love, and without you, none of this matters.

The journey's not over yet!

List of Characters

Abiga: A new member of the Outcasts, forest-born, lives at Snowshoe Falls. She used to run with the Undesirables.

Adora: An old Outcast from Pocket, village-born.

Altrist: A messenger from the Leader.

Anna: Village-born Outcast who lives at Snowshoe Falls.

Bru: A roaming Outcast, doesn't live at Snowshoe Falls or Pocket, but instead makes camp in various places. He grew up in Pocket though, and has a twin brother named Eldem.

Caton: Undesirable, and a spy for the sentries.

Eldem: An Outcast from Pocket raised by the messenger Olivope. He has a twin brother named Bru.

Eveleen: Plateau Guardian, announcer for Hyperion.

Grouper: Village-born Outcast from the Protectorate. He once served as a guide sentry. Now he lives at Snowshoe Falls.

Hyperion: The absolute ruler in the Oblate. He is credited with having set up their society when the outside world fell apart, giving people a safe, fair place to live. Also known as Tatief by his equals.

Huzzah: Village-born Outcast and Pocket-dweller.

Ixon: Pocket Outcast with a very unusual gift.

Jahn: Snowshoe Falls Outcast, matched with Liza.

Jasper: Head sentry in the Protectorate.

Jonas: Guide in the Propagate Building. He wants desperately to have a higher position.

Jun: Pocket Outcast, matched with Ixon.

Leader, The: The chief of the Outcasts.

Liza: Snowshoe Falls Outcast, matched with Jahn. She has two gifts from the Leader.

Melkin: Wanderer.

Mullin: A supplier from the Viand Village who has aspirations for change.

Norwood: Worker in the Propagate Building. She is second in command under Jonas.

Olivope: Messenger from the Leader.

Overseer Hillton: Guardian in charge of appearances, fashion, and design.

Roxan: New plebe in the Propagate Building. Desperately enjoys being outside and loves her new life free of the raising home.

Sprout: Derogatory term for a person who was raised in a village.

Tatief: Another name for Hyperion, known only to those who are his equals.

Thim: Snowshoe Falls Outcast. Kind-hearted, understanding, and strong, in love with Abiga.

Wessel: Guide in the mail division of the Propagate Building. Low moral character.

Whitlock: Chief overseer in the Propagate Building. He is Jonas's boss and Roxan's ally.

Wortman: Overseer of the mail room in the Propagate Building. Known for underhanded deals and circumventing policy.

Glossary of Oblate Terms

Adjustment: A disciplinary action conducted by the sentry guards. Adjustments normally occur in the village where the violation took place; however, for major infractions, the person can be sent directly to the Plateau for adjustment. Adjustments involve punishment and behavior modification.

All-in: The curfew for the people living in the villages. It is enforced by the sentries. All-in changes according to the seasons, but is always mandated by the Guardians.

Attainment: The point in life when a village-dweller may retire and forever enjoy the paradise village called the Plantanate.

Caftywater: Caffinated water fortified with vitamins and herbs.

Calciwater: Purified water fortified with calcium and iron.

Clingman: A code word used by the Guardians to identify any person who possesses a special ability and could pose a danger to himself or others.

Cover-up: The official clothing of the Oblate. Each cover-up has two pieces: a top layer and a bottom one. Some are only shirt length and are worn with pants. Another style is knee- to calf-length, and is worn without pants. Cover-ups are color-coded according to which village a person is assigned and what rank they hold within their employment.

Cycle: A period of time equivalent to one month and based in the phases of the moon.

Drone Pod: A messenger's instrument to see things remotely when he or she can't actually be there. It observes and filters images, deciphering a scene, and then returns to its master with a report of its surveillance. Shape, color, and composition of the drone pod vary according to each messenger.

Balustrade: The wall surrounding all the regions/villages of the Oblate. It serves as a barrier between the land of destruction and the livable world.

Flash: A small increment of time akin to a minute.

Fixed to a Pitch: The state of being very angry.

Gift: An attribute or ability given to an Outcast by the Leader that will help the overall health and well-being of the group. Abilities can be physical manifestations of strength, speed, transporting, etc.; keen awareness of feelings; insight into the heart; or adeptness in various artistic talents.

Gold Horizon: The area surrounding the opening to the main underground transport directly connected to the Plateau. It is called "golden" because the fire bowls, which line the perimeter of its expanse, cast a fiery glow, which can be seen from a distance.

Guardians: The body of leaders stationed at the Plateau. They decide what's for the good of all and keep the world in order. They only answer to their master, Hyperion.

Guide: A managerial position. The guide has some power and responsibilities, but reports to an overseer.

Lumen: Lantern used by outcasts and travelers, powered by a combination of fire and a chemical source that is scraped from the rocks.

Mantra: Phrase repeated by the people who live in villages. It is said in two parts. One person says, "For the good of all." And the other person responds, "We give ourselves." Once the first part has been spoken, it is mandatory that the reply be made. If the responder refuses to answer, he/she receives an adjustment.

Marker: An order given to a worker requiring them to do a particular job, no excuses, no time off. If the person does not complete the task in the time given, the worker is held responsible by the Plateau officials. This could mean a few days in an underground cell or an adjustment at the Plateau.

Matchment: When the Guardians find two people suitable to produce an offspring that would be genetically beneficial to society, a matchment is formed. The pairing lasts as long as the Guardians deem it necessary.

Nanny: Men and women who care for and raise little ones (children) from birth until graduation at fifteen turns. Nannies are also responsible for teaching basic education requirements and life skills lessons.

Ness: Clear liquid that tastes like milk with honey; it's found only outside the villages.

Nutrivia Bar: Compressed bar of food, loaded with protein, vitamins, and grains.

Oblate: The only inhabitable land in the world. It is where Hyperion and the Guardians retreated to when the outer lands succumbed to mass destruction. The Oblate is protected by a wall known as the Balustrade, which separates and protects the villages and provinces from the destroyed world outside.

Obdon Bluff: A bluff situated between Pocket and Willow Way outside the villages.

Outcasts: People who live outside the village boundary. Some of them were Undesirables, some were born in the wild, and some of them came from the villages. All of them follow someone who they only refer to as their Leader.

Overseer: The highest position in every village except for those appointed directly by the Plateau. Overseers are the chief officers in their division. They only report to the Guardians.

Pairing: See Matchment.

Plantanate: One of the five villages in the Oblate. It is considered a paradise and the place people go when they've completed their required amount of service and reached attainment.

Plateau: Underground hub of the entire Oblate. Highly fortified tunnels and underground facilities. All Oblate leadership resides here. Considered a village, but it may only be entered through invitation.

Plasma Globe: The most elite light fixture in the villages. It casts an orangey, white glow and hums. Usually only found in office settings.

Plateau-bonded: A label applied to a person when the Guardians have a desire to promote him/her to a position at the Plateau. It is normally applied to little ones who move directly to the Plateau from the Raising Home, but occasionally a plebe will be marked with the label and sent to a village to be observed until he/she has developed the skills needed to be of assistance to the Plateau.

Plebe: A worker who is new on the job. There is a hierarchy of plebes, which is usually determined by the guide.

Pocket: An Outcast hideout in the forest. A large rock ledge juts out from an embankment creating a pocket-like cave. It is surrounded by trees.

Pomper: An elite group within a pack of Undesirables that controls and manipulates the others. Usually consists of three to five people.

Progenate: One of the five villages in the Oblate. It houses three areas— Gentest; Pairing/Matchment; and the Raising Homes.

Propagate: The name of the building and the division in which rules and legislature is written down for the people. It is also the headquarters for mail distribution.

Protectorate: The second most important village of the Oblate (behind the Plateau). This village trains and equips sentry guards and houses the main sentry post. This is also where information is compiled and printed to relay the desires of the leadership at the Plateau. The Propagate is located in the Protectorate.

Raising Home: A section of the Progenate village where all children are schooled and raised.

Replicator: The person who crafts orders from the Plateau to make them more appealing to the common people.

Roll: Equivalent to one full day. The light roll is when the sun is out; dark roll is nighttime.

Roll-Expansion Card: A card that allows its holder to be out later than all-in, thereby circumventing the curfew.

Scinter: Plateau-sanctioned weapon. All sentries are issued one upon their graduation. Every scinter is specific to each sentry and grows more and more responsive to the sentry as they develop skill. It has a flat silver blade that serves as a conduit for energy. When flicked on, it pulsates with variously colored lights. If jabbed with a lit scinter, death could be instantaneous. The weapon has several energy settings though, and can be programmed to merely stun. Nannies are equipped with scinters too; however, their weapons do not possess the same power level as those carried by the sentries.

Season: A period of time rooted in the seasons each turn and determined by a major shift in the weather. The Oblate experiences four seasons: warm, hot, cool, cold.

Sentry: Guard and law enforcement division of the Guardians.

Shikes: A derogatory expression of surprise. Usually used in connection with a put down or negative news.

Snowshoe Falls: Hideout for the outcasts. A cave tucked in behind Snowshoe Waterfall.

Solar Globe: Underground globe of light connected to above-ground solar panels and used in the subterranean villages of the Progenate and the Plateau as a primary light source.

Solar Rod: Cheap shanty lighting fixture known for not being dependable.

Solar Sticks: Tall cylinder-like poles that click on at twilight to cast a glow on the pathways within the villages, powered by energy from the sun.

Sprout: Slang for a person who was raised in a village.

Stave: Hand-held light, powered through solar batteries.

Tatief: Another name for Hyperion, known only to those who are his equals.

Taxar Bush: Thorny bushes containing a deadly poison that can paralyze and kill a person within a flash.

Time of Attainment: The time in a person's life when the officials at the Plateau reward him/her for a life of good service. At the time of attainment, a person retires to the Plantanate to finish out their life as they wish.

Tog: Article of clothing that is one piece with a tie at the waist. Tog reach to the knees and can be worn with pants or without.

Turn: Equivalent to one full year.

Twig it: A phrase meaning to get something done quickly or get on with something.

Undesirables: A band of people living beyond the boundary to the villages. They run in packs and have no particular leader. Many of them have become animal-like in their behavior and can be dangerous.

Viand: One of the five villages in the Oblate. The Viand provides food and supplies to the other villages, and contains fields and factories.

Vitawater: Purified water fortified with vitamins.

Author Bio

M.B. Dahl discovered her love for writing in elementary school. At eleven, she wrote her first play, "The Nativity," which was performed at her little country school. She is an award-winning author who has written short stories, devotionals, essays, Sunday school curriculum, and church dramas. She is a member of American Christian Fiction Writers. This is her first YA novel.

When she's not writing, she's volunteering with the children's arts programs at her church or spending time with her sweet family. One of her favorite jobs has been working with students at Holman Middle School. She sees life to be a grand adventure where hardships serve to guide her to the heights.

Dahl lives in Richmond, VA with her darling husband, "swonderful " daughters, and three ferocious mutts.

Visit the author's website at www.marybethdahl.org for her blog and more information about Through the Balustrade, including character studies, reading group questions, and study guides.

CPSIA information can be obtained at www.ICGtesting.com
Printed in the USA
BVOW080359130513

320520BV00001B/1/P